*continued . . .*

# NAUTIER AND

*Wilder*

## LORA LEIGH
and
JACI BURTON

BERKLEY BOOKS, NEW YORK

5115 6510 5/13

**THE BERKLEY PUBLISHING GROUP**
Published by the Penguin Group
Penguin Group (USA) Inc.
375 Hudson Street, New York, New York 10014, USA

USA / Canada / UK / Ireland / Australia / New Zealand / India / South Africa / China

Penguin Books Ltd., Registered Offices: 80 Strand, London WC2R 0RL, England
For more information about the Penguin Group, visit penguin.com.

This book is an original publication of The Berkley Publishing Group.

Library of Congress Cataloging-in-Publication Data

Nautier and wilder / Lora Leigh and Jaci Burton.—Berkley trade paperback edition.
    pages cm
    Two novellas.
    ISBN 978-0-425-24339-8
1. Erotic stories, American.   I. Leigh, Lora. Nauti siren.   II. Burton, Jaci. Riding to sunset.
    III. Title: Nauti siren.   IV. Title: Riding to sunset.
        PS648.E7N355   2013
    813'.01083538—dc23                              2012050114

PUBLISHING HISTORY
Berkley trade paperback edition / April 2013

PRINTED IN THE UNITED STATES OF AMERICA

10  9  8  7  6  5  4  3  2  1

Cover art by Don Sipley.
Cover design by Lesley Worrell.

# CONTENTS

# NAUTI SIREN

LORA LEIGH

Mountains majestic.

Waters of the clearest blue.

Pine, Elm and Ash standing as beacons along towering ridges surrounding you.

What peace can be found?

What joy can be attained?

What happiness awaits those whose hearts can open, whose spirit can draw in the great richness of the land?

Not the home of my birth, rather the home my heart chose.

Not a land bequeathed, but a land enchanting, seducing my loyalty and yes, mesmerizing my senses.

This land where I laughed as a child.

This land where I loved as a girl.

This land, how do I love thee as a woman, love thee as a child raised within your tender embrace.

This land . . .

Yes, this land of my heart.

Kentucky.

EVE MACKAY
Somerset, Kentucky

# PROLOGUE

This wasn't supposed to happen.

Not in a million years. Not even one day past forever.

Because she knew the kind of man he was and she knew he was exactly the kind of man she had sworn she would never allow herself to have.

Yet it was happening.

Suspended between complete disbelief and mind-numbing pleasure, Piper Mackay found herself mesmerized by Jedediah Booker's kiss.

Her lips parted.

Her fingers curled around his wrists, though in protest or simply to find something to hold on to, she wasn't certain.

What she was certain of—she hadn't expected this.

His broad fingers splayed into her hair as his palms cupped her cheeks, holding her in place for his kiss. His lips slanted over hers, rubbing sensuously, and sent spikes of heat burrowing through her senses.

It wasn't supposed to be like this.

It wasn't supposed to be so sexy.

The feel of his hard, muscular body against her smaller one, pressing her against the wall at her back, had her knees weakening at the eroticism of the position. The feel of the hardened length of his shaft as it pressed against the towel covering him, throbbing against her stomach, was almost too intense to bear.

She wanted to touch him.

She wanted to run her hands over his hard, powerful body and feel the flex of muscle beneath the darkly tanned flesh. She wanted to do more than stand, frozen, on the verge of fleeing in fear as his tongue flicked against her lips, teasing her to taste him in turn.

Just one taste.

She could take just a moment to experience what she had promised herself she would not tempt.

The wild, erotic promise of Jed's possession.

Her tongue peeked out, touched his, then lingered.

A moan slipped free; completely against her will and her better judgment as she allowed his lips and tongue free rein in the kiss they were initiating.

A deep, rough male growl sounded in his throat as his hands slid from her face and moved quickly to her hips. Before she could process the move, before she could make sense of it, Piper found herself lifted, her legs parting, the soft material of her skirt falling back over her thighs, and the broad, fiery heat of Jed's cock throbbing, hot and naked, free of the towel, against the silk of the panties shielding her sex.

She could have protested.

She would have protested.

But it was so good.

Everything was just so good.

The lush eroticism of the kiss, the heat of his hands against her flesh, the seductive, sensuous pleasure beginning to blaze through her senses. It was so good that resisting was impossible.

His hands clenched on her rear, kneading the rounded curves as his hips rocked against her, sending shudders of pleasure racing through her.

He slanted his lips over hers, one hand sliding from the curve of her ass, and she found herself gripping his thighs with her knees as his hand pushed beneath the soft cotton shirt she wore.

Piper fought to breathe.

She was lost in a world of sensation and pleasure. He held her to him as his hand slid up her side, calloused palms rasping against her flesh just before his fingers curled around the bare mound of one breast.

Finding the hardened tip with his thumb and rubbing against it, he found another way to throw her senses into complete chaos. Her nipples were so sensitive, so responsive, that even her own touch had the power to make her gasp.

Jed's touch, so much more experienced and knowing, had the power to do much more.

His touch against the ripened bud had the power to bring her nearly to release. Playing with the little bud, he rolled his thumb over it before gripping the pebble-hard tip between his thumb and forefinger. Sharpened spikes of sensation tore along the nerve endings to her clitoris before slamming into her womb.

Piper tightened her thighs against his hips, rocking with him, rubbing herself against the broad thickness of the heavy cock throbbing against the heated folds of her sex. Sharp waves of hunger rushed along nerve endings that seemed newly awakened, created only to respond to Jed's touch. Sensitized and now greedy for sensation they throbbed and ached for more and more.

It was so good.

It was too good.

"Piper, sweetheart . . ."

His breathing was as rough as her own, ragged; he was fighting to draw in air as he tore his lips from hers and buried them at her neck.

Tipping her head back, Piper fought to increase the sensation of his lips brushing against the sensitive flesh at the curve of her shoulder. The feel of the tip of his tongue tasting her and awakening a sensual hunger she hadn't known existed inside her.

Digging her nails into his bare shoulders, she told herself *just a few more seconds*. She would allow herself to experience the pleasure, the incredible building heat burning through her body, for just a few more seconds.

His teeth raked against the side of her neck as she felt his body tighten further. A low groan of male pleasure echoed at her ear.

"I could lose myself in you, Piper," he groaned in building lust. "So fucking easy."

Oh, God, what had she gotten herself into?

She had known not to enter his room.

Some part of her had known he was still there.

The temptation had been overwhelming.

Like some damned ninny in a suspense novel, she had crept right in. At the very moment she had closed the door behind her, certain he must be gone, he'd stepped from the bathroom, obviously having just left the shower.

Had she had the good sense to leave?

Hell, no.

"Jed." Whispering his name, she fought to hold on to him, fought to remember why this was a very bad idea.

"Piper. Sweetheart . . ."

The room was spinning—no, Jed was moving. Wrapping one

arm around her hips, he turned, bearing her to the bed and laying her back against the sheets he'd slept on the night before.

The subtle scent of male warmth and the dark hint of the
cologne he wore lingered on the bedclothes, surrounding her and
sinking into her senses. She felt surrounded by him, overwhelmed
by him, and unwilling as well as unable to fight against the pleasure clouding her mind.

Before she could even consider protesting, the soft cotton
shirt she wore was pushed over her breasts and the sensitive, tight
peak of her nipple was suddenly surrounded by the wet heat of
his mouth. It happened so quickly, with such heat that her senses
immediately exploded with sensation.

Piper jerked upward, a moan rasping from her lips as her eyes
closed in rising pleasure.

The lash of his tongue over the sensitive peak sent sensation spiraling from her hardened nipple straight to the clenched,
aching depths of her vagina. The tight, swollen bud of her clit
pulsed with need. Heat flushed her body, and the slick dew of
arousal dampened the swollen folds of her sex and the silk of her
panties.

Pushing her fingers into the overlong strands of his hair to
hold him to the tingling, heated bud of her nipple, Piper felt herself giving up—giving in.

The pleasure was too intense.

The need that had risen over the past year since her sister had
moved out of the inn their mother owned to live with her fiancé
was only burning with a greater, fiery hunger.

Had she been insane when she had taken her mother's offer
to move into Eve's suite just days after Jed had moved into the
room beside it?

Had she known this would happen?

God, she had.

She'd known she would end up in his bed, and she knew he'd break her heart.

He wouldn't be able to help it. He would destroy her.

That thought, that fear, had a reality check suddenly clicking in her mind.

"Jed. Jed . . . not a good idea," she cried out, even as she lifted her hips to grind the mound of her sex more firmly against his cock while he palmed both breasts.

"My best idea yet," he muttered, his voice hoarse as one hand slid to the bend of her knee to lift it higher along his hip.

His hips pressed and rolled, grinding his shaft more firmly against her clit and soaking her panties with her juices as he used both hands to press her breasts together. His lips moved from one hardened nipple to the other, licking and suckling, pulling repeated moans from her lips as her ability to fight against the pleasure dissipated.

She'd dreamed of this.

She'd fantasized about it for far longer than the past year.

"God, I love how you taste," he muttered, his head lifting, his lips coming back to hers as he gripped her nipples between fingers and thumbs and played with them erotically.

His tongue pressed against her lips, parted them, met hers, and stroked against it with heated demand.

He wasn't asking for anything, definitely not the right to have her.

He considered her his due.

That thought sent a wave of trepidation racing through her, only to disintegrate beneath a harder, deeper kiss as one hand left her breasts to stroke her thigh.

"Damn, Piper." He tore his lips from hers to blaze a trail of fire down her neck to her breasts once again as strong, knowing fingers pressed beneath the elastic of her panties.

Lifting her hips, angling them to the fingers pressing closer to her clitoris, Piper could feel the slickened fall of damp warmth spilling from her, preparing the sensitive flesh for his touch.

She was so ready for him. So ready to have his fingers delve into the feminine folds that ached for his touch that she felt poised on a pinpoint of agonizing arousal.

He was so close to touching her clit. So close to caressing that heated bud of sensitized nerve endings that she could swear she could feel the warmth of his fingers as they neared her.

So close . . .

A heavy knocking at the door had them stilling.

Piper struggled to open her eyes, meeting his gaze as his head jerked up from where his lips had strayed to her midriff.

"Hey, Jed, we have to run." Elijah Grant was on the other side, his knuckles rapping against the glass of the patio doors across from the bed once again. "You ready?"

"Please," she whispered, suddenly desperate that she not be seen here, with him, all but naked and fucked in his bed.

Oh, God, what was she doing?

Jed could see the sudden panic flaring in her gaze. The instant withdrawal the second she consciously realized just how close she was to having given in to him wasn't lost on him. The hunger that kept them bound to each other wasn't going to go away. No matter how hard he fought it, no matter how desperately she denied it.

"Give me ten minutes," he called out to Elijah. "I'll meet you at the bikes."

She was trembling beneath him.

The feel of the subtle tremors racing through her delicate body had the power to piss him off as nothing else could. It was like this every time he neared her, every time the hunger flared between them. She would tremble, get that look of wariness in her eyes, and instantly retreat.

He was damned sick of her retreating.

"Why are you scared of me?" Focusing his gaze back on her, careful to keep his voice too low to carry beyond the room, he demanded an answer.

"I am not scared of you." Determination and fiery stubbornness filled the deep sea green of her eyes and tightened the kittenish features of her face.

"Then what are you scared of?" Lowering his voice further, Jed brushed his lips against the swollen curves of Piper's while fighting the nearly overwhelming need to steal another kiss. To forget his partner was awaiting him and that now was not the time to make slow, easy love to her.

He would never pull himself from her if he did.

Elijah could walk in on them and it wouldn't stop Jed from having her.

"Don't you have to go to work or something?" she muttered instead as she pushed at his shoulders. "Let me up, Jed, before Elijah starts picking the lock."

Elijah sure as hell wasn't above it if he thought the situation warranted it.

"What makes you think he would pick the lock?" He knew Elijah would do it, but what made *her* think he would?

Piper rolled her eyes up at him.

"Do I really look that stupid to you, Jed?" Mockery filled her gaze as he levered himself from her body.

He watched silently as she hurriedly pulled the shirt over the swollen mounds of her breasts and pushed the material of her skirt back down her legs before sitting up quickly.

A second later she was standing and sliding her feet back into the sandals she had somehow managed to lose. Or had pushed from her feet as he picked her up moments ago.

"You don't look stupid at all." Arching a brow, he strode to the chair across the room where he'd laid his clean clothing earlier.

Pulling boxer briefs over his legs and then the raging erection that refused to soften, he sat down, never taking his eyes from her, and pulled white socks over his feet.

She wasn't saying anything more.

Her arms were crossed beneath her breasts in a classic defensive posture as he almost gave in to the urge to sigh wearily.

Standing, Jed picked up an ink pen from the table next to him before moving to her once again.

She always carried her date book, with a small sketch pad in it, with her. At the moment, it was tucked in the side of the cleaning carryall she'd placed on the floor when she entered the room.

Bending, he pulled the five-by-seven leather-bound journal from the side pocket, flipped it open, then quickly scrawled his cell phone number in the back. The sketch pad enclosed with it was filled with colorful sketches of clothing designs and scrawled with notes. He would have loved to flip through the new designs he only glimpsed, but knew from experience she'd become immediately defensive.

"What's that for?" she questioned warily as he finished.

Tucking the book back in place, Jed straightened and stared down at her with a sense of heavy disappointment.

"When you decide you can give me a chance to prove that I have no intention of tying you down, Piper, then give me a call." Yeah, he knew at least part of her problem.

Strong men, men born with the same arrogant determination her Mackay brother and cousins possessed.

Capping the pen, he tossed it to the bureau close to the bed, then turned and moved back to the clothing he'd abandoned moments before.

He was aware of her watching him as he pulled on his jeans, secured the belt he'd already pushed through the belt loops, then pushed his arms into the white, long-sleeved dress shirt he'd chosen to wear.

White was for meetings; dark colors were for on the job. And all of it was bullshit, despite the sense of fulfillment he was getting from it. Far more fulfillment than the daily lies and undercover crap he was forced to practice.

"Why would I be afraid you could even come close to tying me down, Jed?" she finally asked, her lips curling into an amused little smile of disbelief. "Really? Do you think I'm attaching more to this"—she waved her arm toward the bed—"than what you intend?"

Using the chair once again, he sat down, pulled on his boots, and never took his eyes from her.

"Let's hope you were," he told her as he finished and rose to his feet once again. "Because, trust me, Piper, I have more intentions than you could ever imagine."

There was the fear.

It flashed in the bright green of her eyes and tightened her expression as she fought to hold back the response. Hell, she was fighting to hide that fear from him, and he hated it.

"Good Lord," she muttered, suddenly reaching down for her bag. "I'm out of here. Remind me to make damned sure you've left before I come in to clean your room again."

"I wouldn't put chains on you, Piper."

She paused, her hand on the doorknob, her face turned from him as her head lowered.

"I don't know what you're talking about." The edge of anger in her voice wasn't nearly as well hidden as he was certain she would have liked.

"Yeah, you do, Piper." He rejected the instant denial she gave the moment she turned her back on him. "You think if you take me as a lover then you'll be exchanging your brother's protectiveness for one far more permanent."

"My brother's protectiveness? Is that what you call it?" She turned back to him then. "Trust me: They named my brother well when they nicknamed him Dawg. He's tenacious, and guards his territory like a junkyard dog. And he sees every damned one of his sisters, as well as our mother, as his territory. It wouldn't matter who we took as lovers, he'd still be hovering over us like a damned pit bull."

There was no anger or heat in the words, only a sense of regret and uncertainty. In the past year, her life hadn't exactly been her own, as her brother did everything in his power to ensure the danger that had threatened her older sister didn't touch the younger ones.

"Nevertheless," he said softly. "I wouldn't put ties on you. I wouldn't treat you as though you didn't have the good sense to understand whether your life was in danger or not, and the intelligence to know whether you can live life as usual, sit tight, or just plain hide."

She watched him warily. "You're the same type of male Dawg, Rowdy, and Natches are." She finally informed him, and it was clear she believed it to the bottom of her soul. "Having you for a lover would be like sleeping with human handcuffs."

God help him, he swore he could see the pain and disillusionment filling her very soul. It was in the weariness of her voice and the soul-deep certainty that filled it.

"I would defend you with my life," he admitted. "But I would also defend your right to a life, Piper. When you decide you're tired of being a frightened little girl rather than the independent woman I know you are, then let me know. Perhaps once you've figured out which you are, then we can resume all the pleasure we were interrupted in this morning."

Her shoulders tightened, defiance and denial immediately flashing in her gaze.

Jed didn't hang around to hear her argument or her reasons for her beliefs; they would just piss him the fuck off.

He knew the past year had been hell on her and her younger sisters. Eve, the eldest, had pranced from the suite she'd lived in for the past five years and moved in with the government agent she was now engaged to, perfectly content to fight her battles of independence and keep her opinions private within the secured houseboat they were currently living in at the lake.

Eve had left her younger sisters to face the fallout with her brother and cousins. Her sisters, though, had never been given a full explanation of why that overprotectiveness had suddenly increased, or when it would end. Though he knew Piper had her suspicions.

Jed couldn't explain what had happened either, not yet, not until he knew Piper understood his intentions where she was concerned.

But hell, in order to make her understand them, he was going to have to figure them out himself.

One thing was certain: He intended to have her in his bed. And he sure as hell didn't intend to let her go anytime soon once he had her there.

Hell, why couldn't he imagine ever letting her go, period?

# ONE

She was going to cave.

Piper could feel it coming. She could feel that bond of pleasure Jed had created four weeks before tightening between them, pulling them together.

She'd taken Eve's suite on the first floor of Mackay's Bed-and-Breakfast Inn after her sister had moved in with her lover, Brogan Campbell.

Brogan had been staying in the suite next to Eve's for the two years he had been there doing whatever it was he was doing. She had a feeling he was a hell of a lot more than a building contractor or supervisor or whatever the hell he claimed to be. She was all but certain he was a covert agent and working directly with her mother's lover, Timothy Cranston.

And she highly suspected both Jedediah Booker and the other contractor staying at the inn, Elijah Grant, were Brogan's partners.

There had been strange things going on in Somerset—hell, in

Pulaski County, period—for the past few years: thefts that didn't make sense, strangers who knew far too much about the people and the mountains where Piper now made her home. And far too many "disappearances" of several of the criminal elements in the county.

It was damned freaky.

And she knew Jed was involved in it.

She watched them, she listened to the gossip and rumors that moved through the county, and she had a hell of an ability to tie together things that at first might not appear connected.

It was a talent she'd often heard Dawg had as well.

It didn't matter what kind of talent she had. She could be as fully trained as any agent who had ever worked with her brother and he'd still treat her like a five-year-old.

And so would Jed.

Pulling the older-model Jeep into the driveway of the post office, she set the parking brake before turning off the ignition and moving from the vehicle.

Sliding the small orange notification card from her purse, she looped the bag's strap over her shoulder and pushed open the glass door leading into the building.

"Hey there, Piper."

"Piper, how's it goin' . . ."

"Hello, Piper, missed you last weekend. . . ."

"Hey, Piper, Dawg going to let you come out and play this weekend?"

She heard it every time she ran into the usual crowd of summer weekend partiers. Because Piper, normally the life of the party, had been absent or joined by her brother or cousins every time she tried to slip out to one of the lake parties. A Mackay always arrived within minutes of her showing up, and what was the point of staying if she was being guarded? She returned the greetings, answered where she had to, and waited patiently in line to sign for the certified letter she'd been notified was waiting for her.

The New York City address hadn't really meant anything to her; neither had the name of the sender: S. Chaniss.

Accepting the envelope from the young clerk behind the counter, Piper thanked her quietly before making her way back to the Jeep.

Closing herself in and restarting the ignition, Piper flipped on the AC and quickly tore open the envelope.

She scanned the letter first; then, as disbelief set in and her heart began racing furiously, she read it more slowly.

Her hand began to tremble. Excitement began to build.

She'd been making her own clothing designs since she was a child, and for nearly as long she had been sewing those designs together. She'd learned early how to use a needle and thread, and she'd torn her fingertips to ribbons as a child to perfect each and every stitch.

Now . . . now someone had noticed them. Someone of such renown in the fashion world that she had never imagined he would show an interest in her work.

Eldon Vessante, one of the biggest names in the New York fashion scene, had, for several years, been bringing in hot new designers, up to three a year, and staging exclusive runway shows for them.

By mentoring new talent he'd made an even bigger name for himself, and each designer he'd mentored was still a hot topic among the fashion world. And their designs were still being worn by models, movie stars, and the rich and famous.

Piper had sent several of her designs to the Vessante panel more than a year ago.

No one knew she had submitted the required six designs to

the Vessante team. She hadn't even told her mother. Hell, she'd forgotten about it months ago when no response had been forthcoming.

His assistant had sent the letter—she quickly checked the date—two days ago?

Oh, my God—they had chosen her designs!

She wanted to scream.

She wanted to jump out of the Jeep and announce it to everyone on the street as they made their way into the post office and various businesses that lined the sidewalk.

She wanted to call her mother and Dawg. . . .

*Whoa.*

Bad idea.

Very, very bad idea.

She really wanted to call Jed, and that was an even worse idea, because there was no way, despite his promise, that he wouldn't let Dawg in on where she was going and what she was doing.

She read the letter again.

The excitement was about to get the best of her.

This was her dream. It was that one-in-a-million shot to realize every dream she'd ever had of what she could accomplish with the talent she had.

And she couldn't tell anyone.

She lifted her head, moving her gaze from the letter to stare through the Jeep windshield, her excitement suddenly overshadowed by a heavy sadness. If she dared to say anything to anyone, then she would end up with more bodyguards on that trip than the queen of England. And wouldn't that make a hell of an impression?

If she thought for a moment that Dawg, Rowdy, or Natches would consider just one of them accompanying her, then it might have swayed her. She knew better, though. For the past summer, they seemed to be everywhere together. Piper had even gone so far as to ask them whether they were married to their wives or to one another.

She'd even questioned why. Why had her sister been kidnapped the summer before? Who had done it? Why had they done it? All she'd received in answer was a closed expression and change of topic. And the certainty that her brother and cousins, along with Timothy Cranston, were involved in something far more dangerous than they wanted their sisters to be aware of.

Carefully pushing the letter back into the large envelope it had arrived in, she turned it over and stared at the address once again.

S. Chaniss, the address read. New York City.

There was no way anyone at the post office could really place exactly whom the letter was from or what it contained. Hiding it and the contents from curious eyes wouldn't be too hard.

Putting the Jeep in gear and pulling from the post office parking lot, she turned the vehicle toward home.

This sucked.

The rebellious resentment that had been brewing inside her for the past year flamed through her senses with a suddenness that made it nearly burst into full-fledged anger.

It simply wasn't fair. She should have been able to shout this accomplishment far and wide. At the very least she should have been able to race to the boutique where she sold many of the unique clothing designs she created.

She couldn't even do that.

Her fingers tightened on the steering wheel as she drove out of town and made the turn toward Mackay's Bed-and-Breakfast Inn.

As the renovated farmhouse came into view, Piper couldn't

help but acknowledge the fact that had it not been for her brother Dawg, then her mother would have died and she and her sisters would have been worse than homeless.

They'd been abandoned by Chandler Mackay long before the Department of Homeland Security had found the small house he'd purchased for her mother when he'd brought her from Guatemala. When they'd been thrown from that home, her mother, Mercedes, had been horribly ill with a lung infection the doctors had been unable to treat.

It was only after Timothy Cranston had brought them to Somerset and introduced them to Dawg that their lives had changed. Dawg had ensured that her mother's medical care was paid for while Piper and her sisters had found security, and they had all found a family unlike any Piper could have imagined.

There was another side of that coin, though.

With the security, acceptance, and love the Mackays had given her and her family there was the heavy-handed overprotectiveness her brother and male cousins exhibited.

It was so heavy-handed that for the past year she and her sisters—except the eldest, whom Piper actually blamed their present state on—had no hope of actually living outside the stifling watchfulness they were suddenly surrounded with.

Slip out to a lake party and what happened? Before they could finish their first beer either Dawg, their cousins, or one of their cohorts—Sheriff Mayes, Chief of Police Alex Jansen, or some other tough-assed Mackay male friend—was there with an eagle eye.

Forget even considering the unmentioned search she had begun for a lover. She was fated to remain a virgin for the rest of her days, evidently.

At twenty-four, Piper considered herself far too old to have not taken a lover. And as much as she would have loved—

*loved*—to have taken Jedediah Booker to her bed, the last thing she needed was one of her brother's watchdogs keeping a leash on her.

Pulling into the inn's parking lot, Piper tried to push back the regret and the hunger she couldn't keep from building inside her body. The sensitive flesh between her thighs felt swollen, aching for a touch. Her clit actually throbbed, and she knew damned good and well that only a man was going to put out that particular fire.

God help her, she didn't want a man as restrictive and just as protective as her brother and cousins. She wanted a lover, a friend, and a partner. She didn't need a keeper.

It was Saturday night.

She had a week to make plans to slip from Somerset and make her way to New York. She was going to have to essentially escape. If that was possible. Because if Dawg had even a suspicion she was leaving town for any reason, then he would have one of his buddies and/or employees or agent-type acquaintances on her ass so fast it would leave road rash on her senses.

That, she didn't need.

She knew the world she wanted to move within, and she knew for damned sure that neither her brother and cousins nor their overprotective friends would move well within it.

So, how to escape a town where the Mackays had eyes and ears everywhere?

Everywhere.

No doubt it wouldn't be easy.

It would require a small amount of lying through her teeth.

Piper smiled.

Hell, she could do it.

She was, after all, a Mackay.

# TWO

"You are up to something."

Piper froze at the sound of Jed's voice as she answered the call on her cell phone.

Lowering the smart phone, she glared at the number.

Piedmont's Pizza.

"Since when did you begin using the phones at pizza houses?" Mockery filled her voice and she knew it.

A chuckle rasped across her senses. Even through the phone lines it had the power to weaken her knees.

"For some unknown reason my caller ID refuses to behave properly," he drawled. "Perhaps they had the number before me."

Yeah. Okay. She'd let him get away with it, but she was highly dubious of the explanation.

"What do you want?" She tried for a vein of irritation in her voice, but she couldn't help the fact that she was pleased he'd called.

And she shouldn't be. He was bad news and she knew it, especially where her determination to hold on to the secret of her upcoming trip was concerned.

She'd wanted to tell him so badly—him more than anyone else, she was beginning to think.

"I want to know what you're up to, of course." His voice lowered, the question carrying an interesting sexual connotation.

Or did she just want to imagine there was something sexual there?

"What do you think I'm up to?" she countered, rather than denying the statement.

He was like her brother: He'd never believe an instant denial. It was their mind-set or something. They knew the sound of a denial in truth and in deception. And Piper wasn't much of a liar.

She much preferred simple evasion.

"What do I think you're up to?" Amusement filled his voice. The sound of it had a smile tugging at her lips.

"Yeah, what do you think I'm up to?" she repeated. "Surely you have an opinion on what it could be."

He was fun to talk to; she'd known that years ago, after he'd first taken up residence at the inn.

"Sweetheart, when it comes to a Mackay, it could be anything and everything," he drawled.

"You're talking about my sisters, not me," she surmised playfully, though her tone was completely serious. "I'm the quiet Mackay, remember?"

She almost gave in to a light laugh at his disbelieving snort. "Quiet one? Nah, you're just the sneaky one."

She shook her head at him as she began folding her silk-and-lace panties and bras and placing them in the small suitcase.

"Shouldn't you be in bed asleep?" she asked as she noticed the time was well after midnight. "I thought you worked on Mondays?"

"Inspections tomorrow," he told her. "My foreman and the job supervisor know what they're doing. I think I'll take the day off."

Oh, great. Just what she needed: Jedediah suspicious and possibly keeping an eye on her.

"The job is near completion then?" His company, along with several others, was building the new industrial office park and warehouses outside of town. Jed's family's company, Booker and Son's Construction, had won the bid to build several of the huge industrial buildings.

"About halfway," he answered her. "You get to put up with me another couple of years whether you like it or not."

"I think Mom has adopted you," Piper reflected as she carefully folded one of the frilly skirts and its matching bag that she'd made into the luggage next. "You've been here since the inn opened."

"Yeah, and she gave us a hell of a deal for the long term," he agreed.

"I'll tell her to consider raising the rent," she threatened, holding back her own laughter as his chuckle echoed across the line.

"I think she wants to adopt me *and* Elijah," Jed teased her. "She likes us."

"Not after Brogan took Eve out of the house," she informed him. "She's still not happy over that one."

Neither were Dawg and their cousins, Piper thought. As a matter of fact, "irate" was a mild description of how they felt about it.

Mercedes Mackay was taking it particularly hard, though. Letting her daughter go hadn't been easy for Mercedes, despite the fact that she dearly loved the man Eve was currently living with.

"We're not related to the bastard," he said with a grunt.

"Aren't you?" she questioned him lightly. "You could have fooled me. You, Elijah, and Brogan play a good game, Jed, but I'm starting to wonder if you're not brothers or something. The three of you are definitely cut from the same cloth."

"Meaning?" Now, wasn't that tone just slightly arrogant?

"Dominant, domineering, stubborn, intractable, opinionated— shall I go on?"

"Hell," he muttered, though she caught the slight vein of amusement in his tone. "I was just hoping for a little sex, Piper, not a complete assassination of my character here."

"Phone sex? Why, Jed, I'm a good girl," she exclaimed as though scandalized. "I can't believe you'd call me for such a thing." Her voice dropped. Piper let it become breathy as she allowed herself to remember his kiss, his touch. "It's none of your business if I'm lying here playing with just the most amazing little toy."

"Huh?"

His surprised little exclamation had satisfaction curling her lips.

"Shame on you, Jedediah Booker," she chastised him, barely holding back her laughter. "My momma would be heartbroken to know what a dirty dog you are. Just simply heartbroken."

"What kind of toy?" The growl in his voice had her stomach tightening. "Come on, Piper; just tell me what it is. What are you doing with it?"

The wicked, sensual, sexual pitch of his voice made her wish she *were* playing with a toy.

"Why, that's just none of your business, Mr. Booker," she informed him with all the sweet Southern-belle charm she could inject into her tone. "I guess you'll just have to find some other way of satisfying your curiosity."

"I can pick the lock on your door," he told her then. "I'll steal the damned thing."

"Even if it's you I'm thinking of when I use it?"

She disconnected the call.

Tightening her thighs as her clit pulsed in time with the throb of need in her vagina, Piper covered her face and fought back the highly unwise action of answering the phone again as it buzzed repeatedly.

This was dangerous.

Jed was far too dangerous.

She might be as bold and just as damned adventurous as any Mackay, but Piper liked to think that unlike her older sister, she also had enough common sense to keep from jumping into the fire.

Nope, the frying pan suited her just fine.

Pulling in a deep breath, she finished packing the suitcase and garment bag she'd chosen to take to New York with her.

She would catch the train in Louisville, and once she got to New York City she'd rent a car.

She didn't much care for driving in Manhattan, but sometimes a girl just had to do what a girl had to do. If she dared to rent a car in Somerset or in Louisville, then the chances were far too great that Dawg would find out. He had too many friends in far too many places. And she knew firsthand that he was on a first-name basis with every reputable car-rental agency in a five-county radius.

That meant just getting to New York City without her brother or her family learning she'd left would be chancy enough.

Luckily, there was one friend she could depend on.

She couldn't tell her mother, her sisters, Tim, her brother or cousins, or her nearby friends or neighbors—she sighed at the thought of it—but she'd managed to make a few friends among the tourists who traveled through Somerset each summer and stopped at the small boutique her designs sold in. Once they sold, it wasn't unusual for the buyers to contact her, interested in other unique wardrobe items. From those buyers, she had made several friends.

Those tourists didn't live in Kentucky, and they had no idea how powerful her brother thought he was. A quick call to one of them, Amy Seavers, had resulted in a fake ID and a train ticket, as well as a ride to the train station.

She was all set and ready to go. All she had to do was slip out with her bags and be waiting at the designated location when Amy's sister, Gypsy, arrived.

Blowing out a hard breath, Piper glanced at the patio doors, her heart beating hard and fast with the thought that Jed didn't make idle threats. There was no doubt in her mind that he knew exactly how to pick the locks on her doors. There was no doubt he would pick them if he were in the right mood.

She rather doubted he'd learned that trick in the construction business. Just as she doubted her sister's fiancé, Brogan Campbell, was slipping into the upper story of the inn in the middle of the night because he missed anyone there.

Hell, no. Those nights Piper had watched the shadowed figure easily pull himself to the second-floor balcony and slip through the glass doors that led to Tim's office, she'd known exactly why he was there.

Timothy liked to tell anyone and everyone who dared to ask that he was retired. *Learn the definition of the word*, he'd growled at the lawyer who'd shown up several weeks before in regard to the deaths of several suspected homeland terrorists the summer before.

Piper had heard the words "Eve" . . . "kidnapping" . . . "boat," and "Campbell" just before he dared to say, "Special Agent Cranston."

She bit back a smile at the thought of how quickly Tim had

cut him down and informed him in no uncertain terms that retirement was a glorious thing.

Retirement, her ass. Timothy, or Tim as she and her sisters often called him, was about as retired as Dawg and her cousins were. Just retired enough to be able to claim they weren't involved in anything, but involved enough to ensure they all knew exactly what was going on in their little corner of the world.

Closing the cases quickly, Piper moved to the closet and stored them out of sight, just in case Jed decided to make a midnight visit.

If he saw her bags and realized they were packed, he would immediately demand to know where she was going. Once he knew . . . hell, she may as well take out an ad.

There wasn't a doubt in her mind that Jed would tell Dawg just as fast as he could make the call. Then Dawg and her cousins would arrive and insist on accompanying her.

If she allowed it to happen.

There wasn't a chance in hell she would allow it, she thought wearily. The very thought of it was enough to send a shudder racing through her body.

She closed the door and moved toward the bed, then came to a hard stop.

Swinging around, Piper moved to the door that led to the sitting room of the suite and swung it open as her heart began pounding with enough force that she swore she could feel it in her throat.

And there he stood.

She crossed her arms beneath her breasts and leaned against the doorframe that connected the sitting room with the bedroom.

"What the hell are you doing here?" It was all she could do to fight back her amusement as well as the surge of sexual intensity sweeping through her.

He wasn't wearing a shirt.

The broad, muscled expanse of his chest was bare. A light covering of dark blond curls feathered over the dark flesh and arrowed into the snug band of his jeans. And he was aroused.

Standing in the middle of her sitting room, bare chested and barefoot, he stared back at her with pure sensual intent burning in his dark, navy blue eyes.

"You're dressed," he accused her, his voice rough as he paced closer to her. "I thought you were naked and playing with toys."

"No, you didn't." Piper could feel herself trembling from the force of the need racing through her. "That's just an excuse, Jed."

"Yeah, it's just an excuse," he agreed as he stopped before her. "An excuse for this."

She hadn't expected it to happen so fast—that his lips would be on hers, his fingers curving around the back of her neck, holding her in place as his lips took possession of hers.

She hadn't expected she would weaken so fast. That her nails would dig instantly into his shoulders, that she would lean into him, against him, so eager for him that her body was quivering in excitement.

What the hell was this? What was he doing to her?

Then thought became impossible. Any possible chance of a denial evaporated as pleasure began to build with a fiery force.

Oh, hell, yes.

Desperate to get closer to him, she wrapped her arms around his neck as he lifted her against him, holding her close in his arms as he lifted her from her feet.

She was weightless.

Gravity couldn't touch her, and neither could the reality of common sense.

"Whoa. Oh, hell, no!"

Piper found herself suddenly spun around, released, and

pushed protectively behind Jed in a move so powerful she knew she'd never figure out how he managed it. But one minute she was in his arms kissing him for everything she was worth, and the next second she was pushing past him to confront her big brother.

The big lug.

He was staring at them as though he had never witnessed such a thing.

"Forget what a couple kissing looks like?" she snapped as he suddenly lost that surprised look and turned a glare on Jed instead.

Moving to Jed's side rather than behind him, Piper crossed her arms over her breasts and stared back at Dawg furiously. "When are you going to learn to knock at the doors to our suites rather than barging in, Dawg Mackay?" she demanded. "I could have been naked or something."

"In the living area?" he demanded, outraged. "And I've never knocked, dammit. You have a bedroom for this crap anyway."

"It's my suite," she informed him. "I could be naked in either room if I want to be. And why should I have to do everything private in my bedroom? I had the door locked. I did not tell you to unlock it. Try knocking."

He didn't even look at her. He was too busy glowering at Jed.

Neither man blinked.

"I was going to say good night," he snarled, finally sparing a short glance her way before turning back to Jed with a killing look.

"Good night, then." She waited for him to leave.

Jed was glaring at Dawg just as fiercely as Dawg was glaring at Jed, and she was getting tired of it.

Dawg's disapproval was clear.

Piper sighed in irritation.

"Both of you get the hell out of my room," she suddenly ordered, anger beginning to flare inside her. "Get out. Go away. Leave me the hell alone."

She had a ride to catch, and she had no intention of missing it. Especially not so she could babysit two grown men who were suddenly acting like two dogs over a bone.

Jed turned his glare on her. "We weren't finished."

"The hell you weren't," Dawg answered for her.

Propping her hands on her hips, she turned a fierce stare on both of them.

"Get out of my room," she snapped again. "If I have to ask one more time I'm calling Mom and Tim and you can deal with them."

"That little bastard Timothy doesn't scare me in the least," Dawg informed her, his celadon gaze sparking with anger.

"Well, Mom does scare you," she reminded him. "And trust me, if she knew what was going on right now she'd have both your heads."

They both grimaced and began retreating.

Jed moved for the connecting door as Dawg backed to the door that led to the hall. As each door closed Piper moved to it quickly and locked it securely.

Good God, how the hell was she supposed to slip out of the house and out of the state with this mess going on?

One thing was for damned sure: if she'd had second thoughts about how her brother or even Jed would act if one of them were to go with her, then she had her answer now.

They'd act just as they were: like two Neanderthals with nothing better to do than beat their chests and roar out their aggressions.

Not what she needed this week.

Oh, God, she didn't need it this week.

The week she was going to find the dreams she'd worked for all her life.

She was slipping out, making her way across the darkness of the porch, two traveling bags in hand.

Jedediah lowered his head for a second before lifting his gaze and forcing himself to watch her make her way from the inn. Curling his fingers into fists, he held back the urge to follow her. To stop her.

If he stopped her, he'd be no better than her brother or her cousins. They were doing all the wrong things for all the right reasons, but that didn't make it bearable for the impulsive, bright, beautiful little star they were smothering.

Crossing his arms over his chest, he leaned against the heavily leafed tree he hid beneath and just watched her. There was no need to follow her. She wasn't headed to a party, a friend's house for a night out, or even one of the local bars.

He'd known that when he'd talked to her on the phone as he'd watched her through the closed-circuit wireless camera that had been installed in the bedroom when her sister occupied it. It hadn't been removed when Eve had moved out.

As he had watched her pack he had known she was heading out of town.

With a friend? Most likely a lover, he thought wearily, wondering at the sense of possessiveness tightening his gut.

Hell, he'd waited too long to secure her to him, left it too late. He'd sensed that as he watched her packing earlier.

He was always careful when checking on her. He never interfered, never looked in on her when there was a chance of embarrassing her if she found out he was watching.

Sometimes, he just wanted to see her. See her relaxed, sleeping, or amused. Sometimes, he just wanted to make certain she was safe, nothing more. He'd seen her packing, though, and he'd been unable to resist calling her, hoping she'd confide in him. Hoping that talking to him, remembering the pleasure they'd shared, would change her mind if she was heading out to stay with a lover.

It hadn't.

She disappeared around the side of the house.

Lowering his head, he stayed in place. He didn't dare move, even under the pretense of returning to his own room. Because he knew he wouldn't make it there.

Hell, no, he'd end up following her, and he'd make her hate him when he couldn't help himself and persuaded her to stay. Persuaded her in a way that would ensure her pleasure—and her hatred.

Fuck, it was hard letting her go.

Rubbing at the ache in his chest, frowning at the tightness there, he wondered at the feeling he'd identified years before as a premonition, a warning of danger.

Who or what could be in danger?

Maybe it was better that Piper was leaving for a few days after all. Her sister had nearly died the year before because she was too close to his partner, Brogan Campbell.

God help anyone who dared to threaten Piper Mackay. He would kill. Perhaps not for the first time, though it would definitely be the first time he'd killed over a woman.

She was worth killing for.

She was worth dying for.

The brilliance that was Piper Mackay couldn't be contained. She was wild and free, bright and burning, and there were already too many men determined to tame that fire. To lock it in. To take the freedom she fought so valiantly for.

He refused to become one of them.

Jed forced himself to move, to walk slowly and easily across the stretch of lawn that led to the inn and the suite he had taken next to Piper's.

She was gone and he had no choice but to let her go.

That didn't mean he liked it.

It sure as hell didn't mean it was easy.

# THREE

Amy's sister, Gypsy Seavers, was waiting exactly where Piper had directed her to the day before.

The small clearing just past the inn was far enough away that if the other woman had turned her lights off before pulling in, then there was no way in hell Tim could possibly see them. Yet it was close enough for her to jog to, even carrying the two bags she had brought with her.

"Trunk's open." Gypsy's voice came from the other side of the vehicle as Piper moved for the car.

By the time she reached the trunk, Amy's sister was standing next to it, lifting it for her as Piper threw her bags in. She took a good look at Gypsy's face in the trunk's light. Just to be certain she was who she was supposed to be, Piper told herself, realizing some of Dawg's lectures on safety might have actually stuck in her mind.

The second Piper moved back from the trunk, Gypsy had it closed and was moving around her to the driver's side.

"Ready to roll?" the other woman asked, glancing back as Piper watched her.

"Ready to roll." A quick nod and Piper was opening the passenger door and sliding inside quickly before pulling it closed.

Gypsy's door didn't so much as squeak as she closed it and restarted the vehicle.

She resembled Amy, Piper decided as the car pulled back out onto the main road and headed toward town.

The same amber or caramel hair, streaked with much lighter strands by the sun. She was slender, compact, and the jeans and racer-back T-shirt she wore showing off her lightly tanned, well-toned upper body made her appear smaller and more fragile than her diminutive five-foot-four frame already did.

"Amy and I were betting you wouldn't make it out after she told me who your brother and cousins were." Gypsy flashed her a quick, rueful grin. "I don't know if I would have followed through after I learned Natches Mackay was your cousin if I hadn't already promised."

Piper stiffened, turning to stare back at Gypsy warily. Great, she knew Natches. Piper wasn't even going to bother asking how yet. Only one question was uppermost in her mind. "Did you contact him?"

"Natches?" Flicking her a questioning look, Gypsy efficiently navigated the curvy mountain road that led to the interstate.

"Yeah." Piper could feel that sense of freedom slowly disintegrating.

"Not hardly." Gypsy grimaced. "Picking you up might piss him off at me, but calling him and letting him know would only add a shadow of distrust to my name if he ever actually meets me."

Neither the resignation in Gypsy's voice, nor her explanation, made sense.

"What do you mean?" Piper shook her head. "Wouldn't it be the other way? He wouldn't trust you if he learned you had helped me? Wouldn't he trust you more if you contacted him?"

"Doesn't work that way." The other woman rejected the suggestion, her expression still a bit stiff, with an air of secretiveness. "I promised I'd help you before I knew who your cousin was. You don't appear to be in any trouble, and my own sources verified how protective your brother and cousins are. If I called him without cause, no matter how much he would love to know where you are and who you're with, then he'd count that as a betrayal of confidence. I'd be deemed untrustworthy, unless you were in trouble." She threw Piper a quick, amused look. "Are you in trouble?"

"No trouble," Piper promised her, breathing out a sigh of relief. "I just don't need company, you know?"

She hoped Gypsy understood. Just as she hoped the other woman didn't call Natches later.

"Sometimes a girl just has to do what a girl has to do. And sometimes she just has to do it alone," Gypsy agreed as the lights from the dash emphasized the unsmiling expression she wore.

"Exactly," Piper stated. "The New York fashion scene isn't a place where any of them would get along well. It would be like placing a herd of bulls in a roomful of china. Forget the china shop. They would raze the shop and head for the warehouse."

Gypsy gave a small, surprised laugh at the description before her amusement was quickly pulled back.

"I've heard that about Natche." She gave a light laugh. "He was a legend in Afghanistan while he was there. One of the best damned snipers the Marines had, and better at covert intelligence than he had any right to be."

Yeah, that sounded like Natches.

"How do you know him?" Piper asked. "Are you with Homeland Security, too?" That would be just her luck.

"Not hardly." Gypsy's lips tilted into a crooked smile. "I was with the Marines myself. Many of Natches's missions in Afghanistan and Iran are used as training points now."

Piper had heard Tim mention that several times, while Natches seemed rather proud of it.

"What are you going to do when they find out you're gone, then?" Gypsy asked as Piper stared into the darkness and wondered what the trip would have been like with Jed.

"Hopefully, they won't find out," she stated irritably. "Because, trust me, New York City would never be the same if those three showed up there."

She shuddered to even imagine the chaos the Mackay cousins could still manage to create.

"Best-laid plans and all that," Gypsy pointed out. "Surely you have a plan, just in case?"

"I'm a Mackay; what do you think?" She grinned back at her friend's sister.

"I think you have one," Gypsy reflected. "But I think you're not so sure of it, and I think you're really afraid it won't work."

"And what makes you think that?" Unfortunately, she was right.

"Six years in the military. The last two in the investigative side of the military police. I can hear it in your voice, and I can see it in your face. You're a piss-poor liar, aren't you, Piper Mackay?"

"Unfortunately, that's far too close to the truth," Piper agreed.

It didn't surprise her to learn Gypsy Seavers was some sort of investigator. She had that air of secretiveness and quiet watchfulness. "I left Mom a note. She'll find it in the morning, and I begged her not to say anything. And for the first time in my life I lied to my mother. I told her I needed to get away from the male portion of the family and I was staying with friends." She grimaced at the lie. "What she'll actually end up doing is anyone's guess."

"And how long do you think it will take for your brother and cousins to find you?" Rueful amusement reflected in Gypsy's voice.

They would find her far too soon if she didn't get very lucky.

"Let's hope it takes a while," Piper suggested, terribly afraid that if she wasn't very, very lucky, then her brother and cousins would find her far too quickly.

"What the hell do you mean, she's not here?" Dawg rubbed his hand along the back of his neck in irritation as he faced Mercedes the next morning, barely holding back a glare. He needed to talk to Piper about what had happened the night before. Catching her with Jed Booker had reminded him all over again of what had happened with Eve the summer before. He didn't want another sister in danger because of her association with one of Timothy's agents. He also didn't want her endangered because she was trying to hide it from him. And he definitely didn't want to piss Mercedes off as he tried to find out where the hell she had gone.

Timothy, the quarrelsome little bastard, got all kinds of out of sorts if he managed to upset Mercedes over her "babies." But he'd be damned if those sisters of his weren't going to drive him to drink.

Their antics were making him seriously consider a nunnery for his daughter.

"Dawg, give her a break," Mercedes ordered, though her voice was calm as she moved around the kitchen and cleaned up from that morning's breakfast preparations. "You've hounded her, Lyrica, and Zoey for almost a year now. Everywhere they go, everything they do, and everyone they talk to is reported back to you so you can fuss at them over their friends, potential dates, and acquaintances. I warned you last year they were going to get sick of it. Piper just got fed up with it first."

Her arms crossed over her breasts as she stared up at him, her expression tight with defensiveness as her determination to stand in his way became more than apparent.

"And you know why I've done it," he reminded her. "Hell, I remember a time when you were all for it."

Now that those stubborn, independent young women were crying on "mommy's" shoulder, she was backtracking from the protective atmosphere just as quickly as she had agreed to it.

"A year ago." One hand propped on her rounded hip as she faced him with fiery dark eyes. "When there was a chance she was actually in danger. Even you admit there's nothing going on now, no one is watching you or the girls, nor is there any apparent backlash from what happened last summer. I believe, Dawg, you can't let yourself accustom to life without that danger. It's not fair to make the girls live such a life as well."

He was not going to allow her to draw him into this argument, not after having this exact confrontation with Christa after returning home the night before, furious at finding Jed in Piper's room, and Piper in Jed's arms. His own wife had been quick to rip a strip of his hide, first for not knocking, and second for daring to butt his nose into his sisters' sex lives again.

He did not want to know his sisters had sex.

He especially didn't want to know who they were having sex with.

"Where's she at, Mercedes?" He wasn't going to give her the satisfaction of this argument. They'd already been down that road far too many times.

"I'm not telling you." Pure stubbornness pulled at her expression.

As much as those girls looked like they could belong to him or his cousins, Rowdy and Natches, he had to admit there were times, like this, when he realized they looked just like their mother.

"Then I'll have Alex put out an APB on her," he warned, trepidation beginning to tighten the back of his neck.

Hell, he hadn't expected levelheaded Piper to be the one to test her safety first.

"No. You will not. Attempt it. Dare to take this from her, Dawg Mackay, and I promise you neither I, my daughters, nor Timothy will ever allow you to forget it."

He turned away from her, rubbed at the back of his neck, and grimaced in frustration.

"I don't feel good about this," he muttered as he turned back to her. "Mercedes, I don't feel good about this at all."

The anger beginning to brighten her brown eyes dimmed, but he could see the concern in them as well.

"I don't like it myself," she admitted quietly. "She didn't tell me where she was going, Dawg; I found out by accident. All she told me was that she had to get away. She slipped out in the dead of night because she trusted none of us to allow her the freedom she hungers for. Let her have her freedom, before we smother her to death."

"A freedom that has the potential to get her killed?" he asked her wearily. "I understand the need, Mercedes, more than you know. But you know what nearly happened to Eve last summer. If someone targets one of the other girls in retaliation, and there's no one there to protect them, what do we do then?"

"We pray that doesn't happen," she whispered as the concern in her gaze threatened to turn to pure fear. "But you also have to understand, Dawg: Piper's not a liar; nor is she one to make decisions such as this rashly. She was driven to it."

He had driven her to it. He could hear the accusation in her tone.

Christa had warned him more than once that the girls were going to rebel against his protection and begin making decisions that would only endanger them. He hadn't believed they would do so without first confronting him.

His sisters were fighters; they weren't cowards.

"How can you be certain she's safe?" he finally asked her worriedly.

"I can't, Dawg." Her smile was gentle, compassionate. "All I can do is pray that if she's in trouble she'll call me. That and trust in the man Timothy has watching her." She winked at him. "Watching her, Dawg. Allowing her to do what she has to do, what she wants to do, while an impartial third person stands ready to protect her rather than standing between her and what she needs. That's the difference."

He shook his head, worry tearing at him as he stared down at her, wishing, just as he had over the past six years, that he'd been able to protect Mercedes and the sisters he'd grown to love so much from his father's cruelties before he had died.

He hadn't known about them. No one had known about them but Chandler Mackay, and Chandler had done nothing to ensure their protection should anything happen to him.

"They'll still get hurt." That was part of what he couldn't bear. "If not physically, then otherwise. They're too trusting, Mercedes, and too innocent. If we don't watch out for them—"

"Then they might get their feelings hurt or their hearts broken?" she suggested as she turned and began cleaning the stove. "We can't keep them from getting hurt, Dawg. It's life. You know that as well as I do."

No, he damned well didn't know that.

They were innocent, gentle, and deserved far more than he knew they had waiting for them if no one was close enough to protect them.

"You do know it, Dawg," she stated as she turned back to him, watching him as though she could read the silent denial raging through him. "You don't like it. You don't want to admit it, but you know it."

He refused to accept it.

"I won't let them get hurt, Mercedes. I promised you that when you brought them home to me. I told you I'd look out for them."

He had promised them he would look out for them, and he was breaking that promise.

She shook her head slowly. "There's only so much you can do, Dawg." The compassion in her expression tightened his chest as he suddenly wished he had brought Christa with him for this confrontation. Maybe she could have talked some sense into Mercedes. On the other hand, she would have probably agreed with her.

"Dawg, give her this time, she needs it," Mercedes said softly. "More than you know, she needs it."

She needed it.

But what happened if it was the chance an enemy needed to strike out at her?

What was he supposed to do then?

# FOUR

Piper loved New York City.

The pace, the energy, the sense of excitement that seemed to permeate every corner of the city sank into her senses. Her heart beat faster. Blood rushed quick and furious through her veins, and the ordered chaos, the shopping throngs and ever-present sea of faces channeled a chaotic pace inside her own body and filled her with elation.

The first time Dawg and his wife, Christa, had brought her to the city had been to introduce her to the many and varied bolts of fabrics and exquisite costume jewelry and fake gems available in the small, out of the way shops and fabric stores there. Rhinestones, glittering crystals, clear sapphire- and emerald-colored stones—the choices seemed almost unlimited.

Now, five years later, she still found the little shops and stores impossible to leave once she began searching for the items she needed for each design—those already sketched and those that built in her imagination as she found hidden bolts of unique or discontinued fabrics, bows, ribbons, and glittering stones.

It was the first place she'd headed the minute she had rented her car that morning after arriving at the hotel.

The black four-door sedan was actually much smaller than she preferred for a four-door, but the latest trend in economy and fuel efficiency had also inspired a new generation of car designs that she simply wasn't as fond of.

Driving in New York City wasn't always safe, but it was rarely dull. Piper found her senses tuning in to the traffic, the bystanders, the lights and sounds of the streets as she drove outside the city toward the mountains that Eldon Vessante's assistant had directed her to. The interview would take place at Vessante's estate, rather than the hotel, and though she hadn't anticipated the drive, she found it relaxed her, at least. Her nerves were less than settled at the thought of the upcoming meeting.

As she drove out of the city and entered the less congested interstate, she could feel her excitement building.

The change in time and location of the meeting was unexpected, especially considering the fact that his assistant had seemed less pleasant than she had when Piper had spoken to her the first time.

Following the onboard navigation, she found herself turning from the highway and moving onto a two-lane road that climbed slowly into the surrounding mountains. Another turn and she passed the sign for Vessante Way, the designer's estate the assistant, S. Chaniss, had told her they were meeting at.

Piper was feeling more confused than excited as she pulled into the curving driveway in front of the three-story estate and gazed up at the stone steps leading to the massive double front doors.

There were no attendants present. No one was rushing to park her car, and only a small, bright red little sports car ahead of her was present.

Stepping from the rental car, she pulled free the wide portfolio she'd brought with her and gazed around the heavily forested area for long seconds before moving slowly to the steps.

As she reached the top, the doors swung slowly inward to reveal a towering butler.

Standing at six and a half feet at the very least, his brown gaze icy, his expression implacable, he gave every indication of being ex-military, and as hard as granite.

"Ms. Mackay." He nodded down at her with a slight inclination of his head. "Mr. Vessante is awaiting you in the drawing room."

The drawing room? Those actually still existed?

"If you'll follow me." It may have been worded as a request, but the tone was a straight-up order.

Her brother and cousins had ensured that she recognized the difference.

Before he turned away, his gaze raked over her with a glint of sudden curiosity, or familiarity. She'd met a lot of men over the years whom her male kin knew, and she was certain she had never met this man, yet that look gave her the uneasy feeling that he knew her.

Turning, he indicated she should follow him.

Dressed in black, perfectly creased slacks and a pristine white shirt that didn't have a single wrinkle, he led her through the wide, steel-colored marble foyer that seemed to extend a mile or more. Reaching the end of the room-size entryway, he turned sharply to the right and a set of doors at the end of the short hall.

A sharp rap of his knuckles was answered in seconds. The

butler gripped the doorknobs, pushed the doors open, then stood back for her to enter.

The heavy Gothic design of the room was a shock. Piper stepped from the more contemporary foyer and tried to control her amazement as she stared around the room. Dark, heavy woods, leather furniture with carved clawed feet, and thick, dark draperies over the windows that blocked the early summer sunlight and sent a rush of trepidation rushing through her.

She jumped, startled at the heavy snap of the doors closing behind her before swinging forward again. From the corner of the room, a light chuckle drew her startled gaze and she watched as Vessante rose and moved slowly into the center of the room. He approached her slowly, his head tilted to the side, icy blue eyes regarding her mockingly.

"You seem nervous." His tone was less than sincere as he attempted to put on a friendly expression.

What was going on here?

"Where are the other designers?" Piper blurted, then winced. Not exactly the most graceful greeting, but this private meeting wasn't what she'd been expecting at all. She had to force herself to stay in place as he moved within inches of her, his gaze dropping to her breasts as his right hand reached out.

Piper accepted the handshake, the sensation of his damp palms giving her a slightly queasy feeling.

Something wasn't right here. As a matter of fact, something felt very wrong.

"The others couldn't make it." Pitched low, his tone still grated against her senses.

He wasn't much taller than she was. At five-seven, Eldon Vessante was so skinny he was bony. There was an effeminate air about him that the overly long white-blond hair did nothing to dispel.

His face had a skeletal appearance, with high, sharp cheek-bones and a long blade of a nose. The photographs she had seen of him had definitely given him more of a substantial air.

God, he reminded her of a rat.

Where had his reputation as a playboy come from?

"I see you brought your portfolio." He glanced to the large, square design folder she carried.

"Yes, I did." Gripping the folder with both hands now, she wondered at the sick feeling of panic growing inside her. "I assumed your assistant and the other designers with your company would be here."

She wished they were.

She hated the feeling of being trapped, alone with him.

"We don't need them, my dear," he drawled, the slight, feminine pout of his lips more apparent as he smiled slightly.

He might not need them, but she did.

"Come, shall we sit and discuss our new venture?" With a wave of his hand he indicated the sitting area on the other side of the room. "I wasn't really considering another designer this year." He turned as though her acquiescence were a foregone conclusion. "One must be certain to choose carefully. To ensure the market doesn't become overly glutted, you understand."

Piper followed, but she did so warily, listening to the precise, self-important tone of his voice rather than the words themselves.

"You're not contributing to the conversation, my dear. That's quite rude of you."

Eldon paused in the middle of the sitting area, one hip jutting forward as he lifted his left hand, palm upward, as though giving her the floor.

"I was listening," she excused her nonparticipation, still watching him carefully as she moved into the sitting area.

"Have a seat, please." He gestured to the sofa with an outstretched hand. Piper perched on the edge nervously as he remained standing.

"Would you like coffee? Or perhaps tea?" he asked, still standing with one hip jutting slightly forward, the position, as well as her own, ensuring her a perfect view of his thighs, should she want to look.

She didn't.

"No, thank you." Clearing her throat and glancing around the room she wished she could push back the panic attack still threatening to shorten her breathing.

She hadn't had one for years, not since arriving in Kentucky, actually. Now her insides were shuddering, her throat tightening, the unreasoned fear rising inside her like a fast-moving sickness.

"Why not?" The hand he had been extending went to his hip in a classically feminine gesture of irritation that did little to ease her apprehension.

Blinking back at him, she fought to come up with an answer other than the fact that the thought of anything in her stomach made her want to throw up as the panic built inside her.

"Tea," Eldon stated, finally shifting his stance and brushing the thin strands of white-blond hair back from his rodentlike face. "You look like the tea sort." Shifting his attention from her to the door, he yelled, "Broecun!"

The door opened.

His expression as impassive as moments before, the bodyguard, butler, whatever the hell he was, stepped just inside the room.

"Mr. Vessante?"

"Have Leda bring in a pot of tea, please."

Cold, cold brown eyes flickered over her for the briefest moment before he backed out of the doorway, closing the doors behind him.

Piper tightened her grip on her portfolio.

Eldon moved closer, taking a seat on the sofa with her. It placed him far too close to her.

"Shall we talk terms then?" he asked, the ice blue of his gaze suddenly hardening.

"Of course." She nodded.

She'd just as soon get this done and have it over with. Lifting the portfolio closer, she was suddenly stopped by the touch of Eldon's hand on her wrist.

Her stomach tightened as dread began to wash over her.

"I don't need to see the designs. They'll be accepted if you play the game properly."

Ahh.

Her stomach pitched alarmingly.

"Excuse me?"

His smile was oily and far too sinister.

"I think you heard me perfectly, actually," he said softly. "We'll enjoy a nice cup of tea; then we'll retire to my suite. Be a nice little fuck until I grow tired of you and we'll see about that show you want so badly."

This wasn't happening.

This couldn't be happening.

"Are you insane?" Had she really said that aloud?

Eldon sat back slowly, his expression tightening further, but thankfully his hand lifted from her wrist.

"You don't want to piss me off, Ms. Mackay," he warned her, his tone low, echoing with anger.

"I don't?" She really didn't, but the churning in her stomach assured her she was going to end up doing just that.

"Do you want that runway show, darling?" He stared back at her with such a chilling lack of emotion that a shudder raced down her spine.

Did she want that runway show?

She was shaking her head before she realized it and rising slowly to her feet.

"You *are* insane," she decided, much calmer than she should have been while facing a madman. "Business isn't done like that anymore."

A mocking laugh parted his lips as he rose slowly to his feet.

"Don't be a fool, Piper," he warned her, his hip jutting once again, as if he hoped she'd glance at his sock-stuffed crotch.

She'd gone to high school; she knew what it looked like.

"Looks like I'm going to be a fool." Clutching the portfolio tighter in her hands, she backed away from him.

She'd not just gone to high school; she'd been raised in East Texas, and she damned well knew better than to turn her back on a rattler.

Unfortunately, he was advancing on her.

"The opportunity of a lifetime?" he asked silkily. "You're letting it ride right on by you." He gave a little waving motion with his hand. "Are you sure you want to do that?"

Was she sure?

Gripping the doorknob, she turned it and pulled the door open quickly.

"Am I sure I want to tell you to shove your offer up that sock-stuffed ass of yours?" she asked archly as she escaped into the foyer.

He paused, but only for a second.

Piper saw the blow coming and only barely managed to evade it as his fist came flying out.

"Bitch!" he snarled.

"Bitch? Because I know the difference between a sock and a dick?" She sneered back at him, quickening her pace as she walked backward.

"You'll never get out of that backwoods town where you're hawking that shit you sew together," he snarled, his face flushing a brilliant red as his eyes bulged to the point that they threatened to pop out of their sockets.

"And you'll never be anything but a fake dick," she threw back at him as Broecun entered the foyer from another room, leaned against the doorframe, and folded his arms over his chest lazily as he watched.

Asshole—he could have at least appeared surprised rather than plain amused.

"Bitch!"

She watched Eldon's muscles bunch, knew he was going to move, and she knew she would never be able to evade the punch.

Jed was going to be pissed.

Dawg would go ballistic.

They would both travel to New York and start taking off heads if she came home with just the faintest bruise that came from a male hand.

She tried to evade it.

She jumped, tried to run, but she was too damned scared to take her eyes off him.

Just before his fist launched, it stopped.

She didn't know who was more surprised, her or Eldon, when he found his fist suddenly captured in the hard, huge hand of Broecun.

"Get out of here, girl." Hard, emotionless, the order was voiced without heat or any sense of warning.

Still, Piper turned and ran for the front door.

She couldn't believe this. She couldn't believe the chance she had dreamed of had come to this.

To lose it all because of some asshole with a sock for a dick.

# FIVE

Pulling into the back lot of the rental car agency, Piper was still fuming hours later.

It was too late to be in an area that appeared deserted in New York City, and far too late to do anything but turn the car back in.

At least the cab she'd called was waiting for her.

She'd stopped to let the driver know she just had to park the car; then she'd be ready to leave.

What she hadn't anticipated was that when she'd thrown her portfolio and her purse to the back of the car earlier, she'd also managed to knock the bag containing her morning purchases over on the back floorboard.

Rhinestones and colored crystals were scattered along the carpet, twinkling merrily beneath the interior lights as she scooped them up and threw them back into her bag without bothering to return them to the small plastic bags they'd been in when she'd bought them.

That took far too long, as far as she was concerned. The damned cab was charging by the frickin' half minute, if she remembered her last trip to New York correctly.

She had only so much cash on her, and her own credit card was barely going to cover her hotel room. The trip was supposed to be all expenses paid, but Piper knew the type of man Eldon Vessante was now. No doubt he had already called the hotel and informed them that he wasn't paying for anything. That meant she'd better have her own card ready and waiting when she walked through the front doors.

Tossing the last of the colored crystals and stones into her bag, Piper stepped back, slammed the door, then hurriedly locked the car before rushing back to the front of the rental agency.

Depositing the keys in the night box, she all but ran to the taxi and gave the driver the address to the hotel.

Just as the vehicle pulled out, the first raindrops began pelting the yellow-and-black vehicle.

"It's finally raining," the driver commented as he turned at the corner and headed for the hotel. "You in town for long?"

"Not really." She stared straight ahead, fuming.

"Business or just a visit?" he asked then, obviously in the mood to chat.

Every cabdriver she'd ever known had spent their time either on their cell phone or talking to the company about waiting fares. This one would have to be the chatty type.

"A little of both," she answered, staring out at the rain as she tried not to cry.

Not yet.

She'd made certain she hadn't cried on the way back to the rental agency. God forbid she get pulled over for any reason, even this far away from home, because she knew it would take less than an hour for Somerset's chief of police, Alex Jansen, to learn about it. What Alex knew, his wife, Janey, would be quick to find out.

And Janey, being Natches's sister and Dawg's cousin, would find it impossible not to tattle.

Piper should have known better. She should have known it couldn't be this easy. She'd worked far too long and too hard for it to happen as she had imagined once she'd received that letter from S. Chaniss.

*"If it walks exactly like a duck and quacks exactly like a duck, then watch out for the explosion, because no two ducks walk or quack exactly the same,"* she'd once heard Dawg say with a laugh.

She should have been prepared for the explosion.

The cabdriver chatted about the rain while Piper answered where she had to. She was aware the trip back to the hotel took much longer than it had going from the hotel to the rental agency, but she always added in for the detours and "scenic routes" the cabbies took to add to the time and mileage they charged, no matter where they were.

There was only so much of a delay he could make, though. It may have seemed like hours before he was pulling into the front of the well-lit hotel, but it had actually taken no more than fifteen minutes. Which was way too long, considering it was close to midnight and the streets, with the exception of Times Square and a few other tourist-heavy areas, were all but deserted of traffic.

Pushing his fee and a larger tip than he deserved through the small opening in the divider between the passenger's and driver's areas, Piper stepped from the cab and moved quickly into the hotel.

"Ah, Ms. Mackay." The young, blond receptionist caught her

attention. The girl's expression was apologetic, her pale blue gaze faintly concerned. Just as Piper expected.

"Yes?" She should have kicked Vessante while she had the chance.

"The manager would like to speak to you." The receptionist's smile was compassionate. "He's coming now."

As she stepped to the reception desk, the night manager moved from his office and slid behind the desk as Piper waited.

Stocky, his face weathered with laugh lines at the corner of his eyes, his brown gaze was concerned and compassionate. It was firm, though. He knew what he had to do, and he may hate it, but he would do it.

"My apologies, Ms. Mackay," the manager, Charles, appeared genuinely apologetic. "I'm aware your stay was to be taken care of by another party, but." He grimaced. "I'm terribly sorry, ma'am, but I was informed before your arrival that that is no longer the case and the party is now refusing to pay."

She couldn't let the manager finish demanding the payment. It wasn't his fault, and she could tell this was one part of his job he definitely didn't like.

"I'd prefer to take care of my room myself, Charles." She smiled back at him as relief gleamed in his gaze.

He was a nice guy; she liked him. He had checked her in during the wee hours of the morning and ensured she had a cab waiting that morning to take her shopping. He'd arranged her morning coffee and joked with her about the weather when she'd stepped into the lobby to leave for her shopping trip.

Taking her date book/planner from her purse, Piper opened it and pulled her credit card free before laying it on the gleaming marble counter in front of the young woman standing at his side.

"Thank you." The young woman—Brittany, her name tag claimed—ran the card before giving her a bright smile as the payment went through. "Will you be staying with us the full length of the reservation?"

So much for Dawg being unaware where she had stayed.

Piper shook her head as she slid a tip to the girl. "I'm checking out tonight. Could you please have a car waiting in about an hour to take me to the train station, and send the bellhop up for my luggage?"

She should never have gone shopping that morning. There were bags of additional materials in her room that she would now have to try to stuff into the single extra duffel bag she'd packed rather than purchasing another, as she'd planned.

"I'll make certain of it." Brittany's smile was too cheerful.

Piper quickly turned and headed for the elevators as she tucked her card back into the planner's clear zippered pocket.

As she did so, a phone number caught her eye.

Jed Booker. The number was scrawled under his name in the neat, no-nonsense handwriting he used.

She should have invited him to come with her, she sighed wearily to herself. Eldon Vessante would have never tried anything so stupid if Jed had been with her. She had a feeling Mr. Vessante would have been far less likely to stuff that sock in his pants, or to make such an outrageous demand.

He would have simply told her he had changed his mind the first chance he had, which would have suited her fine.

Stepping into the elevator, she told herself it didn't matter. If it was meant to be, it would be; it was that simple.

That phone number glared back at her, though, until she snapped the planner closed. She didn't push it back into her purse, however. She held on to it even though she'd already both memorized the number and programmed it into her smart phone.

Yes, if she had brought Jed, she had no doubt the night would have been far less disappointing and much more interesting.

One thing was certain: Jed so did not stuff his crotch with anything but what God had given him. And God had been generous.

Rudy Genoa stared at the disgusting, bloodied face of the car rental agency manager with bitter fury.

He was tied, in a rather clichéd style, to an old-fashioned wooden office chair, because he was too damned cheap to buy the nice, if inexpensive, computer chairs that were so easy to find.

It had worked to restrain him, though.

Duct tape secured his wrists to the arms of the chair and his ankles to the legs. His face was swollen and pale beneath the blood that marred it. The top of his balding head was splattered with his blood, calling attention to the fact that perhaps he'd lost more hair since the last time Rudy had seen him several months ago.

Chester's head lolled to the side a bit, while small, bloody bubbles filled and deflated at his nostrils with each breath.

He really was a distressing sight, but it couldn't be helped. Rudy was furious. The loss of the delivery had the potential to do far more than just embarrass him. The loss of that delivery could bring some very nasty individuals into his town looking for him. The type of men one preferred not to piss off. Even one with Rudy's power.

He couldn't believe the stupidity.

This was what you got for trying to trust family to do a job right.

"Did you think I would just let this go, Chester?" Rudy asked as he straddled the chair he'd pulled over to the balding, overweight little bastard.

"Rudy, please." Sloppy, bleeding, one eye swollen shut, his

lips split by the heavy fist that had pounded into them, Chester wept pitifully. "I did like you said; I swear. It was that new girl. She rented the car out."

"And now the delivery that came in with that car is missing," Rudy stated softly. "We checked it thoroughly."

"Please." Chester choked. "You owe me, Rudy. You owe me. I'll get them back. I swear I will."

He owed him.

Rudy agreed with his cousin for a change.

A six-year stint in prison for a crime he had been nowhere near had earned Chester a hell of a boon. But this . . .

Rudy shook his head as he propped his arms on the back of the chair he was straddling. Six years in prison for the rape of Rudy's rival's mistress came nowhere close to the millions of dollars in diamonds, sapphires, and rubies that were now missing.

The slightest awareness of another presence behind him had Rudy waiting patiently, the familiar lack of sound in his son's movements pleasing.

"I checked the security tapes. She arrived about ten minutes before we did, messed around in the backseat, looks like she knocked over a bag onto the back floorboard. We found a receipt pushed beneath one of the seats for a craft seller for colored crystals and stones. There's a chance the woman doesn't know what she has." There was no opinion either way in the boy's voice.

Well, perhaps Andre wasn't a boy anymore, but as his mother would say, he would always be Rudy's boy.

"And her name?" Rudy asked.

At his son's lack of an answer, Rudy turned to stare back at him with a frown. Rarely had Rudy seen this expression on Andre's face.

That look of concern.

Trepidation began to tingle in Rudy's gut.

"Piper Mackay, from Somerset, Kentucky." The words were a harsh rasp of anger from a man who rarely allowed himself to show any emotion. "The investigation I did on the family after Marlena's disappearance says she's James 'Dawg' Mackay's sister."

But now, Rudy knew why his son had hesitated to give him the information.

Dawg, Rowdy, and Natches Mackay had not just been instrumental in foiling Marlena Genoa's plot to kill John Walker Jr. for breaking their engagement, but had also managed to kill Gerard Andrews, the sponsor backing her acceptance into the Genoa family.

"Coincidence?" Rudy asked.

"She's staying at a hotel no more than two blocks from here," his son answered. "Chester knows the manager there, from what I've gathered."

Andre didn't confirm or deny the theory of coincidence, though Rudy knew he didn't believe in such a thing. Rudy believed, though. He'd seen far stranger occurrences in his lifetime that could be explained no other way.

"This is a complication." Rudy sighed, turning back to glower at Chester. "Why is she here, in the city?"

"According to our contact at the hotel, she's a clothing designer. She was here for a meeting with a backer," his son informed him as Rudy stared at Chester, his eyes narrowed with a fury he found hard to control. "Getting into her room won't be a problem. Once I get in, I'll restrain her and reacquire our property. That should be the end of it."

"Take two men with you," Rudy ordered as he glanced at the brute standing behind Chester. "Send them in. This is a matter you oversee, not one you do yourself."

The boy had a tendency to micromanage shit.

"I'll take care of it," Andre promised, and Rudy knew he

could depend on him. Of all the men he commanded, it was Andre he trusted above all others to ensure the job was taken care of quickly and correctly.

"Very well." Rudy sighed. "And, Andre, don't let your men kill the girl. Make it look like a random burglary. We don't need the Mackays and their government sidekicks in our town."

"Agreed." Andre nodded shortly before turning and leaving the room once again.

Rudy turned back to Chester.

"See, it wasn't my fault, Rudy. It was that girl you hired. She let the car out and I told her not to," Chester whined. "You don't have to kill me."

"True," Rudy agreed, ignoring the hope that suddenly filled his third cousin's abused features. "This is very true."

The girl was Rudy's illegitimate daughter. She was his favorite child, and this incompetent fool thought to place the blame on her? The poor bastard had just signed his own death warrant.

His gaze flicked to the heavily muscled ex-boxer, the Brute, as Rudy called him, standing behind the other man. The one whose fists had made hamburger out of Chester's face earlier.

The large head nodded as the ex-boxer, Jones Morley, read the silent look in Rudy's eyes. The weapon he carried with its silencer attached came up as Rudy moved away from the other man.

A second later, a heavy pop sounded behind him, and Rudy knew he would never have to worry about Chester screwing up again.

The nerve of him anyway, blaming an innocent child for a mistake that should have never happened.

"I hardly think my precious little Asta was at fault in the least," he said as Jones followed him from the room. "What do you think?"

"Asta's no dummy," the other man stated, bringing a glow of

pride rushing through Rudy. "I kind of doubt she would have rented the vehicle if she was told specifically not to do so."

Moving ahead of him, Jones quickly opened the door leading from the office and stood back as Rudy stepped through.

"Get rid of the body," Rudy ordered the two men waiting outside. "Then return to the house."

Striding from the office, Rudy left the building and walked quickly to the black SUV his driver, Danny, was standing beside.

The moment the doors to the office had opened, his nephew, Danny, was striding around the vehicle. Tall and imposing, Danny was as much a bodyguard as a chauffeur. Dark Italian heritage was reflected in his features, while strong American stock was reflected in his tall, stout body. Before Rudy could reach it, his door was open, the comfortable leather interior and an even more comfortable silk-skinned mistress awaiting him inside.

The mistress held no appeal for him tonight, though. The potential for disaster was rising with each minute that Andre hadn't called him to report he had the gems. Every second those jewels were out of his possession, the closer disaster came in the form of some very nasty members of the Russian Mafia.

The Mackay woman would end up destroying Rudy's base of power if he wasn't extremely careful.

Or rather, the woman's family would.

That damned brother, Dawg, and her cousins, Rowdy and Natches, and the men and women they called friends who were part of the Department of Homeland Security were dangerous. Especially that little misfit Timothy Cranston.

They were a force no criminal wanted to call the attention of. Rudy'd lost a very influential lawyer and a rather promising family member he was very fond of to the Kentucky natives.

His niece Marlena Genoa, and her sponsor back into the fam-

ily, Gerard Andrews, had been taken out with such efficiency it
had been shocking.

They had gone to Kentucky to seek retribution against Marlena's ex-fiancé when he had broken their engagement five years
before. Neither had returned, and Marlena's body had never
been found.

Poor Marlena. First her father had turned against the Genoa
family, effectively ensuring she was no longer part of the base of
power and wealth Rudy controlled. Then, she had let the prominent fiancé she had managed to snare slip from her fingers. Which wouldn't have been so bad if she hadn't promised to
secure him, and his father's prestigious law firm, for the Genoa
family. When a promise was made, it must be kept. Or retribution must be established and restitution made. Once John Walker
broke their engagement, the Genoa family demanded restitution,
a small portion of the promised funds and prestige John Walker
would have brought to the family, or Marlena had to seek retribution to prove she was strong enough to be part of the Genoa
family in an age of betrayals, double dealing, and technological
deceptions.

The family needed insurance that she would never do as her
father had and turn on them—turn evidence over to the authorities and attempt to destroy the family. She was to have killed
John Walker and Sierra Lucas before the life insurance policy she
had taken out on him, and he had forgotten about, expired. The
funds would have been given to the Genoa family, and the blood
on her hands would have given at least a small assurance of her
loyalty.

She had done neither. She had instead gotten a highly successful and very beneficial attorney killed and she had ended up,
most likely, under Timothy Cranston's control.

A very, very bad place to be.

If Rudy wasn't very careful, if his son wasn't even more care-ful, then they would soon find themselves facing that bastard Cranston and those hick Mackays in the worst possible way. That was something Rudy intended to avoid at all costs.

He'd had the family investigated after Marlena's disappear-ance and Gerard's death. What he had learned made him wary. The shadowed vendetta that had played out against his organiza-tion for a year afterward still had the power to keep him awake at night.

The authorities had watched his family much too closely, his sources among the law enforcement agencies began disap-pearing, but when his son had been jerked out of England after leaving the family and nearly imprisoned, Rudy had known they had made enemies the family could ill afford. Word on the street was that the Genoa crime organization had shaken the wrong tree in Kentucky and they were going to pay for it.

It was a tree he had no intentions of shaking again in a way that meant he, or anyone in his organization, could be identified.

The only good thing that had come of it? Homeland Security had pissed Andre off enough to return home and ensure that they could never do so again. He was now learning the ropes and moving in as Rudy's right hand. And a very effective right hand he was.

The bodies Andre disposed of were never seen again. There was no evidence to lead back to Rudy, Andre, or the family, and no loose lips spilling family business secrets.

It was a good life.

Unless those gems weren't in his possession when the owners came looking for them.

Resignation burned a hole in his gut.

Fuck. He was going to have to go after a Mackay.

He wasn't frightened of the Mackays, but he was definitely on guard against them.

So much so that he would have gladly let the disappearance of those stones go, unless the Mackay girl tried to sell them. He would have washed his hands of them if the men arriving soon to collect them would have been willing to do the same. Or if perhaps they would have taken the task of collecting them from Kentucky.

That wouldn't happen, though. At least, not until they wiped every last trace of the Genoa family from existence.

Yes, this definitely had the potential to be very, very dangerous. And that potential was growing by the minute.

# SIX

Andre Genoa stared at the hotel from the driver's seat of the dark gray van with a growing sense of fury as he disconnected the call he'd just taken.

Son of a bitch. He didn't need this, not right now. Not at this point in the game.

"Marcel says she's just called for a bellhop, Dennis," he told the man he'd chosen to retrieve the jewels. "You'll go up. When she answers the door, load her belongings. Maneuver her cart into the elevator first, where Marcel will be waiting for you. He'll block her while the doors close. Take the cart to the room service elevator and out the back entrance. I'll be waiting for you there. We'll just take everything, then go through it later."

Dennis was the less violent of the two men, and the one known to be the most protective of his daughter and wife. He was Andre's best bet in ensuring Piper Mackay wasn't harmed.

"Got it, boss." Nodding his head, Dennis opened the door and slid from the front passenger seat.

As the door closed behind Dennis's bulky form, Nate Ryan, his best friend and partner, moved into the seat, his gray eyes narrowed against the lights of the vehicles moving along the busy street as Andre pulled out of the parking space and headed toward the hotel's back entrance.

"This doesn't feel good, Andre," Nate murmured as they turned down the small street used for deliveries. "It doesn't feel good at all. Who chose Marcel to head to the hotel ahead of us?"

"No, it doesn't," Andre murmured. "Rudy didn't say anything about sending extra men in."

He hoped it was just indigestion, but something warned him this task was a hell of a lot more dangerous than the Mexican food they'd eaten earlier.

Marcel tended to give him indigestion, though. The man was a self-important moron. His arrogance had only grown in the past year, after Rudy and Boris Cheslav had chosen him as an emissary between the two families. Marcel had saved Boris's ass a few years back when he'd learned that a relative of the family working an important drug buy was actually a DEA plant. Boris had immediately moved the other man into the upper level of his organization.

When Boris had approached Rudy with the request to handle the jewels coming into the city, he'd revealed the fact that Marcel, Rudy's third cousin, was actually one of his men, and would be their contact during the transaction. Which meant Andre couldn't get rid of him, as much as he would love to.

Marcel was fucking untouchable until the agreement Rudy had made with the Russian family was completed. If the other man disappeared, then the suspicious, highly paranoid Russian might just slip the leash his own son had on him, and strike out at the Genoa family. They couldn't risk that.

Pulling the van into place, Andre glared at the back entrance of the hotel, willing Dennis to hurry, to complete the theft of the girl's belongings quickly.

"A fucking Mackay," Nate sighed beside him then. "What are the chances?"

What *were* the chances. For a man that didn't believe in co-incidence, he was suddenly being given supposed proof that they existed.

"The chances are pretty much fucking nil," he growled. "After we get back, find out why she's here, and start tying up loose ends. I want to know every fucking move she's made, everyone she's talked to, and every breath she's taken since she made the decision to come to the city alone. Dawg Mackay is too fucking paranoid to let one of his sister's travel here without a baby-sitter. And Timothy Cranston would die and go to hell before he'd let one of them travel anywhere alone without a shadow." He turned and glared at Nate. "I haven't found her shadow yet. That means, she doesn't have one."

Nate's expression hardened. "Someone playing with us again?"

"That's what my gut's telling me." Andre made the realization in a flash. "Someone's definitely playing with us, and I want to know why."


The planner Jed had scrawled his number in lay on the table next to the door, where Piper had thrown it after having to force herself not to call him. Again.

She wanted to call him.

She wanted to rail about the decision to travel to New York alone, and she wanted to curse Eldon Vessante to the pits of hell, and she needed someone to listen to her. Unfortunately, she couldn't think of anyone she could call whom she could trust to keep the details to themselves.

Even Amy, the friend whose sister had given her a ride to the train station, couldn't be totally trusted. If Amy even suspected Piper might be harmed, or had been, then she would call Dawg in a New York minute.

Amy might not know Dawg. She may not have a very high opinion of him after some of the stories Piper had told her about his protectiveness, but Amy had become a good friend over the past few years. She returned to Somerset each summer just to see Piper's new designs, and over the course of those visits, they had become close.

Besides, Amy also trusted her sister, Gypsy, and Gypsy was a female version of the Mackay men. Pure military, tough, and suspicious. She would convince Amy to call the Mackays, if she didn't just call Natches herself.

The only bright spot in the night was that she had been able to get a ticket on a train departing in two hours. It would put her in Louisville five hours later, and from there the price for a rental car home wouldn't give away the fact that she had been in New York City.

Dawg would have pups if he ever found out she had traveled there alone. He was so damned protective and controlling of his sisters' lives that he had even fully vetted their roommates at college. She and her sisters had become so disgusted over the choices he had given them that they had opted to just share an apartment together.

Piper hated it.

She hated having to look over her shoulder at every party she went to and every event she attended. Even worse was how often her dates and potential lovers looked over their shoulders.

The few men Piper had actually considered sleeping with had run so damned fast once they'd realized who she was related to that there hadn't been a chance of finding out whether they were as compatible as she had thought they might be.

The men who hadn't run had been far too much like the male Mackays for her to even consider, once she realized the traits they shared with her family members. She was terrified of ending up with a man just like Dawg, or worse yet, a man who reported to him.

That would be so humiliating.

She couldn't imagine anything worse than being in a relationship where she couldn't trust her lover to have more loyalty to her than he had fear of her brother.

Would Jed really fear Dawg, though?

She couldn't imagine that happening, but she could imagine him reporting to Dawg simply because he believed her brother would have the right to know what she was doing, when, and where.

She glanced to the planner again as she finished packing her duffel bag with the items she'd bought before leaving for the meeting with the bastard who had tricked her into coming to New York. She'd literally upended her purse to get all the little packages of stones and colored glass into the duffel, and stuffed all the fabric and notions in after them.

It would serve Eldon right if she did tell Dawg exactly what he had done. Dawg and her cousins would be in New York City so fast no one would dare realize they were gone. And they would beat the skinny, rat-faced little pervert to a pulp.

The thought of it was immensely satisfying, but she knew she could never do it.

Shaking her head at the pleasurable image and heading across the room to collect her planner, she was brought up short by a knock on the door.

The bellhop was quick. She had called the front desk and asked them to give her an hour before sending him up, but she didn't mind leaving a little earlier than she had planned. It would give her a few extra minutes to settle onto the train and feel a little sorrier for herself.

Mockery curled her lips. If there was one thing she didn't do well, it was feel sorry for herself.

Dawg wasn't really a prison warden, though in the past year, she admitted, there were often times she accused him of being one.

Checking the peephole quickly, she saw a large form dressed in the familiar hotel jacket and quickly opened the door.

For the second time that night, her world went to hell.

She had seen Eldon's attack coming; she wasn't expecting this one.

The second the door parted from the frame it slammed inward with such force Piper found herself thrown back into the room, where she crashed into the room service cart delivered earlier.

Dishes and food were suddenly flung across the floor as the cart took her weight, and Piper let out a piercing scream.

*Don't be quiet,* Dawg had always advised her and her sisters. There was nothing an attacker hated worse than having attention called to his actions.

And evidently it was the truth.

"Shut up, bitch." Enraged, the apelike figure dived for her as Piper fought to scramble away, using every breath she had to scream her lungs out.

A heavy fist caught her shoulder, causing her face to slam into the side of the dresser.

For a moment, her senses were rattled, light flashing before her eyes and exploding in vibrant color as she fought back the dizzying darkness gathering beyond the lights.

A hand attached to her upper arm with bruising force, jerking her from the floor as a hoarse demand was growled in her ear.

"Where is it?"

Where was what?

She screamed again, struggling against him as she tried with every blow to bury her fist or a foot into his balls.

Her knee connected, drawing an agonized grunt a second before she was thrown into the wall hard enough to send her bouncing to the bed.

Voices were raised, outraged, cursing.

Piper was struggling to make sense of it as the sudden explosion of a weapon discharging shocked her senses into an abrupt return to reality.

Every bone and muscle in her body hurt.

Dizziness assailed her, washing through her and weakening her as she struggled to lift herself from the bed.

Was she shot?

Oh, God, Dawg would kill her if she managed to get shot while escaping to New York. She would hear all kinds of "I told you so"s. Her sisters would of course blame her for the additional security that would follow. . . . Who the hell were those men rushing into her room?

Oh, God, they were big. . . .

There were too many of them. . . .

Too big, and too many.

Darkness rushed over her, drawing her into a pit of icy nothingness. The complete lack of sensory information was like being buried alive.

She was aware, yet she wasn't.

There, yet she wasn't.

And one question haunted her through it all: Exactly what was it her attacker had been demanding?

*Where are they, you little cunt?*

Where was what?

Who?

"Lady? Lady you okay? Someone call an ambulance; she's hurt. She's hurt—"

*She's hurt.*

Who was hurt?

Oh, yeah—it was her.

She was hurt.

Then the darkness deepened; that nowhere place grew, sucked her in, and enfolded her until nothing and no one else could penetrate.


Jed came awake instantly, before the first, faint vibrating tremor of the phone against the wood nightstand eased away. The second vibration didn't have the chance to begin before he flipped the cell phone open and brought it to his ear.

"Booker," he answered.

"Jed Booker?" the male voice asked, faintly quizzical, highly uncomfortable, and not yet fully mature.

"It is."

"My name is Bret. Bret Jordan. You don't know me, but I found your name in this lady's journal—"

"Piper." He was out of the bed instantly and dressing. "What happened?"

"Well, me and my friends were staying at this hotel in New York City when the lady in the room next to us started screaming. When we ran to her room this guy was beating the crap out of her. He got away with her purse, but her day planner was still lying on a table and it had your name in it. If you know her, the doctors really need some info."

"Where is she?" Jed growled the single word, having dressed as the kid made his explanation.

He was given the name and address quickly as he jerked his boots on his feet, grabbed his weapon and keys, and headed for the door.

"Look, are you family or something?" he was asked then. "They really need to treat her, but she's unconscious—"

"Comatose or unconscious?" Jed was in the pickup he kept parked at the inn for those times when he needed something besides the Harley.

This was one of those times.

There was a moment's mumbled conversation. "Man, the nurse won't tell me. She says family—"

"I'm her brother," he lied instantly. "Her only family. Now, is she comatose or unconscious?"

"Here's the nurse."

The nurse was, fortunately, more informative.

Identifying himself as her brother to the nurse, he waited what seemed like an eternity as she found the doctor. Pulling from the inn's parking lot, he drove at the legal speed limit until far enough from the inn to avoid drawing Timothy's attention, then hit the gas and increased his speed.

Until he hit the highway he wouldn't be safe from detection, just from being stopped for speeding. Sheriff Mayes's deputies would immediately report the truck speeding if they saw it, just as any Somerset cop would report directly to Chief of Police Alex Jansen.

As he got to the city limits, the doctor finally, thankfully, took the phone.

Piper was stable, thank God. He wouldn't have to call Dawg after all. She was currently severely bruised, concussed, and unconscious, but in stable condition. The hospital needed permission to treat her, though, the doctor explained.

Jed lied once again and told them he was her brother, gave the doctor permission to treat Piper, then asked her to put the young man who called him on the phone once again.

"You didn't give the nurse the planner to call—why?" he asked instantly, suspiciously.

"I don't know." Jed could almost see the uncomfortable shrug he imagined the young man made. "We were the ones who rescued her; I guess we kind of feel responsible for her until someone else gets here. You know? And that dude that attacked her tried to shoot us as he ran out of the room. The police around here are nuts, too. They didn't even bat an eyelash, so no one's watching to make sure the guy doesn't come after her again."

"I'll be there in approximately three hours," Jed told him. "Can you wait?"

"We'll be here until you get to her," Bret promised. "But if you could get here faster, it would be good. I heard the nurse say someone else already called the hospital and asked about the lady attacked at the hotel, so whoever attacked her could be planning to come back."

"How many are with you?"

"Just me, my best friend, Matt, and his girlfriend, Olivia," Bret told him. "We'll wait on you. No one's going to bother her while we're here."

"Thank you." Jed wasn't reassured, but he had to admit he was damned glad to know she wasn't alone.

"Well, if it was my sister, I'd want someone to wait on me," the boy admitted. "Drive careful. We'll be here."

Careful?

Jed hit the interstate and pushed his foot on the gas as he disconnected the call, then made another.

"Control," a well-modulated feminine voice answered.

"This is Agent Booker," he stated before quickly giving his control number. "I'm en route to agency airfield in Louisville, Kentucky. Advise all law enforcement to allow disposition and advise agency pilot to have transport ready. Destination New York City."

"We have you on satellite, Agent Booker," Control advised him. "All law enforcement will be advised and turned away. Proceed with caution to airfield Delta-Bravo-Tahoe, where a pilot will be advised to be waiting in hangar six-four-zero."

"Understood," he responded. "Agent Booker out."

No doubt Timothy would question him once he was given the report of Jed's midnight race to New York City, but that could be days away, possibly weeks, until Timothy called and requested agent maneuver reports. Though that was something he rarely did.

The landscape sped by; the roads, luckily, weren't busy in the hours after midnight until four in the morning or later. It gave him the space needed to travel safely at the speed needed to reach the airport just outside Louisville and to still the sudden, unheard-of terror piercing his heart.

What the hell was Piper doing in New York City?

Whoever the hell she'd been sneaking out to meet had obviously abducted her, hadn't they? Piper surely wouldn't leave the state without letting her brother, Dawg, know she was leaving.

Or would she?

Damn her.

He'd been driving himself insane in his attempt to figure out where she had gone without resorting to official channels or contacts to learn her secrets. She'd left without telling him with whom or where she was going. It was obvious she didn't want to share the information or the identity of her lover.

She hadn't wanted to share it then; she would share it now.

She would share it or he would be on the phone to Dawg.

Piper and her sisters didn't think there was anything worse than having their brother or male cousins pissed. Piper was about to find out there was something far worse.

There was Jed, and he wasn't about to let an attack against her go.

This had nothing to do with protectiveness or control. It had nothing to do with an attempt to dominate her life. What it had to do with was the fact that someone had dared to hurt her, and he would make certain that someone had the favor returned.


Piper stared at the nurse in disgust.

"You can't make me stay here," she informed the middle-aged, kindly looking nurse as the woman stared back at her with concerned hazel eyes.

Standing at five feet, four inches if she was lucky, her gray-and-brown hair pulled back from her face in a tight braid as the small wrinkles at the corners of her eyes drew in with her frown, the nurse watched her in disapproval.

"You've had a concussion, Ms. Mackay, and I doubt you feel much like walking right now, let alone traveling to the train station. If you'll just calm down, the doctor will be in soon; he can check you and let you know what damage has been done."

"I already know what damage has been done," she muttered angrily. "Trust me; I can feel every bruise."

And she could. Every single bruise, scratch, and jab that had been plowed into her undefended body.

"I'm certain you can," the nurse agreed compassionately. "But that concussion could be dangerous. Your brother's due at any time—"

"Excuse me?" Piper knew she'd just lost her breath as trepidation began to race through her system.

*Oh, God.*

*No.*

Not Dawg. Surely to God no one had actually called Dawg.

"Your brother Jed." The nurse smiled again. "His name and phone number was in your day planner, thank goodness." She moved to the bed and, as Piper stared back at her in shock, actually managed to wrap the blood pressure cuff around her arm. "Your purse was stolen. If it hadn't been for his name and number in your planner, then we'd have had no idea whom to contact."

Her brother Jed, not her brother, Dawg? No doubt Jed had called Dawg. Dawg, Rowdy, and Natches were probably just ahead of his arrival and blowing fire and brimstone. And once they stepped into the hospital, hell would have no fury like the Mackay men pissed off.

"God, this isn't good." Lying back against the hospital bed, Piper closed her eyes wearily. "How long ago did you talk to him? Forget it." She gave a quick shake of her head. "Doesn't matter; he could be here in two minutes or in two hours." Opening her eyes, she levered herself up on the bed. "Where are my clothes?"

Nurse Dade widened her eyes in surprise. "Ms. Mackay, where your clothes are doesn't matter," she informed Piper. "You need to rest."

"I'll find the damned things myself then." Piper sighed.

She really didn't feel like finding anything, especially her clothes, but sometimes a girl just had to do what a girl just had to do, right?

"Ms. Mackay, you're in no shape to leave the hospital alone."

"Nurse Dade, you really have no idea the forces of nature getting ready to rip through this hospital," she informed the nurse as dread began to fill her. "The Four Horsemen of the Apocalypse have nothing—and I mean absolutely nothing—on my brothers. Famine, pestilence, war, and disease are a kiddie playground in comparison, and I have no intentions of hanging around for the fallout."

Nurse Dade's eyes widened. "Sweetie, I talked to him myself." She gave a small, nervous little laugh. "He was as nice as he could be. I think you may have hit your head harder than the doctor thought."

Struggling from the bed, Piper ignored the nurse's disapproving glare as she shuffled to the small cabinet next to the end of the bed.

Aha, clothes.

"Ms. Mackay, this isn't advisable." The nurse sighed as Piper struggled past the roommate who had been listening in amused interest.

"It's not advisable to be here when Dawg Mackay arrives either."

"Who is Dawg Mackay?" The nurse was all but laughing at her. "His name is Jed."

"You really don't want to know. Trust me."

"You're going to hurt my feelings, sis. That just wasn't nice."

Piper came to a slow stop no more than a few feet from the bathroom door when Jed stepped slowly into the room.

His voice was gentle, amused, and patient. The look in his eyes was damned scary, though.

Scary, that was, if her attacker ever had the misfortune to stare into them.

She could see murder in those eyes. As Jed took in the bruised, swollen condition of her face, the hesitancy in her stance as she stood before him, then the livid bruises on her arms, the navy blue of his eyes flickered with a deep, black rage.

Shaking his head slowly, he advanced on her, all lean-hipped, predatory male grace and dark intent.

"How far behind you is Dawg?" Resignation slumped her shoulders.

If she had been on a leash before where her brother was concerned, no doubt it would feel like prison even before they left the hospital.

"Oh, I'd say about twelve hours or so," he drawled, then leaned close, staring into her wide eyes as he whispered, "He doesn't know, sweet pea. Want to keep it that way?"

Piper nodded. Oh, God, she really wanted to keep it that way.

"Then you're going to cooperate, right?" he suggested softly.

Piper nodded again.

To keep Dawg in the dark?

Oh, hell, yes, she would cooperate.

At least to a point.

After all, she'd hate to mar the Mackay reputation for cooperating only when it suited their own interests.

Right now it suited every single interest she could think of, though.

"Good then." He straightened, his hands settling with airy gentleness just above her shoulders. "Turn around, march right back to that bed, and we'll just wait for the doctor, shall we?"

She moved for the bed.

"That's a good girl," he commended her as Nurse Dade smiled with an awestruck girlishness Piper found nauseating.

Good girl, was she? she thought, sitting back on the bed carefully as she glared up at the smirking, far too self-satisfied Jedediah Booker.

Oh, she'd just show him what a good girl she wasn't.

As soon as the doctor released her, that was.

# SEVEN

Jed hadn't prayed in years, but as he drove from the small airfield outside Louisville the next evening, he found himself praying for patience.

He'd found a chance to question Bret Jordan and his friends Matthew Grace and Olivia Camfield. From their report, they'd heard Piper screaming in the suite next door and had come to investigate. Her door had been opened and a man they described as a "mountain" had been pounding on Piper as though he intended to beat her to death.

He also had the bastard's description. The three had been amazingly observant and were able to provide several valuable details in regard to the assailant's appearance. One of his contacts in the city had made a visit to the hotel and questioned the staff before going to the room and doing the job it seemed the police hadn't, collecting what evidence of the attack had been left.

And there was the reason for the prayers. Patience wasn't his strong suit. The second he had Piper safely at home he'd launch his own investigation. God help the bastard who had dared to touch her.

Once the assailant was found, Jed prayed he could keep from attempting to kill him with his bare hands. From showing the "mountain" what it meant to really hurt.

"Why didn't you tell Dawg where I was?" Piper finally deigned to speak to him, something she hadn't done since they'd left the hospital unless he'd simply left her no other choice.

"I promised to keep your secrets, Piper; I meant it." Glancing at her, he drove the truck he'd parked at the airfield the morning before toward Somerset. "I won't tell Dawg anything I know you'd want me to keep to myself."

The flight back had been short, but Jed hadn't wanted to arrive back in Kentucky until well after midnight. He'd spent the day getting her ready to leave and ensuring someone was investigating her reason for being there and why she had been attacked.

He hoped—hell, no, he was praying—that Dawg wouldn't be anywhere near the inn when they arrived.

She shifted against the leather seats, no doubt trying to find a comfortable position.

His fingers tightened on the steering wheel as he fought back the anger he was determined she wouldn't see.

"And that's why you didn't call Dawg?" She obviously didn't want to believe him.

"That's why."

Dawg would have charged into New York City with Rowdy, Natches, and no doubt Chaya, Natches's wife; the chief of Somerset's police force, Alex Jansen, and Pulaski County sheriff Zeke Mayes; as well as Special Agent Timothy Cranston and Piper's mother, Mercedes Mackay, ready to kill.

Dawg wouldn't have left the city until Timothy had buried her attacker. If that attacker hadn't been found, then Piper would have returned under such heavy guard she would have been smothered before ever reaching Kentucky again.

Silence descended between them, one that stretched until they had nearly reached the exit to Somerset.

"There's no way to hide the bruises," Piper stated, her voice low. "Dawg's going to see them."

Yeah, he would; there was no way to hide the damage to her face, though thankfully, her left eye was no longer swollen shut.

"What are you going to tell him?" Taking the exit to Somerset off the interstate, he knew Piper's time was definitely running out.

Dawg had all but haunted Mercedes and Timothy, demanding to know whether Piper had called her mother yet. Elijah, Jed's partner, had called earlier in the afternoon to report Dawg had contacted several agents at the surrounding airports and had her name run for flights out.

He'd told her earlier about the conversation he'd overheard between Mercedes and Dawg, as well as the fact that Dawg was questioning everyone he could think to question about her whereabouts.

"You can't hide this from him, Piper," he warned her when she didn't answer him.

"I know I can't," she answered wearily.

The tiredness in her tone coincided with that unfamiliar tightness in his chest—something he experienced only with Piper.

"He's been beside himself with worry," he told her. "Christa's accused him of running headlong into a stroke as he attempts to protect all of you."

"If he would just wait until we need protecting." Frustration immediately tightened her body as she pushed both hands through her shoulder-length black hair before clenching them in the deep waves.

God, he would kill to feel all that lush, warm silk against his body. Against his thighs as her lips parted and his dick pierced the heated dampness beyond. That particular portion of his body throbbed in painful hunger as the need for her began to grow impossibly.

Impossibly, because he hadn't believed he could hunger for her more than he already did.

Impossibly, because she was hurt, bruised, and no doubt the last thing on her mind was sex. She was definitely exhausted. She'd slept the whole of the flight, waking only as the plane taxied to the private hangar DHS leased.

"Why won't he wait until we need him, Jed?" she questioned with hurt anger. "Why can't he just let us live a little bit?"

"Because he's seen the monsters." Jed knew exactly why. "He knows what's out there, Piper, and the nightmares haunt him now—the fear of not protecting the four of you, of being off guard and missing a threat, gives him nightmares. That's why he's driving himself to a stroke. That's why he has trouble letting you live your life. Because he knows that in that one moment that you relax your guard, that's when the monsters strike and attempt to steal everything you love in life."

"Did they steal something you love?" she asked.

How had she guessed there was more to his life than he'd allowed her to see so far?

"Not quite." Glancing at her, he saw the need in her eyes—not a sexual need or a physical hunger.

She needed to see more of him than he'd allowed so far.

Intimacy. That connection that had the ability to bind two people together or tear them apart.

"No one knows I have a sister." He had to force himself to

share with her something that even Timothy Cranston was unaware of.

"You hide your family." She nodded as though it made sense.

"Well, my mother hid me from them first," he admitted with
a flicker of amused remembrance. "She didn't want my father to
know about me, didn't want me to be threatened by his career in
covert intelligence or his enemies. Father knew about me, though.
When I was old enough, he found me, and drew me in like he
does so many others and gave me one task: Protect my sister."

He could laugh about it now; at the time, it hadn't been
nearly so funny.

"You say that as though it were an impossible task," she observed curiously.

"You would have to know Mary Elizabeth to be amused," he
said with a grunt. "She taught me a long time ago that you can't
surround those you love in bubble wrap and expect it to work.
First they burst the bubbles; then they find an escape route. Once
they escape, they don't tell you where they're going or why."

Piper watched as that crooked little smile she loved touched
his hard lips and gleamed in his dark blue eyes.

"You tried to surround her in bubble wrap then?" she asked.
"Guess you learned the hard way, huh? I wish you could teach
Dawg and my cousins the fact that it simply isn't possible to lock
us away until it's time to bury us."

"That's your job, sweetheart." He sighed as she watched him,
her gaze meeting his for the second he glanced at her, yet feeling
the effects of the amused heat in his eyes for that tiny moment in
time.

"How is that my job?" She couldn't imagine teaching Dawg
anything. The man gave stubborn a bad name.

"Most sisters start when they're babies," he admitted. "But
you're on the right track. Live, laugh, have fun, and go head-to-

head with him whenever you have to. But don't disappear on him again, Piper. Do it again, and next time I promise I'll help him find you."

"And what makes you think you can find me if Dawg can't?"

"Because Dawg doesn't want to admit you would actually leave the state without telling him," he pointed out as guilt flayed her once again. "I don't have that problem. I saw you leave the inn when you snuck out. I heard the car stopping just down the road. I knew why you were doing it, though. I didn't follow; I didn't run a check on the car. I went back into my room and stared up at the ceiling the rest of the night, wondering who was the man you left with."

The man?

Piper almost smiled. She could hear the probing question he was doing nothing to hide.

"It wasn't a man," she admitted. "It was the sister of a friend giving me a ride to the Louisville train station. I tried to cover my tracks so Dawg wouldn't follow me."

He nodded once.

"It didn't work out so well." She sighed, completing the thought.

"No, but I'm going to assume the circumstances were unusual," he stated.

"How the hell do I know?" She still didn't understand why, who, or what. "One minute I'm waiting on a bellhop and a ride to the train station, and the next second I'm being pounded on, then waking in a hospital with a concussion and so many bruises that breathing hurts."

There was the faintest memory of a demand. A demand for what, she wasn't certain. It wasn't even a memory, not really. It was a confusing collage of something, amid a blast of pain, fear, and her own screams.

"Did you remember the people next door who rushed in to help you?"

She didn't remember the rescue at all.

"I remember meeting them at the hospital after I woke up." She answered him, wishing she could hold on to whatever it was her attacker had said in those chaotic moments. She had a feeling if she could just remember . . .

"They were good boys," he told her gently. "A lot of young men would have waited, or been too wary of poking their noses in where they weren't wanted."

"Oh, they were wanted." She breathed out roughly.

God, what would she have done if they hadn't poked their noses in?

Watching the landscape roll by, Piper realized they were only miles from the inn now.

"Do you think Dawg will be there?"

He was going to be so hurt, and she knew it. He wouldn't understand her need to breathe, to have done this alone, even though it hadn't been the chance she had believed it was.

"Why were you in New York, Piper?"

She'd wondered how long it would take him to get to the one question she knew he wanted to ask.

Forcing back tears of disappointment and humiliation, she let a bitter smile pull at her lips. "I thought I was going to get an offer for a showing of some of my designs," she finally admitted.

"Thought you were?"

"It didn't work out." Staring down at her hands, she wondered whether he would consider it no more than she had deserved for the childishness she had displayed in the deceptive way she left.

"What happened, baby?"

The gentleness in his voice and the fact that he hadn't told

Dawg when the hospital had called him had her raising her eyes as she shifted in her seat to look at him.

Thank God it was dark. The last thing she wanted was for him to see the tears she had to blink back.

"There's this famous designer sponsor," she told him, clearing her throat to hide the hoarseness of the hurt she fought to hide. "He showcases several designers a year, helps them put on a show, and he's never had one who didn't become successful. I received a letter from him last week that he wanted to meet with me after seeing some of my designs that I sent in."

He nodded, showing he was listening as they moved ever closer to the inn.

"I could have had the show and sponsorship if I'd agreed to be his little sex toy until he got tired of me."

As though revealing that much opened a floodgate, Piper told him about Eldon Vessante, and the fact that his pants and his opinion of himself were overstuffed.

His expression never changed; the tension in his body didn't visibly increase. None of the signs of vengeful anger that Dawg and her cousins were known to display were present.

"Two attacks in one day then." He breathed out heavily, the concern in his voice easing something inside her she hadn't known had been knotted with tension.

Piper nodded. "Fortunately, his butler or whoever he was, was there. Some guy named Broken or something. A hell of a name for a person. He kept Eldon from actually hitting me and helped me get away."

"Do you think this Vessante guy was behind the attack at the hotel?"

Piper shook her head. "I don't remember what was said, but he wanted something." She wished she could remember, wished the harshly grated demand would come into focus within her memories. "I can't remember what he said, Jed, or what he wanted, but it didn't have anything to do with Eldon Vessante."

Broecun.

*Fuck.*

The security field was a close-knit one, especially for those agents of John Broecun's caliber. Jed knew Piper had taken the sound of the name literally, but Jed knew the other man, as well as the spelling of his name. And he knew if Broecun was with this Eldon Vessante, either the man was important to some very influential government types, or he was under investigation by them.

At least he had a place to start, and a face to shove his fist into. Eldon Vessante may not have been behind Piper's beating, but the only reason he hadn't been was because Broecun would have stopped him.

Broecun wouldn't stop Jed from teaching the other man how to treat a woman. And blackmailing Piper with her dream of a big-time fashion show and an exclusive sponsorship was something Jed would exact a little atonement for.

"Well, you're home now." He pulled into the Mackay Inn's lot, parked the truck, then shut it off. "Let's see if I can sneak you into the house and get you settled before Dawg gets his first report that you're home."

He sure as hell didn't need Dawg around right now, or Timothy Cranston. He'd talk to them both in the morning instead. Dawg and his cousins were going to have to step back a pace or two, regardless of whether or not they liked it. If they wanted to know the trouble—or potential trouble—his sisters got into or were headed for, then the girls couldn't be afraid to let him know what they were doing.

Her fear of being smothered during what she believed was an

important event had almost cost Piper her life; he wouldn't allow it to harm her more in the future.

"I'm scared for him, Jed," she whispered as he cut the engine, then turned back to her, confused.

"Scared for whom, honey?"

"For Dawg." He could see the tears in her eyes, the faint tremble of her lips in the dim light of the moon.

"Dawg and his cousins take care of themselves and one another just fine, Piper," he promised her.

She shook her head at his statement. "That's not what I mean."

"What do you mean?"

"He's going to be very alone," she told him softly. "He's becoming out of control, Jed. He makes me frightened of him when he starts standing over us like guard dogs. He can't keep telling us what to do or how to live. I know Lyrica and Zoey, too. If he doesn't stop, I swear, we'll all end up leaving. We talk about it more and more often. He may well be headed for a stroke, but Lyrica, Zoey, and I are headed out of town if it keeps up."

"He worries, Piper." His hands clenched on the steering wheel in an instinctive protest at the thought of her leaving.

"I would have been in your bed a year ago if he hadn't been watching us all like hawks. I'm terrified to show any interest in a man, and God forbid I should actually consider taking a lover after the grief he gave Eve." The words were out of her mouth before she could hold them back.

A wave of heat flushed through her at the sudden, brilliant gleam of lust that lit his gaze.

He may not have tightened with the information she'd given him about Eldon's attack, but the moment she mentioned being in his bed, his entire body seemed to jerk in abrupt interest.

Or perhaps "interest" was far too tame a word. It was as though every thought, every emotion, every particle of his being was suddenly intently, greedily focused on her.

"Did Dawg order you to stay away from me, Piper?" he asked her calmly, but what she saw in his gaze was anything but calm.

She shook her head slowly. "No, but who I sleep with isn't up for debate, Jed. And I won't let it become a family point of interest that I'm fighting my brother over the man I want for a lover because he disapproves of him as he did with Eve. It shouldn't be like that, and I can't stand the thought that Dawg would turn it into such a battle."

He'd nearly broken Eve's heart.

Her sister had finally told her of the fight she'd had with Dawg when she had taken Brogan as her lover. Dawg had gone so far as to use the worst sort of emotional blackmail to keep her from giving in to the man she'd been fascinated with for years.

Piper had been terrified he would try the same tactics with her. If he had tried such a guilt trip with her, she would have gone ballistic. Eve had had far more patience than Piper could have ever found in the same situation.

"I was beginning to wonder if you even wanted to find yourself in my bed." He reached out, his palm cupping the uninjured side of her face.

"I didn't say you wouldn't have to seduce me now," she informed him tartly, despite the heat rushing through her body at his touch. "I simply said I may have ended up there sooner."

"You call that little tease a month ago being in my bed?" He came closer, his gaze focused on her lips as Piper brushed her tongue over them, wishing her attacker had kept the back of his hand away from them.

"You call that a little tease?" she whispered roughly. "I'm

going to have to show you a real tease, Jedediah Booker, so you'll know the difference."

"And exactly what would *you* call a little tease, Piper?" he asked, his lips moving close, oh, so close to hers.

"What you're doing right now, maybe?"

She could barely breathe.

Okay, she was sore, swollen, but her lips weren't really that swollen. Most of the blows had actually been against the side of her head, according to the doctor. Not that she remembered a whole lot after she had been slammed into the dresser, due to the concussion.

"This is a tease?" His lips were only a whisper against hers.

"Please, Jed," she sighed his name roughly. "Don't tease this time."

*Don't tease this time.*

Jed stared down at her, seeing the shadow of bruises against one side of her face, the faint swelling of her eye and her lower lip.

"I don't want to hurt you, Piper." He sighed, drawing back. "And I don't want you coming to me out of fear. When the bruises have healed, then we'll talk."

Before he could change his mind, Jed forced himself from the truck and strode to the passenger side of the pickup. Pulling her door open, he did as he had at the hospital: Rather than allowing her to walk to the inn, he simply scooped her from the seat and carried her to the front porch.

Turning from the front door, he was heading for the side of the house when a shadow detached itself from the corner and the front door opened.

"God, no." Piper buried her head against his shoulder as he recognized the height and breadth of the shadow before he actually glimpsed the hard lines of the savagely hewn male features in the dim light of the moon.

"Well, at least they're not trying to run," Natches drawled as he moved to Dawg's side.

"I don't know; I think I'd rather he'd run." Amusement filled Rowdy's voice as Jed let his gaze lock with Dawg's.

"Now's not the time, Dawg," he warned the other man. "Let her rest first. Morning's soon enough."

Piper grunted against his shoulder. "Good luck with that one," she muttered, her voice so low it barely reached his ear.

"Yeah, Jed, good luck with that one." The low, slow cadence of Dawg's voice had the hairs at the back of Jed's neck lifting in warning.

Dawg was pissed, and he was suspicious. His gaze slid to Jed's hold on her slight body, narrowed and intent, his look taking in the protective hold and Piper's determination to hide her face.

"Put her down, Booker," Dawg ordered, his voice dark and warning.

"Don't do this, Dawg." There was no weakness in Piper's voice as her head lifted quickly, her obvious sense of security with the darkness surrounding them apparent.

Jed could have told her the mistake she was making, if he had had a chance.

What he saw instead was Dawg's face.

The widening of his eyes, the paling of his flesh, the immediate awareness that one side of his sister's face wasn't shadow, but swollen and obviously bruised.

Just as quickly, Piper saw the reaction as well, if her sharply indrawn breath and the tension invading her body was any indication.

"No." The harsh order that left her lips as Dawg stepped forward surprisingly had him stopping in his tracks. "It's none of your business, Dawg."

Rowdy and Natches were quick to move around them, their reactions no less as shocked as Dawg's.

"None of my business?" Dawg all but wheezed, his expression tortured, as his cousins, positioned for a much better view, stared at her in horror as the sensors on the motion lights caught the movement and flipped on overhead.

"Oh, my God, Piper . . ." Agonized, Dawg's voice roughed to a harsh, gut-clenching rasp.

Anguish filled the three men's gazes and tightened their expressions as they stared down at her, obviously fighting to process the bruised condition of her face.

As though in one movement, their heads jerked to Jed, their gazes piercing as they stared at him.

Hell, his face was likely to take the brunt of six fists pounding on it before the night was over, because he was damned if he could give them what he knew they were silently demanding.

An explanation.

Now.

"She's your sister," he told Dawg, his gaze connecting with the other man's, knowing he could make an enemy of him in this second. "You want answers, you'll have to get them from her."

"Let me down." Piper struggled in his arms.

Put her down? Was she insane? The second Dawg saw her limping, he'd go damned ballistic.

"Fuck! I'll be damned if I will." Tightening his hold on her, he moved forward, more than surprised as the Mackays parted and allowed him to pass.

Pulling her keys from where he'd tucked them into his jeans at the hospital, he called back to the three men following them, "Her bags are in the truck, if you want to make yourselves useful and bring them in."

At least one set of footsteps paused behind them.

"Like hell," Dawg growled. "She can have them later."

Jed shrugged.

"I should have stayed where I was," she whispered. "Why didn't I stay where I was?"

"They would have found out," he warned her. "Want me to tell you how many contacts Timothy has on the police force there?"

"Where?" Dawg snapped behind him. "I thought you were just the fucking chauffeur?"

Holding her securely as he unlocked her door, Jed glimpsed her expression from the corner of his eye and restrained a sigh. She was shutting down fast. He could feel it, and he hated it. When Piper shut down, her rational and logic went out the fucking window, especially if she was dealing with her brother. She didn't do confrontations well, though he knew she would never admit to it. She buried her fear instead and faced the world with a brutal ice that sliced her deeper than it did those she was facing, once she had time to think and consider what she said during those moments.

Stepping into her bedroom, he strode to the bed in the center of the small suite, laid her on it, then watched in resignation as she jumped from the mattress to face the three men entering the room behind them, the moment he placed her on it.

"Go home, Dawg."

The lights flipped on, and for the first time Dawg had a full, unobstructed view of her face.

"God, Piper." It was Natches who breathed out the protest. "Sweetheart, what the hell happened to you?"

Dawg looked like he had taken a blow to the balls and was having trouble catching enough breath to even fold to the floor.

"Don't the three of you have wives and children of your own to torment?" She questioned them harshly as she tugged at the soft cotton material of the blouse she had worn home.

The light, neutral tone of the gray blouse did nothing to hide the damage done to her fragile face, or where it extended along her shoulder and into the scooped neckline of the garment.

It was one of her creations, he knew—one she was exceptionally proud of. Unfortunately, the light color only emphasized the darkness of the bruises.

"Who did this?" Dawg grated, his voice harsh.

Piper drew herself up, the last hint of any emotion leaving her face.

"I said leave." The demand in her voice was impossible to miss.

Just as arrogant, just as condescending as Dawg could be himself, she faced him with icy refusal, her gaze never flickering beneath the fury in his.

"Dawg, let her rest." Jed placed himself between them. "Ordering her isn't going to get you anywhere."

Dawg's fists clenched at his sides, the need to strike out, to take vengeance, clear in his expression and the tension in his large body.

"Get out of my way, Jed."

"Get out of her room!" Jed countered, determination hardening his voice. "You're not going to yell at her, and you're sure as hell not going to attempt to force answers from her. Just go home and see if you can't ask nicely next time."

Who was more surprised, he wondered, when the three Mackays did just as he ordered—turned and left without another word—himself or Piper?

"This isn't good," Piper muttered, suddenly aware that she could have pushed her brother right over an invisible line none of them had known existed. "Dawg never just leaves."

Jed turned back to her. "I think you should have told him, baby. But we'll see what hardheadedness gets you first."

The smile he gave her was as chilly and polite as her tone was to her brother, but far more mocking.

She stood there staring back at him, the vulnerability he could see her fighting—and the need and the hurt hiding behind the chilly facade—breaking his heart.

He turned and left, just as the Mackays had. He had no other choice. Because as pissed as her brother and cousins were, she had no idea he was even more so.

She had left without him, faced danger without him, and been determined to handle it all on her own—without him. And now, even knowing he would have to face the full force of the Mackay fallout, she wasn't volunteering enough information to her brother and cousins to even give him hope that Dawg, Rowdy, and Natches wouldn't try to kick his ass to hell and back.

And he still couldn't imagine betraying the trust she had placed in him. Even knowing the enemies he could make, the budding friendships that could be destroyed. The Mackays were strong friends to have, but they could be brutal enemies, too. But, Jed had realized the second he had walked into that fucking hospital room that nothing mattered more to him than being with Piper. Protecting her, touching her, having her.

Nothing else mattered.

No matter what.

# EIGHT

Dawg stood next to the pickup, his wrists hanging over the edge, his head bowed, and he had no idea how to unknot the burning fist growing in his chest.

Where was Christa? God, why hadn't he brought Christa with him? She could have talked to Piper, could have made her understand that he had—he *had*—to make certain whoever hurt her never—fucking never—hurt her again.

He felt as though every breath he was trying to take was restricted.

"Fuck, hurts to breathe," he muttered.

"No shit," Rowdy was hoarse.

Natches wasn't speaking.

As he wiped his hand over his face, car lights sliced into the parking lot, drawing his gaze as he found himself staring at the little car he'd bought Christa several months before.

As it pulled to a stop behind the truck, it wasn't just Christa who stepped from the car. Rowdy's wife, Kelly, and Natches's wife, Chaya, moved slowly toward them.

It was Natches who moved first.

Two steps and Natches was pulling Chaya into his arms, burying his face against her neck and holding on tight as Christa moved slowly to Dawg.

"Jed called," she told him. "He told us everyone was safe, but you might need us?"

Her hand, so delicate and fragile, settled against his arm.

"What's wrong, Dawg?"

His throat was so fucking tight. Hell, he hadn't felt like this since the night he learned Christa had lost their child so long ago. Like tears were burning in his gut and refused to be shed.

"Someone beat her." His voice was grating, so rough he barely recognized it as he turned to her and pulled her to his chest. "Christa, someone beat her face and she won't let me help."

He couldn't understand it.

It was tearing him apart. His guts were being ripped straight out of him and he couldn't make it stop.

"Who? Who, Dawg?"

"God. Piper," he snarled, so furious with her, so broken inside he had no idea how to find all the pieces. "Piper, Christa. She just fucking disappears, then comes back, her face swollen and bruised, and she won't let me help."

"Did you offer to help, baby?" she asked gently, her expression understanding, knowing. "Or did you demand?"

He had asked. Hadn't he?

"You demanded, didn't you, Dawg?" she guessed. "All ready to charge ahead and exact vengeance."

"Someone hurt her." It didn't make sense that she wouldn't want vengeance.

"Come on, Dawg. Let's go home."

He shook his head fiercely. "You have to make her tell me—"

"Dawg, you can't make Piper do anything." She sighed. "She's home; you know she's safe. Give her time to come to you."

He shook his head.

"You're just going to piss her off," Chaya stated as Natches lifted his head from her shoulder and moved away several paces. "She's too strong to break down and cry, or let herself be treated like a child. You've hassled her for a year; now it's time to go home."

"She won't stay safe." He shook his head; it didn't make sense to him.

"And here she's a Mackay. Go figure," Christa murmured.

"We'll find him." This time it was levelheaded, "think about it first" Rowdy. "We'll find him, Dawg, and when we do, he won't be able to hit another woman."

Natches, Rowdy, Chaya, and Kelly moved to the truck Dawg had driven to the inn as Dawg moved to the car with his wife. For the first time, Christa noticed, she didn't have to fight over driving.

Dawg moved to the passenger seat as she slid under the wheel.

"I need to go home." He breathed roughly. "I need my girls."

Her and his daughter.

She held back the secret she'd learned earlier. The news that their daughter would have a brother or sister. News that she feared would only make Dawg more protective, even as it made him more loving.

The drawback?

His feared inability to protect those he loved was breaking his heart, and that was breaking her heart. Because there was nothing she could do to ease his pain or to make those he loved, besides herself, understand the demons that tormented him.

Perhaps it was time she, Kelly, and Chaya had a talk with the stubborn and just as determined Mackay sisters.

ONE WEEK LATER

"Good morning, Mr. Samson; I hope you enjoyed your breakfast?" Piper met Guido Samson in the hall outside his room and gave him a warm smile.

The new lodger was a bit portly, his black hair thick, with a slight wave in the shortened length that was brushed back from his face to reveal a hint of gray at the temples. Dark, swarthy, just showing the lines of advancing age, he looked to be in his late fifties, though Piper bet he was in his early sixties.

He'd been at the inn four days and was already making his presence known, mostly by pissing Tim off. It seemed Guido couldn't help but flirt outrageously with Mercedes Mackay.

"Ah, Miss Mackay." He stopped, holding his hand out to her.

As Piper extended hers he took it, raised it to his lips, and pressed a light kiss to it with charming ease before releasing it.

"And here is your young man." He looked over her shoulder, a broad smile pulling at his lips as Piper swore she could feel Jed coming up behind her.

"Morning, Mr. Samson." The deep, controlled drawl—controlled hunger, anger, and determination—sent a shiver racing down her spine.

That tone had only intensified over the past days, just as the gleam of determination in the navy blue gaze had only hardened and, at certain times, intensified.

"Ah, Mr. Booker, good morning," Guido greeted him. "I am out for a day of sightseeing. I believe my son, Rhylan, is arriving this evening and hopes to find the best spots for a few days of fishing."

"The fishing here is excellent, Mr. Samson; I'm certain your son will find plenty of excellent spots." Edging around Guido's portly frame, Jed curled his fingers around Piper's upper arm. "Excuse us, please. Piper and I need to talk."

"Of course," Guido murmured, amused. "Young people have many things to discuss privately."

His soft chuckle followed them up the hall as Jed led her to her room. Opening the room and stepping in, Piper quickly pulled her arm from his grip.

"Since when do we have things to discuss?" Piper asked roughly as the door closed behind them, very well aware of the fact that he let her go. She wasn't free because she wanted to be; she was free because he let her be.

Crossing her arms beneath her breasts, she glared at him, wishing she could push back anger, guilt, or any of the other emotions tearing through her, as she could with her family.

She could stare back at Dawg and freeze any response to the knowledge that he was frightened for her, hurting for her, worried about her, or just plain pissed off at her.

Her sister Eve had always been so thankful to be accepted and loved by her brother and cousins that she would have done just about anything—anything but deny the man she loved.

Lyrica, a year younger than Piper, had such a guilt complex that she worried constantly that she would never be good enough, act properly enough, or be strong enough to be part of the Somerset Mackays. God only knew what their youngest sister, Zoey, felt. She rarely talked about it, and if asked would just laugh and say she was where she belonged. But Piper had always felt there was so much more beneath that statement.

Of the four of them their eldest sister, Eve, had handled Dawg best. They all loved him, but each of them had different ways of dealing with him.

Him, or any other man.

Unfortunately, the defenses Piper had built over the years didn't work with Jed.

"Have you talked to Dawg yet?" he asked.

Piper looked away and shrugged. "He hasn't been around for a while."

Guilt was lashing at her now.

God, she remembered the look on his face when he'd seen the bruises on hers. He looked as though someone had died. Or something inside him had died. She hadn't seen him since.

"I'm going to talk to him," she promised.

What the hell was it with Jed Booker?

He was just staring at her. There was no force, no guilt-inducing comments, just those dark, dark blue eyes watching her with that silent, deep curiosity.

"Are you?" Jed asked.

It was a simple question. No mockery, no sarcasm, nothing offensive, but Piper could feel the guilt growing inside her.

"You don't understand what he's like, Jed," she burst out, pushing her fingers through her hair in frustration as she turned and stomped to the other side of the room before turning back. "This is how he gets you. He knows how to work every damned one of us."

"Does he, Piper?" he asked her quietly. "Or is he just struggling with his inability to protect four girls he loves nearly as much as he does his own daughter? Four girls whose abandonment and hardships as children torment him?"

She shook her head fiercely. "That wasn't his fault."

"Fault doesn't matter, Piper," he said calmly, moving to her, making her all too aware of the sudden sensitivity of her body whenever he was around.

His voice was steady, every movement deliberate, but his eyes were like deep pools of sexual heat. His gaze licked over her as his hands curved against her bare shoulders. They slid down along her arms, then back up, the rasp of the calluses against her softer flesh so erotic she was forced to bite back a moan.

"What does matter, Jed?" she asked, unable to break her gaze from his. "Should I give in to him as Eve tried to do, and refuse to end up in your bed? Should I promise not to live or have a life so Dawg can sleep at night?"

Tears filled her eyes at the thought. "Don't you think I've learned how I have to handle him by now? If I don't defy him, then I won't have a chance at having a life myself."

"And there are those times you could defy him and lose your life, Piper."

"Then he has to learn to talk to us." Frustrated anger hoarsened her voice as it tore through her emotions. "Why do we have to automatically give in and bury our heads against life or risk dying? Jed, I can't do that. If I'm in danger then I have to know, and I have to know why. Just as you would."

His gaze flickered and she knew he understood that.

"If I go to Dawg, then he'll see it as a weakness; don't you understand that? I'll be giving in and he'll take full advantage of it. Not out of cruelty." She held her hand up to delay whatever argument she could see brewing in his expression. "Not out of manipulation. That's his instinct," she argued. "Just as it's yours."

It was the way they were, the type of men they were. If Dawg didn't come to her first, seeking answers, then he wouldn't be in a frame of mind to discuss what had happened to her while she was away. He would dictate her security instead and try to lock her so far out of sight she would have a hard time finding herself, let alone anyone else finding her.

"You forget: I came for you." His head lowered as he voiced the reminder, his lips brushing against her ear and causing her eyes to close at the pleasure of the touch. "No questions, no demands. I came for you, Piper, and I'm the one forced to field questions from your friends and family. If I have to take Rowdy or Natches Mackay's fist for you, because I keep refusing to answer their questions, then you are going to owe me. Big-time."

The words were a breath of warning against her neck as Piper felt her knees weaken.

Lifting her hands from where they hung at her sides, she tentatively gripped his upper arms, feeling the play of his biceps beneath her fingers.

"They won't hit you." She knew her brother and her cousins. They were hard men, but they weren't unfair.

"Perhaps I should have a taste now." His lips brushed against her jaw. "Show me what I'm going to take that punch for, Piper."

Her head turned; her lips parted.

She'd dreamed of his kiss since that first one six weeks before. Each day, each time he spoke to her, teased her, silently rebuked her, had built the need for it.

She needed his kiss.

She needed his touch.

Her lips accepted his, parted, and Piper found herself dragged into a chaotic storm of pure heat.

Pleasure raced across her flesh like ribbons of electric sensation. From her lips to the tip of her toes and back to the crown of her head, his lips against hers created a reaction she couldn't have expected.

She should have expected. She'd felt it before. But how was she to know that the first time hadn't been just a fluke? She had never predicted the intensity of the pleasure to repeat itself or—incredibly—to begin building higher, stronger.

Faster.


Jed barely controlled the gut-deep groan of instant, overwhelming hunger.

Son of a bitch, it couldn't be this good. There was no way this unusual depth of pleasure was real.

He'd convinced himself it had been a figment of his imagination, but as he lifted Piper against his chest and bore her to the bed, he knew the pleasure was doing just that.

It was burning brighter, hotter, and deeper than anything he'd ever known.

She wasn't doing anything different. It wasn't that experience filled each tentative lick of her tongue against his or each heated brush of her body against his.

Piper was anything and everything but experienced, and he knew it. He'd made it his job to know everything about her that a man could dig up.

But he hadn't known the effect she'd have on him.

A low moan slipped past his lips. Her knees were hugging his hips, the thin material of her panties beneath the ankle-length silky skirt she wore rubbing against the denim of his jeans as it covered the tormented length of his dick.

God, he was hard.

So hard he felt as though his cock were seconds away from becoming pure steel, throbbing furiously, his testicles drawn tight beneath it. He knew he wouldn't last long. Hell, he'd be lucky if he got inside her before he embarrassed himself and spilled his release into his jeans.

Laying her back on the bed, Jed couldn't force himself to

break from the kiss that seemed to be feeding the flaming lust burning between them.

Fuck, it was good.

She was good.

She was as sweet as sunrise and as hot as the Texas heat waves he remembered from his childhood.

Rolling his hips against hers, the hardened length of his cock pressing against the tender mound of her pussy, Jed worried at his lack of self-control.

She wasn't experienced. Hell, it would surprise the hell out of him if he learned she wasn't a virgin. But she had the power to strip him down to the core of who and what he was. A male animal. A sexually hungry, sexually determined, sexually intent male animal, and he couldn't seem to pull himself back.

That powerlessness was so alien to his character, to his very nature, that shock resounded to the depths of his senses.

Yet it wasn't enough to stop him.

One hand pushed beneath the loose, sleeveless top she wore. One of her own creations yet again: a soft white silk with a handkerchief hem that perfectly matched the hem of the skirt.

Tiny, tiny mother-of-pearl buttons held the material over her rapidly rising and falling breasts as his hand slid beneath the top, his palm cupping the underside of one breast perfectly.

The excuse for a bra was little more than silky lace, easily pushed aside by his fingers as his thumb searched out the hardened little point of her nipple.

It was swollen tight and hard, and the caress he gave it had Piper arching to him, a muted cry falling from her lips as pleasure arced between them like a live electrical connection.

With his free hand Jed struggled to undress her. The tiny buttons were instruments of torture as his fingers fumbled and slipped on them. It seemed to take forever, but finally he released the captive tip of her nipple to lift her to him and push the blouse from her shoulders.

Reaching behind his neck, he gripped her wrists, pulling them free of the hold she had on him and dragging them down to allow him to remove the blouse and lacy bra.

Hard, sipping kisses kept them connected as he hurried to undress first Piper's lush, heated body, then his own harder, fiercer one.

If he didn't have her, if he didn't sink his cock inside her soon, then he was going to die of the hunger clawing inside him.

"So fucking pretty," he growled against her lips as he finally had her naked beneath him, had himself naked and ready to take her.

But the silken peaches-and-cream flesh distracted him.

He meant to spread her thighs and sink inside her while he still had the control to take her slow and easy.

He made the mistake of lifting himself from her, releasing her lips to rise above her, his gaze lowering to the full, tempting globes of her breasts.

Tiny hardened cherry red nipples topped the firm flesh, and the temptation to taste them was too much to resist.

"You're killing me," he groaned. "God help us both, Piper; I'm dying for you."

The need to taste her had his mouth watering, the hunger obliterating everything else. His head lowered, lips parting, and when he captured one tight, swollen peak, he swore he could feel her losing control along with him.


Piper jerked at the sudden suction of his mouth against the overly sensitive tip of her breast. The sensation was so sharp, so brutally

erotic that her hands rose quickly to his shoulders, her nails biting against his flesh.

She had to hold on.

Oh, God, it was so good.

She whipped her head against the comforter beneath her, her
hips lifting against him, feeling the brush of the heavy width of
his cock against her thighs—there were so many sensations. So
much pleasure.

The tugging of his mouth around the tender bud of her breast
was an agonizing pleasure. One hand cupped the curve of her
flesh as the other moved slowly down her waist to the rounded
curve of her thigh.

"Part your legs," he ordered hoarsely as his lips moved to the
opposite peak. "Ah, God, let me in, baby. Let me have you."

She was really going to do this, wasn't she?

There was no turning back; she could feel it.

After years of wondering why she'd been unable to take a
lover, the mystery was now solved.

She hadn't taken one because she'd needed Jed. She'd waited
for him, ached for him—somehow she'd known he was out
there; she'd known he'd come for her.

Her legs parted, urged by the powerful fingers at her thighs as
his lips lowered and covered the other hardened tip of her nipple.
Suckling it, he lapped at it with his tongue, then rasped it with
his teeth.

Piper felt as though she were being devoured.

That thought was amended as his lips began a path down her
torso. Hungry kisses, tasting licks set fire to her senses. Caresses
stroked pure exquisite pleasure to her nerve endings and had her
waiting in painful anticipation as he moved ever closer to her
trembling thighs.

"You know what I want, baby." He groaned as he found

her belly button and felt her tremble in response. "I want all those sweet juices gathering at your pussy."

Her breath caught and held in her chest as his lips moved farther, kissed, stroked, licked.

A breath of air brushed over the bare flesh of her pussy, the dew-slick folds sensitizing further at the thought of the coming caress.

She couldn't help but watch.

His gaze caught hers for long, erotic moments before his eyes dropped, drawing her eyes to the swollen folds.

His lips parting, Jed's head lowered, his tongue reaching out for her, then burying in the slick, swollen flesh of her pussy.

"Oh, God. Jed." Her hands slid into his hair, gripped and held on tight as her upper body jerked upward in response.

Spreading her knees farther, Piper dug her feet into the bed and lifted her hips, pressing closer, muted, hoarse cries leaving her throat as his tongue began a sensual, delicious dance in the plump, slick flesh he'd found.

He pushed his hands beneath her hips to lift her closer, and Piper lost the strength to hold her shoulders and head from the bed. Falling back, she strained against the pleasure, eyes closed, reaching for the brilliance of the supernova of fiery heat she could feel building in her pussy.

Wicked and erotic, his tongue lapped at the juices spilling from her vagina before easing up, licking and stroking, pushing her further, deeper into the maelstrom gathering inside her. Rasping, probing, the devilish instrument of torturous ecstasy began licking around her straining clit, testing the swollen tenderness, inciting it to a desperate ache that had her crying out for release.

When his lips covered the distended little bundle of nerves, Piper felt the shock of it explode through her system. Shuddering, her hips jerking against his hold, against the sucking heat, she felt

her senses begin dissolving in a release of such pure ecstasy that
she swore she could feel herself flying.

Drawn tight, arching to him, racked by primal internal shudders of a climax that shocked her to her woman's core, she
fought to cry, to scream out the pleasure, only to find enough air
to give a low, ragged moan.

And still it wasn't enough.

For all the strength and power of the climax gripping her,
still, that building ache in her pussy drove her to reach for more.
To beg for more.

Her eyes jerked open as he pulled himself to his knees.

Eyes wide, Piper's gaze focused on the thick, engorged crest
of his cock. He quickly pulled the condom from the side table,
tore it open, then rolled the protective sheath over himself, before he came over her once again.

"Jed . . . ?" She could feel the trepidation building inside her.

"I have you, Piper." She was only barely aware of the words
whispered at her ear as he buried his lips in her neck. "It's okay,
baby; I have you."

Everything inside her stilled then.

The feel of the hard, thickened crest of his penis pressing into
the quivering entrance of her vagina held her poised on a rack of
desperate need and building fear.

"Jed. Jed, I haven't—" A groan tore through her as the throbbing width of his cock breached the clenched opening of her
pussy.

"I know, sweetheart." His head lifted. "Look at me, Piper. Let
me see you."

She forced her eyes open, watching his eyes as he stared down
at her, the blue so dark it now appeared black.

"Hold on to me." He groaned as her hands clenched in the
comforter. "Hold on to me, sweetheart."

Lifting her hands, she gripped his upper arms, stared into his eyes, and felt him advance further before pulling back.

"Wait." The protest was instinctive.

"Shhh, I'm not going anywhere," he promised, his lips lowering to hers. "Just hold on to me. Just for a second."

The muscles of his hips bunched, the head of his cock throbbed inside her, and a second later a hard, heavy thrust had the iron-hard length powering through the shield of an innocence she knew she'd saved for him.

His lips caught her cry at the shock of the entrance.

Holding the kiss, he pulled back, then pushed inside again, burying deeper as pleasure and pain began to build with equal intensity.

Lifting her legs to get closer to each heavy thrust, Piper gave herself to him, knowing that from this moment on, she no longer completely belonged to herself.

Each hard thrust inside the clenched depths of her pussy pushed inside her with increasing strength, faster, to an edge of a fiery abyss she was both terrified of and reaching for.

Pleasure radiated through her body, stoked by each piercing impalement of his cock inside her, stretching her, burning the sensitive depths with the heavy heat of his possession.

Moving over her, stroking inside her with quick, deep thrusts of the steel-hard, heated flesh, Jed pushed her harder, faster. Her hands clenched on his arms as the flared crest parted her flesh and drove to the depths of her before quickly retreating, then stroking over flesh so sensitive that the pleasure was agonizing with each stroke.

Each thrust was harder, faster. Each was hotter, more demanding, until that abyss reached out for her, the flames exploding around her and tearing through her senses with such blinding ecstasy that she knew she would never be the same.

Harsh, quaking shudders of sensation attacked her body. Unprepared for their strength, for the sheer destruction of her senses, Piper could only do as he'd told her: She held on tight.

She gasped, crying out his name as her body clenched and shuddered beneath him, her pussy tightening around his shuttling cock until he thrust in hard and deep and gave himself to his own pleasure.

She hadn't imagined it could be like this. She'd never conceived of such pleasure, of such deep, overwhelming waves of pure ecstasy streaking through her, possessing her.

She wouldn't have believed that in one moment of rapture her soul would open and her heart would give itself totally, completely, to a man as fierce, as hard, and yet as gentle as Jedediah Booker.

# NINE

Eve had told her that once Brogan had touched her, once she had learned what real pleasure, real intimacy were, then she'd been caught.

*Hook, line, and sinker, sister.* Eve had grinned unrepentantly the day Piper had berated her for moving from the inn and leaving her, Lyrica, and Zoey—well, mostly her and Lyrica—to face the fallout.

The fallout being Tim, Dawg, Rowdy, and Natches becoming so damned protective that Piper, Lyrica, and even Zoey—the most spoiled of the sisters—were feeling the bite of the males' overprotectiveness.

Lying in Jed's arms that afternoon, Piper wondered what she was getting herself into this time, and just how it would affect not just her, but also her unattached sisters.

"Stop thinkin'," Jed drawled, and for just a second there was a hint of the Texas upbringing he'd once told her he'd had.

"You're starting to sound like a cowboy." Turning against his chest, she propped herself up and stared at him from where she lay against his shoulder.

Jed grunted lazily. "Yeah, it creeps out now and again."

"This is the first time I've actually heard it," she pointed out. "I was starting to wonder if you'd lied to me about being born in Texas."

That Texas drawl was unmistakable. And she'd never heard it pass his lips.

So why now?

She was almost glowing at the possibility that perhaps sexual satisfaction and male contentment had managed to relax him enough that he'd lost a moment's control over something it seemed he'd deliberately suppressed.

"I don't lie to you." The simple statement had her stomach tightening in a feeling akin to, but not exactly, the panic attacks of the past.

This wasn't panic. It was terrified anticipation, petrified hope. It was something it shouldn't be; that was for damned sure.

"You've never lied to me?" Forcing the disbelief into her voice wasn't easy.

It was almost impossible simply because she wanted so desperately to believe him. Wanted to believe him, and she was too scared to allow herself to do so.

"I've never lied to you, Piper. And I never will."

Was he lying to her? He had to be lying to her.

"I won't lie to you," he continued. "But that doesn't mean there aren't questions I can't answer. If I can make the commitment not to deceive you, then I expect you to make one not to ask the questions you know would be off-limits."

Could she ask for more than that?

She didn't know whether she could, or whether she should, but she knew she had to.

Sitting up, she tucked the sheet around her breasts and stared down at him silently for long moments. With one forearm lifted and tucked beneath his head, his dark navy blue eyes so intent and serious, with long strands of dark blond, gold, and tawny hair falling over his forehead, he resembled the men he employed on the construction job that she knew he used as a cover. Rugged and hard, lean and naturally muscled.

"How am I supposed to know what questions are off-limits?" Tilting her head to the side, she watched him curiously now, wondering whether this was how Eve and Brogan made their relationship work. Did they have an understanding that there were parts of his life and what he did that she couldn't question?

Could she live with that? Really?

She loved Jed. She'd known that for a while now.

But did she love him enough to abide by such a rule?

"I think you'll know which questions those are." His gaze dropped to her breasts as they rose over the edge of the sheet.

"I think that if those are the rules, Jed, then I have to know who and what you are. If that information is off-limits, then you may as well climb that cute ass right out of my bed before one of us gets pissed off."


God help him, but he loved her.

Jed stared up at Piper Mackay and knew she owned parts of his heart and soul that he hadn't even known existed. There was no denying that they belonged to her, either, because as he watched her, he knew he'd trust her with every secret he had inside his soul.

He'd trust her with them, but he'd never tell her some secrets. The secrets that were far too dangerous to her safety should she know them.

Because he knew beyond a shadow of a doubt that to save her, he'd betray each and every one of those secrets, and he knew she'd do the same for him.

"I'm an agent for the United States Federal Protective Service," he told her. "We're tasked with protecting and investigating any threats to the possessions of the United States government and, in some instances, government employees. You knew I was an agent." She nodded her head slowly. "What did Eve tell you happened last summer?"

"That several former members of the Freedom League believed Dawg had something Chandler Mackay had stolen years ago, and they kidnapped her to attempt to make him turn it over."

Jed nodded. That was the story they had come up with, not that the majority of it wasn't true. It was. It just wasn't the full explanation; neither did it include Eve's fiancé's part in the situation, or Jed's and Elijah's.

"Those members were stealing confidential files from military and government offices to locate a cache of gold Chandler hid years ago. They believed Dawg would know where it was stashed."

Dawg probably did know where it was stashed, Piper thought. Hell, he probably had it hidden himself once he found it.

She knew he'd taken to keeping the things Chandler had stashed away as he found them, out of pure spitefulness toward the government, once he'd learned how Piper, her mother, and her sisters were treated after Homeland Security had found them.

"I guess telling me the truth means you intend to stick around for a while?" she asked, trying to hold on to the charade she'd played since meeting him.

That unspoken lie that what he did or where he went wouldn't matter to her.

Uncurling his arm from beneath his head, he slid his hand behind her neck and pulled her to him.

"What do you think, Piper?" he growled against her lips. "Do you think there's a chance in hell that I'll ever let you go now?"

He didn't give her a chance to answer him. The teasing brush of his lips turned serious, burned through any objections she might have, and left her too hungry, her body too heated to deny him.

Possessiveness rang in his tone, gleamed in the midnight blue of his eyes, and filled the power and dominant strength of his kiss.

Did she think he would let her go now?

Not for a while, perhaps.

Not until the hunger began to dim. Not until the flame of lust began to cool. And wasn't that the way of it?

The questions, the uncertainties and insecurities of the emotions raging through her became suppressed by a pleasure she couldn't deny.

A pleasure she didn't want to deny.

His lips rubbed against hers, his tongue licking at hers, tasting her and allowing her to taste him in turn.

The wild, erotic flavor of his kiss was one she was certain she would never be fully prepared for. The heat and wonder, the incredible pleasure and full, chaotic sensory overload were unlike anything she had ever known before his touch.

She'd waited for this since she'd first realized how sensual a male's touch could be, or how pleasurable a kiss could be. She'd waited for this kiss.

She'd waited for Jed.

Easing back, Jed slid kisses from her lips to her jaw as his arms wrapped around her, pulling her closer to his aroused body.

Heat surrounded her. Flames licked over her nerve endings and pierced her pussy with a force that had the tender muscles clenching violently.

The feel of her juices easing along the sensitive portal, and the fierce ache in her clit as it built rapidly, pulled a low, desperate moan from her lips.

She needed him. She ached for him.

Smoothing her hands along his shoulders to the heavy strength of his biceps, Piper held on tight as she felt herself being lowered to her back. Anticipation began to build, along with pleasure and the driving need for more.

Always for more.

Surely the day would come when the instantaneous need for his possession would ease. When he would touch her and she would at least have a moment to think, to consider, before her hunger for him overrode any other consideration.

At the moment, she couldn't imagine it happening, though.

His lips slid along her neck, and she felt the rasp of his beard, the feel of his hand stroking against her stomach, moving higher, cupping her breast. Each sensation built in pleasure and in heat until Piper was moaning beneath him, her hips lifting, pressing the mound of her pussy against the hard muscle of his thigh as he came over her.

"I get drunk on you, Piper," he muttered against her breast, his lips brushing against the tight, sensitive peak of her breast a second before his tongue rasped over it with erotic hunger.

"Please, Jed," she whispered, desperate. "Don't wait."

She wanted him now. Foreplay could come later.

He moved closer, his legs parting hers as his head lifted from her breast.

Piper forced her eyes open.

She wanted to watch, wanted to see him take her.

She was on the verge of begging when the world suddenly upended.

One second she was lying beneath Jed, anticipation tearing through her senses.

In the next second it felt as though she were flying through the air before she landed against Jed's hard body, only to be rolled quickly to the floor.

Everything happened so fast. Too fast.

Wide-eyed, shocked, she let her gaze follow his hand as he reached beneath her bed, jerked out a lethal black handgun, then leveled it over the top of the bed with steely-eyed intent.

As she rolled to her stomach to push herself from the floor, she heard the lazy, less-than-amused drawl.

"Jed, do you have a fucking death wish?"

Dawg didn't sound pissed, but he didn't sound approving either. It was a dangerous tone of voice that assured all those listening that his mood could swing either way.

He was ready to talk, and in true "Dawg" style, he was barging right in.

Lips tightening, Piper jerked the sheet Jed had dragged off the bed as they rolled, and wrapped it quickly around her naked body. Peeking over the side of the bed, she growled back at her brother.

"Why are you sneaking into my bedroom?"

Dawg's brow lifted. "Little sister, I wasn't sneaking. Your door was unlocked."

"The hell it was." Struggling with the sheet with one hand to keep it around her, Piper used the other to push her hair back from her face as she glared at Dawg.

She was all too aware of Jed moving to his feet, completely at ease with his nudity and not the least bit ashamed as he collected his clothes. Dawg's expression tightened, his mood shifting toward that dangerous mark.

"Don't call me a liar, Piper," Dawg warned her then. "I said the door was unlocked. Trust me; it was unlocked."

"I locked that door earlier, Dawg," she told him, suddenly aware that something simply wasn't right where his entrance was concerned. "I remember securing it. And neither Jed nor myself has gone out of it since."

Dawg's gaze narrowed. "I wasn't exactly quiet when I pulled in and called out to Mercedes to tell her I was coming around to your room." His gaze swung to Jed as he laid his shirt across the table before securing the belt on his jeans. "I guess there's not a chance in hell you heard anything?"

Jed cleared his throat. As he glanced at her, Piper felt her face flushing heatedly.

She knew exactly why they hadn't heard anything.

"Figures." Dawg grunted, drawing Piper's attention back to him. "You're certain the door was locked?"

Tipping her head to the side, she stared back at him with mocking disbelief. "Really, Dawg?"

They both knew she was certain. Piper was the one often found checking all the doors and windows in the middle of the night, to be certain no one could slip into the suite.

Lifting his hand, he pushed his fingers through his hair in agitation before staring back at her, his celadon gaze filled with concern. "Piper, please God, tell me what's going on before someone does more than bruise your face."

She knew that door had been locked, which meant someone had unlocked it at a time when they would have believed she was otherwise occupied.

They were there looking for something.

She just had no idea who or what they were searching for.

# TEN

Staring into her brother's face and seeing the fear and worry for her reflected in his gaze, Piper was forced to admit that her suspicions regarding the attack couldn't be ignored any longer. There wasn't so much as a sliver of a chance that the attack in New York had been random, and she knew it.

It hadn't been an accident that her room was the one a burglar had targeted. She hadn't been randomly picked out of a crowd and then followed to her room. She wasn't just a faceless nobody someone had decided to torment.

And the nightmares . . .

Those vague, shadowy horrorscapes she drifted into once she fell asleep couldn't be ignored either. Just as the unlocked door couldn't be overlooked. Someone was desperate enough to get to her that they had picked the lock on her patio doors in broad daylight.

Breaking contact with Dawg's fierce look, she glanced at Jed, and knew he had reached the end of his patience as well. If she didn't tell her brother now, then he would.

"As you know, I slipped out of town last week." She sighed in resignation as she stared back at her brother once again. "A friend drove me to Louisville, where I caught a train to New York City to meet with someone interested in my designs. I was getting ready to leave to come home when I asked the front desk to send up a bellhop to help with my luggage. I had bought lots of materials at the fabric stores." She waved her hand toward her worktable. "It wasn't the bellhop who arrived. When I opened the door, I got a faceful of fist, and if it hadn't been for the kids in the adjoining room, the damage would have been much worse."

Dawg sat down slowly in the chair beside him before wiping his hands carefully over his face.

"I need to get dressed." She breathed out roughly. "You can question me when I get back."

Gathering her clothes, she strode quickly to the bathroom and snapped the door closed behind her before leaning against it and dragging in a ragged, fear-filled breath.

She knew she had locked that door.

She remembered locking it, just as she remembered Jed checking those locks when he'd risen from the bed after they had caught their breath.

What if she had been alone and Dawg hadn't shown up?

What if she had been attacked again? Or one of her sisters, or her mother?

God, what had she managed to draw back to Somerset and her family?


Dawg stared at the closed bathroom door before turning his gaze on Jed.

The other man was playing with one of the little glass gems Piper was so fond of. She'd bought a shitload of stuff, evidently, while she had been in Manhattan. Enough that she'd not wanted to carry it all herself to the cab.

She had instead opened her door to some bastard pretending to be a bellhop.

"What do you know, Jed?" he finally questioned the other man.

Listening to Jed's account of the night the kid had called him, and his arrival at the hospital, Dawg had to admit that his gratitude toward the other man was overwhelming.

There was no doubt in his mind that Piper would not have called him or one of their cousins. She was so wary of their protective tendencies, and so certain, according to Jed, that the attack had been random, that she would have never watched her back.

Fortunately, Jed had been watching it for her.

"Did you suspect she would be followed?" Dawg asked when he finished.

"If I had suspected it, she would have called you long before now," Jed informed him.

Jed turned his head as the bathroom door opened and Piper walked slowly from the room.

It was then that Dawg saw the expression that transformed Jed's face.

Hell, he'd hoped it hadn't gone that far.

No, he'd known it had gone that far, he amended as he watched Piper's gaze meet her lover's and saw the unconscious devotion that filled her face and eyes as well.

Those two were already so fucking bonded that he doubted even death would separate them. And he was certain neither of them was even fully aware of how deep it went.

*    *    *

Jed straightened as Piper moved from the bathroom. Intending to reach out for her, he was more than a little surprised when she moved to him instead.

Snagging his arm around her waist and pulling her to him, Jed ignored Dawg's dark expression and instead gave Piper the silent security he knew she was reaching out for.

"Do you remember anything the attacker said? Anything he did? Any odd scents, or an accent?" Dawg asked her as Jed felt the subtle tremor that raced up her spine.

"He said something."

Jed tightened at the admission but didn't berate her. It was the wrong time to do so, with Dawg standing there watching so closely.

It would hurt her to be embarrassed in such a way in front of her brother. And it would embarrass her, at the very least subconsciously.

"What did he say?" Dawg urged as he pulled his cell phone free and, Jed suspected, hit the record feature.

"That's just it; I don't remember what he said." Frustration filled her voice, thickened it and hinted at her inability to make sense of whatever she remembered. "He was demanding something, and I didn't know what the hell he was talking about."

Jed rubbed her lower arms gently, forcing himself to hold back the fury burning in his chest.

"You can't remember a single word?" Dawg questioned her again, his tone smoother than it had been moments ago, less angry, as though he too sensed the effect their anger had on her.

"Something about a car." She sighed, shaking her head as another tremor raced up her spine. "I just can't remember, Dawg."

"I have a few contacts in the city," Dawg murmured. "And a

few spread out through the police department. I'll make some calls and see what I can find out."

"I'm sorry, Dawg." Guilt was lashing at Piper's senses now.

Dawg was doing everything he could not to explode, to hide his anger.

Those bright celadon eyes seemed darker than normal, his expression almost haggard, and she realized the past week had been just as hard on him, perhaps, as it had been on her.

"For what?" he asked then.

"I shouldn't have reacted as I did when you saw my face. I was terrified you'd try to lock me away somewhere, though. You don't know how scary you get when you're in protection mode."

"That's still a possibility." He grunted as he leaned back in the chair and crossed his arms over his broad chest.

The black T-shirt he wore stretched across his powerful biceps created an impression of vast strength. "The nightmares have been brutal, Piper."

And they had been, she knew. The Mackay wives, Christa, Kelly, and Chaya, had arrived the day before and, along with her sisters and mother, berated Piper for refusing to tell any of them what happened.

Christa had told her that Dawg had been awakening from nightmares ever since, certain that Piper was in grave danger, and he had no idea how to protect her.

"I love you, Dawg." What more could she say? "You, Rowdy, and Natches saved us. But you've also smothered us this last year. Smothered us to the point that there's no privacy at all. And I just couldn't handle it any longer."

He leaned forward, his arms dropping from his chest and resting against his knees as he clasped his hands between them.

"Piper, if I ever end up having to bury one of you because I faltered or because I didn't know one of you was in danger, I don't know if I would survive the guilt. You're a Mackay. Your sisters are Mackays. Trouble and danger will always follow the four of you because of the covert jobs you hold. Unless . . ." He gave Jed a long, hard look. "Unless there's someone strong enough, someone dangerous enough, to deflect it."

Oh, Jed was strong enough. And he was dangerous enough. . . .

"Perhaps you should teach us properly how to protect ourselves, Dawg. I'm certain you and Jed would like to sleep sometime. And I do like going to the ladies' room without some hulking male standing outside the stall."

She shot him a tight, hard smile as irritation flashed in his expression, and Jed's arms tightened around her.

Dawg could only shake his head. "God, and here I thought you were the least stubborn sister."

"Just the quietest one," she amended the thought. "Trust me, Dawg: No matter the impression Eve gave you, neither Lyrica, Zoey, nor myself are willing to live like fugitives or witness protection candidates. You're going to have to come up with a solution other than some strong, forceful caveman to keep us from attracting trouble."

"No kidding." He grunted, rising to his feet. "I'm going to get out of here and make a few phone calls, catch up with Natches and Rowdy, and see what we can figure out." His gaze sliced to Jed's. "Make sure she's either not in this room, or that her locks are secured against anyone determined to get in."

She felt Jed shift behind her and glanced back.

He was staring at her worktable again, only this time, as he released her, his fingers went to the dark green glass jewels scattered amid the red and clear cut crystals.

"Those will be so pretty on the dress I'm designing." She sighed.

He rolled several in amid another batch whose color didn't seem as deep or rich.

"Where did you get them?" He picked a few up before moving across the room and handing them to Dawg.

Piper watched them curiously.

"A craft shop in New York, in the Garment District." She shrugged, catching Dawg's eye. "You've taken me there before."

Dawg rose slowly to his feet, his gaze on the pieces of colored glass.

Closing his hand quickly around the stones he held, he flipped the cell phone open again and made a call.

"I need you down here in Piper's room, ASAP. And if you have a jeweler's loupe or a strong magnifying glass, bring it with you," he ordered—Tim, Piper assumed.

She rather doubted he was ordering one of her sisters or her mother down here.

Flipping the phone closed, he moved to the table next to her bed and flipped on the light.

Holding his hand beneath the brightest area of the lamp's glow, he turned the stones with a finger, studying them carefully.

"What the hell is going on?" Piper whispered as trepidation began to rise inside her.

The panicked feeling that tightened her stomach shortened her breath and left her with the sensation of being unable to fill her lungs.

"Piper." Dawg lifted his gaze as Timothy rushed into the room, magnifying glass in hand. "These aren't glass." Lifting his gaze to Timothy Cranston, he motioned him over. "Tell me what these are."

Dropping the stones in Timothy's hand, Dawg stared down at him with a dark glower.

Holding his hand beneath the light, Timothy moved the magnifying glass over his hand and studied the colored objects with a frown.

"Where did you get these?" he asked Dawg, never taking his eyes from his palm.

"Piper brought them home from New York." The growl in Dawg's tone was a dangerous rasp. "She says she picked them up at a craft store."

Timothy didn't bother to lift his head or his gaze from the magnifying glass.

"She didn't get these at a craft store," he murmured. "Where else did you go?"

"What are they?" she questioned him warily.

"Emeralds, rubies, diamonds, and sapphires, Piper. These aren't pretty crystals and colored glass, sweetheart. Now, tell me where else you went."

Piper shook her head, swallowing tightly.

Diamonds, emeralds, rubies, and sapphires?

God, no wonder she'd thought they looked so much more brilliant after she got them home than they had when she first picked them out at the craft store.

"I rented a car and drove outside the city for a meeting, but I never had that shopping bag out of the car. When I returned the car, everything had fallen out of the bag to the floor, and the stones I bought were scattered on the back driver's-side floorboard."

Timothy jerked his head around to glare at her then.

"A rental car?" he questioned her, his tone icy.

Piper nodded slowly. "It was a rental."

"What was the name of the agency?" Tim asked.

"Riley's Rentals."

Tim nodded slowly before lifting his gaze to Dawg's. "That's Genoa property."

Genoa property.

Piper had heard of the Genoa family and the Mackays' run-in with them six years ago, just before Piper and her family were brought to Somerset.

The crime family had first butted heads with the Mackays when a family member, the niece of head of the family Rudy Genoa, had come for vengeance against John Walker Jr. and his lover, Sierra Lucas, for a broken engagement.

Marlena and her associate, Gerard Andrews, had been responsible for the half million dollars Rudy Genoa had advanced them to ensure Marlena caught John Walker's attention and kept it.

Expensive clothes, salons, and an apartment on Park Avenue. She'd been plucked, polished, and perfected—until the night John had learned she was also fucking his friend and fellow attorney, Gerard Andrews. The same man who had assured the Genoa family that if John married Marlena and had a child with her, then the attorney would willingly put his name behind the defense of Genoa family members in court.

"How did they get in my car?" she whispered.

"The Genoa family's rumored to be bringing jewels, gold, and cash into the States for another family—a Russian crime family they're trying to build ties with. The Russians are shipping the contraband into Italy, where the Genoa family has ties, and then members of the family are taking over. Homeland Security and the FBI have been trying to figure out exactly how they've been doing it. If Riley's Rentals is involved, then they're likely shipping them in vehicles that are coming through as cargo. Riley's has a reputation of shipping vehicles overseas and back again for wealthy clients. No agency has been able to tie them to anything illegal, though, until now."

"What do we do?" Panic was beginning to edge through her senses as fear began to build.

"We'll take care of it, Piper." Jed's arms tightened around her as Piper felt the fear beginning to overflow her tenuous control.

What had she managed to get herself into? Why had she allowed this to happen? She could have just told Dawg, Jed, and Tim what had happened and they would have figured this out a week ago. Before someone had attempted to break into her room.

"Don't worry, Piper. We have the contacts to fix this," Dawg promised her as he turned back to her. "You stay with Jed; Timothy and I will take care of things."

This wasn't what she wanted.

"I didn't want you to have to risk yourself," she whispered. "None of you. I just wanted to be able to take this meeting without everyone breathing down my neck."

"You were being protected for a reason, Piper," Jed stated as Dawg and Tim began to move toward the patio door, where Dawg was pointing out where the lock had been picked.

"For a reason I was never allowed to understand." Turning, she faced him, her gaze meeting his, irritation flooding her as fear and confusion fueled the panic tightening her stomach. "Maybe, Jed, if something—anything—had been explained to me, then I would have been more prone to listen a little more closely."

"Now you're sounding like a child." He sighed.

"Why shouldn't I?" she mocked him. "That's how I'm treated. Treat me like an adult and see if I don't try to act like one."

# ELEVEN

Nothing could possibly be easy, Piper thought as midnight rolled around before she was able to extricate herself from her mother, sisters, cousins, and various family members.

"Dawg couldn't just keep his mouth shut?" she muttered as Jed escorted her into his room. "He could have kept all this to himself for a little while longer."

"Dawg usually knows what he's doing," Jed assured her, locking the door behind them before turning and striding through the living area. "Stay here; I want to check out the bedroom again."

Crossing her arms over her breasts, she watched as he disappeared into the bedroom, closing the door behind him.

So Dawg usually knew what he was doing, did he?

"You are aware that Dawg is the one whom Tim accuses of constantly living by the seat of his pants, right?"

She didn't quite catch Jed's response, but it was something along the lines of, "That's when Dawg is at his best."

At his best, her ass.

It was when he was most dangerous.

She was still standing there glaring at the door when it opened and Jed walked through, his chest gloriously bare, his shirt conspicuously absent.

She didn't need this right now.

Hell.

Tightening her thighs, Piper fought to hold back the ache beginning there. The swelling of her clit, the throb of her pussy. The fiery, desperate need to be filled by the hard thrust of his cock.

Dark blond hair fell over his brow, while the navy blue of his gaze seemed to deepen and gleam with heated hunger as he stared back at her.

"He didn't have to tell the whole damned family," she muttered, her mouth drying out as he paced closer.

"Would you want to know if one of your sisters were in danger?" he asked softly.

Dark, thick lashes lowered over the gleam in his eyes as predatory awareness filled them.

He knew she wanted him.

It wasn't as though she could hide the hardness of her nipples as they pressed into the thin material of the blouse she wore. Or the heavy pulse of blood in her throat.

His gaze, heavy with latent lust and intent, flicked to the throbbing of the vein at the side of her neck, then back to the hard tips of her nipples.

Sensation raced over her flesh as heat built in her womb and fired a need she still had no idea how to handle. Hell, she didn't even know how he managed to do this to her. What she did know was that resisting him wasn't going to happen.

"You didn't answer me, Piper." He stopped just in front of her, his wide chest separated from the hard tips of her nipples by no more than a breath of space.

"What was the question again?" Oh, Lord, she was supposed to keep up with the conversation?

With him walking around with his broad naked chest? Oh, dear Lord, she didn't think so.

"Would you want to know if your sisters were in danger?" he asked again.

"I remember the question." She glared back at him, determined to bluff her way through having not heard it the first time. "That's not the point, so why answer?"

A knowing smile curled his lips.

"Really?" Settling his hands on her hips, he brought her body flush against his.

Broad, fiercely erect, the length of his cock pressed against her belly behind the denim covering it.

"Really." Trying not to appear too greedy to touch him, she let her fluttering fingers press against his chest.

"Beside the point, huh?" he asked.

Piper closed her eyes, hoping to find some measure of control against the hunger flooding her system.

"It really is."

Closing her eyes didn't help.

Oh, God, it only made it worse.

Jerking them open, she fought to catch her breath as his lips settled against the side of her neck for a heated kiss.

"Jed, what do you do to me?" she whispered, needing to know, to understand why she couldn't deny the fire raging between them.

"The same thing you do to me, sweetheart, maybe?" His teeth raked against her neck as he finished the question, bringing a low, keening moan from her throat as she arched her neck.

"Do I make the world burn for you, too?"

Jed lifted his head, staring down at her, amazed by the question.

God, was that what he did for her? Did he make the world burn down around her? Because he swore that was exactly what it felt like to him as well.

It felt as though the world were burning down around him, and nothing mattered but the flames edging closer toward them.

"Baby, the world doesn't even exist for me when I'm touching you." Were those words really falling from his lips?

What the hell was she doing to him?

Moving his hands from her waist, he lowered them to the belt that cinched her waist loosely and released it. He dropped it to the floor, and his fingers moved to the buttons of her blouse.

Was that him actually fumbling with a button as his lips touched hers?

But, hell, her kiss was fire itself. It was the flame burning the world around him and searing him with pleasure. It was the fuel feeding it, and the only hope he had of surviving the effect on his senses.

Parting her lips further, tasting the teasing heat of her tongue against his, Jed had to force his fingers to work. To remove each button from the exquisite softness of the blouse she'd made with her own delicate fingers.

Fingers that were curling against his chest, blunt little nails rasping against his flesh as she dragged them to the jeans riding low at his hips.

Hell. She was tugging at his belt, releasing it, dragging it apart slowly as he deepened the kiss and drew in the rich essence of her feminine need.

The last button parted, the material separating and slowly

drifting from her shoulders as he pushed it back from the rapid rise and fall of her breasts.

Soft, silken lace encased her breasts in a bra as light as air. Sliding the clip between her breasts open and pulling the fabric from the swollen weight of the firm curves, he was forced to pull his lips back from hers, to drag in air as the button of his jeans released.

His self-control was going to hell in a handbasket.

"Come here, baby." Swinging her up into his arms, he strode quickly through the sitting room to the bedroom door.

Opening it and pushing through, he moved to the bed he'd turned back when he'd entered the room earlier to check the doors. Laying her against the cool white sheets, he moved his hands to her delicate legs, where the skirt she wore had fallen back above her knees.

The midcalf length of the full skirt shouldn't have been so damned sexy, but it had tormented him all day with the knowledge that it covered flesh softer than the material over it.

Stroking his hand down one leg to her fragile feet, he removed the sandals covering one before moving to the next.

"Beautiful." Running his hands back up the inside of her legs, he parted them gently, watching as the paisley print of the skirt fell back to her thighs. "Do you know how hard it was to keep from dragging you to this bedroom today? To keep from pushing my hands beneath this skirt to find all the sweet, hot flesh beneath?"

Piper arched beneath him, watching through lashes that refused to open fully, fighting to breathe through the incredible pleasure pouring through her.

Pushing his hands beneath the skirt, he curled his fingers beneath the elastic of the low-rise bikini underwear she wore and began pulling them down with exquisite slowness.

"Jed, you're teasing me," she accused him, her body tortured with the need for his possession.

"I'm teasing me." Hot, rich lust echoed in his voice, filled the dark sound with wicked hunger as he pulled her panties free and tossed them to the floor.

Pulling back, he rose quickly beside the bed, and before she could do more than draw a sharp breath, he'd shed the denim and snug boxer underwear containing the fierce width of his straining erection.

Heavy veins throbbed forcefully along the shaft as he came to her, while the wide crest, flushed and dark with lust, gleamed with a layer of precome.

Rather than pushing her legs immediately apart and coming into her, as she'd expected, he lowered himself carefully over her. Rough with an overnight shadow of a beard, his cheek brushed against the side of her breast.

"So pretty," he whispered as her hands gripped his shoulders, her legs parting to encase the muscular strength of his thighs.

Arching to him, Piper bit back a demanding moan. She needed to feel his lips against her breasts. Needed to feel the heavy draw of his mouth and the flick of his wicked tongue.

"You're going to make me beg, aren't you?" she demanded, a moan slipping into her voice as his lips brushed against the tight, sensitive point.

"Never."

She would have, if he would just—

"Oh, God! Oh, Jed. Yes. Please." Her hands lifted to his head, her fingers fisting in his hair as she strained against him, arching into the heated possession of his mouth as it wrapped around the sensitive peak of her breast.

The tender bud of her nipple throbbed in agonizing pleasure as he drew on it. Fierce, pleasure-sharp spikes of sensation raced to her clit and the depths of her vagina as the feel of silken warmth eased from the clenched portal.

Drawing on the tender flesh, he flicked his tongue against it with lashing warmth. Pleasure struck repeatedly at her womb, clenching her pussy and pounding through her clit with exquisite sensation.

"Oh, God, Jed, it's so good." She arched closer, desperate to feel his touch between her thighs. Piper's senses became focused on nothing else but each fiery, rapturous tug of his lips and each suckling motion of his hot mouth as his fingers eased slowly, teasingly up her thigh.

"Jed, please." Begging was so not beneath her as his fingers brushed against the silken folds of her pussy.

He parted the intimate lips, his touch too slow, almost taunting as she arched and ached for more.

The pad of his finger rubbed against the clenched entrance; he ignored the desperate motion of her hips as she fought to force his finger inside her.

"Greedy, baby," he whispered, the tips of two fingers now rubbing against the entrance to her pussy.

"Greedy?" She panted. "More like tormented. You're tormenting me, Jed."

"I'm loving you." The words were whispered against her midriff as his lips moved lower and one hand pushed her skirt higher. "I'm loving you, Piper."

Before she could counter his declaration, his lips lowered and covered the straining, tortured bud of her clitoris.

"Oh, God, yes." Twisting against the sudden grip he had on her hips, Piper's hips jerked in reaction. "Jed. Oh, Jed, yes, please."

Lavish licks surrounded the straining bundle of nerves as Piper cried out, pleading, begging, desperate for release now.

Nudging at the little bud, licking at it, suckling it into the heat of his mouth, he pushed her toward an abyss of ecstasy that threatened her sanity.

As he stroked and laved the sensitive bundle of nerve endings, the fingertips stroking at her entrance began to slip inside, stretching her flesh and opening the little portal. Swift, heated flares of sensation raged through her flesh, striking at her womb, at her clit, and stealing her breath.

The feel of his fingers pressing inside her, separating the tender tissue and caressing hidden nerve endings, had muted cries escaping her throat as she fought for release.

She didn't want to wait.

She'd waited long enough.

She'd waited twenty-four years for this man, for this pleasure, and waiting one second longer for her release seemed entirely uncalled-for.

"Jed, please." Her fingers kneaded his scalp as her hips lifted, her thighs spreading wider as his fingers fucked slow and easy inside her. "Please don't make me wait."

A muted groan of male pleasure was her only answer as his tongue rolled over her clit, pressed against it, and threatened to ignite the explosion she was reaching so desperately for.

God. She couldn't wait much longer. She was going to melt into a mass of pure sensation at any second. Waiting was only intensifying the painful eagerness now building inside her.

"More." Lifting to him, rolling her hips against the invasion of his fingers inside her vagina, against the probing, wicked tongue and suckling lips at her clit, Piper fought to hold on to her sanity as the need became a driving, desperate ache to fly into the heated rapture she could feel awaiting her.

"Please. Jed . . ." She couldn't take much more.

Oh, God, he was going to pay for this. She was going to make certain he paid for this.

His lips lifted; his fingers eased back.

Forcing her lashes open, Piper watched as he dragged himself to his knees before bending to the side of the bed and reaching for a condom.

The heavy length of his cock jutted out from his body, flushed and eager and tempting a hunger she'd never had the chance to give in to.

She had the chance now.

Her body was humming for the penetration she knew he was preparing for.

But she wanted . . .

As he straightened before her, Piper pushed herself into a sitting position.

"Not yet." Her fingers curled around his wrist as he moved to roll the condom over the throbbing, flared crest of the fiercely erect shaft.

"Piper, baby." The warning in his voice was clear. "I don't know if I have the control for this."

"Sure you do." She breathed out, one hand curling around his erection, marveling at the fact that her fingers couldn't encircle it, yet her body could accept each hard thrust made into it by the fierce shaft. "Just like I did."

Leaning forward, she tasted him.

A hard, primal groan sounded above her as her tongue licked over the engorged crest.

Parting her lips, she covered the width of his cock head, taking him into her mouth as her lips hugged the hard flesh and drew on it with pleasure.

Salty, male.

The explosion of taste had a moan tearing from her throat, vibrating against his dick and sending Jed's senses into overdrive.

Damn her, she was destroying him, and he couldn't stop her. She was sucking his control straight from him by the simple act of sucking his dick as though it were a favored treat.

With her tongue lashing at his cock and her lips tightening around it, her wicked, seductive fingers cupping his balls in one hand as the other stroked the heavy width of it was nearly more than he could bear.

"God, Piper, I'm going to come, babe." He groaned with a desperation he swore he'd never felt before this woman.

Her tongue rubbed at the head of his cock. It probed at the oversensitive nerve endings just beneath the head, then sucked the engorged heat with such pleasure he swore he was going to lose control and spill his release into her suckling mouth.

He had to tighten his fingers, had to grip her hair and try to force her head back from the shaft.

Her eyes darkened.

Seeing her staring up at him with the light green of her eyes darkening imperceptibly was nearly too much for the tenuous control he was barely holding on to.

Yet he couldn't stop.

His hips moved even as he told himself he'd hold still.

He watched the head of his cock pull back, sink inside. Watched as he fucked her mouth and those pert, pretty lips reddened.

He watched until he couldn't take it any longer.

Pulling free despite her protesting moan, Jed moved back, and before she could react, he managed to turn her to her stomach, his hands gripping her hips and lifting them before him.

"Damn, your ass is so pretty." Sliding his hands back to the rounded globes as he positioned his cock at the slick, heated opening of her little pussy, he couldn't help but marvel at the pleasure slicing through his senses. "I love this pretty ass, Piper."

"You're killing me," she cried out desperately.

"Then we'll go together." He groaned as he pushed the head of his cock into the fiery heat of her juice-laden cunt and had to clench his teeth to fight back the release building in his balls. "God, Piper, we'll go together, baby, because I never knew pleasure could be this fucking good."

He couldn't hold back.

He couldn't hold on.

Gripping her hips firmly, Jed pulled his cock back, then in one fierce thrust buried the eager erection halfway inside the gripping, lush little pussy he was certain would steal his sanity.

Pure, unadulterated ecstasy began building in his senses.

Blood pounded in his veins, and on the second thrust, nothing else began to matter but the pure, mindless race to shattering rapture.

Piper tried to scream.

As the fierce, pleasure-pain sensations began whipping through her pussy, attacking her clit and racing through her senses, she swore she would never survive the cataclysmic pleasure building through her flesh.

She couldn't struggle against it; hell, she didn't want to.

She gave herself over to it, reaching ever harder for it, poised on the edge of an abyss she wanted nothing more than to fly into.

"Jed, please." She forced the cry past her lips. "Harder. Please. Please fuck me harder."

She wanted that release.

She wanted it now.

God, if she had to wait she might not survive it.

Fingers curling into the sheets beneath her, she held on tightly.

She thrust back to him, panting for air, as flames burned through her system, licking across her flesh and attacking the rapidly rising sensitivity of her clit and the aching depths of her over-stretched vagina.

As she fought to break the bonds holding her to reality and to jump headlong into the flames, she felt Jed above her. His lips were at her neck, stinging nips and heated kisses attacking the bend of her shoulder a second before he caught the tender flesh between his lips and delivered a heated kiss that became a cata-lyst to pure ecstasy.

The explosion tore through her.

Rapture ripped her from her place in reality and threw her headlong into the cataclysm of flames awaiting her. Destructive, the tidal wave of pure ecstasy overwhelmed her; as she flew through that place of searing sensation, she found the man who had taken her there.

Piper felt him inside her, covering her, not just taking her body, but sinking inside her soul.

His groan echoed around her.

His cock buried deep one last time, pulsed and throbbed; then her muscles clenched around him further as he found his own release.

Crying out his name, locked in a world of blinding color and overwhelming rapture, she could do nothing but trust him to hold her, to keep her secure as the pleasure pounded through her, tore past the deepest reaches of her heart and invaded the very depths of her soul.

She was his.

There was no denying it. There was no fighting it.

She belonged to him.

But as she felt him sinking inside the abyss with her, Piper knew he belonged to her as well.

He was hers.

There was no denying her, just as she knew there was no longer any chance of denying him.

For the first time in her life, she knew exactly what it meant to belong.

Now if she could just live long enough to enjoy it.

# TWELVE

"What now?" With a towel wrapped around her, her damp hair lying along her shoulders, Piper stepped from the bathroom after showering, the reality of the danger facing her threatening to overwhelm her optimism.

The chest-tightening panic was returning, waiting, preparing her for Jed to walk away. . . .

Like her father had walked away and left her, her mother, and her sisters unprotected and alone. Just as she was afraid Tim and Dawg would walk away.

Was that why everything inside her shut down whenever she and Dawg moved toward a confrontation? To prepare her heart, to steel herself against the abandonment?

"We wait and see," he answered, the towel he'd wrapped around his waist earlier still in place.

He hadn't dressed.

Heated need for his touch was threatening to weaken her need for answers as she watched him toss their dirty clothes into the hamper next to the bathroom door.

"Since when do you sit around and wait on anyone or anything, Jed?" she asked, frowning at the feeling that there was much more going on than simply waiting. "What are you and my brother up to?"

Tightening in response to some imperceptible feeling of dread, her heart began to beat at a sluggish pace.

The impending panic was a result of the look on his face, the darkening of his navy gaze that made his eyes appear almost black.

"We're not just waiting; we're watching," he finally stated, his expression hardening just enough to warn her that she was going to hear something she didn't want to hear.

"What are you watching?"

"Your room." Jed paced to the television, retrieved the remote, and hit the power button.

Watching the screen, she was surprised as he reached behind the unit, and a second later, the split view of the screen showed both her bedroom as well as her sitting room.

"Brogan had the cameras installed just after he started sleeping with Eve," he revealed. "He was afraid his or Dawg's enemies would attempt to strike out at her, or take her from him. There were cameras in her room, and GPS on her car and her cell phone."

The cameras had been there since before Brogan and Eve moved from the inn? And they were still there?

"I was supposed to move them," he told her. "And I was going to until I learned you were taking her room after she moved in with Brogan."

"So you've watched me when I didn't know you were?"

Controlling her? Maneuvering her?

Was he so much different than she had begun to believe he was?

"Only once or twice." Broad shoulders shrugged as he watched her carefully. "The night you were packing to leave for New York."

Holding the towel close to her breasts, she sat up, watching the view on the television, wondering what she should feel.

Was the need to deny that he would do such a thing to control her normal? Was she simply trying to make excuses for him?

"Why?" she whispered. "Why were you watching me?"

He rubbed at the back of his neck, frustration tightening his face. "I worried about you. I wanted to see you. Hell, Piper, you've made me fucking crazy since I've moved in here, as you've tempted me, then run from me. There were days I wasn't certain I could keep from playing the caveman I knew you were waiting for me to reveal lurking inside me."

Biting her lip, she glanced to the screen again.

"So why show me now?"

"Because I don't want any secrets at all between us any longer," he stated. "Not secrets like this." Flipping his hand toward the screen, he moved to the dresser and pulled his clothes from the chair next to the bed as she watched, then began dressing angrily.

"I don't want to take your fucking freedom," he growled at her as he shoved the white-and-gray-striped shirt into the waistband of his jeans and quickly buckled his belt. "I don't want to control what you think or feel or what you do." Glaring at her, he sat down in the chair next to the bed and pulled on dark leather boots. "I just want you."

He just wanted her?

"And now you've had me," she said, feeling kind of hollow inside. "Did you change your mind about wanting to control me and my life?"

Had she made a mistake? The one mistake she had sworn she would never make—had she fallen in love with a man unable to resist the urge to completely take her life over?

The look he shot her was one of such scorn that anger immediately flared inside her.

What the hell did he expect her to think?

Stomping to the end of the bed, where he'd laid the clothes he'd collected from her room earlier, Piper pulled on her own jeans, soft cotton tank camisole, socks, and sneakers.

"Maybe I should just return to my room." She felt a bit hollow inside now, as though some part of her had just been cruelly ripped from her chest.

He wasn't saying he loved her. He wasn't mentioning caring for her. There was no hint of commitment or anything other than the fact that he had been watching her and she had driven him crazy.

"What the hell do you want from me?" she asked as she finished dressing and turned back to him, aching inside with the knowledge that she could be losing what she hadn't even known she'd so desperately needed.

"I want you to stop being frightened of me, to start with," he demanded.

"Then don't pull this crap on me." Turning on him fully, her arms propped on her hips, Piper confronted him as she had never confronted her brother. "For God's sake, Jed, I never knew what the hell you've wanted from me. You flirted, you smiled, yet you never asked me out or gave me so much as a hint that you wanted more than a one-night stand. Or is that all you wanted?"

Heated anger was brewing inside her, rising to the surface and threatening to break free of the shield she normally kept surrounding it.

"What do you think I wanted?" Dark emotion filled his expression and his eyes, warning her of the thin ice she might be stepping onto.

She'd never heeded the warnings from Jed, though, so why start now?

Why should she even attempt to make excuses to herself, let alone to him, Dawg, or anyone else? she thought furiously as she watched him hit the remote, turning the television off before throwing the remote to the bed.

"You think I've driven myself insane trying to hold back, trying to ensure you have the space you need to deal with your brother and decide what you want with me, just to stop with a fucking one-night stand?" Jed growled.

He moved so fast there was no avoiding him.

His hands were on her shoulders first, jerking her to him before one arm wrapped around her waist to hold her against his hard body while his free hand slid into her hair, clenched, and pulled her head back.

"You make me feel like a fucking caveman," he rasped. Power, hunger, and something much deeper echoed in his voice and gleamed in his eyes. "Son of a bitch, Piper, you make me feel things I've never felt before, and I have no idea how to fucking deal with them."

Her eyes widened.

"What do I make you feel, Jed?"

His lips parted, but what he would have said, she didn't know.

"How very sweet."

That voice.

Grating. Harsh.

She knew it. It echoed in her head and slammed through her memories with the force of a sledgehammer.

Jed's eyes narrowed as he released her, turning as he used one arm to keep her behind him.

It was the nightmare she'd had nightly since the attack in New York. The face she could never remember. The vision of horror and pain she hadn't been able to escape.

The man was pockmarked, a scar running through the left side of his upper lip and bisecting a weak chin. Thinning dark brown hair and muscular shoulders combined with mean, cold hazel eyes and a gun leveled at Jed's chest.

"You're a stupid man." Jed seemed to sigh, but she could feel the dangerous fury building in his body.

"How do you figure that?" Thin lips curled into a sneer as bulky shoulders shifted beneath a light jacket that strained across them. "I slipped in on you, didn't I?"

"Did you?" Was that amusement in Jed's voice?

The other man chuckled. "Why don't you just move away from the little girlie there," he suggested. "She can run over to the next room and collect all those jewels she got in New York and bring them back to me. I might let you live if she hurries. And if she brings them all."

Jed was slowly shaking his head. Piper gripped his waist with one hand as the other balled into a fist and pressed against his back. Fear rose inside her and threatened to steal her breath. An ugly flash of life without Jed slammed through her imagination and left her fighting back tears.

"How do I know you don't have someone waiting in her room?" Jed asked, as though he hadn't just been watching the complete emptiness of her suite.

"Doesn't matter; we'll both want the same thing," the man

stated, his voice harsh as he advanced another step. "Now, does she go after those jewels or do I kill you? Then her." A smile twisted his lips as the mocking question passed them. "Or I could just hurt you a little bit to show her I mean business." He aimed the gun at Jed's kneecap.

"No need to go that far," Jed drawled, as though it were all a game. "She can just do as you ask."

She knew Jed's voice. She knew the passion-rich sound of hunger in it as well as the icy slide of a warning. And the warning in his tone was unmistakable.

"I thought that might be the case." The intruder's smile was a terrifying grimace as he glanced to Jed's side to peek around at her.

He chuckled with a grating rasp. "It's nice to see you've healed from our last meeting. I've always thought it a rather wasted effort to add more damage before the old bruises have healed."

And he appeared to enjoy the thought of adding those bruises.

He had every intention of killing them. Piper could see it in the pure anticipation in his gaze. Cruelty was inherent in the man's face, and in her memory of his heavy blows landing against her undefended body.

"Go on, Ms. Mackay," he ordered her softly, waving the gun toward the door between Jed's room and her own. "Collect all the jewels now. Miss any and he'll die."

"How would I know?" Licking her dry lips, she didn't have to pretend pure terror; it was there, slapping her in the face. "They're mixed in with the rest of the stones."

Evil hazel eyes narrowed. "What do you mean? Mixed in with the other stones?"

"The stones I bought at the craft store." Forcing the words past her lips, she tried to hold back the quaver in her voice. "I thought they were the fake stones I'd bought."

For the briefest second surprised disbelief filled the man's gaze before a cackle of laughter left his lips.

"Son of a bitch." The laughter was almost a wheeze. "Why am I even surprised? You look about that stupid, bitch."

Stupid?

The gun still aimed at Jed's knee was all that kept her mouth shut as she stared back at him.

He might think she was stupid, but she knew he was fucking ugly. She could fake smart if that were true, but there was no way in hell he could fake pretty, she thought mockingly, fighting to hold back her fear.

She wasn't stupid, though. What she was, was doing everything she could to buy enough time for Jed to figure their way out of this one.

"Well, I suggest you learn how to identify the real stuff and separate it from the fakes really fast," he suggested, his voice lowering and echoing with cruelty. "You have about four minutes to get that cute little ass back in here before I start putting holes in your man." He waved the gun at Jed's knee before lifting it to Jed's heart and smiling back at her.

Everything inside her was shaking, trembling in fear now, while Jed's complete stillness had wariness growing inside her.

He was up to something; she could feel it.

She knew Jed. He wasn't moving; nor was he taunting.

"I'll just get them all."

"Make sure you turn the lights out," Jed suddenly advised her.

Piper paused.

"What fucking lights?" Fury echoed in the gunman's voice. The lights went out and the darkness exploded around her.

Piper found herself thrown to the floor a breath before the explosive report of a weapon echoed through the room.

Riding close on the sound of the gun's discharge, shattering glass from the mirror above the dresser began raining down on her, biting sharply against the bare flesh of her arms.

She covered her head until the stinging storm ceased, then scrambled across the room on her hands and knees, glass pricking into her palms and knees as the sound of an enraged fight could be heard ahead of her.

She had to find Jed.

"Stay in place, Piper," Jed yelled out a second before a hard grunt was heard. "Stay where you are, dammit."

She pushed herself against the wall as she glared into the darkness, her hand pressing against a large shard of the glass on the floor. Curling her fingers around it, she lifted it, holding it against her just in case she might need it.

A second later a shadow hurled itself toward her as though propelled by some unseen force.

Or Jed's fist.

The wide body of her assailant—or her would-be killer— slammed into the wall beside her.

Fury surged through Piper at the knowledge of who it was bouncing against the wall. Gripping the glass tighter in her hand, she struck out and buried the arrowed point of the glass into the brute's back. Or maybe it was his shoulder?

She wasn't certain which.

The second she slammed it home she tried to move out of his way. The fist was faster than her self-preservation instincts, though. A hard fist in her direction slammed into her shoulder, throwing her off balance and sending her pitching to the floor, her hands scraping against the glass that covered the carpet.

"Dammit, Piper." Affectionate frustration filled Jed's voice and covered that underlying well of complete fury she sensed.

She couldn't see a damned thing, but suddenly Jed was picking her up and throwing them both to the side as the report of the weapon blasted through the room once again.

An animalistic growl left Jed's throat as he pushed her halfway beneath the bed, then jumped across it.

The gun went off again as raised voices outside the room could be heard. A high-pitched male scream sounded, and then for the space of a few short seconds, there was unbearable silence.

Piper stared across the bed, desperate to see Jed's shadow moving, to see some kind of movement that she could attribute to him.

Without him, she was lost.

She felt lost.

Terror squeezed her heart like a furious vise and left her breathless as she glared over the bed, determined to see him alive. She had to see him alive.

Her lips parted to call out to him at the same moment the lights flipped on, shocking her senses.

Piper dropped down and beneath the bed, rolling to peep from beneath the bed skirt at the overly large feet suddenly rushing around the room.

"Dammit, Piper." Hard hands shoved beneath the bed and gripped her wrists, and she glimpsed Jed's bruised face as he pulled her from beneath the bed and dragged her against the hard width of his chest.

Piper pressed one hand against his heart as she pressed her face into his neck, concentrating on the beating of his heart against her palm.

He was alive.

That was all she could think, all she could allow herself to focus on.

He was alive.

"Hell!" Tim's voice echoed above her with his characteristic mocking frustration. "Only a Mackay could cause this kind of commotion and still fucking live through it."

"Hey." Dawg's protest was a rasping growl. "I think I resemble that remark."

"Resent, Dawg," Rowdy repeated the response he'd been repeating for years. "You're supposed to resent that remark."

"I'll resent it when it stops happening." Dawg sighed.

Lifting her head from Jed's shoulder, Piper looked around, her eyes widening.

The large mirror over the dresser was shattered and lying in bits and sharp pieces in front of the oak dresser. The window across the room was missing a wide section and spiderwebbed with long cracks.

The flat-screen television was missing its screen and hung lopsided now, its pieces littering the floor. The chair was upended, along with the bedside table, lamp, and clock. Amid all of it, unconscious or dead—she didn't care which—the broad form of the man who had attacked her in New York lay sprawled, still and silent.

"I know this one." Tim kicked at a limp, thick leg, his expression reflective. "Marcel Genoa. He's one of Rudy Genoa's fists, and Marlena's cousin."

"I thought we had that organization taken care of, Timothy?" The question rumbled from Jed's throat, the irritation in his voice heavy.

A stranger's voice intruded into the conversation then. "It's according to your definition of 'taken care of,' Agent Booker."

Piper's head jerked up as Jed rose to his feet immediately, lifting her along with him to his side. But no one was moving to defend themselves.

"Mr. Samson?" Swallowing tightly, she moved her gaze from Rhylan Samson, Guido Samson's son, to the men filling the room around her.

Rhylan stepped into the room, his thumbs hooking into the pockets of his jeans, lean, muscular shoulders shifting beneath the dark gray silk shirt he wore.

"Marcel was a bit of a wild card who we were unaware was lurking in the dark," Rhylan said, moving one hand to close the door behind him before lifting the other to prop both on his tapered, muscular hips.

Staring down at Marcel Genoa, he shook his head wearily. "We've been looking for him since the attack on Ms. Mackay."

"You could have informed us," Timothy snapped, his gaze swinging to Piper. "It's not as though she was forthcoming with the information."

Piper refused to flush.

"Perhaps, Tim, if I'd been allowed an opinion or a choice in the past year where my security was concerned, then maybe I would have been forthcoming with the information."

"She's not going to stop blaming us," Dawg muttered behind her. "Let it go, Tim."

Letting it go was the best choice her male family members could have made.

Rhylan chuckled at the response, his gaze moving to Jed's. "Good luck, Agent Booker. You may need it if you continue dealing with Mackays."

"I rather doubt it." The confidence in Jed's voice had Rhylan inclining his head with a grin.

"What's going on, Rhylan?" Tim asked.

"Why the hell do all of you seem to know this man far better than a few days' stay would warrant?" Piper asked. Wasn't it just like Dawg and their cousins, along with Tim, to know it all while leaving everyone else in the dark?

She was fucking sick of being left in the dark.

"Piper. There's information you can't have, and there will be times your questions will not be answered."

Tim lifted his gaze to Jed as Piper felt her chest tighten in pain. She was the one who had carried the bruises, who could have died. Who deserved this information more than she? "Take her to her mother; she's waiting in the hall. We'll figure this out—"

"No."

Piper had never been so happy to hear that rough, growling refusal come from Jed's throat as she stared back at Tim in re-crimination.

Tim grimaced, his face appearing more lined, his expression more concerned than ever.

"You know the delicacy of this information—"

"Drop it, Cranston." Rhylan breathed out roughly as he gave his head a hard shake. "He's right. She's the one who's been in danger, not the rest of you." He turned to her again. "I'm sorry, Ms. Mackay; you were caught in a web of deceit that had nothing to do with you, other than the fact that you were in the wrong place at the wrong time, and ended up with belongings we were unaware were in that car. The jewels you inadvertently ended up with are the belongings of a particularly sadistic Russian mobster. They'll be returned to him, so we can then track where they end up and what they're being used to pay for." He turned to Tim. "If you'll gather the jewels together for me, I have the paperwork you need."

Timothy's lips thinned as the situation was explained to her. "That's information that could get her killed, Rhylan."

"Only if she tells anyone what she knows," Rhylan objected.

"And I think she's proven she knows how to keep her mouth shut."

No, he was wrong; she didn't need to hear this particular argument.

Jed had tensed to a breaking point, and Dawg, Rowdy, and Natches looked as though they were facing the gallows at the thought of her hearing whatever information this man had to give.

"Mom's waiting for me." Turning to Jed, she felt the tension slowly easing from his body. "I'll be in the kitchen."

"I'll be there soon."

His head lowered, and his lips touched hers with a gentleness that filled her soul with a warmth that went far beyond arousal, need, or hunger. It filled her with a knowledge she hadn't understood until now.

As Jed released her she moved quickly to Dawg, threw her arms around him, and immediately felt him enfold her in his arms.

"I understand," she whispered in his ear quickly. "I never understood how you feared for our safety until now, Dawg."

"Understood what, sweetie?" How could she have ever thought it was just arrogance and male superiority that caused him to hover over her and her sisters so closely?

"Why." Her arms tightened around his shoulders. "Why we have to stay safe for you." Leaning back, she stared into his eyes and saw the bleak knowledge he held in his soul.

The knowledge of all the ways she could die, and all the ways he couldn't protect her, her sisters, and her mother if he weren't always diligent.

It was the curse of loving men such as this, whether they were lovers or the best damned brother and cousins anyone could have.

His jaw bunched, emotions whipping through the light green of his eyes and clenching the muscles of his face before he nodded sharply.

A quick hug to both Rowdy and Natches, and Piper hurried from the room.

As Tim had said, her mother was waiting in the hall, but she wasn't alone. With her were Lyrica and Zoey, and moving up the hall Eve and Brogan strode toward them quickly.

Brogan's gaze surveyed her swiftly before he nodded and moved past her, leaving Eve to give her a firm hug as their mother wrapped her arm around Piper's waist.

They were all safe—this time.

But they were Mackays. The sisters were Dawg's, Brogan's, and now Jed's weaknesses. They would always live beneath the shadow of the Mackay males' strength, as well as the strength of the men they loved.

A strength that had acquired enemies for them through their dedication to justice.

Flashing a grin first to Lyrica, then to Zoey, she warned them with amused reflection, "I'd acquire ninja training if I were you. Otherwise they'll never stop hovering. So give in, or get tough."

Lyrica slumped against the wall.

Zoey just stared back at her with eyes a fierce celadon and an expression of complete rejection of such a thought.

"We're Mackays," Zoey stated then. "We don't give in."

"Hell, no." Eve laughed lightly.

"Not in this lifetime," Lyrica assured them all.

"It looks like it's time to get tough, then," Mercedes stated as she had so many times in the past, her smile bright and filled with anticipation as they turned and moved quickly to the kitchen.

Coffee, a sweet, and a game plan. That was how they dealt with the problems life had thrown at them for as long as Piper could remember. Her mother would prepare hot drinks, some sweet she had baked, and they would figure out the best way they could handle the situation. The best way to get tough and fight back against whatever problems they faced.

It was time to get tough.

# THIRTEEN

The Mackay women had learned how to fight back—if not in strength then with their intelligence—fight silently, and fight with success years before Chandler Mackay had died. They had perfected the art.

Until now, Piper, her sisters, and her mother had been certain they could make their male family members back up and stop hovering so closely. Piper could see now that it wasn't going to happen.

But she could also see why.

With Eve sitting with them, coffee and a slice of Mercedes's coconut cream pie in front of them, they began to plot and to plan.

Not for their freedom.

Not for their independence.

They were plotting, planning, and they would do all they could to defend all they loved, however they had to.

No matter what it took.

TWO DAYS LATER

Stepping into the upstairs bedroom Piper's mother had moved them into, Jed closed the door quietly behind him and stared at the woman still sleeping deeply.

The quilt had been pushed to the bottom of the bed and nothing but a soft cotton sheet covered her naked back.

Piper was stronger than he'd ever imagined. Stronger and more fierce than he'd ever given her credit for.

In the past two days she'd given them as many details as she could remember about the rental agency, the young girl who had given her the car, as well as the location of the packets of jewels as she'd found them.

Her purse had fallen from the backseat, knocking over the shopping bag containing the rhinestones and crystals she had bought that morning. She'd thought nothing of the packets she'd found beneath the seat. She'd simply gathered them all together and thrown them into her bag before rushing to the cab waiting for her.

Why should she think anything of it? They were the same plastic packs the crystals and rhinestones she'd bought were packaged in.

There was nothing unusual about finding the packets, and nothing that could have tipped her off that she had anything that wasn't hers.

Now Homeland Security had answers they'd been searching for for years: how the Russian mob was smuggling the gold, jewels, and drugs that were funding the criminal organization they were building—and the terrorists it was suspected were backing them—into the United States.

It wasn't over, but neither was it a threat to Piper any longer, and that was all that mattered to him: making certain she was no longer in danger.

Now that the task was completed, his body was reminding him of another task that needed to be taken care of.

Two days without her touch, without having her, and his cock was like an iron wedge in his jeans, demanding relief.

Unbuttoning the shirt he wore and shrugging it from his shoulders, he allowed it to fall, forgotten, to the floor. Stopping at the bed near the stool positioned at the footboard, he sat down to remove his boots.

Standing seconds later and releasing his jeans, he shed them and the boxer briefs he wore, discarding them on the floor where he stood. A smile curled his lips, the fingers of one hand gripped his dick, and he moved to the side of the bed to pull the sheet from the silken body of the woman he reckoned he loved more than life.

As the sheet cleared the rounded globes of her pert ass, her hips shifted and she rolled to her back. Jed felt his breath still in his chest for precious seconds as he stared down at her, still marveling that such beauty was laid out for him, tempting him, hungry for him.

Firm, cherry-tipped breasts drew his gaze. As he watched, she parted her creamy thighs, revealing the sheen of slick dew on the lush folds of her pussy. Above, the moist, swollen little bud of her clit peeked out at him and tempted his tongue as her nimble little fingers stroked up his thigh before cupping the taut sac of his balls.

Fuck, her fingers were like hot silk.

Cupping, stroking, fondling the tense flesh beneath his hard dick, she drove him to complete distraction and had him panting as she slowly sat up on the bed. Her fingers moved from his balls, brushed his fingers aside, then slowly curled around the tortured length of his dick.

He clenched his teeth, fighting for control, yet a moan still slipped past his lips as he watched her lips part as she eased forward and slowly—fuck him, so damned slowly—covered the engorged crest of his cock and sucked it inside.

It was like being immersed in white-hot pleasure.

Hell, this wasn't just pleasure. It was pure fucking rapture.

The deep draws of her mouth had shards of incredible heat raking across the too-sensitive flesh, while her wicked little tongue flicked and tasted the throbbing head she held captive.

Thick lashes closed over her green eyes as he buried his fingers in the thick, black length of her hair. Creamy cheeks hollowed as she suckled him like a favored treat, moaning around the width of the throbbing head and lashing at it with her hungry little tongue.

"Ah, fuck." The words were dragged past his lips as she began stroking the tortured shaft with warm, silken fingers. "Piper, sweetheart, I'm going to end up coming in your mouth instead of that hot little pussy."

She moaned around the head, a hot little sound of hunger and need that had his stomach tightening as he fought to hold back his release. He wasn't ready to come. Not yet. Fuck, he just wanted to feel this a little longer. Just wanted to luxuriate in the pure ecstasy of each suckling motion of her mouth, each lick of her tongue and stroke of her fingers.

Staring into her face, seeing her pleasure and arousal, was more than he could stand. He could feel his balls tightening. The head of his cock flexed and clenched in her hungry mouth, and before he could push back the driving spikes of tortured pleasure, a spurt of release washed over her tongue.

It was like giving her a taste of rapture rather than a taste of his seed.

Desperate moans fell from her lips. Her fingers milked the hard shaft as her lips and tongue searched for more of the rich, male taste, clearly eager—no, craving—more.

Pulling back took every ounce of control that he possessed.

Watching the slow release of his cock from the hot moisture of her mouth was like tearing out a piece of his soul.

But there was so much more pleasure to be found.

Coming to her, he covered her lips with his, his tongue slipping past her lips and dancing against hers as he moved between her thighs. With one hand he quickly rolled the latex condom over his cock, then twisted against the hold of her thighs and found the slick entrance he was searching for.

It was pure heat raining down on the head of his cock as he tucked it against the clenched opening of her heated cunt.

Soft as luxury, as hot and tight as pure sin itself, the clenched tissue milked at the head of his cock, tightening with each shallow thrust, then spasming with delicate greed as he thrust heavily inside her.

Control.

God help him, just a little control, because he wanted nothing more than to sink inside her and hold himself there forever.

"I love you, Piper." The words were torn from his lips, pulled from his soul, and whispered against her lips as he thrust inside her, hard and deep, burying himself to the hilt in the milking grip of her pussy. "Sweet God, I love you."


Piper felt her breath catch.

Holding tight to the strength of Jed's shoulders as she fought to adapt to the width of the iron-hard cock throbbing inside her, she hadn't expected the declaration. Nor had she expected the emotion that filled it.

Forcing her eyes open, meeting his gaze, and seeing the love in his eyes had her own gaze dampening.

"I love you, Jed," she whispered, her breath hitching, her heart catching at the depth she knew that her love filled her.

There wasn't a cell in her body that wasn't filled with the ever-deepening love she felt for him.

Tears blurred her vision and wet her cheeks, and as his lips lowered to hers once again, the tears infused their kiss.

Piper caught her breath as his hips shifted, his cock retreating from the tightened depths of her pussy. His kisses fed the hunger raging inside her. Each fierce, deep thrust of his cock sent searing pleasure racing through every nerve ending.

Her clit, swollen and throbbing, ached for relief as each thrust of his hips pressed his pelvis into it, and each heavy penetration inside her tender cunt pushed her closer to release.

She was on the verge of begging.

Oh, God, it was like being immersed in pure pleasure.

Flames burned inside her, whipped over her flesh. They tore through her pussy, wrapped around her clit, and with each stroke inside her pushed her closer—

"Jed, please," she begged, her neck arching, knees lifting to grip his hips tighter, to push closer with each stroke inside her. "Oh, God, please. Fuck me harder. . . ."

A harsh groan rasped from his throat.

One hand gripped her hip as he buried his face at her neck, stinging kisses pressing against her flesh as the pace increased. Rapid-fire thrusts impaled the tender, sensitive flesh. The heat built inside her, raced through her womb, struck at her clit and in the depths of her pussy. Blinding, white-hot, and intense, the orgasm exploded inside her, flinging her from the edge of reality and tossing her into a chaotic storm of pure sensation that seemed never-ending.

Like a supernova, it expanded and burned, searing everything in its path as Jed buried himself deep inside her, stilled, then, with a heavy growl against her neck, gave in to his own release.

What she felt in that moment shouldn't have surprised her: The feeling that suddenly she and Jed inhabited the same soul, the same body, the same storm of emotion and pleasure, shouldn't have been a shock. But she had a feeling it was something she would never get used to. It was something she would never tire of experiencing.

It was a bonding, she realized as tears spilled from her eyes once again. A bonding she would never be free of. One she never wanted to be free of.

"I love you, Piper." His voice was a mix of hope and desperation as he held tight to her. "Beyond my last breath, I love you."

Beyond his last breath, and beyond forever itself . . .

They loved.

# EPILOGUE

It was that deepest part of the night.

That time when sound carried its best and revealed the secrets others would prefer remain hidden.

For Lyrica, it was that time of night that haunted her the most. The time that seeped into her soul, filled her with chaos, and left her staring into the darkness and hearing the secrets she had no desire to know.

It was that time when she ached for what she now knew she could never have, yet was forced to acknowledge that settling for less wasn't going to happen.

It was that time of night when, no matter the locks on the doors, or how tightly the windows were closed, still he found a way to her. . . .

"Pretty Lyrica," he whispered from the darkness. "Did you really think I'd let you hide . . . ?"

"Please—don't." She shook her head, helpless as she felt his weight on the bed, watched his shadow come over her as he slowly drew the sheets back from her naked, aching body. "Please . . ."

"You're mine . . ."

# RIDING TO
# SUNSET

JACI BURTON

*To Lora Leigh—as always, thank you.*

# ONE

"Hey, the newbie's back."

"Survived the latest mission, huh? Did Diaz hold your hand so you wouldn't be scared?"

"I'm pretty sure Diaz said that Jed was afraid of the dark."

"I give him a year and he's going to run back to the FBI, tail between his legs."

Jed Templeton cracked a grin, not at all insulted by the ragging he'd been getting from General Grange Lee's crew of veteran Wild Riders. On the job for about a year, Jed was still the new guy. And when you were the newest of any crew, you took shit until you proved yourself.

He dropped his bag and headed into the kitchen of Wild Riders headquarters to grab a beer before moving to the living room, where Mac, Lily, Diaz, Jessie and Spence were huddled up watching a football game on the big-screen TV. He grabbed one of the available seats, unscrewed the top off his bottle of beer and propped his booted feet onto the scarred table.

"So?" Jessie asked, leaning forward to clasp her hands together. "Diaz said it got rough."

"He would say that, being a pussy and all. I had to do most of his job for him, but I'll cover for him when I file my report to the general."

Jessie snorted. Diaz scowled, but didn't say anything.

"So really, Diaz, how did he do?" Mac asked when the commercial came on.

The room went silent except for the sound of a manic announcer on TV, selling car insurance.

Diaz shot a glare to Jed, who smiled at him.

Diaz shrugged. "He can hold his own. Kicks ass in a gun fight and hand to hand. He'll do all right."

The rest of them nodded and tilted their drinks in his direction. He nudged his bottle of beer toward all of them, and when the game resumed, they argued over teams.

That was it. With Diaz's endorsement came acceptance.

Lily came over to sit next to him on the two-person love seat. She laid her hand on his forearm. "It's hard to dig into this group," she said. "I was the first, and a woman at that. When I joined, I had to prove myself. So did Shadoe. Even Jessie, though she'd been mostly brought up here, had to prove she could hack it on her first assignment. We all have our trial by fire."

"Yeah, good thing you didn't suck worse than the women," Spence said, grabbing a handful of chips.

"I did not hear that, Spencer," Lily said. "You don't want to upset me and my hormones."

"Sorry, oh pregnant one."

Jed leaned back and cocked a brow. "A baby, huh?"

She grinned. "Yeah. Mac and I are having a baby."

His gaze shot to Mac, who grinned. Jed lifted his beer. "Congrats to both of you."

"Thanks," she said. "Hence the reason for all the mad recruiting the general has been doing over the past year. With a lot of us getting married, and now Mac and I having a baby . . . obviously I'll be taking some downtime—"

"Retiring," Mac said.

"Maternity leave," Lily argued.

"Retiring," Mac said again, his gaze focused on the game.

She rolled her eyes. "We're still discussing that part. Anyway, we're so glad to have you on board, Jed. Diaz already told us you did a great job on the Montana assignment. How do you like working for the Wild Riders?"

No one had ever cared whether he liked his job or not. Not when he was in the Marines, not when he was in the FBI. He did what he was assigned to do, like it or not. This was a different atmosphere entirely.

"It's fine."

She laughed. "You're going to have to loosen up, Jed. I promise we don't bite."

"Jessie does," Diaz said.

"And you like it," Jessie shot back.

Jed shook his head. "Are all of you paired up?"

"Yes," Lily said. "Like I said, that's why the general needs some new blood. Some of us are moving on and out and it's time for the next generation. That's you, Jed."

He didn't know about the whole "next generation" stuff, but he liked the job. It was adventure, it took him around the country, and it beat the hell out of the boring shit he'd done for the FBI. When General Grange Lee had recruited him, he'd jumped at the chance to have a little more leeway in what he did for a living, while still doing a service for his country.

For the past year the general had trained him, put him through grueling evals. Then he'd let the other guys run Jed through maneuvers and practice scenarios, which meant time out here at headquarters in Dallas. He'd gone on a couple light assignments, nothing major, followed by the big one with Diaz—a harrowing undercover in Montana.

It had gotten ugly. He and Diaz had gone full throttle when the bullets had started flying. They'd taken down a group of survivalists, pulled in all the gunrunners and tied up the mission with a bright red bow. And hell, he'd done it all in his leathers and riding his Harley.

He liked this job.

"Templeton."

He stood when the general came in. "Sir."

"First thing, I keep telling you not to call me 'sir.'"

"Sorry, sir." Shit. Old habits died hard. "Sorry, General."

Spence snickered. The general shot Spence a look that would freeze the devil in hell.

"You want dishwashing duty for the last month you're working with me, Spence?"

"Nope."

"Then mind your own fucking business."

"You got it. Minding my own fucking business here, Grange."

"You're with me in my office, Jed."

Jed got up and followed the general to his office, shutting the door behind him. He stood and waited while the general took a seat.

Grange rolled his eyes. "You're not in the military anymore, Jed, and neither am I. And I'm getting tired of reminding you. You don't salute me, you don't stand at attention, so just relax. Call me Grange or General. I don't give a shit. But pull the stick out of your ass and sit the hell down."

Jed pulled up a chair in front of the general's desk.

"You know, kid, I get that you thought you were going to be career military, and that you went straight from two tours in the Marines to four years with the FBI. And you suffered doing nothing with the G-men because they're stick-up-the-ass regimented asswipes, but here we're more relaxed and nobody jumps unless I'm pissed off. And when I'm pissed off, Jed, you'll know it. Understood?"

"Yes, si . . . General."

"Good. Now, for your next assignment."

Thank God. The last thing Jed wanted was downtime. He was ready to go.

The general clasped his hands together. "This one's a little different. I want you to fly to Florida. Daytona Beach. Your target is Elena Madison, age twenty-six."

"Undercover?"

"You'll be undercover. Sort of."

Jed cocked a brow. The general raked his hand through his hair. "It's hard to explain. I know Elena's mother, Carla. She's gone missing, but Elena doesn't know that."

"And you do."

"Yes. Carla has always been sort of a free spirit, very New Age. Kind of a hippie, back when hippies were the thing. She comes and goes as she pleases, takes off whenever she feels like it."

"So Elena wouldn't think anything of it if her mother was gone."

"Right."

"But you—being friends with Carla all these years—have kept tabs on her."

Grange nodded. "You could say that."

"How do you know she's missing?"

Grange stood, rubbed the back of his neck and turned to look out the window. Jed could tell he was uncomfortable as hell. Obviously having some kind of personal relationship with this Carla was doing a number on him. From what he knew of the general, he left his personal life out of all his dealings with the Wild Riders. Why he was giving Jed this assignment, he didn't know. But he was going to be patient and listen.

"I've kept tabs on Carla for years. I always know where she is. But this time . . . I've lost her."

"Lost her?"

"Yeah. And that's not good."

Whatever was between Grange and Carla Madison, it was something deep and meaningful, or at least that's what Jed was taking away from that comment. "Okay. Have you . . . lost her before?"

"On occasion, but I always pick her back up. This time I haven't been able to."

"Oh." Well, hell. How was he going to do this mission without stepping on the general's toes?

"Ask your questions. Nothing's off-limits. I'm not going to send you into this blind."

"Who is Carla Madison, General?"

He blew out a deep breath. "She's my sister."

"Okay, which means Elena is your niece."

"Yes."

"Can't you just go to Elena and the two of you try to figure out—"

"Elena doesn't know about me."

Jed frowned. "Why not?"

"Because we didn't want her to."

Jed scratched his head. "You're her uncle, sir."

"I know I'm her uncle, dammit. But I've kept my family away

from who I am and what I do because of my lifestyle and career choice. My enemies. It would make both Carla and Elena targets."

Jed nodded. "Okay, that I understand. Tough choice for you."

"It was, but it was the right one."

"So what do you need me to do?"

"We need to find out where Carla is, and keep Elena safe."

Now the light was beginning to shine on this mission. "You think one of your enemies has figured out that Carla is your sister and has targeted her?"

"Possibly. I don't know and won't until I get down there and try to find her. But I can't go hunt for Carla and protect Elena at the same time. So I need you to help."

"Why me, General? I'm the new guy. Why not one of the others?" This was a pretty deep secret to share with the most recent recruit.

"Because I haven't told them this secret. And because they've built up relationships with each other and stand to lose a lot if this goes wrong."

Now he got it. He didn't have the ties they all had—they all had someone to love. He was a loner, and therefore the easiest to take along on this assignment. "Understood."

"I knew you would. Pack it up, we're leaving in an hour. I'll fill you in on Elena on the plane down there."

Jed pivoted and left the office, realizing he'd just gotten royally fucked.

The general's niece? And she didn't know?

Yeah, this one had no-win scenario written all over it.

# TWO

Elena Madison put the finishing touches on the display case just in time to open.

It was a lovely day, warm and sunny, and the ocean breeze swept into the shop as the doors were opened. Traffic was light so far, but having an upscale shop near the beach meant the more discerning clients had to fight the tourist traffic to get here.

She didn't mind. She had repeat customers who didn't mind the drive to the beach. And she liked the location, loved the view and wouldn't sacrifice it. Her mother's influence, no doubt. The only thing they shared in common—their love of the ocean.

She'd modeled her gallery after the beach and the water, always brought in pieces that reflected the ebb and flow of the tides, the way the landscape was always changing, just like art. Good designers knew this and changed with the tides, the seasons, the years.

The doorbell tinkled, and one of her favorite—and richest—

customers stepped in. Louise wore colorful button-down shirts and khaki capri pants along with white tennis shoes. She looked like a tourist, but the woman was made of money. She had a condo overlooking the beach, and she was loaded. She loved to come in and share her stories about her husband and how the two of them had made a fortune in the real estate market in New York. Louise loved this area as much as Elena did, so they had a lot in common.

"Louise." Elena smiled at the woman. Louise was in her seventies, and Elena admired Louise's pep. "Finish your walk early today?"

"It's such a glorious day. I walked all the way here from my condo. It's my exercise for the day and I couldn't resist stopping in to see if you had any new pieces."

"You know I do. Come see." She led Louise to the case where she highlighted the latest arrivals.

Louise's eyes widened, and she slipped on the glasses she kept on a jeweled string around her neck. "Oh, these are lovely, Elena."

Elena stood back and let Louise bend over to examine the necklaces.

"Who did the coral pieces?"

"James Waymire."

Louise pulled her gaze away from the case only long enough to cast a gleaming smile at Elena. "Stunning."

"I thought so, too. He brought them in over the weekend and I bought several pieces. You also need to see the new glass sculpture Triana did. I have it back here when you're ready."

Louise went over several of the necklaces that Elena pulled out of the case, finally settling on the coral that had caught her eye at first. Then Elena made her some tea and the two of them sat at the back of the shop and admired Triana's five-foot-wide blue glass sculpture of a jumping dolphin. Elena had set it up on one of the side windows where the light could show it off to its full effect.

"It's breathtaking," Louise said. "And if I came home with a piece like that, Leo would kill me."

"But you won't be bringing it home. I'll have someone deliver it to you." Elena winked, and Louise let out one of her bawdy laughs.

After Louise left, Elena was busy with other clients. The morning passed in a blur of activity, just the way she liked it. When Marco came in to relieve her, she had just enough time to run out and grab a bite to eat. She headed upstairs to her apartment over the store, kicked off her shoes and fixed a sandwich, then stepped outside and ate on the balcony so she could enjoy the beach view.

She'd worked hard to open this store, had gone to school, scrimped and saved every penny she owned working three jobs in order to come up with the money to rent the gallery. And she still hadn't had enough, until her mother—her mother of all people—had handed her an envelope with the cash to not only rent the property but buy the building outright.

She'd been stunned. Her mother was as flighty and undependable as they came and, as far as Elena knew, rarely held a job for more than a month. Where she got the money, Elena didn't even want to know. She'd tried to give it back, but her mother had said it was a gift and gifts weren't to be returned. Elena had hoped her mother hadn't done a drug deal or robbed a bank.

She'd still like to know where that money had come from. Her mom eschewed money and property, only had enough to get by and often had to mooch off Elena, causing her to dip into her own meager savings.

She took a bite of her sandwich and focused on the calming waters of the ocean, the cloud-free sky, the screams of laughter from children playing in the sand at the water's edge. Anything but the enigma that was her mother.

She heard the low throaty rumble of a motorcycle as it roared down the street, tearing into her idyllic rest. She followed the sound as it grew louder and pulled to a stop in front of her shop.

Oh, yum. Hot guy on a Harley. Now that was almost as good a sight as her ocean. Baggy jeans, sleeveless muscle shirt, and the muscles to show off in it, he was tall, with black hair and a strong chin she could see from all the way on the second floor. Mirrored sunglasses gave him a bad boy look that should have turned her off—she never went for guys like him. Yet she couldn't deny wanting a closer look.

He shoved off the kickstand with the heel of his boot and climbed off the bike, slid the keys into his pocket and headed inside her shop.

Huh. She didn't get too many bikers in her shop. It wasn't typically their style.

She looked down at her watch. Technically she had a half hour left to her lunch hour.

Then again, she did have inventory coming up at the end of the month, so no sense wasting time when there was so much work to be done. Besides, Marco might be overwhelmed with clients.

Right. And that happy button between her legs hadn't been touched in far too long, so the sight of testosterone on a Harley just might have gotten her motor running, which surprised the hell out of her. She much preferred men who were more refined—the suit-wearing *Wall Street Journal* type—not the grease-under-their-fingernails type.

But she had a need to get a closer look. Men who looked like that guy could be considered art, and art was her job, so why not?

She did a quick brushing of her teeth, smoothed her hair and her dress, slid her heels back on and headed back downstairs, through the back door and into the shop.

Mr. Good Looking was in the shop, sunglasses tucked into the neck of his shirt. Marco was currently leaning next to him, showing him the metal sculptures.

Hot and Sexy looked up at her as she walked through the gallery. His lips curved upward in a hint of a smile that made her fully aware of herself as a woman. She hadn't felt that kind of draw toward a man in a very long time.

Marco could handle this customer, but since the place was currently empty, no reason not to be polite, especially since he'd smiled at her and all. She headed over.

"Marco."

Marco's head shot up. "Oh, Elena, hi. I was just showing Jed here some of our welded art pieces. Jed, this is Elena Madison. She owns Eclectic Designs."

Elena held out her hand.

"Nice to meet you, Elena. Jed Templeton."

His hand was calloused. And really big, but gentle in hers. Sometimes big guys liked to prove their masculinity by nearly crushing her hand. Good to know he could power it down.

"Welcome to my shop, Jed. Are you here for the bike rally?"

He laughed. "Yes and no. I moved here to start a business, but I see you saw my ride, so yeah, the bike event should be fun."

"Oh? What kind of business?"

"Security."

Her brows went up. "That's interesting."

"Hope it's interesting enough to businesses around here."

"Do you have clients yet?"

"A few. Are you looking for security?"

"No. We have a system already in place."

He nodded. "Good for you."

She liked his voice. Deep and gravelly, the kind of voice a woman would like to hear whispered to her in the dark.

Wow, it *had* been a long time for her, hadn't it? "So, Jed, what are you looking for today?"

"Nothing in particular, but these designs caught my eye. I need to furnish my new place."

"Oh, really, where's your place, if you don't mind me asking?"

"I'm renting one of the new Oceanview condos just across the road. I have the furniture but it needs something more."

She smiled. "We can certainly help you with that."

The bell jingled over the front door. Marco met her gaze, then shrugged. "I'll go see to the new customer."

Normally she'd never take a prospective sale away from Marco, but this guy intrigued her. If he bought something, she'd give the commission to Marco anyway.

"Tell me what you're interested in."

His brow popped up and he gave her a flash of a smile.

"I don't know. Not much for art, but the place is nothing but white walls. When I rode by, I liked what I saw in the window. And this is interesting." He motioned to the mermaid made out of metal, rising out of waves and leaning against the rocks.

"She is stunning and would be an interesting conversation piece. But I have to be honest—she doesn't come cheap. Perhaps we should discuss your price range first?"

"I don't have one."

Now it was her turn to raise a brow. Was he really here to buy an art piece, or was he hitting on her? She was picking up all sorts of signals, especially the way he was looking at her with the intensity in his steely eyes.

She found herself unable to look away.

"All right then. She sells for three thousand, five hundred."

He gave a short nod. "I also like this one. It has a hard edge to it."

She turned and smiled, liking his taste as he pointed out some of her favorite pieces. Jed might not have a knowledge of art, but he had a good eye.

"How long have you owned the gallery?" he asked as they moved to yet another piece.

"Four years."

"Successful?"

"I do well enough." She lifted her gaze to his. "Where are you from, Jed?"

"Dallas."

"And what brings you here to start a business?"

"I like the beach and the ocean."

"There's a beach and ocean in Texas."

He glanced outside, where the clear blue sky met the impossibly cerulean ocean. "Not with water this color and weather like this year round. It's amazing."

"It is, isn't it? That's why I wanted my shop here instead of in town. I wanted to spend my days being able to look over the water. I live above the shop, too, so I take whatever breaks I can and go sit on the balcony and watch the waves. It's the most calming thing."

"Better than any tranquilizer, I imagine."

"Ocean waves are tranquilizing. They bring a peace you can't find anywhere else. And after work I can run along the sand, or play in the water." She realized she'd been staring out at the ocean so she dragged herself back to his face—he'd been watching her. "Sorry. Obviously the ocean and I have a love affair going."

His lips lifted. "No, I understand. And I'll take the mermaid."

"Good choice. And welcome to the beach, Jed."

"Can you have it delivered? Obviously I can't strap her to the back of my bike."

"Of course. Just give me your address and I'll have her sent to you at your convenience."

They did the paperwork and Elena arranged to have the art sent to Jed's condo the next day.

She hadn't realized how much time they'd spent together until shadows began to fall over the water and the crowds began to thin. She'd tuned everything and everyone out but him.

"How about dinner tonight?"

She lifted her head up from the credit card slip she'd shoved into the cash register.

"Excuse me?"

"You close soon, right?"

"Yes."

"Have dinner with me."

"Oh, I don't think—"

"Are you married?"

"No."

"Seeing someone?"

"No."

"Then have dinner with me. I'd like to get to know you. I liked talking to you, and I don't really know anyone here. You can tell me all about your city."

She had no reason to say no, and every reason to say no. But she didn't really want to. "All right."

"I'll pick you up at eight. You like to ride?"

She never rode. That was one of her mother's things, not hers. "I never—"

He grinned. "That's okay. I'll go easy on you. See you at eight."

He left, and she finished up work for the day, mostly in a fog. Marco was thrilled to have the commission on the sale.

"He asked me out," she mentioned when they were going through receipts.

"He did not." Marco's dark eyes widened. "Tell me you didn't say no."

"I didn't say no."

Marco feigned disbelief. "Why, Miss Elena. I'm shocked. You always say no. Mr. Muscles must have the magic touch. Too bad he's not gay or I'd have lusted after him myself."

She laughed. "Yeah, and Torrance would have kicked your ass all the way to Miami."

Marco sighed. "True. But just because I'm in a relationship doesn't mean I'm dead. I can still look."

Marco left when she closed up the shop. She locked up the windows and doors, enabled the alarm system and headed upstairs, changed clothes and put on her tennis shoes to head outside for a run.

It was a cool night so she threw on a hoodie, stretched and started off easy, relishing the brisk air. She crossed the street to the beach side, enjoying the crowds that had gathered for bike week.

Motorcycles zoomed by, their engines roaring as she got into the rhythm of her run.

Her mother was a bike fanatic, had always gotten so excited whenever the bikers came to town. She'd make tie-dyed T-shirts or some kind of jewelry to sell to the bikers, happy to be a part of the throng of incoming tourists. Sometimes she'd hook up with a biker group and go off riding. Elena would worry they'd kidnap her and she'd never be seen again. Her mother told her she worried too much. She told her mother she wasn't careful enough. It was a common argument.

She hadn't seen her mom in a few weeks, was surprised she hadn't popped into the store. Her mother always managed to show up during bike week. Elena wondered where she was, though tracking her mother down was something she'd long ago given up hope of ever being able to do. Though she had a cell phone, she rarely answered it and often lost it. For a grown woman, she often acted like a child.

Elena had long ago given up hope of ever changing her mom. Her mother enjoyed her free-spirited lifestyle, the ability to pick up and charge headfirst into whatever new adventure caught her fancy. It was probably why Elena chose to be so grounded in one place, in one career, determined never to live with her head in the clouds.

Dusk had settled over the ocean, the sun sinking fast over the vast array of hotels to the west. She made a quick turn and headed back to her apartment, took a shower and dried her hair and surveyed her closet, trying to decide what to wear to dinner tonight.

No dress since she'd be riding a bike. Now there was a departure for her. She was going out with a biker tonight, one of her strict taboos.

But oh, what a sexy biker he was. And it was just dinner, right? She could deviate from her hard rules for just one night.

# THREE

lena Madison was one sexy package of slender curves, tanned, long legs and a perfect face with mesmerizing green eyes all rolled into intelligence, wit, charm and—oh yeah—the most kissable full lips Jed had ever seen.

And she was hands off because she was General Lee's niece. Didn't that just suck?

But he was in, had done the job of getting his foot in the door. Now he just had to stay there. He'd had his eye on her for a full day, watching the shop, monitoring her clientele and how she related to them. She was no nonsense but nice to her clients. She took her lunches on the rooftop of her business, which doubled as her living quarters. Nice digs, too, with a beach overlook.

The general had set him up right next door at this kick-ass condo with a balcony view directly onto her shop and apartment.

Considering some of the assignments he'd had with the military and the FBI, this one had definite benefits.

And now he got to take the hot girl out to dinner?

Beat the hell out of eating sand or being bored to death by paperwork.

Except for that whole "hands off" thing. But he'd deal.

He left the condo, climbed on the bike and rode the short distance to Elena's shop, curbing the bike on the side street. He went to the side door and rang the bell. She came outside and everything that made him a man tightened.

Some women instinctively knew how to dress for riding on a Harley.

Elena wore skinny jeans, a white T-shirt and a short leather jacket along with a pair of leather boots. She'd pulled her hair back in a ponytail, and it swung back and forth as they walked toward the bike.

"What?" she asked as he handed her a helmet.

"You look hot."

Her cheeks stained a blush. "I do not. Did I dress right?"

"Perfect." He tightened her chin strap and climbed on the bike. She got on behind him and snugged her thighs against his, wrapping her arms around him.

Yeah. Perfect fit.

"Ready?" he asked, slanting her a look over his shoulder.

"Ready."

He started the engine, goosed the throttle and headed out, rolling out past the myriad of hotels on Atlantic Avenue. He wanted to get them out of the tourist area.

Bikers were out in force already, and he blended in, weaving in and out with them as they moved along with the flow of traffic. Elena was quiet and he wondered what she thought of all this. She hadn't moved since they'd taken off. Her legs were still pressed along his, her arms still wrapped around his middle. He reached down to touch her leg and she reacted by squeezing her thighs against his and leaning forward.

"This is wonderful," she said.

He grinned and picked up a little speed once they got past the heavier traffic. He took them out onto Highway 1 and toward Ormond Beach, finally pulling into a seafood grill he'd read about.

Elena climbed off and took off her helmet, shaking her hair free of her ponytail. "Great choice," she said as she wound the ponytail holder onto her wrist.

"How was the ride?"

"Surprisingly exhilarating."

"Surely that wasn't your first time on a bike."

"No, but it's been a very long time. I'd forgotten how fun it could be."

He smoothed a few stray hairs away from her cheek and tucked them behind one ear. "I'm glad you enjoyed it. Let's go eat."

They went inside and got a table right away since he'd made reservations. He ordered water since he was driving. She ordered a glass of white wine.

"Are you sure you don't want a glass of wine or a beer?" she asked.

"Not when I'm riding."

"Oh. Good point. Aren't you the careful driver."

"Not always, but with the rally in town there are enough people boozing it up and getting on their bikes. I like to keep a clear head."

She tilted her head to the side and took a sip of her wine. "So tell me about yourself, Jed Templeton."

"What would you like to know?"

"Oh . . . everything."

And this was where he'd have to make up a pack of lies. Now

all she'd have to do was take the bait. "I was born and raised in Dallas. Pretty middle-class stuff. Average neighborhood. Only child. My dad was an engineer, my mom stayed at home. I went to college at UT, studied business and graduated decently. I tried the whole corporate thing but I was bored, so I went to work for a private investigation company down there. I was always into gym stuff so I liked the physical aspect of the work more than the paperwork side and I became a P.I."

"A P.I., huh? I'll bet that was interesting."

"It was. Lots of lowlifes, cheaters and scammers. Never a dull moment."

"I can imagine. Is that how you got into the security business?"

"Yeah. We had a client who was a little too zealous in wanting the goods on his ex-wife. She wasn't doing anything wrong, so we dropped the client but he didn't drop the harassment. I didn't like the guy at all—he was scum, and since we initiated the contact, I offered protection for the ex-wife on the side. I installed a state-of-the-art security system for her and bodyguard services. She had a restraining order on him and we caught him breaking and entering at her house, so he went to jail."

"A good day's work for you, I'd say."

"Yeah. I felt bad about that case, and my boss at the P.I. firm kept taking clients on like that because money was money to him, so I left him and started my own company. I'm a little more selective about the clients I take on. I do more thorough background checks."

She leaned back and swirled her wine around in the glass. He liked the way she looked at him. When a woman looked at you like that, it made you glad to be a man. Too bad this was an assignment.

"So tell me about your life, Elena Madison."

She shrugged. "Not much to tell other than what you've already seen. I own my shop and run it. It pretty much consumes most of my days. We're open Tuesday through Saturday. And when we're not open, I'm usually out shopping for new inventory by meeting with artists, or doing paperwork. My life isn't exciting."

"I don't know about that. You love what you do, and that's always exciting. So how did you get into the business?"

"I like art. Always have. Especially unique pieces that reflect the area, like sand, water, air. It calls to me."

"Understandable. Family?"

"Just my mother."

"Does she live nearby?"

She smiled over the rim of her wineglass. "She comes and goes as she pleases."

He cocked a brow. "Not sure what you mean by that."

"My mother is what you'd call a free spirit. She's not really grounded in reality or things like a permanent job or a home. She chooses to eschew the establishment and go her own way."

"Oh, so she's a hippie."

She choked out a laugh. "Yes, I guess you could say that. She's a holdover from days gone by."

He held out his water glass in salute. "Good for your mom."

"You wouldn't say that if it was your mother. You didn't have to be raised by her."

"Was it hard for you?"

She shrugged, but he could tell it bothered her. "Sometimes. When there were events in school that required parental attendance, my mother would be off painting, or she was chasing a band, or an art show, or she'd forgotten because she was at the beach engrossed in the sunset and had to get the colors just right for the latest sculpture. And sometimes she'd go off for weeks at a time and I wouldn't know where."

He frowned. "She didn't leave you alone when you were a kid, did she?"

"No. She had lots of friends and she left me with them. I was well taken care of. There was just no . . . stability."

"I'm sorry."

She lifted her gaze to him and smiled. "Don't be. I survived it just fine."

He reached across the table for her hand, covered it with his. "Yes, you did, but it still couldn't have been easy for you."

Elena looked down at Jed's hand covering hers. "No, it wasn't easy. At times I resented her for it."

"I would have, too. What about your dad?"

"He took off when I was a baby, and they divorced. He was in a band, wanted to work on his career, didn't much want to be saddled with a wife and kid. Mom got full custody, he signed off on it, and that was that."

"So you don't know him? He's never come back and tried to find you or get in touch with you?"

"No."

"That sucks. I'm sorry."

She shrugged. "I got over the no-daddy-in-my-life thing a long time ago. My mom and I did just fine."

"No other family members to help you?"

"No. It was always just me and my mom."

He took a drink and studied her, wondered if it bothered her more than she said. "You didn't even have anyone to complain to about the way she abandoned you."

That was the word that always lived in the back of Elena's mind—the word she never gave voice to. One dinner and a short conversation, and Jed had it pegged.

Abandoned. First her father, and then her mother. Her father she never knew, so she never cared. He couldn't hurt her. But her mother had abandoned her for most of her life. And she couldn't believe she'd just spilled all that to someone she didn't know. She never talked about her family.

"Well, enough about that," she said with a smile. "I'm very excited you bought the mermaid today. I hope you'll let me see how it looks at your condo."

"I'll be glad to invite you to my place to see it. Maybe you can help me organize the furniture there. It needs a woman's touch."

And he easily let her back out. He was her hero tonight.

Their food arrived and conversation turned to less touchy subjects, like the bike rally.

"Have you been to the rally before?" she asked.

"Not this one."

"You go to others?"

"I've been to plenty around the country."

"The one here is rowdy and attracts hundreds of thousands of bikers. It gets crazy."

"Do you get a lot more business during the rally?"

"I do, though my shop doesn't really attract the biker clientele."

He laughed. "Hey, I'm a biker."

She lifted a forkful of rice to her lips. "You're a unique kind of biker. Most of them want commemorative T-shirts and biker-type souvenirs, not one-of-a-kind pieces of art. But yes, we do get bikers popping in to check things out."

"I'll have to send some people your way, then."

For some reason, she believed he would. "Thank you."

Elena didn't quite know what to make of Jed. He was nice, polite, easy to talk to, and he listened when she talked. And of course he was also sexy, so hot her toes curled, and he rode a Harley like it was part of his body.

He was quite possibly perfect, which meant there had to be something wrong with him; otherwise there would be some woman stapled to his side at this very moment. He looked to be early thirties, and no way a man this good-looking and this nice could have managed to escape the clutches of a woman for this long.

Which meant he was probably a love 'em and leave 'em kind of guy.

That would work out well for her, since she wasn't looking to settle down now. Or ever.

He probably only wanted sex.

And good God, she really needed sex. She'd really like to have sex with Jed. A delicious, no-holds-barred, all-night-long sex session with someone like Jed should hold her for the next six months or so. Then she could concentrate on her work again.

She wondered if he'd go for it.

Duh. He was a guy. He had a penis. Of course he'd go for it.

They finished dinner and Jed paid the check. They went outside and she started for the bike, but he grabbed her hand. "Let's go for a walk."

"Okay."

He led her across the street to the walkway by the ocean. They strolled in silence for a few minutes, the only sound the crash of the water hitting the shore.

"I can see why you like it here," he said. "I like the sound of the waves."

"I leave the door to my balcony open as often as I can just so I can hear them."

He turned his head toward her. "Probably not the safest thing."

"Probably not, but I'll take the risk to hear the beauty of the ocean. No manufactured ocean waves sound can duplicate the real thing. It lulls me to sleep every time." She stopped and moved in front of him. "Put your back against the wall here."

He did.

"Now close your eyes, and just listen."

She moved into him so she could get closer and whisper in his ear. "Couldn't you fall asleep to that sound every night?"

He didn't answer right away. Instead, his arms wound around her waist and drew her against him. He bent and whispered in her ear. "Honestly, it's hard to concentrate on the ocean waves when your body is pressed up against mine."

She laughed. "You're not paying attention."

"Sorry, you're distracting."

He opened his eyes, and she was again struck by the utter masculinity of his features. She reached up and traced her fingers over the slight beard stubble that gave him such a bad boy look, but his face wasn't a pretty boy one to start with. He had too many harsh lines and angles. His jaw was too square, his nose a little too wide. He was the kind of man to grab onto a woman and hold her tight, just like he was doing now.

"Jed."

"Yeah."

"Would you come home with me tonight and sleep with me?"

His lips curved just a little. "You mean like a slumber party?"

"No. I mean like have sex with me."

That teasing little curve to his lips disappeared. He threaded one arm all the way around her waist. The other dove into her hair the second his lips touched hers.

She was going to take that as a yes. And oh, God, the kiss. An explosion of sensation that sent Fourth of July fireworks skyrocketing through every nerve ending. Her lips tingled, and when he deepened the kiss and tightened his hold on her, her nipples throbbed, and her sex pulsed and moistened with need and expectation.

This was what she missed when she focused too much on business and not enough on pleasure. A man's touch, the way it felt to be held, to feel his large hand at her hip and the other massaging her scalp. He turned her around and placed her up against the sea wall, moving in to press the length of his body along hers. She reached for his chest, laid her hands on him, felt his heart beat a wild rhythm, the same as hers.

He tore his mouth from hers, his breathing staccato and heavy as he pulled back to search her face. "I probably shouldn't have started this out here. This is worse than having a glass of wine. I don't think I can drive now."

She laughed. "I'm not going to say I'm sorry you did."

He swept his thumb across her bottom lip. "Good. Let me take you home."

"Okay."

It was going to be a long ride home with a throbbing motorcycle between her legs.

# FOUR

The cool air blowing on his face on the ride back to Elena's house did nothing to bring Jed's temperature down. Not with her breasts mashed against his back, her hands pressing in on his abs and her thighs nestled against him.

All he could think about was that kiss, about the way she tasted, the way her body curled into his when he'd pulled her into his arms.

She'd asked him for sex. Goddamn. What the hell was he supposed to do about that—say no? He was undercover, his assignment to get close to her. This would bring him close to her, wouldn't it? He'd just be completing the mission.

In a sort of unorthodox way.

He had to keep his head in the game. Unfortunately, the only head doing the thinking right now was the head of his dick, and it was like a divining rod. It wanted sweet, hot pussy, and knew it was right behind him. All the blood from his brain had rushed south, and his dick was doing all the thinking.

The assignment could wait. He was going to have sex with Elena tonight. Tomorrow he'd get back on task.

He rolled around the corner to the gallery, his eye instantly drawn to a dark flash skirting around the edge of her building. He laid on the throttle and Elena's body tightened.

"Hold on," he said to her as he kicked it into high gear, tore up the length of asphalt and careened around the corner, sliding to a stop. He threw the kickstand down and flew off the bike, tearing his helmet off.

The first thing he saw was the broken glass. He drew his gun, his gaze shooting to a shocked Elena, who climbed off the bike.

"Shit," she said, surveying the damage.

He lifted the gun and half turned to her. "Call the cops."

She stepped over the glass. "My alarm has an autodial to the police."

"They cut your alarm or it'd be going off right now."

She looked at him and nodded. "You're right. Of course." She dug into her bag and pulled out her phone, made the call, gave the police the information.

"Come with me. Stay right with me, right behind me. And don't touch anything."

"Okay."

Normally he'd leave her outside while he went in to check everything out, but he wasn't taking a chance on leaving her vulnerable until he knew whether or not this had been a simple breaking and entering, or something else.

He stepped through the wrenched open door and walked inside.

It was a mess. The glass case in front was broken. It had been a smash and run. They hadn't wanted to linger too long. Probably someone looking to make a quick score and get out, but they knew enough to bypass her security system and bust in through the front door. He inched in farther, looking through the shop toward the back rooms. Nothing disturbed back there. By then he heard the sirens and moved back outside, sliding the gun into his pants.

Elena was right on his heels.

"You have a gun," she said.

"Yeah. I'm in the security business, remember? And I'm licensed to carry."

She nodded. "Right. Of course." She pulled her hair back with both hands. "I'm not thinking clearly right now."

Jed gave a long look to the broken glass and then to the street before turning his attention back to her. "They're long gone, probably took off as soon as they saw my bike."

"Goddammit. I've never had a break-in before."

The police arrived, and Jed stayed out of the way while they did their job and took Elena's statement. Jed told them what he knew, that he'd seen only a shadow of movement as they turned the corner, but nothing else. It took a few hours for them to fingerprint the place. Jed made arrangements for boards to go up to cover up the broken glass, and he got a replacement lock and put that in on the front door.

When the police and fingerprints unit left, he turned to Elena. Purplish circles shadowed her eyes.

"You look wiped out. I should let you get some rest."

"Wait."

He stopped.

"Would you mind coming upstairs with me? I know they cleared everything including the upstairs, and I know I'm being a big baby about this, but this whole break-in freaked me out."

"Come on. I'll go up with you."

Her shoulders slumped in relief. "Thanks. It's silly, I know."

He put his arm around her and walked toward the back of the shop. "It's not silly. It's scary for you to know someone broke in down here. And now you have a nonworking alarm, so I'm sure you feel vulnerable."

She turned to face him as they were halfway up the stairs. "Thanks for understanding."

He stepped in front of her. "Let me go in first and clear the area."

He opened the door and stepped inside her apartment, switched on the light. He knew the cops had been up here already checking things out, but she didn't feel safe.

She needed to feel safe in her own home. And right now she was hovering at the landing, still on the stairs, afraid to step foot inside.

Not good. It was a small place—kitchen with living area right off it, and one bedroom and one bath. He had everything checked out within a minute and came back to her with his hand held out.

"Come on."

She slid her hand in his and allowed him to pull her the rest of the way inside. Then he led her around each room, opening closet doors, checking in the shower and the pantry.

"No one's here. They were never here. They never even made it to the back of your shop."

She wrapped her arms around herself. "This really freaks me out. Normally I'm fearless."

He put his hands on her shoulders. "Tonight you have a right to be scared. Tomorrow you can be fearless again."

She sighed. "You're right. And I will be."

Then she raised her gaze to his. "I had such great plans for us tonight. Dammit."

He swept his knuckles across her cheek. "I think you need some sleep."

"I think you're right. God, I'll never sleep now."

"Yes, you will. You're exhausted. Come here."

He took her hand and led her to the south window. "See the condos there?"

"Yes."

"That's where I'm staying. I'm on the third floor. I can see your place from my place, so I'll keep watch over you tonight. And if you hear any bumps in the night—what's left of the night—call me and I'll come over." He took her phone and punched in his number.

Her lips lifted. "That helps. But I'm a big girl and I can handle it. Now you go home and get some sleep, too."

She led him down the back way and to the door. "Thanks for being here."

"Thanks for coming to dinner with me." He pulled her into his arms and kissed her, reminding her of what they were about to do when some asshole had broken in.

When he pulled away, her face wasn't pale anymore.

"Good night, Elena."

She licked her lips. "Night, Jed."

He walked away and climbed on his bike, figuring he'd done way more than just make contact on his first night.

Probably way more than he should have, but as far as the mission, he was in.

# FIVE

Elena had to close the shop for the day, which sucked for business but was a necessity. She had to clean up, inventory what had been stolen, call the insurance company, get the glass and door replaced and do a hundred other things that had nothing to do with sales.

Her mind was running in a million directions.

She'd called Marco and told him about the break-in. He'd rushed in to help with the cleanup, horrified by what had happened, but also eager to hear all the details.

"You're lucky only a few pieces were taken," Marco said as they finished up the inventory.

She nodded. "Obviously someone busted in to make a quick swipe."

"Probably wanted jewelry to pawn for drugs."

"That's what the police said. I have to take photos of the

stolen inventory to them and they'll alert the pawn shops. If any of the pieces show up, the shops will notify the cops."

Marco took care of running over the photographs and descriptions of the stolen jewelry, while she met with the insurance adjuster there at the shop. He had just left, as had the glass company, when a van pulled up on the side street.

Jed got out, grabbing a bunch of equipment. She went out to greet him.

"Where's your bike?"

He smiled at her. "The bike is for play. This is for work."

He dragged the equipment inside her shop.

Uh . . . what the hell? She pivoted, went inside and locked the door and found him at the back of the shop.

"What are you doing?"

"Installing a new security system. Your old system sucked."

She crossed her arms. "I don't recall ordering one."

"You didn't. This one's on the house."

"Jed, really, I can replace the alarm system myself. That was going to be my next call, as a matter of fact."

He didn't look up from the pile of gizmos and wires. "Now you don't have to."

"Jed."

"Busy here, Elena."

The doorbell rang. "Dammit. Stop what you're doing. I'll be right back."

It was a customer—one of her regulars—and she had to spend some time telling her about the burglary and letting her client know everything was all right. By the time she got back to Jed, he had the alarm system mounted on the wall.

"Remove that system."

He finally stopped and gave her an exasperated look. "Why

would I do that when it's already installed? I'm testing the connections now."

"Jed. I don't want your charity."

He laughed. "This isn't charity, Elena. It's advertising."

"What?"

"You just had a break-in. I'm installing my security system. See? Great advertising." He sidestepped her, bent down and connected a few wires. "All set. Let me walk you through it."

Elena had been bulldozed and she obviously wasn't going to win this argument. And she did need an alarm system. Why not take the gift that was offered? It was a win-win for both of them, right?

He showed her how to use the system, then asked her to enter a code. Once she did, they locked everything up from the outside, and she opened the door without entering the code. In fifteen seconds an earsplitting alarm blared, much louder than the one she had previously. Her cell phone rang within a few seconds.

Jed took her phone and completed the testing with the alarm company, then handed her phone back to her.

"You're set. This one won't fail. It has two backup systems, so if someone manages to cut through the main lines, the backup will kick in and automatically trip the alarm. Sirens will go off, alarm company will be dialed. You don't verify that it was an accidental trip of the alarm, the police will be on their way within two minutes."

"Wow. Awesome. I'll take it."

His grin was like a little boy with a new toy. "Thought you might like it."

"You're very good at this."

"Thanks." He put away his tools. "When are you reopening?"

"Tomorrow."

"I talked to the police. There've been a rash of burglaries for the past few weeks. Fast smash and runs. They've had to beef up security in the area, but with the rally in town, they're short staffed."

"That's bad for business owners, but should be good for your business. I'll be sure to pass your name around. I'm sure there are several who need to beef up their alarm systems."

"You don't have to do that, but thanks."

She laid her hand on his arm. "Actually, our local business owners association meeting is tonight. You should come as my guest. I'll introduce you to everyone."

"That'd be great. Sure you don't mind leaving your place unattended?"

"I have to admit it worries me, but it's a good opportunity to test out your new security system, isn't it?"

"Thanks for the show of faith. I guarantee you it'll work. Plus, unless they're morons, burglars don't tend to hit the same place twice in a row. I think you're safe."

"Good to know. Cocktail hour is at six-thirty, so I'll pick you up this time, say around six?"

"I'll be out front waiting. I'll even take a shower," he said, wiping the sweat from his brow.

"Ha ha. Everyone will appreciate that, I'm sure."

He packed up his tools and took off, and sweaty or not, she couldn't help appreciating how mighty fine he filled out a pair of jeans.

This guy was too good to be true. She wished her mom was around to meet him. Flighty she might be, but she could read people and was always a good judge of someone's character. She knew when a guy was full of shit and who had a hidden agenda. Elena had lost a lot of prospective boyfriends that way, but her mother was usually dead on in her assessments. She might not remember what day of the week it was, or forget that she and Elena had a lunch date, but she knew people.

She grabbed her cell phone and dialed her mother's number. It rang a few times and went to voice mail.

"Hey, Mom, it's Elena again. Just wondering where you are. The bike rally is this week so I thought maybe you'd be around for that. Call me. Or stop by." She hesitated before adding, "I love you."

She and her mom weren't exactly close. Her mother frustrated her more often than not. She could always count on her showing up, usually when she didn't want her to.

But she always showed up.

She was starting to get worried.

Jed took a shower, then threw on a pair of shorts and checked on Elena's shop and house via the monitors he'd set up when Elena hadn't been looking. It hadn't been hard to sneak up to her place and get everything installed. Breaking and entering was his specialty, and now that he had his own alarm system on her property, even easier.

Everything was locked up tight, nobody skulking around. He felt better about having his eyes on her shop and her house.

He grabbed his cell and contacted Grange, who answered on the first ring. He told Grange about the break-in.

"Suspicious?" Grange asked.

"I don't know. It looked like a regular break-in. Some jewelry stolen. Police reported an increase in burglaries in the area over the past few weeks, so I don't think it has anything to do with someone targeting Elena, but I'm sticking close to her. I have a camera set up in her store and in her apartment, too. Also, I'm escorting her to a business dinner tonight."

"Good enough. Glue yourself to her if you have to, but don't let her out of your sight."

"You got it, boss. Anything on Carla yet?"

"No. Tracking her cell phone. It's still on, and shows her in the Daytona area, right on the pier. I went to that location but she's not there, and phone shows no movement. I didn't find her phone, either. Her credit card has shown no activity in the past month, so there's nothing to track. And since she's always on the go with no permanent address, it's hard to narrow down her last location. It's a lot of footwork, but I'm going to hit up an old friend in the area for some help. I'll keep you posted."

"I'll do the same."

He clicked off and grabbed some clothes to get dressed. A business dinner meant no blue jeans. Instead he chose black slacks and a white long-sleeved shirt, then took along a sport coat just in case he needed to be a little more dressed up.

He was outside waiting when Elena pulled up in her car, surprising the hell out of him.

He expected her to drive an economy car. Something with four cylinders, or maybe even a hybrid. Not a smoking hot black '66 Chevelle SS. Just the sound of the engine purring made him want to climb into the driver's seat and see what she could do.

Instead, he had to get into the passenger seat.

"Are you kidding me?"

She looked over at him. "What?"

"This car."

Her lips curved. "I like muscle cars. It's my only nod to my mother's crazy lifestyle. She used to date a guy who was into restoring old cars. I fell madly in love with Chevys, and the love affair has continued throughout my life."

He arched a brow. "Now *that* I want to hear about."

"Maybe I'll tell you, but we don't want to be late for dinner."

The engine rocketed them forward when she pressed on the gas and drove off. Jed leaned back and watched her as she maneuvered the beast through the heavy traffic.

The steering wheel was oversized, the car a monster. But Elena manhandled it like she knew what she was doing, didn't abuse the Chevelle's awesome power.

Oh, man, he really wanted to drive this car.

"You ever take it out and really run it down the highway?"

She flicked her gaze to his. "Sometimes, when I need to let off steam."

He laid his arm over the back of the smooth vinyl seat, watching her as she concentrated on her driving. She wore a short-sleeved black dress, snug at the top, loose at the bottom. It hit just above her knee. Conservative enough for a business dinner, but she still looked sexy as hell wearing it.

She pulled into a hotel and parked. He came around to her side of the car and opened the door for her. When she stepped out, he got a good look at her outfit. She grabbed a short-sleeved jacket that she pulled on over the dress.

"Thanks."

"You look nice tonight."

She stepped closer to him, laying her hand on his upper arm. "So do you. The other women of the association will want to drag you away from me."

He grinned. "Not a chance. I'm all yours tonight."

# SIX

Elena had been right. As soon as she and Jed had walked into the conference room where the business association was meeting, every set of female eyes had zeroed in on Jed.

Of course they would, since many of the men in attendance were overweight, middle-aged, balding, or married. The pickings for single women were slim to none, so bring in a hot young guy like Jed and any available woman—hell, even the unavailable ones—started salivating.

She'd like to think she wouldn't have pounced on him like the current pack of circling wolves. She was focused on her business, not trying to find a man. She ran into good-looking available men all the time and her pulse didn't jump in the least.

Until she'd met Jed.

Poor guy. He was surrounded, though seemed to be holding his own, drink in hand, engaged in conversation with no less than six women. Every one of said women were doing the hair flipping, lip licking and lash batting like tomorrow was Armageddon and tonight was their last chance to get laid.

And these were solid, upstanding, levelheaded businesswomen, many of whom were her friends. She didn't understand how the presence of hot testosterone could reduce them to fourteen-year-olds.

Then again, as she watched Jed slide one hand into his pocket and affect a casual stance, then laugh at something one of them said, maybe she did understand it. There was something about him that captured her like no man ever had before. Part of her wanted to storm into the middle of the pack and plant her mark on him, to declare him off-limits to the rest of the sex-starved she-wolves before any of them got their claws into him.

Wow. *Get fucked recently, Elena?*

No, and that was obviously her problem.

"Who's the guy?"

She looked up to see Todd Bishop next to her. "Jed Templeton. Just moved into town."

"Boyfriend?"

She laughed. "No. He installed a new security alarm in my shop so I offered to bring him with me to the meeting tonight and introduce him around. He's trying to get his new business off the ground, and with the recent string of burglaries in the area, I figured he could meet some of the owners."

"Huh," was all that Todd said, no doubt irritated to be usurped as resident cock of the block. One of the few decent-looking single men in the association, Todd was usually popular, but he was a manwhore, and rumor had it he'd slept with quite a few of the available women in the group. He'd tried a few times to get Elena to go out with him. She'd always declined.

He was good-looking—tall, with dark brown hair and a great build. The problem was, he knew it and made no bones about the fact that he enjoyed the single life, which normally wouldn't bother her, but she hated his attitude toward women. He owned several car dealerships in the area and he had the whole slick salesman mantra down a little too well for her liking.

"We have a good alarm system already," was all Todd said.

"That's what I thought, too, until my shop got hit last night."

Todd raised a brow. "You did? That's too bad. Did they take a lot?"

"A few pieces of jewelry. Made a mess of the shop."

He picked up her hand. "I'm so sorry, Elena. I should introduce you to our security team. They're the best around."

"That's nice of you, Todd, but as I told you, Jed installed a new system today, so I'm up and running again."

His gaze narrowed. "But you're not dating him, right? Because there's this weekend trip to Orlando I'd love to take you on."

Ugh. How many times was she going to have to tell him no before it sank into his thick, Neanderthal head?

"Actually, she's dating me."

Shocked, Elena could only stare as Jed moved around Todd and put his arm around her waist. He put his hand out. "Jed Templeton. And you are?"

Todd didn't look at all happy, but shook Jed's hand. "Todd Bishop."

"Of Bishop Motors? I've seen your dealerships all over the place."

That puffed Todd's chest out. "Yes, that's me."

Really, it was Todd's father who owned all the dealerships and had all the money. Todd was just good at spending it and putting his perfect hair and football player body and God only knew how many thousands of dollars in orthodontia to get those perfect teeth in front of the camera to do the commercials she saw on television every day.

"Business must be great for you," Jed said, affecting a casual, couldn't-give-a-shit stance.

Todd nodded. "We do all right. So you have an alarm company?"

"Alarm and security services." Jed pulled out his card. "If there's anything we can do for you, just let me know."

"We have a good security team of our own. Been in business for over fifty years and haven't lost a car yet."

"That's great." Jed pulled Elena closer to him.

Todd got the message. "Well, I think I'll see what kind of food they have on hand. Elena, I'll talk to you later."

"Bye, Todd."

"Nice guy," Jed said after he left.

"He's a dick."

Jed laughed. "Someone you've dated?"

She cast him a horrified look. "Bite your tongue. I have standards."

"Good to know."

"How about you? Make any dates with your new female fan club?"

"They're all very nice."

"Uh-huh. You didn't answer my question."

He led her over to the table where the food was being served. "I'm starving. How about you?"

She tilted her head back and studied his face. "Avoidance and poker face. Now you have me worried. You have to be careful with those women, you know."

"So you're jealous. I like that."

"I'm not jealous. Should I be, given that you and I are apparently dating?"

He laughed at her reminder of his declaration to Todd. "Nope. I'm all yours, totally devoted."

She rolled her eyes. "I give up. You're on your own."

He took a plate and handed it to her, then got one for himself and leaned in to whisper against her ear. "I'm here with you. I want to be with you, not them."

She felt ridiculous for the spot of jealousy. "I really hate you right now."

He slipped an arm around her middle and tugged her against him. "No, you don't. You think I'm charming."

"I think you're a pain in the ass and I regret bringing you here."

He laughed, the low rumble vibrating through her body. "I'll make sure I'm appropriately grateful the entire night."

She shook her head, filled her plate and did her best to ignore him, which was difficult considering the death stares she received from all the women who she was certain would gladly change places with her.

The speaker during dinner was from the local police, a last-minute fill-in for the president of their local chamber of commerce, who asked them to talk about the burglaries in their area. The detective from the burglary division spoke to them about being vigilant and aware of any usual activity or people hanging around their establishments, as well as making sure their security systems were up to date.

Elena leaned over to Jed. "This will be a great opportunity for you."

Jed smiled at her.

After the presentation, Elena took Jed around and introduced him to as many of the local business owners as she could. There were several that appeared interested in upgrading their systems, so they took his card. By the end of the night, Elena was certain he had at least two or three new sales. She beamed, glad she was able to help him out. He was even taking calls on their way out, so it seemed his new business was already starting to take hold.

"I hope you get a lot of business out of this," she said as they left the hotel.

He seemed distracted, looking outside to the parking lot. "Yeah, it should be great."

Odd that Jed didn't seem nearly as excited as she was for him.

"Jed. You do want new business, right?"

That snapped his attention back to her. "What? Oh, sure I do. Thanks for bringing me along. This really helps a lot. You ready to go?"

He didn't sound excited. They headed outside to the parking lot. She rolled her eyes and dug into her purse for her keys. Men were so hard to figure out.

His fingers were on hers and she hadn't even realized he was behind her.

"Mind if I drive?"

She tilted her head back. "Is this a male thing? You can't stand to let a woman drive you?"

"No, it's an 'I want to get my hands on your engine' thing."

She turned around and cocked a brow. "Is that a euphemism for sex?"

"Well, it wasn't, but now that you mention it . . ."

She laughed and dropped the keys in his hand. "One scratch and you pay for it, and this baby's a classic."

"Don't I know it."

He started up the Chevelle, and Elena watched as he closed his eyes.

"What are you doing?"

"Shhh. . . . I'm listening to her purr."

"Stop that or I'll get jealous."

His lips curved and he put the car in gear and drove off, giving the car just enough gas to make the ride a thrill. As she suspected, he didn't take her right home, instead drove north, taking them for a ride parallel to the shore. The night was cool, but the windows were down, the car was rocking and she was with a man who knew exactly what to do when he manhandled all the horsepower of the Chevelle. He let her loose and pressed on the gas and they went flying.

For the first time in as long as she could remember, Elena sat back and let someone else do the driving. She enjoyed every minute of the wind in her hair, the salty smack of ocean breeze on her face and the beauty of a man's chiseled features in the driver's seat.

He pulled in front of an empty stretch of beach and parked, leaving the radio tuned in to the oldies station.

She took off her seat belt and half turned to face him. "This is very sixties, park and make out."

He turned and put his arm over the seat. "Really? I thought you'd never ask."

She laughed. "Yeah, except for the bucket seats."

He cast his gaze behind him. "These bucket seats are plenty big enough."

"Are you serious?"

"You never made out in the car?"

"No."

"What a shame. This is a great make-out car."

She rolled her eyes. "Wouldn't it be more comfortable to go to my place?"

"Where's your sense of adventure, Elena?"

"My mother lives the life of adventure. I'm more into being normal."

"You mentioned your mother before. What's up with her?"

"She's a leftover hippie from the sixties who never grew up."

He nodded, and reached for a strand of her hair that had fallen over her shoulder. "I see. And you're the staid, grounded polar opposite of your mother."

"Exactly."

He leaned over and swept his hand behind her head, cupping the nape of her neck. "I'm going to kiss you now. In your car, right here on the beach."

His breath swept across her cheek, and her lips parted. He pressed his mouth to hers—a soft, gentle kiss that made her breath catch, made her want more. She reached for him, pulling at his shirt to draw him closer, wanting to feel his warmth, his body against hers.

He dragged her across the seat to his side of the car. Suddenly she was straddling his lap, and the kiss had deepened.

This was so not her. She did not make out with men in the front seat of a Chevelle. On the beach, no less. No, she was boring and predictable. Men brought her home and they had a glass of wine and conversation, and then they kissed and moved into the bedroom, where they had . . .

Boring, predictable sex, whereas Jed was rocking her ever-loving world right now. His fingers dove into her hair, removing the barrette she'd put into her hair to hold it back. He rested his hand on her neck while he kissed her, and she could feel her pulse pounding against his fingers. All she could think about was his mouth and his tongue and how amazingly talented he was at deep, soulful kisses. She laid her hands on his shoulders, and wow, he was just solid muscle everywhere.

He swept his hands down her back and she shivered. He lifted his lips from hers and the goose bumps intensified at the blatant desire reflected in the dark blue of his eyes.

"Cold?" he asked.

She shook her head. "No, but do you really think we should be doing this here?"

There went that smile again. Cocky, self-assured. "Where do you think we should be doing this?"

"My apartment."

He swept his thumb across her bottom lip. "You like to play it safe."

"And you're just a little dangerous."

He moved his hands down the sides of her rib cage and let them rest on her hips. "So if you've never made out in your car, you've probably never had sex in it, either."

The thought of it, the images it evoked, were more than her already fried brain could handle. "No."

He squeezed the flesh of her hips, and she bit back a moan. When he started to raise her dress, her panties went damp, and her body undulated against him. A total involuntary response to being on top of a very hot—and very hard—male.

His lips quirked. He lifted against her, his erection pressing against her sex. "I could make you come without even undressing you, Elena. You'd be perfectly safe."

Her lips parted and she let out a soft gasp. How long had it been since she'd had an orgasm? A while, and too damn long for one that hadn't been self-induced. "I don't think that would be a good idea."

"You don't like sex?" His fingers played along the hem of her dress, sliding an inch or so underneath.

She swallowed, her throat gone dry. "I like sex just fine."

He kept his focus on her face as his fingers continued to dance upward, along the front of her thigh, then inward. "Fine? Oh, sex needs to be more than fine. It needs to be great. Awesome. The best damn thing you've ever had."

His thumb teased the edge of her panties, sliding so near her pussy she thought she was going to die. Her muscles were so tense her legs trembled.

"Hold onto my shoulders, Elena, and let me," he said, keeping that contact with her eyes as his fingers slipped inside her panties.

She gasped and dug her nails into his shoulders.

Jed's lips curved and his eyes went dark. "Yeah, like that."

His hand was warm despite the breeze blowing in through the car windows. Her nipples were aching, throbbing tight points of need. She wanted him to suck them into his mouth and make her scream, but she couldn't form words because his hand was inside her panties.

"You're hot here, Elena. And wet."

She rose against his hand, not sure whether she wanted to escape or grind against him. Her pussy quivered, her clit a tight knot of nerve endings so close to bursting it was embarrassing. She licked her lips and his hot gaze watched every movement of her tongue, making her wish they were naked and sprawled out on her bed so she could taste every square inch of him. She wanted to lick his skin, to feel his cock in her mouth.

And when he slid a finger inside her, she whimpered.

"You need to come. Your pussy is tight around me, trembling. You want me to make you come, Elena, right here on the beach, in your car?"

She fought through the rising haze of need and desire to nod her head.

He pulled his finger out and used her moisture to coat her aching clit.

"Tell me," he said. "Tell me what you need and I'll make it happen for you."

She had to swallow to coat her parched throat. Her heart thrummed and beat so hard she was afraid it was going to explode.

"Touch me. Make me come."

He drew her head down to his, kissed her and cupped her sex with his big, hot hand, his fingers tucking inside her pussy at the same time he ground the heel of his hand against her clit.

A fiery explosion of sensation burst inside her. She moaned against his lips, sucked on his tongue and came, rocking against his hand. He shoved his fingers inside her harder and she rode them, feeling every thread of her orgasm in every part of her body. It made her light-headed and giddy and it felt so damn good she never wanted it to end.

Jed took her down easy, kissing her lightly, licking at her lips and rubbing gently at her pussy until she felt like she could breathe again. When he removed his fingers, he licked them, his gaze riveted to hers. She shuddered and sat down on him. He was hard as stone, reminding her that only one of them had been satisfied.

He looked at her, smiled at her, the heat still evident in his eyes.

But he lifted her and put her back in the passenger seat and started up the car.

"Jed. We're not finished."

He slanted a grin her way. "No, we're not. But I'm not going to push my luck by lingering out here too long."

He drove them back to his condo and got out, opened the door and came around to her side to open the door for her.

He wasn't going to come to her apartment. She didn't understand.

Before she could say anything, he pulled her into his arms and kissed her deeply, then pulled away with a smile on his face.

"I'm going to smell you on me all night, remember what you looked like when you came."

Her nipples tingled. She laid her hands on his chest. "We're not finished here."

"No, we're not, Elena. We're just getting started."


The first thing Jed did after he got back to his condo was check on Elena's place using his surveillance equipment. Everything was locked up tight. He watched her use her alarm code to get in and rearm it once she was inside.

Her apartment was clear, too, and when he ran through the tapes of the area from when they were gone, nothing came up.

He undressed, turned off the lights and got into bed, staring up at the ceiling. The crash of the waves outside didn't help him drift off to sleep. Nothing would, since his cock was throbbing and his balls ached.

He could have taken Elena home and gone upstairs to her apartment. She wouldn't have balked. He'd seen her look of surprise when he'd driven to his condo instead. But something stopped him.

He didn't want to push things with her, didn't want her to think he was only after sex.

What a joke. This wasn't a relationship. This was an assignment. He wasn't dating her, for Christ's sake. Once Grange found Elena's mother, he was outta here. So what the fuck did he think he was doing? He was supposed to stick close. Sleeping with her was as close as he could get, even if it wasn't part of the assignment.

He got out of bed and stared at the laptop, watching Elena in bed.

What a sick voyeur he was. She was asleep, the covers pulled up over her.

He could be in bed with her right now. And she wouldn't be sleeping.

He didn't need to be a nice guy. He hadn't been a nice guy earlier when he'd had his fingers inside her.

God, she'd been hot and wet and smelled so damn good. His dick had been pounding so hard he was surprised he hadn't come in his pants. He wanted to be inside her so bad he'd ached with it.

He still wanted it. His cock was hard, throbbing, demanding release.

He walked away from the image of her sleeping and lay down on the bed, closed his eyes, and thought about Elena, her sweet body writhing on top of his as she came.

He fisted his cock and squeezed, stroked it slow and easy, imagining her delicate hands surrounding the shaft as she sat next to him, her lips parted as they'd been earlier tonight when she'd been so hot and turned on. She'd kept the connection between them, left her eyes open while he'd slid his fingers inside her and made her come.

He brought his hand up, let his thumb slide over the crest of his cock. Fluid spilled from the tip and he swept it over the head. He ached, his balls tightening. He was so primed, so pumped with the need to let go that he could come right now. Images of Elena arching against him pummeled his senses as he got a stranglehold on his cock and pumped it up and down, wondering what it would feel like to have Elena's hot, sweet mouth sliding over the head of his dick.

He groaned, arched his hips and propelled his cock into his fist. Her mouth would suction over the head, tight and wet, her tongue swirling over him as she took him in, inch by inch, sucking him deeper until she had a mouthful of him.

He wanted to grab her by the back of the head and feed her his cock, pump against her tongue, feel the soft velvet rasp of it as she squeezed his dick with her mouth until he couldn't take it anymore, until he was ready to shoot his load right into her willing mouth.

"Fuck!" He let go, thoughts of Elena sucking him prominent in his mind as he shot come all over his stomach.

He went to the bathroom to clean up and came back, doing one more check on her. She had rolled over and kicked off the blanket, showing off her fine ass covered only by a pair of black panties.

Dammit, he was going to have to stop looking at her or he'd get hard again.

And then he'd never get any sleep tonight.

# SEVEN

It was a joy to reopen the store the next day. Elena's regular customers came in by the droves to check on her and make sure she was all right and that the store hadn't suffered too much damage after the burglary. Really, they came to gawk and gossip, which was fine by her. She loved her clients, and she and Marco enjoyed catering to them, because they typically bought a lot.

They didn't disappoint today, either, obviously thinking she'd been robbed blind and would be out of business within a week if they didn't help her out. Who was she to tell them otherwise? She couldn't think of a single client who hadn't left the store with something.

Business was booming today. She should get burglarized more often.

Okay, maybe not.

She hadn't seen Jed today, or heard from him. Not that she missed him—much. But after last night's incendiary interlude in her car, followed by his quick exit, she wasn't sure what the next step was going to be.

Then again, he did give her a hot kiss good-bye. But he hadn't called her last night. Or this morning. Or showed up.

She rolled her eyes. He had a job, a new business that he was trying to get off the ground, and a pocket full of business cards from the meeting last night. He was probably on the phone or in person marketing those contacts today, like he should be. And since when was she so interested in a guy?

She'd always vowed never to let a man become front and center in her life. That was her mother, not her. Her mother chased men, chased dreams like they were wisps of smoke. Elena's life was her business and staying grounded in reality.

She was never going to follow love. She would never become her mother.

Work settled down after three. Marco had a doctor's appointment, so she sent him off for the day. The shop stayed fairly busy until about an hour before closing when she finally grabbed something to eat and had a chance to sit down behind the counter. She nibbled on some fruit and cheese, then went to work on the day's receipts while she had a few quiet moments.

She figured it was going to be a slow last hour, unlike the rest of the day, giving her time to catch up, when the door chime signaled. She looked up and two men came in. Biker types in leather chaps and jackets. She came around the counter and headed toward them.

"Hi, can I help you?"

They split the counters, one going one way, the other the opposite direction. Neither said anything, or even looked at her, just observed the art on the walls and the sculptures scattered around the shop.

Her radar went up immediately. She took a step back and let

them observe. Not everyone was a talker. They were probably just in there to browse.

She stood by, hands clasped behind her back, when one of them lifted his head. "Tell me about this."

He was referring to the glass wave sculpture in the case. "Sure." She came over to the case. "This piece was made by one of our local artists. She's very popular for her use of a mix of colors."

"Let me see it."

"All right." She went behind the counter and unlocked the cabinet, conscious of the man's friend on the other side of the counter.

These guys made her nervous. Not because they were bikers, but because of their demeanor. She wished Marco were here to help her keep an eye on them.

She placed the thick velvet presentation mat on the counter, then deftly pulled the piece out of the cabinet and laid it on the overlay.

"As you can see, it's quite spectacular."

"Uh-huh. How much?"

"Eight hundred."

He didn't look up at her, didn't blink, didn't balk at the price. She half turned to see what the other guy was doing. He was inching closer to the front door at a very slow pace, still not making eye contact.

She didn't like this. Her stomach knotted. She needed her phone. She suddenly wanted to call Jed.

She kept her focus on the guy moving toward her front door. "Are you interested in this piece, or can I show you something else?"

"Show me something else," the guy said.

Reluctantly, she turned her gaze back to the customer. "All right. What would you like to see?"

"This one."

She tucked the glass piece to the side, ready to smash it and use the shards as a weapon if need be. She pulled out the shell.

That's when she heard the distinct click of the lock at her front door. Her gaze snapped to the man at the door. "Hey!"

She dove for the glass and came out with it in her hand, ready to break it over the counter and stab the asshole nearest her.

"Hey yourself, babe. What's going on here?"

She sagged with relief at the sound of Jed's voice. He sauntered in from the back of her shop. How he'd gotten in that way, she had no idea, and frankly didn't care. All she knew was the look on his face was lethal, and his right hand was resting on the butt of the gun tucked into his pants, sending a clear message to the two guys in the store he was ready for whatever they had in mind.

"I don't think we want anything today," the one by the door said, quickly unlocking the door.

The two of them left in a hurry.

Jed was at her side in two seconds and she sagged against him.

He took the glass from her hand. She hadn't even realized she had a death grip on it.

"Hell of a weapon here."

"It could be if I'd broken it."

"I'm not disagreeing with you. Who the hell were those guys?"

"No idea. I didn't like their vibe from the second they walked through the door. No eye contact, and I could tell they weren't really interested in any of the inventory."

He tipped her chin up with his fingers. "They were interested in you."

"I guess."

"You're shaking. You need to sit down."

He took her to the back of the shop and put her in the chair. "I'll be right back."

She nodded.

He was right. She was shaking. She clasped her hands together and tried to force the tremors to stop, but every time she did, the thoughts of what could have happened with those two men came barreling at her, and the shivers started again.

"Okay, come on. I'm taking you upstairs."

Her head shot up. "But the shop—"

"Is closed. Locked up tight. It was almost closing time, anyway."

She wanted to argue, but she knew he was right. She'd be useless to her customers right now. Dammit.

He helped her up and on shaky legs she climbed the stairs to her apartment, where she collapsed on the sofa.

"Got any coffee or tea?"

"Both."

"Tea would probably be better for you."

"Far-left-hand cabinet. I don't need you to wait on me. I'm all right."

He shot her a disbelieving look from the kitchen. "Yeah, you look all right. If you stood up, you'd probably fall over. Just sit there and I'll fix you something."

"Fine. And I'm not helpless, you know."

"Never thought you were."

"I was ready to bean that one guy with the glass sculpture. I also have a pretty decent right arm. I would have pitched the coral at the door guy, and would have likely hit him, too. Or at least injured him enough to go for the alarm. Or I could have hurt or disabled them both enough to give me time to run upstairs and lock myself in the apartment or gotten to my phone in time."

"Uh-huh. I'm sure you could have taken them both down single-handed."

"Now you're making fun of me."

"Am I?"

Jed handed her the cup of tea. She looked up at him and smiled, then took it with shaky hands.

"Thanks." She took a sip, and the warmth spread throughout her body. She'd needed this.

He kneeled down beside her. "You're pale."

"I'm tougher than you think." Or maybe she was just trying to convince herself so she wouldn't be scared out of her mind.

"Obviously. You had an entire plan in mind to kick their asses. You didn't need me."

She put the cup on the table beside her. "I so did. You're my hero. I might have had a plan, but who knows if I would have been able to carry it out. At the time I was terrified."

"Hey, you didn't fall apart like most people would have. I give you a lot of credit for that. You weren't a babbling baby and you held yourself together. I'm sure you would have executed whatever you had in mind with precision. I'm just glad I showed up and made them change their minds about whatever it was they thought about doing."

"What do you think they had in mind?"

He shrugged. "No idea, but whatever it was wasn't good."

She shuddered and wrapped her arms around her herself, feeling suddenly chilled.

Jed reached behind her for the blanket and laid it over her.

"Thanks, again. And how did you get in the shop?"

"I was on my way over to see you. Saw the dude flip the lock and knew something was up, so instead of busting your front door in or shooting the lock, I came around back and used the code to get in."

"Oh, that's right. I forgot I'd given that to you."

He swept his hand over her hair. "You can change the code if you want to."

"Are you kidding? You saved my life today."

He sat on the sofa next to her. "I don't know about that, but I'm glad I could be here for you."

"It was handy timing. My shop seems to have been targeted."

Or Elena was the target. Jed wasn't sure. He'd been in the condo, and once he spotted the two guys pulling up in front of her store, he'd zeroed in on them. They'd waited until Marco left before going inside, a sure sign they were scoping her out. He'd hightailed it out of the condo, got a scan of their bike tags and headed for the front door. That's when he saw the one lock it, so he'd hurried around the back and used the code to slip inside.

He wasn't sure if these guys were part of the burglary ring going around, or if they'd been after Elena. He intended to find out, but his first priority was making sure she was safe.

He stood, went to the window and looked out. Lots of bikes cruising by slowly, some appearing to look into Elena's shop. A few people walking by stopped at the door, then walked away. There was no way to tell if they were just shoppers or if anyone was dangerous.

"You can take off now," Elena said, drawing his attention away from the traffic outside. "I'll be fine. I really should reopen the shop."

He leaned against the windowsill. "Not a chance."

She pulled her legs up behind her. Yeah, she didn't look ready to run back downstairs and open that door.

"I can't stay closed, Jed. I have a business to run."

He knew she was right, but he'd stick closer from now on. "You're still pale, and it's almost dinnertime. How about I fix dinner?"

She raised a brow. "You cook?"

"Uh, by fixing dinner, I meant we could order a pizza or something."

She laughed. "I like pizza."

"That's good, because I don't really cook. I can make eggs and bacon and toast. And I fix a mean bowl of cereal."

She laughed. "I'm a great cook."

"Then I might just have to keep you around so I don't starve to death or blow my budget on take-out food."

She directed him to her stash of take-out menus and he ordered them a pizza. Thank God the woman liked to eat. They agreed on a pizza loaded with sausage and pepperoni, and they each got a salad to go with it.

While they waited for the pizza to arrive, Elena went to change clothes. Jed sent a quick text to Grange, letting him know what happened along with the tag numbers of the two bikes. He told Grange he was sticking close to Elena. Grange texted him back and told him he'd check up on the bikes and get back to him.

Jed really wanted to go after those bikers, but he couldn't be in two places at one time, and his main job was to keep Elena safe.

Normally he liked the action—chasing down the bad guys. He'd left his job at the FBI because there hadn't been enough of the action. Too much time in the office, too much research work. Now he was stuck inside with Elena—protection duty basically.

Yet for some reason he didn't mind, and he knew it was because he was attracted to her. He was going to have to pull back on the attraction and do his damn job, quit letting his dick rule the mission.

"That's better." She came out in a white tank top with some skimpy other strappy thing underneath it in pink, and some black yoga pants that came to her knee. The whole ensemble shouldn't have been sexy, but it was, because when she went into the kitchen and rose up on her toes to grab for paper plates, her top rode up and gave him a glimpse of tanned, flat stomach.

And his cock noticed.

His cock could just damn well remember that Elena was a mission, not a potential fuck buddy.

He went to the window instead of ogling her.

"Something interesting out there?"

"Yeah. The pizza guy. I'll be right back."

After he fetched the pizza, they sat at the kitchen bar. He liked watching her eat. She didn't put much dressing on her salad, but dove into her pizza like she was starving. He liked a woman who ate actual food as opposed to pushing food around on the plate and pretending to eat. He'd dated women like that before—the stick-thin variety who thought men liked to date women with the figure of a twelve-year-old boy. He wasn't that kind of a guy—he liked a woman to look like a woman. He never understood the whole starvation thing.

"So how's business going?" she asked.

"Uh, good."

"Did you make some contacts from the business association?"

He hadn't called any of those people. Didn't intend to. And she could verify that. "Not yet. I had some other people I'd gotten in touch with, so I have some alarm installs I'm working on with them first."

"Oh. That's great. Sounds like you're pretty busy."

"Yeah." He bit into his pizza and tried not to say too much. He was going to have to dance around his cover and hope she wouldn't send anyone else his way.

Her phone rang. "It's Marco."

She answered it, and filled Marco in on what happened at the store while she ate and reassured him that Jed was there with her and she was safe. He listened to the dynamic.

"No, don't come over. Jed's here and I'm fine . . . Yes, I was scared, but I swear I would have taken one of Bondino's corals and beaned him with it."

She laughed. "I know how much it's worth, but it's not like I carry a gun, and even if I did, I wouldn't shoot them . . . Well, okay, maybe if it was him or me, I would shoot him . . . No, you absolutely will not increase your hours at the shop. You have school, and you have Torrance. You have a life, too."

Then she handed the phone to Jed. "He wants to talk to you."

Jed arched a brow and took the phone. "Hey, Marco."

"Is she all right? I mean is she really all right? She's trying to make me feel better because I wasn't there, but I need to know."

Jed met Elena's gaze. "She's fine."

"I'm afraid for her. This is the second time something has happened while I wasn't there."

"I know."

"Don't say anything to her, but I'm thinking someone's targeting her."

Marco was pretty perceptive. "Maybe. I'll check it out."

"Thank you. I feel better knowing you're there with her. You'll stay the night?"

He smiled at Elena. "If she'll let me."

"Use your charm, man. Coerce her. I won't sleep if I don't think she's safe."

"Don't worry about it. I've got it covered."

He sighed. "All right. I'll be there early in the morning."

Jed handed the phone back to Elena. She finished the call and laid the phone down on the table. "He worries like a mother."

"It's good to have friends like that."

"I know. I don't know what I'd do without him. We've been

together since I first opened the shop. He has a keen eye for art, but beyond that, he's a good friend. He's family."

Because she didn't have any other family around to be her support system.

"You miss your mom?"

She shrugged. "I can't miss her."

"Why not?"

"I got used to her not being around. And I'm an adult now. I don't need my mother."

She was staring at her salad.

"I would think a girl always needs her mother, especially at a time like this."

Her gaze shot to his. "A time like what?"

"Come on, Elena. Your shop was burglarized, and you were nearly attacked today. That's fairly traumatic."

She lifted her chin. "I'm not a child who needs to go running to her mama every time something bad happens. I'm self-sufficient and able to take care of myself."

More by necessity than by choice, he'd imagine. "Because your mother wasn't here for you so you had no choice?"

"I never thought about that. Maybe." She leaned back and took a swallow of beer, then pointed the tip of the bottle toward him. "You're very good at this."

"At what?"

"Playing psychologist."

He laughed. "Just observing. I don't analyze anyone."

"Either way, it's a good point. I don't spend too much time delving into my relationship with my mother. She is who she is and maybe that's made me who I am. I'm not as free spirited as she is. I don't just drop everything and go or try new things, because I never wanted to be anything like her. I wanted to remain planted in one place, doing one thing, because she was always on the go doing a hundred different things."

"And you didn't like that."

Her clear gaze met his. She didn't seem angry, just contemplative. "No, I didn't. I hated her lifestyle, hated the havoc it wreaked on me. Whoever she was, I wanted to be the opposite."

"Are you angry at her?"

She looked away, out the window. "I don't know. Maybe. Probably. Yes. When I was really little, she'd take me with her. We had great adventures, traveling from place to place. I met some pretty cool people. She was so much like a kid herself that it was like hanging out with a best friend. No rules, no curfews, just all this joy.

"But then she decided—or maybe other people decided for her—that I needed to be in school. So she stopped taking me with her and left me with other people. That's when the fun ended."

"Because she got to go off on her great adventures, and you didn't anymore."

She nodded. "Yes. I resented her for that. I was jealous. I had to grow up, be responsible."

"You grew up, and she didn't."

He saw the tears welling in her eyes. She pushed away from the bar, threw her plate in the trash and walked to the balcony.

He'd pushed her too hard, hadn't meant to, but there was so much about her he wanted to know. Just part of the mission, of course. The more he could discover about her mom, the better chance they had of finding her.

And then he could move on to another mission.

He tossed his plate, grabbed both beers, and walked out onto the balcony. It was cool outside tonight, but he liked it. Bikers lined the streets and he wished he could hop on his Harley and join them. Instead, he handed her a beer, grabbed a chair and just watched and listened to the thunderous rumble. All he could see for miles were single headlights in both directions, horns honking, bikers riding or walking on the sidewalks. He got up and looked down the road.

"There are vendor and beer tents set up, and bands, too. You can go. I know you'd rather be out there riding with them."

He picked up his bottle. "Got beer right here, and I'd rather be with you."

She laughed. "Liar. We could go for a ride."

He shook his head. "It's not safe."

"If you think I'm going to become a prisoner in my own house, you're wrong. Just because two assholes tried to threaten me today doesn't mean I'm going to be afraid to go out." She stood. "I'll go change."

He grabbed her wrist and stopped her, hooking her gaze with his. "I've been to plenty of rallies. There's nothing new out there I haven't seen before."

He pulled her down on his lap, swept his hand down her back. "Here now, there's definitely something new and way more interesting than anything down there."

# EIGHT

There was nothing more enticing than a man who focused his entire attention on you. Elena's breath caught as Jed's gaze captured hers.

His eyes revealed so much—heat, intensity and desire.

She'd opened up to him, told him about her mother in more detail than she ever had before with anyone else. She barely knew him, and yet she'd spilled her secret pain to him. Why?

Because he'd made it easy. He'd asked, she'd answered—just like that.

And he was still here.

Most men didn't want all the deep dark secrets. They wanted easy and uncomplicated. Jed had dug deeper, forging a connection she wasn't sure she was ready to forge with him—with any man.

Now he looked at her as if he wanted something deeper, the

kind of connection that would require them to move forward on a physical plane.

Though they already had, at least on her side. Until he'd backed away, and she'd wondered if maybe he'd had second thoughts. But the looks he gave her now told her something else entirely.

"Don't think so much all the time, Elena," he said, sweeping his hand to the back of her neck and drawing her closer. "Just feel."

His breath whispered across her mouth as he fit his lips to hers. She sighed and leaned against the hard plane of his chest and let her fingers slide into the silken strands of his hair.

She was lost in the sensation of his mouth, the way his tongue swept along hers. She breathed in the clean male scent of him, smoothed her hands along the muscles of his arms and felt him tense. When he deepened the kiss, she was lost, wanted to dive in and forget everything but the way she felt right now.

And what was so wrong with that, other than she was always in possession of her faculties. She never threw her sensibilities out the window, was always in control.

She hadn't felt in control of anything since she'd met Jed.

He stood, his arm wrapped tight around her waist until her feet touched the ground. He maneuvered her to the wall of the balcony and moved into her, pressing his body against hers.

And then he pulled back, one hand on the wall, the other on her hip, his eyes locked with hers.

She zeroed in on his mouth. Damn, he had a fine mouth. Her lips tingled as she remembered how good he was at using it to kiss her. She wanted more of that—a lot more of it, which made her mind wander to what else his mouth was good at.

He must have been watching her, because she saw the upward tilt of his lips.

She lifted her gaze to his and was hit by the blast of unshuttered desire in his eyes.

"I want you, Elena." He moved his hand along the side of her rib cage, inching her tank top up, too.

Her body flushed with a sudden rush of heat. "Right here?"

He shrugged. "I don't care. I want to fuck you. Here or inside. Up to you."

She shuddered in a breath and slipped her hand around his neck to pull his head down. She held him an inch from her lips. "Let's start here and see where it goes."

His mouth met hers in an explosion of deep, dark passion, his arm sweeping around her back to draw her against him. He lifted her top and slid his hand inside to rest against the skin of her belly.

Her heart pounded, a loud, crashing beat that drowned out the sound of revving motorcycles and honking horns. All she could hear was her own breaths and the moan she let escape as Jed plundered her mouth with deep kisses.

She'd been kissed before—plenty of times. But this was all consuming, and her head spun, her knees felt weak, and she was dizzy from the sensations blasting her body. There was a chill to the night air but she was hot—all over. And so was Jed, his body a furnace as it pressed full on against hers.

This was no gentle make-out session. It was a power assault, as if all this time he'd been holding back and now he'd unleashed everything he had on her.

And what an arsenal it was. His body was all hard muscle, his thigh wedged between her legs more than capable of keeping her upright. As she grasped his upper arms, she felt the bulge of his biceps and swept her hands over his broad shoulders.

He made her feel safe and made her swoon a little bit, because he wasn't the type of guy she usually went for. He wasn't a buttoned-up business guy. He was an outdoors-and-carved-in-muscle guy. He looked dangerous; he smelled like leather and something primally male that was unique to him. It wasn't cologne, either. It was his masculine scent and it drove her crazy. She had no idea how to handle him.

Fortunately, he was doing all the handling at the moment, because her brain cells were melting under the siege of his mouth and hands. And when he slipped his hand down her pants and cupped her sex, she cried out against his mouth.

He drew his lips away from hers to meet her shocked gaze.

"You're wet and hot in my hand." He teased her with a light stroke, dragging another moan from her as she clenched his shirt between her fingers and held on.

His cock was hard as he rocked it against her hip.

"I'm going to fuck you tonight, Elena. Hard and fast, then easy and slow. I'm going to make you come so many times you're going to beg for mercy."

She rolled her hips toward the magic of his fingers as he dug the heel of his hand against her clit and tucked two fingers inside her. She was so close to coming she could only focus on his movements and the dark, whispered words that spilled from his lips.

"You know, I'll bet you taste as good as you feel. I want you to come in my mouth, Elena."

She was balanced on the very edge of insanity, but held on enough that shock slapped her when he bent down and dragged her pants over her hips.

"Jed. Not out here."

He tilted his head back and grinned at her. "No one's watching, and you have enough privacy out here. You're ready to fly, Elena. Let me."

It was such a wicked idea, and she didn't have the power to move, let alone think. She could only watch as he pulled her pants and panties down to her ankles. The cool breeze hit her feverish skin, but then Jed was there, cupping her buttocks with his hands and tilting her pussy toward his mouth.

She watched in awe and need as he fit his mouth over her clit and sucked.

Oh, God. So, good. His tongue darted out and licked the length of her pussy, and she threw her head back, forgetting about the brick wall behind her. But even the pain didn't dissipate the incredible pleasure of his mouth, his tongue and the delicious things he was doing to her as he dragged his tongue across her tortured flesh, parted her folds, put his lips over the tight knot and took her right over the edge.

She reached for his head and held him there while she came, wanting to scream but not wanting to call attention to herself. Instead, she pushed her pussy at his face and rocked against him while he licked and sucked her through the most intense orgasm she'd ever experienced.

When the wild pulses died down, he helped her step out of her pants and panties, then led her inside and laid her on the bed, only to bury his face in her pussy again.

She hadn't had time even to catch her breath from the last orgasm before he had her primed and ready to go again. Only this time he widened her legs and slid his fingers inside her while he sucked her clit.

"Jed," she whispered, reaching down to tangle her fingers in his hair. She arched against his mouth, and he met her gaze as she came. The contractions were even more intense than the first orgasm he gave her.

She was panting out breaths, trying to come to grips with what had just happened to her, when Jed loomed over her, the hem of her shirt fisted in his hands. He smiled down at her. "These have to come off. I want you naked."

She wanted that, too. "I want you naked, too."

"You, first." He lifted her tank tops off and tossed them to the floor, then climbed off the bed only long enough to shuck his clothes.

She leaned up on her elbows to watch as he discarded his shirt, revealing sculpted abs and a line of dark hair that disappeared into his pants.

Her mouth watered and she licked her lips. That was a most tantalizing line, and she watched it as he popped the button on his pants, drew the zipper down and let his pants drop to the floor.

It was so unfair that a man could be built like that. Narrow hips, amazingly well-built thighs, and his cock was magnificent. She scrambled onto her knees and waited as he climbed back onto the bed.

"You're incredibly good-looking," she said as he came to her.

One side of his mouth quirked. He swept her hair away from her face. "And you're gorgeous."

He threw her down on the bed and followed her. She laughed, but all humor died when he put his hands and mouth on her again. Naked, his body pressed to hers, was a bone-numbing experience. He was hot and hard all over, and she wished she had more hands.

She loved his stomach. She'd never really gravitated toward guys who worked out all the time. All that muscle was kind of a turnoff. But with Jed it was different. Maybe because he had a brain to go with the muscles, and a sense of humor and an—

Oh, God, yes, that amazing mouth. He sucked her tongue deeply into his mouth and she could swear she had a mini-orgasm. Her pussy tightened and her clit tingled, all her nerve endings seemingly connected to what his mouth was doing to hers.

There was something magical about this man. He mesmerized her in every possible way, and his touch had a profound effect on her. Sure, it had been a while since she'd had sex, but she'd never thought of sex as something so amazing it would make time stop.

Jed made everything in her world stop, including her breath. She pushed on his shoulders and he lifted.

"Something wrong?"

"I can't breathe."

He moved off to the side. "I'm sorry. I'm too heavy."

She rolled over and grabbed him. "No. Not like that. I mean I'm overwhelmed, but in a good way. You're rocking my world here, Jed."

He arched a brow. "Is that a bad thing?"

"No. God, no. But isn't it time we take care of you?"

He let out a short laugh. "Plenty of time for that."

"Oh, but I take a certain amount of joy in touching you. You wouldn't want to deny me, would you?"

She traced her finger down his chest. So smooth, but underneath, there were those muscles. She laid her palm flat over his abs and felt them tighten.

She lifted her gaze to his. "Tickle?"

He wasn't laughing. "No. Your hand feels good. I like you touching me."

She slid her palm down his lower belly and wrapped her fingers around the heavy heat of his cock. It jumped against her fist and she began to stroke him.

"Then let me touch you."

Now it was his turn to gasp, and oh, she really liked that. She squeezed his cock harder, loving the rock-hard feel of him.

He released her hand, rolled her onto her back and slid between her legs. "If you spend any more time touching me, I'll come."

Heat coiled deep within her. "I'd like to see that."

"You will. But first I'm going to come inside you when I fuck you."

She was going up in flames. She'd never been with a man so verbal. She liked the verbal. A lot.

He leaned against her and rubbed his shaft across her pussy, sending spirals of pleasure through her nerve endings. She wrapped her legs around his thighs and rocked with him, increasing the tension to her clit.

Jed propped up on his hands and she held onto him, digging her fingers into the corded muscles of his arms as he suspended himself above her. His strength was a turn-on, as was the way he seemed to know how to pleasure her. This easy tease, the way he took her right to the edge time and time again with no thought of getting himself off, was a heady thrill and made her feel like the only woman in the universe.

Or at least the only woman in his universe.

And if he kept rubbing his cock against her like that, she was going to have an orgasm. For the third time.

"Jed."

"Yeah."

"Fuck me."

"I will. As soon as I watch you come again."

She wanted to tell him it was ridiculous, when he hadn't yet had one, but she was so close—so close—and his hot shaft felt so damn delicious, his balls slapping against her pussy as he expertly stroked her clit.

"You're so wet, Elena. It would be so easy to slam inside you and fuck you hard until I came. But do you know how your skin flushes when you're turned on, and your nipples get tight? I want to suck on your nipples when I'm fucking you and make you come when I'm inside you."

She dug her nails into his arm and fell right over the cliff again. He stopped, put his fingers inside her and made it that much more intense as the waves of orgasm intensified. Then he leaned over and kissed her, brought her down easy from the sweet climax he'd given her.

He turned over and grabbed a condom, rolled it on and climbed between her legs.

"I could tease you and make you come all night long," he said. "But I'm about to explode because I want to be inside you."

"I want that, too." She reached for his cock and drew him to the entrance to her pussy. He eased inside her, filling her as he pushed deep, then held, swelling inside her.

She didn't think she'd be able to feel anything after coming so many times, but her pussy quivered to life again, pulsing as he began to move.

He cupped one breast in his hand, leaned in to take her nipple between his lips, his tongue sliding over the tight peak.

She felt the delicious tug all the way to her core. As he sucked her nipple, he half withdrew, then drove his cock inside her, and the sweetest pleasure spiraled through her.

He lifted his head, thumbed her nipple and took her mouth, kissing her deeply while grinding against her. The myriad of sensations drove her ever upward toward another orgasm. She swept her hands along his back, feeling his body tense as he thrust against her.

She knew he was close, and so was she. She wrapped her legs around his hips and lifted against him. His groan was so enticing. She lifted her gaze to his, saw the need there, and it made her pussy tighten around him.

"Christ," he muttered, and reached for her knee, brought it forward and held her leg there while he began to thrust in earnest.

As he drove in deep, she shattered.

"Jed," she said, his name spilling from her lips as her climax thundered through her.

He followed, dropping down on her and shoving deep inside her, then gathering her against him while he shuddered out his own orgasm. He tangled his fingers in her hair and kissed her with a depth that left her breathless. She held onto him as if he were her only lifeline in a storm at sea.

He rolled her to the side but didn't let her go. Instead, they stayed like that for a few amazing moments, with Jed stroking her hair and back and kissing her lips and jaw.

She felt cherished. They might still be strangers and maybe it was because this was just the first time and that's why it felt special, but she still felt cherished, and that was an unusual feeling.

Finally, he got up and went into the bathroom. She expected him to get dressed and take off, but he came back and climbed into bed with her, pulled the covers over them both and drew her against him.

She fell asleep with a smile on her face.

# NINE

Jed woke with a start. Disoriented, it took him a few seconds to remember where he was.

Elena's apartment. He felt her body next to his, pressed intimately against him.

But that's not what woke him.

Something was wrong.

He didn't want to disturb Elena or make any sound, so he stayed still, listening.

There. Downstairs. Footsteps.

He shook Elena awake. She moaned and he leaned near her ear. "I think someone is downstairs."

Her eyes shot open.

Jed took a look at the alarm on the wall next to her bed.

Nothing. No blinking, no alert. Dead silent.

Shit. He knew he'd installed a foolproof alarm system, and that he'd set and armed it. That someone was in the house meant that whoever was inside was good enough to bypass his alarm system.

No routine burglary this time.

He pointed to her clothes and a pair of tennis shoes across the room. She nodded and slipped out of bed as silently as he did. He grabbed his clothes and slipped into them, got his gun and moved over to her. "Car keys," he whispered.

She shifted her gaze to the kitchen. There, on the counter. He nodded and took her hand, and that's when he heard the creak.

Bottom stair. He'd heard it himself a few times coming up and down her stairs. It was a good alert.

She squeezed his fingers. He turned to her and motioned with his head for her to stay quiet, then backed up to the terrace. The night was warm so they'd left the door open. He pushed her outside.

"Stay here."

She grabbed his arm. "Where are you going?"

"To see who's in your shop."

"We should call the police."

He nodded. "I will." He pushed her down. "Stay here and out of sight. I'll be right back."

As soon as he figured out if it was someone after what was in her shop, or someone after Elena.

He stepped back into the room and inched over to the doorway leading to the stairs, listening for further sounds of approaching footsteps. He slowed his breathing down, trying to force the adrenaline to calm so he could hear something other than the rush of blood in his veins and his pounding heart.

Once he was calm, he listened. Nothing. Whoever had made the noise on the bottom step must have changed their mind, at least for now.

Until he saw the movement at the top of the stairs.

Shit. Someone had infinite patience, and after he'd made the sound at the bottom of the stairs, had probably stopped and waited to see if someone came after him. When no one had, he'd continued coming up the stairs.

Jed crouched down as the guy reached the top of the stairs and rounded the corner.

After that it happened fast. The intruder moved in a hurry, spotted Elena and pointed his gun.

Jed pushed off and attacked, kicking the gun out of his hand.

The intruder sent off a kick and Jed's gun went flying, as did Jed. The guy dove for his gun but Jed tackled him, taking an elbow to the face and barely dodging a lethal move meant to kill, not incapacitate.

This guy meant business, and now so did Jed, who hadn't intended to do anything but disable the gunman. But this guy was determined to take him down, then either kill or capture Elena, and Jed wasn't going to allow that to happen.

They rolled across the floor together, strength fighting strength. Jed fought a hard blow to the chin and knocked the guy in the throat with his elbow. As the guy fought for breath, Jed knocked a lamp over, grabbed the cord and wrapped it around the guy's throat.

He fought it off, rolled over Jed and gave him a hard kick to the kidney that had Jed wincing. He struggled for breath, the room spinning, saw the other guy running for his gun. Jed leaped up, dashed for his, turned, aimed and fired.

A fraction of a second faster than the gunman, who went down like a crumbling building, hitting the floor with a thud.

Elena came running in. She fell to her knees next to Jed and put her hands on his face.

"Are you all right?"

Jed nodded, gasping for breath. "Fine."

She shifted her gaze to the guy across the room.

"Is he dead?"

Jed pushed up and walked over to the intruder, kicked the gun away and laid his fingers on the guy's neck.

"Yup. Dead."

"Oh, my God," Elena said, wide eyed, her hand over her mouth.

This whole assignment had gone to shit in an instant.

"I'm going to check downstairs. I'll be right back."

"Okay. Should we call the police?"

"No." At her shocked look, he added, "Not yet."

He raised his gun and hustled downstairs, but he figured this guy had been working alone. He checked the alarm, saw how the guy had circumvented it.

Clever. Dammit.

He searched the entire store. Front door was secure. No one else was here. He dashed back upstairs to find Elena still in the same spot he'd left her. He wanted to comfort her, but now wasn't the time.

"We need to get out of here."

Her gaze shot to his. "What? Why?"

"Because my guess is this guy here isn't working alone, and his backup can't be far behind."

"We're leaving him here, in my apartment?"

"Yeah. Come on, we need to go."

"But the police . . ."

"We need to get out of here now. You're in danger."

He grabbed her hand. She resisted. "I'm in danger? I don't understand."

"I know you don't. But I'll explain on the way."

"On the way to where?"

"Somewhere other than here. You're not safe. Let's go."

She dug in her heels and refused to move.

This wasn't going at all the way he'd planned. Then again, he hadn't planned on someone breaking in to kill her, or kidnap her, or whatever the hell the guy had come in here to do. He wished he had time to sit her down and explain it all to her, but Elena's safety was his number one mission.

He turned to her and took her hands in his. "I promise I'll explain everything to you, but right now I have to get you someplace safe, and this isn't it. I can almost guarantee that whoever hired that guy will send someone else once he doesn't check in."

She glanced over at the lump on the floor. "What was he sent here to do?"

"Either kidnap you or kill you."

She went pale. He hated having to be so blunt, but it was the only way to get her to move.

"Why?"

"This isn't the place to explain. Let's go." He grabbed her keys and her hand and headed to the back stairs. This time she cooperated. Her car was in the garage, so Jed unlocked the garage door and flipped on the light, his gun raised. He checked out the garage and cleared it and the Chevelle before letting Elena climb into the passenger side.

He opened the garage door, checking the outside thoroughly, then got in and started the engine, wincing as the Chevelle roared to life. Any other time he'd feel a thrill at the 396 engine powering up. Now he wished she whispered like a kitten.

But the Harley wouldn't be any quieter and he wanted the safety of four doors and a roof to protect Elena. Plus the Chevy had some power behind her—if they needed to move, she'd haul some serious ass.

He pulled out, dropped the garage door down and locked it, then inched to the end of the alley. It was the middle of the night, and despite the rally, traffic was light, so he pulled onto the main street, keeping his eye on the rearview mirror to see if they were being followed. When he'd made enough twists and turns and gone in circles enough times he was certain he didn't have a tail, he pulled out his phone.

"What's wrong?" Grange asked as soon as he picked up the phone.

"Hey, Grange, it's Jed."

"You can't talk freely."

"No kidding. It's been a while. Just wanted to let you know I was in town. And hey, I know it's short notice, but my friend and I need a place to stay."

"You're compromised. You need a safe house."

"I know. We kind of got run out of our place. If you can't, I understand."

Grange sighed. "I'll give you directions and an address. We'll pick you up."

"You're a lifesaver. I knew I could count on you."

He gave Jed the address and directions. It wasn't far from their current location.

"We'll be there soon. Thanks."

"Keep eyes in the back of your head," Grange said.

"You got it."

Jed hung up and started the trek south. Miles of shoreline flew by on his left, houses and hotels on his right. After a while he plunged into darkness. He hoped he didn't pass the place.

"So that was a friend of yours on the phone?" Elena asked.

"Yeah. Someone I trust."

"Jed."

"Yeah."

"You need to tell me what's happening."

"I will. Once I get you safe." She was just going to have to trust him for now. And he was going to have to make up one hell of a bunch of lies once they got to Grange's place. Hopefully Grange would help him with that, because he had no idea what he was going to tell her.

He'd like to tell her the truth—that she had an uncle—family that cared about her and worried for her safety. But that wasn't his call to make. If Grange wanted to stay out of the family picture, that was his decision.

Jed intended to do his job, which was to keep her safe, and that was all he was going to do.

Though he'd just done more than that tonight, hadn't he?

He'd made love to her. And it'd been damn good. He could still smell her on him, could taste her, could feel the way her body responded to him over and over again.

His cock tightened and he had to push those thoughts away.

He'd screwed up and gotten involved.

Then again, if he hadn't been there tonight, he might have been too late. Someone had punched through his alarm system and gotten to Elena. Jed knew how to wire an alarm, so this guy was an expert. If Jed hadn't been there . . .

He didn't want to think about what might have happened.

"Where are we going?" she asked.

"It's not much farther." He searched for the marker the general had told him would be there. Only another few miles or so.

There it was. A stone proclaiming a historical landmark. Just past that, a turnoff, barely noticeable amid the desolation of the landscape.

He made the right turn into the pitch-black darkness. The road bumped and he wished for his four-wheel-drive SUV.

"If I didn't know better, I'd swear you were kidnapping me."

He sensed the nervousness in her voice. She didn't know him better. She didn't know him at all.

He had to hold the wheel with both hands so he couldn't reach out to reassure her. Instead, he shot her a quick smile. "It's going to be okay. I promise."

It was going to be okay. That was a promise he meant to keep.

Elena had no idea where she was, where they were going, or what had happened tonight. It was all so quick.

She'd been asleep, warm and tucked in against Jed. And suddenly, he'd woken her and her entire world had changed.

Someone was in her house. Someone with a gun. Jed had taken over, there'd been an awful, ugly fight, and he'd had to shoot the intruder. Then he'd dragged her out of her house telling her that her life was in danger.

She didn't know who to trust or what to believe anymore.

She wanted to believe Jed. He'd been her savior on more than one occasion.

Unless . . .

She glanced over at him as he maneuvered the ruts in the road, so confident, so amazingly handsome. She remembered his hands and his mouth on her body earlier tonight, and she warmed past the chill she couldn't seem to shake.

But how much did she really know about him? And how odd was it that he showed up at the same time these things started happening to her? And how convenient that he was in security, and he'd been the one to install the alarm in her shop?

The alarm that hadn't worked tonight.

She wrapped her arms around herself and drew her knees to her chest to ward off the goose bumps.

Had he set her up to trust him? Had this all been some elaborate scheme to put her in this place with him right now?

Just because a man was gorgeous and seemingly capable

didn't mean he couldn't be a bad guy, a thief, a kidnapper or something even worse.

God, had she blindly trusted him and put herself in danger? Was she that stupid? She had no cell phone, no purse, no credit cards, nothing but the clothes on her back and the car Jed drove. They'd been in such a hurry to get out of the house—no, Jed had insisted they move fast; she hadn't even thought about grabbing her phone or her purse.

Stupid move. Now she had no way to call for help. If she even needed to call for help.

She didn't even know where they were. She'd been so lost in her own thoughts she hadn't paid attention to landmarks. They'd gone south on the highway. But now he'd driven into some swampland and they were God only knows where.

Someplace remote. There were no houses, no hotels, no lights. Nothing but a barren wasteland, a remote, single-lane road with water on both sides.

Where the hell was he taking her?

"Jed."

"It's just up ahead."

Her mother would think of this as a great adventure. Elena was going to be downright pissed if she ended up butchered to death by some guy she'd just had phenomenal sex with and not even live to tell Marco about it.

Marco had liked him. And Marco was usually a great judge of people. He frequently pointed out the losers she dated, steered her away from guys he told her were no good for her. He was a lot like her mother in that respect.

So if this one ended up being a serial killer, it was going to be all Marco's fault.

Well. At least she'd retained her sense of humor.

There. They broke through a clearing. They were on a point at a hill, the ocean at a distance.

Jed put the car in park.

"Come on."

She gave him a wary look.

"Elena, I promise you're going to be safe. Trust me."

Ha. Famous last words. Then again, if they'd wanted her dead, wouldn't he have just let the guy with the gun take care of it? Why the elaborate ruse?

Dammit. None of this made sense.

She got out of the car when Jed opened the door.

It was so dark she couldn't see anything.

"Give me your hand. Stay close to me."

She slipped her hand in his and he led her up the hill.

When they reached the top, she saw the helicopter. Jed started toward it, but Elena stopped. He turned to her as the blades began to rotate and the helicopter fired its engines.

"No." She tugged on his hold, not sure what she was going to do, but if she got in that helicopter, he could take her any-where.

"Elena, come on. You have to go with me."

The chopper's blades began to stir up a heavy breeze, blowing her hair into her face. She grabbed onto her hair with one hand while trying to pull her other hand free from Jed's grasp. "No. I'm not going with you."

He wouldn't let her go. "What are you going to do? Go back to your house?"

"Yes. And I'm going to call the police. Why didn't you call the police, Jed? What are you hiding?"

He looked exasperated with her. She didn't care. She wanted the truth.

"I'm not hiding anything from you. I'm trying to keep you safe."

"Calling the cops would have been a good start, instead of leaving that dead guy at my house."

"I promise you'll have the truth, as soon as we get you out of here."

She shook her head. "No. I'm not getting in that thing. And who's "we"?

The next thing she knew she was thrust over Jed's shoulder and he was running for the helicopter. She struggled, but she was dumped in the seat and held there while the chopper lifted off.

Jed finally let go of her. She looked outside the window and all she could see below was ocean. There was nowhere for her to go. A leap out of the helicopter would kill her.

The pilot of the helicopter hadn't even looked at them. Maybe he was used to men throwing women in his helicopter against their will. She doubted he'd help her.

The fight drained out of her and she sank against the seat.

Jed tapped her leg. She turned to look at him. He motioned to his seat belt and she put hers on. He also wanted her to put on earphones with a mic so he could talk to her, but she shook her head.

She didn't want to talk. She wanted to go home, climb in bed and go to sleep, wake up tomorrow and realize this had all been a bad dream. Then she could go downstairs, open her shop, and it would be like any other normal day.

Normal. Her life hadn't been normal since she'd met Jed.

She shot him a glare. He was watching her. He looked tense, as if at any moment he expected her to either leap on him or fling the door open and throw herself into the ocean.

She wasn't that stupid. She was no match for his strength

and she wasn't about to kill herself. She was all about survival, and she'd figure out how to survive this.

Even if she had been stupid enough to get herself into this nightmare.

The drop in the pit of her stomach signaled their descent. She looked out the window to see the first gray fingers of dawn peeking over the horizon, giving her a glimpse of a tiny strip of an island below. And then the copter started to dive. She held on, watching as the island grew larger, and they landed on a clearing just off the beach.

An older guy stood there in camouflage pants, boots and a brown T-shirt. Jed unbuckled and got out first, then helped Elena.

Her ears stopped ringing as the helicopter's rotors and engines were cut.

"Gen—uh, this is Grange," Jed said. "Grange, this is Elena Madison."

The older guy nodded at Jed, then turned his attention on her.

He looked fierce. And mean. Very military, with his precision haircut, rigid stance and his hands clasped behind his back. She felt like she was being inspected and she should stand at attention.

He nodded to her. "Miss Madison."

"Elena," she corrected.

"I'm sure you're tired. Let's go to the compound."

Compound? Where were they, Guantanamo?

Grange pivoted and led the way through the canopy of trees onto a well-worn path. Now that it was lighter out, at least she didn't feel like she was stumbling around in the dark. But she still didn't like that she had no idea where she was, or where they were going.

Or why she was even here or had been flown here by helicopter.

She shifted her gaze to Jed, who was fixated on Grange's back. She tried to get his attention but he wouldn't look at her.

Fine. She stepped up her pace and moved alongside Grange.

"What's going on? Why was I brought here?"

She didn't think the man had any ability of movement in his mouth other than grim straight line.

"I'll explain everything to you after we have you secured."

"Secured. What the hell does that even mean? I own a jewelry store. I'm not military and no threat to national security. Have I been set up somehow?"

She threw Jed a glare over her shoulder and tried to keep up with Grange, but his long strides ate up the path and she gave up.

Jed stayed with her, though, not once leaving her side. But he didn't say anything, either, which only made her dig her tennis shoes harder into the soft, sandy surface of the ground.

She wanted to stop, turn around and head back to the beach. But since she didn't know how to fly a helicopter and she hadn't seen a pay phone around anywhere, that would be kind of foolish. Maybe there'd be a phone inside the "compound," and she could call the police.

She'd never felt more idiotic in her life.

She never trusted strangers, wasn't easy around people she didn't know. She wasn't her mother, didn't give blind faith to everyone like her mom did. But she'd sure as hell acted like her by giving her body and her trust over to Jed.

And look where it had gotten her.

They finally broke through the jungle. A thick stone wall surrounded them.

The compound. She swallowed, some part of her knowing once she walked through those gates, she wouldn't be able to get out.

Grange pulled a remote out of his pocket, pressed the button, and oversized double gates slowly opened. She walked through, then stopped to stare at the sheer size of the building they were heading toward. "Compound" seemed appropriate, though for some reason she had expected to see an austere, prison-like building, when instead it was a mansion.

They must have landed on the back side of the island, because she hadn't seen this when they arrived.

Lush greenery, beautiful walkways, an amazing pool that wound its way through the property and a waterfall at the edge of the pool. The house—if one could call it a house—was magnificent. Tall white archways, marble entrances and flooring, winding staircases, it was like a castle, with a mix of modern. She walked through with awe at the classic cherry wood dining table, then was struck dumb at the ultraexpensive marble layered throughout the expansive kitchen.

"I'm sure you're thirsty," Grange said as he leaned against the kitchen counter. "Coffee, something cool to drink?"

"Coffee, please."

She waited for a bevy of servants to come running, but Grange made the coffee himself.

"Is this your place?" she asked.

"No. It belongs to a friend. He's on a conference call right now. He'll be joining us shortly."

"So he lives here. By himself?"

Grange handed her the coffee. "Cream? Sugar?"

"Just cream."

He opened the refrigerator, grabbed a carton of cream, and handed it to her. Very understated for a place so elegant. She poured some and put it back in the refrigerator.

"Take a seat. We'll wait for Pete."

She sipped the coffee and nearly died. Whatever kind it was, it was heavenly to her sleep-starved and stressed-out body, so she focused on it instead of Grange and Jed, who huddled together just out of earshot for a few minutes before coming back in to sit across from her, staring at her as if she were some lab animal they intended to dissect after breakfast.

"Hungry?" Grange asked.

She shook her head.

"Sorry I'm late. Overseas call and I have to be on their time zone."

She looked up as a man entered the room. Dressed in khaki shorts and a flowered, button-down shirt, he was tanned, with a shock of white hair. Mid-fifties would be her guess.

"Elena Madison, this is Pete Northram, a friend of mine."

Elena nodded. Pete came over to shake her hand. "Miss Madison. So happy to have you as my guest."

So this was his place. "Guest, or prisoner?"

Pete frowned and looked at Grange. "She doesn't know why she's here."

He turned his attention back to her. "I assure you, Miss Madison. You are not a prisoner here. You're welcome to roam the house and the grounds. Make yourself at home."

She leaned back in the chair and wrapped her hands around the mug of coffee. "I kind of liked my house."

"You weren't safe there," Jed interjected. "Or maybe you forgot about the guy who broke in last night. The one with the gun."

She shot him a glare. "I appreciate you being there to take care of him. But we could have called the police."

"We don't want the police involved," Grange said.

This was getting ridiculous. "First, who is 'we,' and why not? And what's going to happen to the dead guy in my apartment? We're supposed to just leave him there?"

"He's been taken care of."

"What the hell does that mean?" she asked Grange. "Who *are* you people?"

For the first time in the short period of time since she'd met him, Grange let down the façade of military bearing. He seemed to slump in the chair and ran his fingers through his hair.

"I know you want to protect her, Grange, but she has to know the truth," Pete said. "Then maybe she can help."

He shook his head. "Not supposed to work that way. I promised. That's why I sent Jed."

"What? Why you sent Jed to do what?" She stood, tired of being the last person to know anything, and having a very bad feeling she'd been used. She cast her gaze to Jed, who was looking at her with a solemn expression that screamed guilt.

She palmed her stomach, suddenly feeling sick. The oversized kitchen seemed to close in on her and she had to get out of there. She pushed away from the table and walked out of the room, eyeing the double doors leading to the backyard, the early morning sunshine and the pool area.

No one stopped her. She didn't see guards, so she headed toward the edge of the pool, kicked off her shoes and sat down, dipping her feet in the heated water.

Thankfully, no one had followed her because her head spun and she needed to process what Grange had said.

*Not supposed to work that way*. What wasn't supposed to work what way?

*I promised*. Promised who?

*That's why I sent Jed*. This was the worst. Jed had been some kind of plant, sent to her to do what? Their meeting hadn't been coincidental; it had been orchestrated to end up this way, to bring her here. Everything that had happened between them had been a lie.

Everything she had been feeling for him had been real. Her stomach twisted and tears pricked her eyes. This was not the time to be a girl wracked with emotions. Not when she was in the middle of something she didn't understand, kidnapped and tossed on an island with three strangers. Her life was in danger and she needed to keep a clear head.

Jed could just go fuck himself.

"Elena."

So much for time alone to think. At least it wasn't Jed. Right now she'd deliver a punch to his midsection that, twelve-pack abs or not, would rock his world.

Grange came and pulled up a chair next to her.

"We need to talk."

She peered up to him. "It's about time somebody said something to me. I've been kidnapped and lied to."

"You weren't kidnapped. You're being protected."

"From whom, exactly?"

"Someone who has a vendetta against me."

She pulled her feet out of the water and turned to face him. "What? What does that have to do with me?"

"It's kind of a long story, and you aren't going to like a lot of it, but bear with me while I explain it to you."

She nodded. "Go ahead."

"Your mother is missing."

Her heart skipped a beat. "Missing?"

"You already know that, don't you?"

She shrugged, refusing to give him any more information than necessary. "I haven't been able to get hold of her, but that's not unusual for my mother. She's often out of touch."

"I know. But this time is different. You can call her phone and leave a message and she'll always get around to calling you back. She hasn't, has she?"

Elena didn't answer.

"And as flaky as she is, if you need her, she'll be there for you. Isn't that right?"

She narrowed her gaze. "You know my mother?"

"Yes."

"Do you know where she is?"

"No. But I've been trying to find her for the past month. She's never out of touch this long."

"What is your relationship with my mother, Grange?"

He looked at her for the longest time.

"She's my sister."

Elena didn't believe it. Not for one second.

"My mother is an only child."

"No, she's not. I'm her brother."

"Bullshit." She pushed off and stood, then started toward the house. Grange stopped her by stepping in front of her.

"Elena, your mother is my sister. She was born Carla Suzanne Lee on January twenty-fifth, 1957."

"Easy enough information to obtain."

"Ask me anything about your mother."

"Who was her best friend in high school?"

"Trick question. It was Bobby Ross. She befriended him in study hall freshman year. They never dated, became best friends and were inseparable throughout high school. Bobby was a war-protesting, antiestablishment, pot-smoking hippie, just like your mother right up until he got accepted to Harvard. Then he had a complete turnaround and decided he wanted to be a lawyer.

And not a people's lawyer, either, but a corporate one. Your mother was devastated because she lost her best friend."

Elena eyed him suspiciously, still not convinced.

"Keep talking."

"Despite her big talk about communing with nature, she loves meat, especially hamburgers. Her favorite is smothered in steak sauce with cheddar cheese on top. She hates tomatoes and is allergic to peanuts. She has a purple birthmark on the back of her neck and a scar on her scalp where her hairline meets her forehead, on the left side. It happened when we were kids. She was eight, I was twelve. We were playing on some equipment at the gym and your mom was a tomboy when she was a kid, so she always played with the boys. I pushed her, she fell and hit her head on the edge of the cement. She got sixteen stitches and a concussion, and I got grounded for two weeks."

"She told me about the scar. Said one of the boys in the neighborhood pushed her. And she never told me she had a brother."

"Because it wasn't safe for her."

Elena frowned. "Who the hell *are* you?"

"I'm a retired U.S. Marine general. I work for the government running an undercover operation. Jed works for me."

Of course he did. And she'd been just a job.

Ignoring the hurt of that revelation, she asked, "What kind of undercover work?"

"I run a crew of Harley-riding operatives. They do some down-and-dirty special ops work as bikers, usually infiltrating biker gangs involved in smuggling, gun running or drug operations."

"Sounds fun."

He laughed. "It can be an adventure, but also dangerous. And in my line of work and the things I've done both in the military and in my special ops work over the years, I've made a lot of enemies. It caused me to cut ties with my family—with your mother—because I didn't want anyone using her—or you—to get to me."

She stared at him, at this man who looked so hard. Could he have that much of a soft side? "You cut yourself off from us to keep us safe?"

"I tried to. I stayed in touch with Carla to the best of my ability so I could make sure you both were taken care of. Our parents died. She had no one to take care of her and didn't exactly do the best job taking care of herself. And then you came along, so I had to make plans for your well-being, but I couldn't play an active role in your life. I'm sorry for that, but it was necessary."

"The money for the shop. That was you?"

He didn't say anything.

All this time she thought the only family she had was her flighty, undependable mother.

She had an uncle. And as she looked at his face, she could see the resemblance between him and her mother. The eyes were the same color, the chin the same. They could even have the same smile, except that Grange had yet to offer one up.

"So what does all this mean? Do you think someone connected my mother to you and kidnapped her? Is that why you sent Jed out to watch over me?"

"Yes. And yes."

At least he wasn't bullshitting her, pretending to be someone he wasn't.

"Why didn't Jed just tell me right off who he was?"

"Because that wasn't his assignment. We didn't know for sure if someone would come after you, and I didn't want to scare you. My intent was for you to never know about me unless absolutely necessary. Until the attacks started up, until someone broke into your apartment with the intent to kidnap you or possibly hurt you, Jed's assignment was to watch over you. If we could have found your mother and no one came after you, you would have never known about me."

And Jed would have disappeared in a puff of smoke after that.

*Way to go, Elena.* She'd guarded her heart so carefully all these years, never letting anyone get close. Then the one guy . . .

She could sure pick them, couldn't she?

"You ready to go inside? We can talk more with the team about strategy."

She wasn't ready to face Jed, but she needed to find her mother. "Sure."

Grange held out his hand. She took it.

"I have an uncle."

For the first time, he cracked a smile. And there it was. Her mom had that exact same lopsided half smile. Her heart tugged.

"You do. I've always been here for you, Elena. I always will be."

She missed her mother, and for the first time realized how serious this all was. She nodded and they went back inside. The smell of bacon made her stomach rumble. She followed the scent and saw Jed in the kitchen fixing breakfast. Pete had disappeared again.

"Smells good," Grange said. "I'm going to go check in at headquarters, see what's going on with the current missions. Don't eat it all before I get back."

"No guarantees, General." Jed was working busily in the kitchen and didn't bother looking up. He had a pan of bacon going, one with eggs, and another with pancakes. The toaster flipped out four slices. He grabbed them, slathered them with butter and threw them on a stack, flipped the pancakes, turned the bacon and stirred the eggs.

"I thought you said you couldn't cook."

He didn't meet her gaze as she stepped fully into the kitchen. "I might have exaggerated that part."

"You lied." She took over the bacon and eggs while he concentrated on the pancakes.

Now he did turn to face her. "Yes. I lied. Part of the job sometimes."

She grabbed the bacon with the tongs and put it on the plate, then added more into the pan, stepping back when it sizzled and popped. "You're really good at it."

"Cooking?"

"Lying."

He stacked the pancakes on a platter, then leaned his hip against the counter. "Look, Elena. I'm sorry about not telling you who I really was."

She couldn't look at him, not when her emotions were so raw. "You could have kept your distance from me."

"I could have." His voice lowered. He moved in and put his arms around her. "I tried to, but it didn't work. And what happened between us wasn't part of the job."

She ached, partly because she was hurt, but also because she needed to feel his arms around her again, to know that what had happened between them had been real.

He tipped her chin up with his fingers, forcing her to meet his gaze. He looked as wounded as she felt inside.

"How am I supposed to believe anything you say now?"

"I don't know. I'm still Jed. I just have a different background and a different job."

"So everything you told me was bullshit."

"Yes."

She sucked in a breath and pulled out of his embrace, grabbed the tongs and turned the bacon. "All lies. Everything."

"No. Not everything."

"That smells great, and I'm starving," Pete said.

She blinked back tears as Grange and Pete entered the room. She and Jed finished cooking. Everyone piled up their plates and took a seat at the kitchen table.

Pushing thoughts of Jed aside, she turned her focus on Pete. "You live here alone?"

He nodded as he munched on a piece of bacon. "I won it from a sheik in a high-stakes poker game."

She laughed. "You did not."

"Actually, he did," Grange said.

Her eyes widened. "Seriously? The sheik bet his house? This house?"

"This house was nothing to him. To people like us, it would be like betting pocket change. Losing it made him laugh."

"As I recall," Grange said, "he wasn't happy when he lost that hand. Or the house."

"That's because he thought he had me beat."

"What did you have to wager?" Elena asked Pete.

"Not a house, that's for sure. I think it was my diving watch. The sheik liked all the bells and whistles on it."

"He put this house up against a watch?"

"It was a nice watch," Grange said.

She shook her head. "So you live out here in this—palace—all by yourself?"

Pete got up and took his plate into the kitchen, started running water. "No. I travel quite a bit for my job. But I come here when I want some privacy."

She leaned back in the chair. "Yeah, I imagine you get plenty of that here."

Grange picked up her plate. She stood. "I can do that."

"You and Jed cooked. Pete and I will clean up."

She turned her attention on Jed. He shrugged. "It's the rule. Whoever cooks, the other cleans up."

She liked that rule, just didn't expect them to follow it. Seeing two men in their fifties doing the dishes kind of surprised her.

She stood and leaned over the counter, watching them. "Your wives must appreciate all this domesticity."

"Don't have one," Grange said.

Pete didn't say anything, and since he didn't offer information, she didn't want to pry. Maybe he had an ugly divorce in his past and was still sensitive about it.

"So how do you two know each other?" she asked Grange.

"We did military time together. Met each other in boot camp, have been friends ever since," Grange said.

"We had the fortune—or maybe misfortune," Pete said with a laugh, "to be stationed at the same places time and time again. We kept running into each other, so we became friends. I never would have made it through some of the tough times in my life without Grange."

Grange squeezed Pete's shoulder. Pete nodded and they went back to cleaning the kitchen, laughing and cracking jokes as if that whole sentimental moment hadn't just happened.

Elena wondered what that exchange was about.

When they finished the dishes, they led her down the hall and into Pete's office. He had a giant screen and multiple computers going. It looked more like a war room. They sat at a large table in the center of all the whirring gadgets and multiple screens.

"Okay, let's see what we can do to find your mother," Pete said, grabbing a keyboard.

"We followed her cell movements, but as far as we've been able to track, her phone was last used at the pier at Daytona Beach over three weeks ago. No activity since, so the cell might have been tossed."

Elena shook her head. "She'd never toss her cell phone. She's always on the move and it's our only way to stay in touch with each other. She might shun other modern conventions—like a regular job, computers, a permanent address and the like—but she does try to stay in touch with me via her cell because she knows I go crazy and worry about her if she doesn't."

"Ditto," Grange said. "We have regular weekly check-ins and she doesn't fail at those, which is why I was concerned when we had no contact. When I found the cell hadn't moved from the pier, I knew she was in trouble."

"You track her via GPS," Elena said.

Grange nodded. "I had to for her own safety. Otherwise, I tried not to interfere in her life, or yours. Once I determined she was off the grid, I sent Jed in to cover you and I came in to try and locate her."

"So you follow me via my phone, too?"

"Yes."

At least he was honest. She wasn't sure she liked that.

"No one follows you around, Elena. You just go about the business of your life. Your patterns are tracked, and as long as you don't deviate from them, then I know you're safe. But if someone took you, I had to know about it."

There were all kinds of things wrong with violating her privacy, but she wasn't going to get into it with him now. Her primary concern was finding her mother. "Your GPS tracking didn't help keep my mother safe, did it?"

He didn't flinch or look away. "No, it didn't. But I'm going to find her."

"How? She has one credit card she rarely uses. She likes to live by the cash rule."

Grange grimaced. "I know. Not that it would matter. I don't

think she voluntarily tossed her phone in the trash and is out somewhere partying and shopping. I think someone took her."

"So how do we find her?"

"We retrace her steps, figure out where she was, who were the last people to see her when she disappeared. If we can get a lead, we can maybe find out who took her. I can't move on anyone until I know that."

"Okay. How can I help?"

"You know her movements better than anyone. Where she goes, who she hangs out with, where she stays."

"She has some friends who might be able to help."

"I'll need names and addresses," Grange said.

"You're going to go talk to them?"

"Yes."

She laughed. "They won't give you any information on my mom. They'll talk to me, though."

He shook his head. "You're not leaving the island. It's not safe for you."

She shrugged. "Go ahead and try, but I'm telling you it's a waste of your time."

She wrote down the names and addresses of her mother's friends, then handed them to Grange. "Why didn't you just come to me right away? We could have done this a week ago."

"It was important for me to keep my distance from you. At the time, I was chasing other leads on your mother, anyway. And we didn't want to involve people she knew. The less people involved the better. Now that someone has targeted you, too, everything has changed, including how we approach looking for her."

She nodded, knowing nothing about how one searched for someone who was missing. Or taken.

Her worry about her mother increased.

Grange and Pete prepped to leave. Pete changed into a pair of khaki pants and another flowered shirt. Grange stayed in his camo pants and beige shirt.

She laughed at him. "Now I'm sure they won't talk to you, at least a couple of these people. If you go in there looking like a general, they'll probably hide their bongs and think you're DEA there to raid them."

"She's right, Grange. You need to look more like a local," Jed said.

Grange frowned. "This is what I wear."

"Think undercover," Jed said, then motioned to Pete.

"You want me to dress like him?"

"Yes. That might at least get you near the front door," Elena said.

"No fucking way am I going to wear a shirt like that."

"Hey," Pete said. "This shirt is comfortable."

Grange crossed his arms, lifted his chin and glared at all of them. "This is ridiculous."

"You want to find your sister, or you want to maintain military bearing?" Pete asked.

Finally, he sighed. "Fine."

Grange trudged off behind Pete.

"Really? That's all he ever wears?" Elena asked Jed.

"Those are the only clothes I've ever seen him dressed in."

She went in the living room and sat on one of the plush couches, grabbing a pillow to her stomach. The sheik lived well. Or, she supposed, now Pete did.

When Grange and Pete came back out, she had to stifle a laugh. He and Pete could be brothers, both in khaki pants, sandals and wildly colored flowery print shirts.

Grange's mouth was twisted as if he were in pain.

"You'll definitely blend in now," Jed said, doing his best to hide a smirk.

Grange shot Jed a death glare. "If you laugh, I'll make it hurt later."

Jed raised his hands. "I'm just saying you're appropriately dressed, General."

"This is the most uncomfortable thing I've ever worn," Grange mumbled.

Pete rolled his eyes and cast a look toward Elena and Jed. "It lacks a sufficient amount of starch for his liking."

Elena snickered.

"We're out of here. We'll report in when we have something," Grange said. "Elena, there are clothes for you in the bedroom down the hall. Jed can show you. Take a shower, a nap, whatever you need to do to feel comfortable."

"Good luck," Elena said.

Within a few moments she heard the sound of the helicopter. Her stomach tightened and her lighthearted mood fled.

She was alone—she supposed she was alone, since she had yet to see anyone else wandering the house—with Jed now. She caught him out of the corner of her eye, leaning against one of the stone pillars in the oversized room.

"Hopefully they'll find a lead."

She nodded.

"Grange is the best at what he does. He'll find your mom."

She didn't answer.

"Elena, I'm sorry I couldn't have been honest with you. I was doing my job."

She shot him a look. "So when you were doing me, you were doing your job?"

His brow furrowed. "You know it wasn't like that."

"Do I?"

She shot off the couch and started to walk away, then stopped, realizing she had no idea where to go. This wasn't her house. So far she'd been outside and in the kitchen. She knew the path to the helipad. Other than that—clueless.

There was no place to run, but she'd be damned if she'd stay here like a trapped animal and make small talk with Jed or listen to his lies.

"Where's my room?"

He lifted his arm and pointed. "Down that hallway. Third door on the left."

She started in that direction.

"Elena."

She paused. "What?"

"At some point you're going to have to talk to me."

Wanna bet? She did a quick-step down the hall, found her room and shut and locked the door.

The room was a palace, just like the rest of the house. It was oversized, ostentatious, with floor-to-ceiling windows overlooking the pool and gardens. She flung herself onto the bed, sinking into the creamy duvet that wrapped itself around her with a comforting caress.

Exhaustion took hold. She wanted to forget everything, to shut it all out like a bad nightmare. Maybe if she took a short nap, she'd feel better. She was bitchy and short-tempered, especially with Jed, who had only been doing his job.

She rolled over onto her back.

His job. Right. A job that hadn't required him to sleep with her, to engage with her emotionally, to smile at her and make her—

Make her what? Start to think she was falling in love with him?

He hadn't *made* her do anything. He hadn't made her any

promises. He'd been there, been available and hot and sexy, and she'd been all too eager to throw herself at him. It wasn't like he'd forced himself on her. He'd done his job by staying close to her. What had happened between them had been mutual, but she sure as hell had been blaming him for everything, hadn't she?

She threw her arm over her head to shut out the streaming light and closed her eyes.

# ELEVEN

Jed held his breath and dove down to the bottom of the pool, skimming across from one end to the other. He pushed off the deep end and broke the surface, his lungs burning as he swallowed in oxygen. Then he turned, dove down and did it again, forcing himself to drive harder, to increase his speed, to push himself past the point of endurance.

When he came up for air the fourth time, he was breathless and wasted, and this time he hadn't been thinking of Elena the entire time he was under.

He swam to the edge and hopped out, wiped his hands on the towel and checked his phone to make sure Grange hadn't called or texted.

Nothing yet, but it had only been a few hours. He wouldn't expect to hear from them for a while.

He turned, pushed off and plunged down again, forcing his body to remain submerged while he swam the bottom of the pool from end to end. When he surfaced this time, Elena stood at the edge, watching him.

He shook the water out of his eyes and stared at her. She was wearing an orange bikini. Nothing overly sexy, just a two-piece thing. Except anything she wore was sexy because of her curves.

And because it was Elena. She could have put a burlap sack on her body and he'd think she looked hot.

She cocked her head to the side. "You trying to drown yourself down there?"

"No. It's an endurance exercise."

She took a seat at the edge of the pool and dangled her legs in the water. "I was beginning to think I was going to have to jump in and rescue you. You were down there a long time."

"I'm used to it."

"Obviously."

She was talking to him. Something had changed from two hours ago when she'd stormed off to the bedroom. Jed didn't want to do anything to piss her off, so he turned and resumed swimming, this time doing regular laps. She stayed at the edge of the pool, watching him.

If that's what she wanted to do, fine. It didn't bother him at all.

Much.

Except when she leaned back on her hands, her body stretched out to the sun, reminding him of what it was like to make love to her. The water in the pool was heated, and so was he. He swam to the edge and climbed out, grabbed his towel and hoped for a cold breeze to chill him out.

Elena slipped into the water, sank in over her head, then popped out and swam. Her strokes were strong and confident as she did laps. He climbed into the chair and watched her body curl from side to side as she took a breath, then put her face back in.

Even at swimming she was elegant and beautiful.

And gave him a hard-on.

He thought about going inside but didn't want to leave her alone out here, so he was just going to have to suck it up and suffer.

She finally stopped, came to the steps and walked out, water dripping off her body. His gaze caught on one line of water running between her breasts. It slid between the thin strip of fabric, down her ribs and over her belly, dipping into the front bottom of her swimsuit.

He shuddered, then lifted his gaze to her face. She'd stopped in front of him, grabbed the towel in the chair next to him and took a seat.

"What's the deal between Grange and Pete?"

He arched a brow. "What do you mean?"

"I saw a moment between them. Something emotional about Grange being there for Pete during a rough time in his life."

Jed shrugged. "Not my story to tell. You'll have to ask Grange or Pete."

She sighed. "More secrets. Great."

"Pete lost his wife in the Beirut Embassy bombing in 1983."

Elena put her hand on her heart. "Oh, no."

Jed nodded. "Yeah. Pete and Grange were both Marines, both of them stationed in Beirut at the time of the bombing. Dina worked at the embassy. Grange was close to both of them, loved Pete's wife like a sister. I think it hit him as hard as it did Pete."

"I can't even imagine how tragic that must have been for Pete."

"Yeah. Grange said he questioned his own dedication to the military at that point, but Pete was determined. He was a strong sonofabitch, and he refused to let Dina's loss cripple him. He served honorably and has dedicated his life to bringing down the bastards who preyed on his country and on the weak. When he left the military, he did some time with the CIA, then special ops work, tracking missing persons, mercenary jobs, anything that served his country in whatever capacity they needed him to. And through it all he and Grange have stayed in touch and remained friends. They're like brothers."

Elena leaned back. "Wow. It's good that Pete had Grange to lean on. What a terrible loss for him. So he never remarried?"

"No. Grange said Pete always felt Dina was it for him, and no other woman could come close."

Elena sucked in a breath and stared out over the water and the jungle beyond it before turning back to face him.

"Okay, Jed. Tell me who you really are."

He swung his legs over the side of the chaise to face her.

"I grew up in Maryland. Went to Georgetown. Wasn't the best student, but I got by. I liked to party and gave my parents a hard time. They were good to me, sacrificed a lot to give me a good education. I didn't appreciate it. They died in a car accident when I was in my second year of college."

She gasped, leaned over and grabbed his wrist. "Oh, God. I'm so sorry."

He stared down at the water dripping on the ground between them, the memories thick as fog rising up to swallow him. "I don't remember much about that time. I tried to bury it like I buried them. My dad had a distant cousin who tried to step in and help, but I didn't want anyone. After my parents died, I lost it at school. I'd barely had the drive and ambition to start with. I dropped out of school and wandered aimlessly for a year, doing a lot of drinking and navel gazing. Then I pulled my head out of my ass and realized I wasn't going to honor my parents by becoming an alcoholic. So I joined the Marines, did two tours of duty in Iraq and Afghanistan. After that I joined the FBI."

She squeezed his hand.

He lifted his head. Her eyes shimmered with tears. Sympathy, not pity. He knew the difference. Thank God. He couldn't handle anyone feeling sorry for him, had had enough of it to last him a lifetime.

"The FBI was okay but boring. No challenge in it, no action. That's when Grange found me and offered me a job with the Wild Riders."

She arched a brow. "That's what his organization is called?"

"Yeah." He quirked a smile. "They're a wild bunch, all right. But good people. Great agents. And I like the job so far. I'm still new at it, but it gives me a taste of adventure and some action instead of desk jockeying or paper pushing."

"You're an adrenaline junkie."

He shrugged. "Maybe a little. I just want to do something to serve my country. And maybe help people."

She grazed her thumb over his hand. "Your parents would be proud of all you accomplished."

Hearing her say that made his heart clench. "I'd like to think so."

"Does it still hurt?"

"Not as raw now as it was in the beginning. I still miss them, wish I could pick up the phone and hear my mom's voice or my dad's laugh. I took it for granted that they'd always be there for me. You don't appreciate what you've lost until you don't have it anymore."

She stood. He figured she was going inside.

"Sit back in the chair."

He did, and she shocked the hell out of him by climbing in the chair with him. The chaises were oversized and could easily fit two, but God, he hadn't expected this, hadn't expected her to snuggle her body against his and lay her head on his chest.

He was afraid to touch her, but when she pulled his arm around her and she moved in even closer, he gave up trying to figure out what the hell was going on and just went with it. He tugged her in.

"Thank you," she said. "I know that wasn't easy for you to tell me, and I appreciate you sharing a little piece of who you are."

"It's okay."

"Do you ever talk about it?"

"Not really. No one to talk to."

She tilted her head back. "No other family, friends, girlfriends or anything?"

He smiled down at her. "No family. Guys don't open up to each other about shit like that. And I don't have girlfriends."

She gave him a dubious look. "I'm sure you've had girlfriends before."

"I've had women in my life before. No one I'd consider a girlfriend and no one I'd want to talk to about this. My lifestyle hasn't been conducive to anything long term."

"I guess that makes sense. Hard to establish a relationship when you're moving around all the time."

She smoothed her hand over his chest. Jed gritted his teeth, trying to remember she was just making conversation and offering comfort. His dick wanted a whole different kind of comfort, which it wasn't going to get. He hoped she wouldn't notice.

"Do you ever want to settle down and raise a family?"

"I guess. Someday."

"What will you do then? Get a job as an in-town bodyguard or something?"

He laughed. "I've never given it any thought. I've been pretty much living for the moment the last ten years or so, not thinking of the marriage-and-family thing."

She swept her hand over his shoulder, down his chest and

across his stomach. God help him, this was torment. The soft hand of a woman over his stomach, knowing that if her fingers crept just a little lower and she'd hit the jackpot? Yeah, that was torture.

"You're getting hard, Jed."

"I was kind of hoping you wouldn't notice."

"Kind of difficult not to. It's rather obvious."

"Is this because you feel sorry for me? Because of my parents?"

She paused, lifted herself up and stared at him for a few seconds.

"No. It's you I want. Did you feel sorry for me because of my mother?"

He pulled her down on top of him and tangled his fingers in her hair. "I never once thought about your mother when I was making love to you. The only person I thought about then was you."

He put his lips on hers, tasting her. He'd missed her flavor, the feel of her mouth against his. After last night, he wanted more. Maybe they didn't have anything beyond just this assignment, but he didn't care. He'd only had a brief taste of her and he wasn't nearly done with her yet. He slid his tongue between her teeth and deepened the kiss, waiting for her to pull away.

She didn't, instead walked her fingers south and rested them on the top of his board shorts, right where his cock was about to burst through the material and leap into her hand.

When she started to rub his cock through the material, he tensed and pressed against her, unable to resist how damn good it felt. He wanted more, wanted the feel of his cock against her hand.

He untied his shorts and shoved them down. His cock sprang out and she sat up, straddled the chair and grasped his dick in her hand. She slid his shaft between her fingers then squeezed him with both hands.

"God, that feels good." He leaned back, not sure whether he enjoyed the sensation or watching the look of utter rapture on her face as she stroked him. Both were making his balls tighten.

He wanted to bury himself inside her and forget she had ever been an assignment—that she still was. This wasn't part of his job. He didn't have to pretend to get close to her anymore, because this was as close as he was ever going to get.

And this time, she was here because it was where she wanted to be.

As she stroked him, she leaned forward, her breasts pressing against the flimsy material of her swimsuit.

"Take it off," he said, motioning to her top.

Her lips curved. She knew damn well she was the one with all the power right now. She released his cock and reached back to untie the string at her neck, teasing him by holding the material while she untied the back. Then she pulled the top away and revealed her breasts.

Her nipples tightened under his gaze. Jed sucked in a hard breath as she leaned forward and captured his cock between her lips, rolling her tongue around the crest. He jerked against her tongue, the strong urge to let go almost more than he could bear.

But her sweet, hot mouth surrounded him, and he wanted more of it, knew he could hold on if she'd just—

Oh, yeah. She took his cock between her lips, took her time sliding her mouth over his cock. It was the sweetest hell. Sweat beaded and ran down his back as he fought to hold on, to keep from jettisoning into her mouth. He needed this to last, wanted to feel every second as she squeezed his shaft with tight suction, only to let go and swirl her tongue over every inch of him as if his cock were an ice cream cone.

He swept his hand over her hair as she rose to the tip and licked the crest. She lifted her gaze to his and smiled, cupped his balls and gave them a gentle squeeze. He swallowed when she gave him a knowing grin, then covered his dick with her mouth and went down on him again, stroking him with her mouth in a way that made him certain this torment was going to end in a hurry.

He gripped the edge of the chaise and pushed against her mouth, feeding her his cock as the freight train of orgasm rushed through his nerve endings.

"I'm going to come, Elena. Fuck, I'm gonna come."

She gripped the base of his cock and stroked him, forcing his shaft deep into her mouth.

He let out a loud groan, wrapped his hand around her hair and held her there while he erupted, shuddering as he climaxed.

Elena continued to suck him as he came, holding tight to his cock while he gave her everything he had. When he collapsed against the chair, she swept her tongue over the head of his cock, then let go and raised her head, licked her lips and smiled at him.

She was a vision. Topless, her cheeks pink, her hair wild around her face and her lips moist. If he wasn't utterly spent, he'd pull her on top of him and fuck her.

But he was going to need a few minutes until he was ready for that, which didn't mean he couldn't get her ready.

He pulled her onto his lap and kissed her, tasting his salty come on her lips and tongue. He licked her lips, then dove inside for a deeper taste of her. He kissed her jaw, licking along the column of her throat.

"Jed," was all she said.

He bent her back, holding her with his arm across her back while he took a nipple in his mouth, flicking it hard with his tongue, then sucking it deeper between his lips.

Elena let out a soft cry and reached for his arms, digging her nails into his skin as he moved from one nipple to the other to suck them.

She liked to have her nipples sucked, the harder the better. His dick began to stir to life again. No surprise, since she was so responsive to everything he did.

He slipped his hand under her butt, lifted her and swapped positions with her, leaning her back against the chaise. He draped her legs on either side of the chair, spread her out, then sat back and stared at her.

He could take a picture of her like this, her legs open, her nipples still wet from his mouth, and her eyes half-hooded, watching him. She tucked her bottom lip between her teeth and he smiled up at her.

"Now I'm going to lick your pussy and make you scream."

Her eyes opened. "Are you sure there's no one else around?"

He shrugged. "Don't know. Don't care. Either way, it's a little late to be worried about that, don't you think?"

She let out a soft laugh. "I guess you're right."

He rolled over to his stomach and fit himself between her legs. He swept his thumbs over her inner thighs and felt her tremble.

"Easy, baby." He reached up and untied one of the strings on the side of her bikini bottoms and pulled it away, revealing her sex. He breathed in the honeyed scent of her, rich with her desire. He rubbed his fingertips over her plump pussy lips. The way she arched toward his touch told him exactly how ready she was for him, so he slid his thumb inside her pussy and gently fucked her with it.

She was wet, and he was hard again, ready to be inside her. He could already imagine her tight walls squeezing his cock.

He twisted his thumb around her pussy, leaned in and licked around her clit.

"Oh, God, that's so good," she said.

He pulled his thumb out and slid two fingers inside her, fucking her while he sucked her clit.

She gasped and shoved her pussy at his face.

"Ohhhh. Yes, Jed. More, just like that."

He loved a responsive, communicative woman. He gave her what she asked for, pumping his fingers inside her, swirling his tongue over the tight knot of flesh until she squirmed against him.

"Jed, that's going to make me come."

Exactly what he wanted from her. Her pussy squeezed his fingers and he gave her more of the same. She lifted her butt, driving against him, pulling his fingers deeper inside. He put his mouth over her clit and sucked, and she cried out. She raised her head and looked down at him, reaching for his hand.

"Jed."

He held onto her as she climaxed, watching her as she let go. The intensity of emotions crossing her face as she gave him her body was amazing.

And when he felt the pulses ease, he withdrew his fingers and scooped her up in his arms. She straddled his waist and held on as he grabbed his phone and carried her inside to his bedroom.

She kept her gaze on his as he walked the long hallway.

"Tired of the great outdoors?" she asked as he pushed the door open.

"No, but the condoms are in here."

She laughed.

He set her on the bed, fished the box of condoms out of the bathroom and came back to her. He dropped his shorts while she untied the other side of her bikini and removed it, leaving her naked.

He got the condom on in record time and climbed onto the

bed, drawing Elena next to him. She threaded her fingers through his hair and he took a moment to just breathe.

Which was all she gave him, because she reached for his cock, caressing him with full, measured strokes. His breathing quickened. He raised her leg and placed it over his hip, then entered her with a quick thrust.

Her eyes widened, then seemed to melt as her heat surrounded him. He paused, feeling her body tighten and pulse, wanting to savor the sensation. But he couldn't hold back the need to move inside her, so he pulled back and drove deep.

She gasped, reaching for him to hold on as he powered inside her.

She pushed at him, so he rolled onto his back, letting her take the lead. She climbed onto him, straddling him.

Oh, yeah. Nothing he loved more than a beautiful woman on top. Her breasts spilled toward him when she leaned forward, giving him access to touch her as he pleased. And he did, reaching for her nipples, plucking them until she moaned.

She laid her hands on his chest and rolled against him, giving them both exactly what they needed. She rocked his world by rising up, then sliding ever so slowly back down onto his dick.

"This is slow torture," he said.

She smiled at him, then surged forward, arching her back and giving him an excellent view of her pussy. He swept his thumb over her clit and she hissed, lifting just enough so he could watch where they were connected, could see her pussy gripping him as she slid back down onto him, his cock disappearing inside her.

Then she increased the tempo, her body tightening around him as she bent over him. His balls tightened—he was close, and so was she. He grasped her hips and began to lift her up and down on his shaft, their gazes locked.

She dug her nails into his shoulders. "Jed."

"Yeah. Come on my dick, Elena. Squeeze me with your pussy and make me come, too."

She was panting, her breath against his face, her lips parted. Their bodies slid together in a sweat-soaked union until Elena laid herself fully on top of him. She pounded his balls as she fought for her orgasm by grinding against him. He gritted his teeth while holding on, wanting her to go first.

Damn, she was beautiful, her face flushed, her breasts thrust forward as she moved against him. His balls tightened and he held onto her hips, rolling her clit against him.

Her lips parted and she met his gaze, her eyes widening as she came. Her pussy squeezed his cock and he let out a yell as she tore his orgasm from him. He felt it come at him from the top of his spine all the way through every nerve ending as he emptied inside her while she bucked against him and cried out, shoving her pussy onto his dick.

She fell forward and lay on top of him when it was over.

Christ, she'd shattered him. Limp and sweaty, all he could do was hold her, stroke her back and listen to her breathe. He sure as hell couldn't move and didn't even want to. Elena didn't seem to want to move, either.

Fine with him, because that had been intense. He'd had great sex before, but something more than just great sex had passed between them.

He lifted her, swept her damp hair away from her face. She looked down at him, not smiling, just studying his face. He wondered if she was thinking the same thing.

What had just happened between them?

"Elena." He rubbed his thumb over her lip.

His cell phone rang.

Shit.

He reached over and grabbed it. "Yeah."

"It's Grange. We got nowhere here. We're going to need Elena's help to find her mother. We'll be back to pick you up in an hour."

"Got it. We'll be ready."

He clicked off, turned his attention back to her. Whatever had been between them, that look in her eyes, was gone now.

"Did they find anything?" she asked.

"No. They need your help."

She smiled. "I told them."

They climbed out of bed.

"I'll go take a shower. When will they be here?"

"About an hour."

She nodded and started to leave. Jed grasped her hand and pulled her against him, wrapping her in his arms for a deep kiss that lasted way longer than it should, considering Grange and Pete were already on the way.

He pulled back and studied her, wishing they hadn't lost that moment.

"One of these days we'll get to stay in bed without being interrupted."

She gave him a curious look. "I'd like that."

# TWELVE

lena took a shower, dried her hair and dressed in some of the clothes that had been left for her in the bedroom—a pair of capri pants and a T-shirt, along with some canvas shoes, which suited her just fine. It was a little creepy they had clothes for her, but whatever. Maybe they belonged to a relative or friend of Pete's. Either way, they fit.

Jed was already in the living room when she came out. He was dressed in dark cargo pants and a sleeveless shirt that showed off his tanned muscles and made her want to lick her lips. Or lick him. And despite having just had sex with him—she wanted to have sex with him.

Again.

What they'd just shared had seemed like more than sex. Afterward, he'd looked at her as if he'd wanted to say something. But then the phone had rung and they'd been interrupted. She wished it hadn't, but that was her being selfish. Finding her mother had to be first priority, not whatever was going on between her and Jed—which was likely nothing other than just really hot sex.

She heard the helicopter coming in.

"Let's go. We'll meet them at the beach," Jed said, sliding his gun into his pants.

She followed him down the path to the beach, climbed into the helicopter and they took off again.

They didn't talk until they landed again at the same spot where they'd taken off in the middle of the night. A beat-up, older-model, four-door sedan was waiting for them.

"Where's my Chevelle?"

"It's been garaged and is taken care of," Grange said. "Don't worry about it."

"And what about my shop? And Marco?" She'd been so wrapped up in her own issues and her mother, she'd totally forgotten about her business and her closest friend.

"We let Marco know—to the extent we can—what's going on," Grange said. "He's taking care of running the shop in your absence. We also have protection there in case someone comes in there looking for you and causes trouble."

She nodded, relieved she wouldn't have to worry about Marco's safety. "Okay. Thank you."

"Now we need your help with your mother's friends," Pete said. "I've been in intelligence my entire life, and I've never not been able to gather information."

"Until now," Grange said with a smirk.

"I told you they wouldn't tell you anything. My mother's friends are very loyal and they don't trust strangers. They must have sensed you were feds."

"Loyal my ass," Pete said. "Paranoid is more like it."

She leaned back and rested her head against the seat. "Same thing."

"Okay, so we'll hit all these locations again," Pete started.

"Wait." Elena topped him. "If they see me coming with you, they might not even talk to me. I need to go in alone."

Grange shook his head. "Not going to let you go anywhere alone. That makes you vulnerable to whoever has your mother. If they grab you, we're fucked."

She sighed. "Well, you two sure can't go with me."

"I'll go with her," Jed said. "Since you've both already been to those places, these people might not say anything, even in front of Elena. I'll be her boyfriend helping to find her mom."

Elena lifted her gaze to Jed. His expression revealed nothing.

"That'll work," Grange said. He looked at Elena.

She shrugged. "I guess so."

They dropped Grange and Pete off at a coffee shop. Jed took the car and they drove to the trailer park where Paco, one of her mother's oldest friends, lived. It was even more run down than the last time she'd been here trying to find her mother, which admittedly had been about five years ago.

Junked-out cars littered the landscape, along with bicycles and more kids and dogs than Elena could count. A few chickens squawked and ran across the gravel road where Jed parked.

"We walk from here," she said.

She started, but Jed grasped her hand.

"I'm supposed to be your boyfriend, remember? We need to look the part."

She looked down at his hand, then up at him. "Right."

He swirled his thumb over her hand. Goose bumps skittered up her arm.

"Stop that."

"You like it."

"I do." She kept walking, ignoring the stares they got as they made their way to Paco's trailer.

"They don't like strangers here, do they?" Jed asked.

"They grow weed in the woods back there. Of course they don't like strangers. Try not to look so much like a federal agent."

He snorted. "Yeah, I'll try."

They finally reached the trailer. Graffiti marked up the sides of the small single wide, mostly written in Spanish and various gang symbols. The screen door hung precariously to the side and there were what appeared to be bullet holes above the windows.

Elena couldn't believe her mother had stayed here.

A rough-looking kid about sixteen leaned against the open door of the trailer, making no attempt to hide the gun tucked in the front of his low-riding pants.

She felt the tension run all the way through Jed's body. She squeezed his hand and hoped he read her signal to stay calm. She'd hate for him to shoot this kid. She knew kids like him. They were more bravado than skill.

"Whatchootwowant?" he asked, a cigarette dangling from his lower lip.

"Paco around?"

"Who wants to know?"

"Tell him it's Elena, Carla Madison's daughter."

The kid threw a sneer at Jed. "Stay right there. You move, someone around here might kill you."

The kid disappeared inside.

"That boy has a bright future ahead of him."

Elena sighed. "I'm afraid not."

A man appeared at the entrance to the trailer, a trail of smoke and the distinct odor of pot wafting from the end of the joint he smoked. He was skinnier than she remembered, his dark pants hanging off him now. His white tank top hung loosely on his skeletal frame, and his dark greasy hair reached to his shoulders. He also appeared to be missing a few teeth as he grinned at her.

"Elena! It's been a long time, *chica*. *Como estas?*"

Elena grinned. "*Bueno*, Paco. How are you?"

He nodded. "Pretty fucking good. Who's the guy?"

"This is my boyfriend, Jed. He's cool. Jed, this is Paco."

Jed nodded. "Nice to meet you."

Paco nodded back. "He looks like a fed."

Jed coughed. "I get that a lot. My mom makes me cut my hair."

Paco laughed. "Ah. I understand. Must please the mamas, no?"

"What can you do?"

Jed was good at this.

"What can I do for you, Elena?"

"I'm out of touch with my mother. I was wondering if she'd passed by this way lately."

Paco frowned. "No, baby, I haven't seen your mama in a long time. Last time she was here was—hmmm, let me think—probably six months or so. Said she was going legit. Can you believe that shit?"

"No. I can't. What did she mean by that?"

"No idea. Said something about wanting to go back to school to finally finish up that degree she'd started. You know me, I'm always half buzzed anyway, so in one ear and out the other. But I haven't seen her since."

She couldn't help being disappointed, but Paco had no reason to lie to her. At least she hoped not. "Okay. Thanks, Paco. If you see her, could you tell her to call me?"

"You know I will. But you know what else, two jokers who also looked like feds stopped by here today looking for her."

She feigned surprise. "Really? What did they look like?"

Paco spat on the ground. "Tried to look like tourists, but I can spot a fed a hundred yards away. I sent them packing. They were lucky I didn't shoot them."

"I wonder why they would be looking for her?"

He shrugged. "No clue, baby girl. I hope your mama isn't in any trouble."

"God, I hope not, either. I guess I'll have to find her before they do."

"You do that. And if you need any help, you come get me. We'll get a posse out looking for her."

She climbed up the stairs and kissed his cheek. "*Gracias*, Paco. You take care of yourself."

"You, too, *chica*."

"Nice to meet you," Jed said with a nod.

"Take care of this lady," Paco said. "She's special."

Jed slung his arm around Elena. "I know she is. And I will."

They headed back to the car. Now that they had Paco's approval, no one watched them.

As they drove toward the next destination, Elena was silent, thinking about what Paco had said.

"What's wrong?" Jed asked.

"Paco said my mother was thinking of going back to school. I never knew she was in a degree program. She never told me about it."

"Maybe she didn't want you to know."

"It's possible. She rarely finished anything she started. And who knows, maybe it was just one of those bucket list items. You know, before I die, I want to climb Mount Everest, go to Italy, get a degree, et cetera, et cetera?"

"Or maybe she had a goal in mind and wanted to change her life."

Elena stared out the window. "Maybe."

An hour later they were in Cocoa Beach, in a completely different environment than the first location. Mitzie Winfield was a rich woman who'd lived a solitary existence since her third husband died in the eighties. Elena never quite understood how Mitzie and her mother got to be friends since Carla Madison was a no-material-things love child and as far removed from wealth and society as one could get.

But Mitzie and her mother were friends, and occasionally her mom would stay over at Mitzie's posh private home on the beach. They'd play cards and spend time on Mitzie's yacht and shop and go to all these parties. Her mother would tell her stories about spending a few weeks with Mitzie and all the wonderful adventures she had. For a while, Elena thought her mother was full of shit, but Carla took her daughter once to meet Mitzie, and Elena had been stunned to find out it was all true.

Mitzie loved Carla, and Elena figured it was the simplicity of her mother's existence that Mitzie appreciated. Or maybe because her mother didn't want anything from Mitzie other than her company. Even when they went shopping, Mitzie bought things for herself but her mom never let Mitzie buy anything for her other than lunch.

They arrived at the coral beach house and parked in front. Elena rang the doorbell. A waft of perfume greeted her.

Mitzie, well tanned, her makeup done to perfection as always, was dressed in a flowing beach dress.

"Can I help you?"

"Mitzie, I'm not sure if you remember me, but I'm Elena Madison, Carla's daughter."

Her eyes widened. "Oh, of course. Elena. Gosh, I haven't seen you in so long." She grasped Elena's hands in hers. "Where are my manners? Come in, dear."

Her kitten heels clapped across the polished floor as she led

them into the sunken living room. Elena felt like she should take
off her shoes when she sank into Mitzie's carpet, which matched
her shoulder-length white hair.

She turned and smiled.

"So tell me, who's your friend?"

"Mitzie Winfield, this is my boyfriend, Jed Templeton."

"Nice to meet you, ma'am," Jed said, shaking her hand.

"Aren't you a handsome devil? Nice catch, Elena."

Elena couldn't hold back the warm blush staining her cheeks.
"Thank you."

"I just made some tea. Would you like some?"

"We'd love some," Elena said.

"I'll just be a moment. It's a lovely day outside. We'll have it
on the terrace. Go have a seat out there."

Elena led Jed outside to the terrace.

"Nice view," he said.

"Yes, it is." She took a seat in one of the cushioned chairs.

Mitzi showed up a few minutes later with a tray.

"Let me help you with that," Jed said, standing to take the
tray from her and set it on the table.

"Oh, and he has manners, too," Mitzi said, watching as Jed
poured the tea and served it to them. "I like this young man."

Elena took the glass from Jed, her body heating as their gazes
met. "I do, too."

She took a sip of the tea. "This is wonderful, tea, Mitzie.
Thank you."

"I'm so glad you like it. So tell me what brings you here.
How's your mother?"

"That's why I'm here. I was wondering if you'd seen her
lately."

"No, I haven't. I was hoping she'd get in touch but I haven't
seen her in about six months."

"I see."

Mitzi laid her hand over Elena's. "Is something wrong?"

"I'm just out of touch with her and hoping to reconnect."

Mitzi waved her hand in the air. "Well, you know how your mother is. Always off on one adventure or another. And she's terrible about checking in. I always admonish her about that when she comes to see me. I try to call my friends once a week, just to chat. I wish your mother and I could do that."

"That would be nice."

"I even invited her to move in with me, you know."

Now that was a shocker. "You did? When?"

"Last time she was here. I told here she was getting too old to wander around like a vagabond. She needed to set down some roots, and I offered my home here as a place to plant her flag. God knows I have more space here than I know what to do with. And since I never had children, I have no grandchildren to come visit, so it's just me, all alone here in this rambling house on the beach. Your mother loves the water. I figured it would be a perfect place for her to settle, since she and I get along so well."

Elena leaned back in the chair with her glass. "And what did she say to that?"

"She thanked me profusely, of course. Your mother is always so incredibly polite. She said she'd give it some thought, but she was considering making other permanent plans with her life."

Again, more secrets. "Did she mention what those permanent plans were?"

Mitzie laughed. "No, she didn't. And despite my pressing her, she said she didn't have everything in place yet, but when she had it all figured out, she'd be sure to come by and tell me all about it. And that was the last time I saw her, the little devil. I've been dying of curiosity ever since."

And now, so was Elena.

Mitzie turned her attention on Jed, scoping him out like one would ripe tomatoes in the produce aisle. "So, Jed Templeton, tell me all about yourself. I need to decide if you're good enough for my friend Carla's daughter."

Elena looked at Jed, who cast a gorgeous smile at Mitzie, then made up a rather dazzling bunch of lies about who he was.

Of course, he was really good at it, but this time she couldn't fault him.

They finished their tea, visited with Mitzie for a while longer then left, with the promise to her that if they heard from Carla, they'd be sure to have her get in touch with Mitzie.

"Your mother has secrets," Jed said.

"Yes, she does. I'd like to know what the hell was going on with her and what she was planning to do to change her life."

Jed pulled onto the highway. "First, we have to find her. And no one seems to have seen her since she's been missing. It appears you're the last one to have had contact with her."

She wrinkled her nose. "That's not good."

The third person they went to see had a story much like the first two. Amanda was a hippie like her mother. She created glass art and Elena bought some of Amanda's work for her shop. Elena saw Amanda rather regularly, so she had nothing much to offer, and she was kind of an airhead.

"Oh, wow, you know, I haven't seen your mom for a while. I can't remember when. I think it was the art fair in November. She helped me with my booth."

Amanda, though in her fifties and her hair entirely gray, still wore pigtails, Birkenstocks and skirts that dusted the floor of her one-bedroom apartment. Her three cats wound around her ankles. And her voice was so soft Elena had to strain to hear her. Jed stood stoically in Amanda's colorful kitchen and let Elena ask all the questions.

"Are you sure it was all the way back in November? You haven't seen her since?" Elena had seen Amanda at least fifteen times since then. She would think Amanda might have mentioned not seeing her mother since then.

Amanda looked up at the ceiling as if she were hard in thought. "Uh, I don't know. We did a Christmas show, too. She might have been there, but that could have been Veronica with me. I can't recall."

How the woman was able to maintain a successful business, Elena didn't know. After spending a half hour grilling her, Elena knew they'd get nowhere with her. She thanked Amanda and they were off.

"What a ditz," Jed said as they left.

"She is, but she's also a brilliant artist."

"If you say so. Her stuff looked like flea market junk."

Elena laughed. "Clearly you don't have a discerning eye for art. There's a big difference in what she makes and your average crap."

"Well, you know what they say. I might not know art, but I know what I like."

They rendezvoused with Grange and Pete back at the restaurant.

"Anything?" Grange asked as they climbed back into the car.

"No solid leads on Carla's whereabouts. Her friends haven't seen her."

"Do you think they were telling the truth?"

Elena noticed he asked the question of Jed, not her.

"Yes. They all know Elena, and seemed to have no reason to lie to her."

"Hell. We're back to square one."

Elena folded her hands together on her lap and stared down at them.

Grange leaned forward in the seat and rubbed her shoulder. "We'll find her. I promise."

She nodded, but the more time that went by, the more she realized how she'd allowed her mother to slip away. She'd gotten so wrapped up in her life, in distancing herself from her mom, that she had no idea what her mother had been doing with her life. Her mom had all these secret plans about changing her life that she knew nothing about, because while her mother had been passing in and out of her life, Elena hadn't taken any time to sit down with her and just ask her what was going on. She couldn't recall when they'd last had lunch or dinner, or taken a few hours to sit down and talk with each other.

That was her fault. She liked her mother to check in now and then so she could be sure she was okay. Other than that, she really wanted nothing to do with her.

Had she subconsciously tried to push her mother out of her life?

Maybe that was why her mom was making all those changes . . . all those plans. She had no idea. And now she might never have the chance to ask her what those plans were. Even worse, her mom might not have the chance to act on them.

Grange's phone rang. He picked it up.

"Okay, when? Where? Two locations? That's not possible. Give me the intel on both."

Elena turned in her seat to see Grange jotting down notes.

"Got it. Thanks."

He hung up and instructed Jed to find a spot to pull over. He was on the beach highway, so he pulled over at a lookout point.

"Carla's credit card is showing usage."

Elena's heart rate sped up. "That's good, right? It's a lead."

"Could be. Problem is, it showed simultaneous usage at two different points of origin."

"You mean the card was used at two different places at the same time?" Elena asked.

Grange nodded.

"Were they online purchases? She shops online sometimes if she borrows Mitzie's computer."

"No. They were in person."

"It's a trap," Pete said.

Grange nodded. "That's what I'm thinking."

"We need to get Elena back to the island," Pete said.

"No," she said. "We need to follow those leads."

"Jed and I will follow the leads," Grange said. "We have to keep you safe."

"I'll get her back to the island," Pete said. "You two track down those credit card leads."

She cast her gaze at Jed. He knew she wanted to go, wanted to be with him when they found her mother.

"You should go with Pete. The island is the safest place for you right now."

Her heart sank. "I want to go with you."

"I know you do, but if either of these leads pans out and we head into danger, being with us is the last place you need to be."

"Agreed," Grange said. "And it's possible whoever has your mother thinks that's exactly what we'll do—that we'll bring you along with us. Which means it's the last thing we're going to do. Go with Pete and we'll report in as soon as we know something."

Jed started the car and headed back to the helicopter.

Pete got out and the pilot fired up the engine.

Grange held her hands. "This is the best lead we've gotten. Even if it's nothing more than a game someone's playing, it's a start, a way to track them and find your mother."

"Please be careful. I just found out I have an uncle. I'd hate to lose you."

He hesitated for a second, then pulled Elena into his arms for a hug. "I'm always careful."

He stepped back, cleared his throat. "Go with Pete. I'll worry less knowing you're with him."

She nodded and he walked away, leaving her with Jed.

She should leave. Pete was waiting for her. But something held her there.

She didn't want to go.

Jed moved next to her. "I know you want to come along, but it's not safe for you."

"I need to be there."

"Your safety has to come first."

The logical part of her knew that. She'd be in the way. She wasn't feeling very logical right now. She laid her hand on his chest. "You stay safe. If it's a trap . . ."

He wrapped her hand in both of his. "I'm good at taking care of myself."

She sighed. "Okay. Take double good care of yourself this time. I don't want anything to happen to you."

Jed cast a look at Grange, who leaned against the car, his arms crossed, staring at both of them.

"Ah, hell." He pulled Elena into his arms and kissed her soundly.

When he broke the kiss, she smiled at him.

"I'll be back soon. Stay close to Pete."

She nodded and squeezed his hand. "I will."

She climbed into the helicopter. As it rose, she watched Jed walk toward Grange.

# THIRTEEN

The silence in the car was deafening. The one thing Jed knew about Grange was that he didn't have to say much—or anything—to speak volumes about how he felt about something.

And he hadn't said a word since the helicopter lifted and they drove off.

Which meant Jed was going to have to speak first.

"I care about Elena."

No comment.

"I care a lot about her."

Still no comment.

"I realize that getting involved with her wasn't part of the assignment. It just happened."

Zero. Zip. Nada. Not even a glare in his direction.

"And frankly, sir, and with all due respect, my personal relationship with her is none of your business."

That got him a look. The death glare. The others had warned him about the death glare. They were right. That was some scary shit.

"You can stay the hell away from my niece, Templeton."

"Kind of hard to do, General, since my assignment consists of protecting her and working this case with you."

"You're off the case. As of right now."

"You're in charge and you have the right to do that. But I won't stay away from Elena."

"I can fire you."

"You can."

The silence this time stretched into five minutes. Then ten. A muscle in the general's jaw twitched. "You hurt her and I'll hunt you down like a rabid dog and shoot you."

"Okay. But I might be falling in love with her."

That got him another look. "Might?"

"Never been in love before, General. Not really sure if that's what this is or not, and circumstances haven't exactly been ideal for the two of us, if you know what I mean. But yes, I might be in love with her. I'd like to get this assignment over with, get a real relationship going with her and see if maybe she feels the same way."

"Hmph."

That was better than the death glare, at least. And the general hadn't shot him, so Jed would call that progress.

Now they had to find Elena's mother.

And he couldn't believe he'd just blurted out he was in love with Elena.

Was he? They barely knew each other. But what he felt was strong, something he'd never felt for any other woman before. When he wasn't with her, he wanted to be. That meant something.

And how did Elena feel about him?

They needed time together. Time that didn't involve danger and assignments, where they could just be two people hanging out together.

The general's niece. He was in love with the general's niece.

Christ, he sure could fuck up his life, couldn't he?

Grange drove them to the garage where Elena's car was housed. He tossed Jed the keys and gave him the address where one of the credit cards had been used.

"We're going to have to split up to save time. Follow this up. Keep in constant contact. I want to know as soon as you find something."

"Yes, sir."

"And knock off that 'sir' shit. I thought we went through that already."

"Okay, General." He headed toward the Chevy.

"Jed."

"Yes."

"I'm not planning to kill you yet. And obviously my niece sees something in you, so try not to die."

Jed grinned and flipped the keys around in his hand. "Will do, General."


Elena paced the path in the living room, her eyes on Pete's cell phone, which sat near him on the table.

It had been two hours. Nothing. It hadn't rung once.

She hated standing around here doing nothing.

Pete had offered to play cards with her, but that would require sitting and she couldn't sit. Pacing was much better.

He was reading a magazine. Reading! Calmly sitting there

flipping pages when who knew what was going on with Jed and Grange.

"How can you sit there so calmly and just read?"

He lifted his gaze and peered at her over the top of the magazine. "What?"

"You. Reading. It's driving me crazy."

"My reading is driving you crazy?"

"Yes. No." She dragged her fingers through her hair. "I'm sorry. I'm the one who's crazy. It's the not knowing anything. Shouldn't they have called by now?"

His lips curved in a half smile. He laid the magazine on the table and put his phone in his pocket. "You wouldn't enjoy surveillance duty."

"What?"

"Patience. Missions take patience."

She crossed her arms. "This isn't a mission. It's my mother."

His smile died and he stood. "Sorry. I didn't mean to be insensitive. These things take time. They'll call as soon as they have something to call about. Come on."

She followed him outside. "Where are we going?"

"If standing around doing nothing is making you restless, I have something you can do to help me around here."

"Anything to keep from watching the clock and your phone."

He led her down the path past the pool and the main house. She hadn't explored this area yet. It went through the woods and beyond the back of the house. There was another building back here.

"What's this?"

"Storage. We'll replenish supplies."

"Okay, great." Something physical would help to allay some of her stress.

It was a two-story stone building. He pulled keys out of his pocket and unlocked the heavy door, holding it open for her.

"Just step inside. I'll hit the light when I follow you in."

She moved in and waited for him. It was cold in there. She shivered, and didn't much like how pitch dark it was in here. She hoped he hurried up with the—

He turned the light on and she saw racks of supplies, mostly nonperishable food and paper items, piled as high as the ceiling.

"Wow. Planning for world domination from your island here?"

He laughed. "No, but sometimes I don't have access to the helicopter, so I have to make do with what I have on hand. I just make sure to have a lot on hand."

"Probably a smart move." She put her hands on her hips and turned to him. "So what do we need to take back with us, and do you have a shopping cart?"

He was scanning the racks, but dragged his attention away. "Actually, I do have a cart. It's in the other room. That way I don't have to make as many trips. Through that door on your left. Down the hall, second room on the right. If you wouldn't mind. I'll get the ladder and start pulling what we need from the racks."

"Okay, sure."

"Light switch is just inside on your right."

She opened the wide door and flipped the light switch on a long hallway with multiple doors. It was even colder back here. She rubbed her arms and headed down to the room where Pete had indicated the cart would be.

She turned the knob and pushed the door open, then fumbled around for a light switch. It wasn't on the right side of the wall, so she stepped farther in, propping the door open with her foot.

She was shoved in the back and went flying to the hard floor, the door slamming shut behind her.

Her knees screamed with pain where she'd scraped them, her heart jamming double time from the fear and shock.

What the hell just happened?

She scrambled to her feet and ran back to the door, pulled on the knob, but it wouldn't turn.

It was locked.

She banged on the door.

"Pete? Pete! I'm locked in. Pete! Can you hear me?"

Her heart pounded. Someone had pushed her down and locked her in the room. Was Pete okay? Had he been knocked out, or even worse?

"Pete!" She banged on the door. "Pete, answer me!"

"He can't hear you."

She whirled around at the voice behind her.

"Who's there?"

"I'm over here."

Her stomach fell, hope and terror mixing as she realized who had spoken to her.

"Mom? Is that you?"

"Elena?"

"Keep talking. I'll find you. Or a light."

"He never turns on the light in here, so I can't see him. Only at the end of the hall out there. So I only see him in shadow."

"There has to be a light in this room."

She fumbled from the door to the wall, using small steps to make her way around the room. The walls were icy cold, made of stone. She wasn't sure if the building was artificially air-conditioned or if the source of the cold air came from somewhere else, but it was frigid in here. She'd made it halfway around the room when she wrapped her fingers around the metal bars.

"You're in a cell?"

Her mother's cool fingers found hers. "Elena."

Tears sprang to Elena's eyes. She slipped her hands through the bars to reach out and touch her mother. "Mom. Mom. Are you all right?"

"I'm fine. What are you doing here?"

Relief warred with worry. Her mother was alive. That's all she had to concentrate on right now. "We came to rescue you. Only we didn't know you were here. How did you get here?"

"I don't know. And who is 'we'?"

"Me and your brother. And one of his employees."

"Grange is here? Grange told you who he was?"

"Yes. How did you end up on this island?"

"I'm on an island? I don't even know how I got here."

Pete. It had to be Pete who brought her mother here, who shoved her into this room. This was his island. But why would he do this? Why her mother? Why betray Grange? "What's the last thing you remember?"

"I had an appointment with a realtor to buy a house. I had seen the house a few times before and really liked it, so I was ready to close the deal on the property. I was going to settle down, get a job, go back to school."

All those things she had heard about, but her mother hadn't told her about.

"We met at the house. He offered me some tea. That's all I remember until I woke up here."

"It must have been Pete."

"Who's Pete?"

"A friend of Grange's, or at least we thought he was a friend. He owns this island we're on."

"Oh, no. I'm sorry you're involved in this, Elena. We've tried so hard to keep you safe. Grange has always been worried that his job would harm you or me. I told him not to be concerned. I guess he was right. I never took him seriously."

Elena squeezed her mother's hand. "It's so cold in here. Are you warm?"

"There's a blanket. And I have a sweater and some socks."

"Are you fed? Do you have water?"

"Yes, to both. It's just so dark in here. I miss the light, the warmth of the sun."

"How long have you been here? Do you know?"

"Without the sun or the night, I have no idea. Weeks, maybe?"

"Oh, Mom. I'm so sorry."

Her mother reached through the bars and caressed her cheek. "I'm the one who's sorry. I haven't taken care of you like I should. I guess I waited too long to grow up and become responsible."

Elena laughed. "I'm responsible enough for both of us. I'll get us out of here."

"This is all so touching," a voice said in the darkness. "Listening to the two of you get reacquainted. It's too bad Grange isn't around to hear it. It would only add to his guilt. But don't worry. I recorded it all and I'll make sure to play it for him."

Pete. Elena's blood boiled at the thought of the torment he'd put her mother through. "Pete, let my mother go. You can keep me as a hostage. Grange will do whatever you want."

Pete laughed. "Why would I let either of you go? I have both of you now, and you mean everything to him. And now that you've got that new boyfriend, the two of them will go crazy trying to save you. And they'll both fail."

"Let my daughter go," her mother said. "You can do whatever you want to me. Let Elena go."

"How sweet that you're both willing to sacrifice yourselves

to save the other. Too bad Grange wasn't so noble. He'll likely let you both die before he puts his own ass on the line."

He went silent.

"Pete?" Elena asked. "Pete!"

She would not let her mother die. She didn't plan on dying, either. Whatever plan Pete had, she wasn't going to go along willingly. No matter what it took, she was going to fight.

# FOURTEEN

Jed entered the restaurant where Carla had allegedly used her credit card. He flashed his I.D. and asked to speak to the manager, then reviewed the video surveillance of everyone who'd been at the restaurant during the time period her card had been swiped.

No one matching her description had eaten or had a drink there. The person using the card was a middle-aged woman with sunglasses and brown hair. She'd worn a scarf, but made no effort to hide her face from video surveillance. She'd stopped at the bar, had a cocktail, used the card and left.

But it wasn't Carla. She had the same build and hair color, but it wasn't Carla.

He'd called Grange, who reported the same thing at the retail store where her card had been used. A woman with the same type of description had bought two blouses, used the card and left the store.

"So two women fitting Carla's description both use her card for small purchases, make no effort to hide from video surveillance then leave," Jed said. "Smells like a setup to me."

"Agreed," Grange said. "It's like someone wanted us to go on these wild-goose chases. Why?"

It hit Jed right away. "To separate us from Elena."

"We need to get in touch with Pete right away. We have to warn him. I'll meet you at the helicopter pad."

Jed broke speeding records on his way to the helicopter pad. When he got there, his heart fell to his feet. The look on Grange's face was grim.

"What?" he asked.

"Pete's not answering his phone. And I can't get in touch with the copter pilot. I've made arrangements to get another helo here pronto. ETA is thirty minutes."

When every second counted, thirty minutes just didn't seem fast enough.

Jed paced, ran his fingers through his hair, watched the sky and paced some more, trying to formulate a battle plan. While he walked in one direction, Grange went in another, neither of them saying anything to the other. When Jed heard the whir of rotor blades, he almost yelled in triumph. As soon as the helicopter landed, they were airborne again and heading to the island.

He hoped they would find the other helicopter standing by and Pete waiting for them with an explanation of cell trouble.

His hopes were dashed when he saw the helicopter gone and no Pete standing there wondering why the hell there was another helo landing on his island. Because if Pete were able, he should be waiting there with a gun in his hand ready to fire on an intruder.

Grange and Jed pulled out their weapons and ran through the jungle.

"I'll take the right, you take the left. Shoot anybody that isn't Elena or Pete."

That was Jed's plan anyway. By the time they got to the house, Jed already knew Elena was in deep trouble. Maybe they were connected in some emotional way, because he knew she was gone. He didn't feel her nearby.

She wasn't in the house. Neither was Pete.

"We tear this island apart," Grange said.

Jed was right on his heels as they moved through the island with precision, looking through the jungle, checking trees, bushes or anyplace Elena could be held. When they broke through the clearing and saw the other house, Jed looked at Grange.

The front door was partially open.

"Supply house," Grange said. "And Pete always keeps it locked."

Jed lifted his weapon as they pushed the door open. It was cold in there.

The main room was clear, so they went in through the next room, a hallway leading to other doors. They checked each door, which was locked. Jed kicked them in one by one.

When they got to the one with the cell, he turned to Grange.

"I never saw this room. Only the main supply room. Pete told me the others were electrical."

Grange walked in, picked up the blanket, saw the simple cot, and then the clothes.

"Carla. Sonofabitch, he's had Carla all this time." Grange picked up the cot and threw it across the room. "Fuck, all this time and I never knew."

"Why?" Jed asked.

"I was supposed to relieve him that day in Beirut so he could pick up Dina. I was delayed, didn't get off in time. If I'd relieved him, he would have picked her up and she wouldn't have been at the embassy when it was bombed."

He lifted sorrow-filled eyes to Jed. "I had such guilt over that, but Pete said he never blamed me, that there was nothing I could have done differently, that it wasn't my fault. He had lost his wife and he was consoling me. Turns out all this time he'd been waiting for this moment to get his revenge."

"Why wait until now?"

Grange shook his head. "I don't know. Maybe he was hoping I'd get married, then he'd take my wife away like his was taken away. Only I didn't. I had a career, never got around to finding a wife. So maybe he got tired of waiting and he figured he'd take the two most important people in my life—my sister and my niece."

"Jesus, Grange, he's one disturbed bastard."

"There's not even a window in here. And it's fucking cold. How could he do this to her? Who knows how long she's been in this room? I'll kill him for making her suffer like that."

Grange started forward, but Jed stopped him. "General, I know you're in charge of this mission, but you're not thinking with your head right now. Frankly I don't give a shit what you do to this guy when you find him, but if you go out there without putting a plan together, you might lose them both. And I don't intend to lose Elena."

Grange stopped, sucked in a breath and nodded. "You're right. We need a plan."

"The first thing we have to do is figure out where he took them."

"Helicopter. They need a flight plan, and radar may have picked them up. We'll hit that first."

They ran back to the house and Grange made some calls. They pulled up area flight radar while Grange got them connected.

"Helicopter took off south. He's headed out of the country. I've got our pilot firing us up and ready to track him, plus military jets on the way to intercept if he's still in flight."

They packed up duffels of firepower and were on the helo in fifteen minutes, in touch with the military trying to track where Pete's helicopter had gone.

"We're in luck. He's still in the U.S. Small island off the coast of the Florida Keys," Grange said. "We're going in hot and heavy. Not sure if he's there alone or he has help. He's amassed a lot of money doing mercenary work over the years. He's made some friends in low places, too. This might get ugly."

Jed was heavily armed and just pissed off enough to put a bullet through Pete's head the minute he saw him, and ask questions later. "Understood."

"I wish we had time to bring a bigger team in. I've called in a few favors, so we'll get some backup, but I don't know when that'll be. There's no police jurisdiction where we're going, so right now it's just you and me."

"I'm ready for whatever he's got, General."

He hoped Pete was unprepared for the hurt Jed was going to rain down on him. Because Pete had his woman and his woman's mother, and that meant he was going down.


Elena hoped that not only Pete burned in hell, but also the pilot who'd helped Pete drag her and her mother out of that refrigerated room and onto the helicopter. She hoped he was paid really well, though she doubted the money would do him any good when he rotted away in some prison somewhere.

Pete had cuffed them, chained their ankles together and tossed them onto the helicopter, then flown them somewhere south and landed on yet another godforsaken uninhabited island, where he'd dragged them off the helicopter, again with the help of his minion, and locked them in the bedroom of a house.

This house wasn't as ostentatious as the last one. It was smaller, less fancy and far less spacious. Not that she cared since they were still stuck out in the middle of nowhere. And chained.

Her mother had cried out when they'd been taken out of the room. After so many weeks in the dark, the sunlight had played havoc with her eyes. Elena had told her to keep her eyes shut tight. That, coupled with the chains around her ankles, meant her mom kept tripping and falling as they were dragged to the helicopter. Pete, finally disgusted, threw her over his shoulder and carried her. When they landed on this island, he told her mother if she didn't get out and walk, he'd shoot her and leave her on the deck of the helipad.

Elena's mother somehow managed to squint and walk to the house, but she was crying now because her eyes burned so badly. She needed medical treatment.

Elena swore she'd find a way to kill the sonofabitch for all the torment he'd caused her mother.

She wished she could help her mom take a shower. She said the only thing she'd had access to was water, soap and a wash-cloth. She craved a shower and a long, soaking bath. But with them being shackled up like this, she couldn't even have that.

Elena sat on the edge of the bed while her mother slept. At least this bed was more comfortable than the cot her mom had been forced to sleep on for so long. And it was warmer here. Her mother slept soundly, no doubt exhausted and likely malnour-ished. She'd lost weight, her dirty clothes hanging loose on her much smaller frame.

Elena raised her cuffed hands and swept them over her mother's hair.

She'd resented her mother for so long, had ignored her, had tried so hard not to be like her. Now she'd do anything to save her.

Elena's hand brushed something metal. She slid her fingers into her mother's hair and pulled out one of those thick hairpins and smiled. Her mother was always sticking those things into her unruly curly hair to keep it away from her face.

Then it hit her. She dipped her fingers into her mom's hair again, searching, and found another pin.

She stared at the two pins in her hand, then at the handcuffs, and grinned, remembering the lessons she'd been taught long ago.

She straightened the hairpin, then bent down and worked at the lock holding the chain at her ankles. She slid it into the hole and began to work it around. After about fifteen minutes she'd worked up a sweat and had gotten nowhere, so she opened the second pin and used two of them, forcing patience when all she wanted was for this damn thing to—

The lock clicked open. Oh, my God, it worked. She resisted the urge to pump her fist in the air and squeal. She pulled the lock off and removed the chains, then set about on undoing the handcuffs, which were a lot easier to pick than the lock. She had those off in a few minutes, climbed off the bed then set to work on the lock at her mom's ankles.

Her mother stirred and sat up, her eyes still shut. "Elena?"

"Shhh, Mom, stay quiet."

"What are you doing?"

"Picking these locks with your hairpins."

"What? How can you do that?"

"I had to amuse myself somehow when you dragged me

over to Paco's when I was a kid. Some of his friends taught me how to pick a lock."

She sighed. "The influences I exposed you to as a child . . ."

The lock released. "Have come in handy. Let's take a look at those handcuffs now."

She had her mother out of the cuffs within ten minutes.

Hope lit a flame inside her. She helped her mother to the side of the bed so she could get her bearings, then stood to look around the room. The windows were barred, so no way out there. She went into the bathroom. Same thing with the windows. She went back into the bedroom and opened the closet door, looking for anything that would help her get them out of there. She rummaged through the racks of clothes hanging there, then bent down and pushed aside the boxes of shoes.

Her breath stopped when she saw the bright red numbers and the countdown on the black box tucked in the back of the closet.

That looked an awful lot like a bomb. And the clock was ticking down. Time left was a little over sixty minutes.

She sucked in a shaky breath and gently shut the closet door, turned to her mother and kept her voice calm.

"We have to get out of here before Pete comes in and realizes we've gotten free. How are you feeling?"

"A little weak, but I can handle it."

"How are your eyes? Can you see anything?"

Her mother tried to open her eyes. "Light hurts still. I'll manage. I'm ready to get out of here and go home."

"Me, too." She was going to have to try the door, which she figured would be locked. She took her mother's hand and led her to the door, tried the knob.

It turned.

"Door's not locked." Why should he when he had the bomb in the closet?

Bastard.

She turned to her mother. "Stay very quiet, and be ready to run like hell. Don't let go of my hand."

Her mother nodded, squeezed her hand. "I love you, Elena. I'm sorry."

Elena pulled her into a hug, tears welling in her eyes. "Nothing to be sorry for. And I love you, too, Mom."

Her first priority was getting her mother as far away from the bomb as possible. That was their best chance at survival. The second option was to find a phone so she could call for help. She knew Grange and Jed would be tearing the world apart searching for them.

That gave her comfort. They'd find her and her mom. In the meantime, she'd do whatever it took to get them out of there and away from that lunatic Pete. She had to get her mother out of this house and now.

She inched the door open and peeked out. The room they were in was at the edge of the hallway. She could see a living area and kitchen. Two men holding guns were in the kitchen having a beer and staring out the open back slider toward the beach. No sign of Pete.

"Stay here," she whispered to her mother, and inched out of the room, wanting to take a look around the edge of the wall.

They were right at the front door. If she could somehow get past those men in the kitchen, or if the men would go outside, she could grab her mom, get out of the front door and make a dash to freedom. She didn't know how big that bomb was, but if they could clear the house, maybe they'd be okay.

Maybe.

She slipped back inside the room and partly closed the door, giving her mother a report of what she'd seen. She kept watch over the guards, hoping and praying they'd walk outside. All she needed was thirty seconds.

Then she heard the loud roar overhead, and the guards went running.

She grabbed her mother's hand. "Let's go now!"

# FIFTEEN

Nothing like a couple of low-flying fighter jets as a diversion. Jed was thankful Grange knew people in high places. The flyover should provide enough of a distraction to get Pete and whoever else was working for him scrambling to figure out what the fuck was going on.

They beached the Zodiac boat on the back side of the island and leaped out, weapons drawn, while a helo and the jets hopefully kept Pete busy on the main side. Jed and Grange ran like hell toward the house, ripping through underbrush, foliage slapping them in the face and arms as they rushed to get to Elena and her mother.

"You see anything that isn't Carla and Elena, shoot it," Grange said, having no problem keeping up with Jed.

That was already Jed's plan anyway. He figured every person on this private island was hostile.

They reached the clearing. Jed didn't even pause as he ran through the open back door.

"Elena!"

No answer. He checked every room in the small house, but she wasn't there. Neither was her mother.

"Front door is open," Grange said, heaving big gulps of oxygen and dripping sweat from their extended run. "Maybe they got out."

"And maybe Pete took them out when the jets flew over."

Grange nodded. "I'll go out the back and retrace. You take the front. Check in."

"You got it."

Jed ran through the front door, down the steps and onto the path, figuring if Elena had escaped, she'd go in that direction, hoping to find a way out. Stones marked a path for about fifty feet, then it was sand and a worn pathway leading through the jungle.

He lifted his rifle, slowing his pace as the jungle thickened around him. He lifted his arm and swiped the sweat from his eyes.

The crack of a twig to his left made him crouch down and focus in that direction. He dropped and rolled when a shot fired at him but missed.

Another shot. He flattened himself on his belly and took aim, looking for the shooter. He followed him with his sight, tracking his movements as he inched through the jungle.

This guy wasn't very good. Jed's finger poised on the trigger, he drew the guy in his sights, about to pull the trigger when a shot rang out and he dropped, his left arm burning. A warm trickle of blood slid down his arm. He grabbed a handkerchief out of his pocket and tied it around his arm to stop the flow of blood, ignoring the pounding pain.

Motherfucker, they had him pinned on both sides.

He went running deeper into the woods, taking fire from his left and right. But he got ahead of them, then found a thick tree to hide behind and waited for them to come get him.

He heard the one on the left first.

Silence wasn't their forte, so he heard the shooter on the run. Jed aimed and fired, and the first one went down with a thundering crash.

He changed position right away so the second shooter wouldn't be able to get a point on his position.

Catching his breath, he found a spot, belly crawled a few feet, trying not to make any noise while listening for sounds of others. He didn't hear anything, so he found a large rock and tossed it.

That's when he heard the other one coming up on the position where he'd tossed the rock.

He rose, moved in behind him, spotted the target creeping through the foliage. He got him in his sights and took the shot, dropping him.

He dove back into the jungle, keeping watch for other shooters.

Time was wasting and he had to find Elena.

Elena was lost. Hopelessly lost. She'd started out on the path, then was afraid that made them an easy target and they'd run into Pete or one of his guards, so she dove into the jungle, figuring they could hide out if they needed to until Jed and Grange found them.

And they would find them. She'd heard the jet overhead. It had to be them.

Her mother's progress was slow. She was tired and weak and mostly blind, so she couldn't run. Elena had to tell her mother where to step so she wouldn't trip over the gnarled roots sticking up out of the ground.

After they'd walked for a while, she finally settled them against a hollowed-out tree trunk to take a rest. She didn't know how long they'd survive out here without food and water, but she'd figure out a way.

And she hoped they were far enough away from the house. She had no idea how much time had elapsed, but it was getting close.

She wanted to get farther, like out to the beach, but she didn't want to get into a clearing. Maybe they'd be safe here.

She heard the crackle of leaves, the snap of wood.

And maybe they weren't safe here after all.

Then again, it might be Jed and Grange, and if she stayed silent, she might miss them.

Tension knotted in her stomach. She didn't know what to do.

"Elena."

She silenced her mother with her hand, and took a peek around the edge of the tree.

The gun pressed against her cheek.

"There you are, Elena. I was wondering where you and your mother had disappeared to."

Pete.

Her heart sank.

"Get up."

She couldn't move. He did, though, coming around to yank her mother up by the hair. Her mother cried out.

"Stop it!" Elena screamed. "I'll do anything you want. Just don't hurt her."

Pete smiled, and she'd never seen anything more vicious, or more insane.

"Good girl. We're going back to the house."

Elena shook her head. "No."

"Oh, yes."

"We're not going back there with you. There's a bomb in the house."

Her mother turned her head. "What? A bomb?"

"That's right, Carla." Pete caressed her face with the gun, his hand still holding her hair tight. "A bomb. I'm going to blow up you and your precious daughter. Grange is here somewhere. He's going to watch and there's nothing he's going to be able to do to save you. Just like I had to watch my Dina die and could do nothing to save her. And once again it's going to be all his fault."

"You're mad," her mother said.

He laughed. "Oh, I'm beyond mad. I'm getting my vengeance. Finally."

"Please let my mother go, Pete. Just take me," Elena pleaded.

"You come with me or I'll shoot her right now, leave her here and take you to the house." He motioned with his rifle.

Defeated, she had no choice but to lead the way, figuring as long as they were both alive, they still had a chance.

She'd figure something out. This bastard wasn't going to win.


Jed had sights on Pete, Elena and Carla. But he had Elena in the front blocking his way, goddamit. He didn't have a clear shot.

He'd climbed into a tree, hoping it would give him an advantage, but he still didn't have the shot.

Then Grange stepped into the path and Pete stopped.

Now there were even more people in his way. But Jed set up. All he needed was a fraction of a second on his target, and he'd be able to take Pete down.

*Come on, Grange. Give me what I need.*

*   *   *

Elena stopped cold in her tracks when Grange appeared in front of them.

Shock, relief and utter terror left her immobile. But something in Grange's eyes calmed her, too.

He knew what he was doing. He only glanced at her for a fraction of a second before turning his attention on Pete, but it was something.

"Pete. What are you doing?" Grange asked.

Pete laughed. "Grange, my old pal. Glad you joined us. You're just in time. Let's go to the house and have a beer."

"I don't think I'll be going anywhere with you. Let them go and then we'll talk."

Pete tightened his grip on Carla's hair. She winced and Grange took a step forward. Pete put the gun to Carla's temple.

"I wouldn't do that. You know how good I am with a gun."

Grange raised his hands. "Fine. Then tell me what this is all about."

"You know what this is about."

"Dina."

Pete nodded. "You need to pay for what you did to her."

"You know how sorry I am about that. But what happened to Dina was circumstance and terrorists."

"Your fault. If you'd been on time, she wouldn't have been there. She wouldn't have died."

Grange nodded. "And I'll live with that guilt the rest of my life. So if you want to blame someone, if you want to kill someone, then kill me. Not Carla or Elena."

"No, they have to pay. They're innocent, and they have to pay. Just like Dina."

Grange turned his attention on Elena. "Come here."

"No," Pete said.

Grange ignored him. "If we're going to die, I want to hug my niece." He reached for the gun on his hip with two fingers, took it out of its holster and threw it to the ground. "Look, no weapons. No tricks. I surrender."

Grange turned his gaze back on Pete. "Now let me hug my niece. I spent my whole life separated from her because I thought I was keeping her safe. Now we're all going to die. At least let me have this."

Pete grinned, obviously sensing triumph. He nodded. "Fine. Then we go in the house, I lock you all up and then you blow up. But hurry, because time's running out."

Elena walked over to Grange.

Grange wrapped his arm around her. She squeezed him tight, but lost her balance when he jerked her to the ground and knocked the very breath from her.

A shot rang out. Carla screamed.

"Mom!" Elena cried out.

Grange rolled her over. She pushed at him and he let go of her.

"It's all right, Elena. He's dead."

She jumped up and saw her mother shoving away from Pete's body. Elena ran over to her mother and threw her arms around her.

"Are you all right?"

"Yes, I think so. What happened? Is he dead?

"He is." She turned to Grange, who came over to help his sister.

"How?" Elena asked.

"Jed," Grange said, motioning to Jed, who swung out of a nearby tree and started toward them, rifle flung over his shoulder. "He's a damn fine sniper. I just had to get you and me out of the way so he could take the shot."

"Jed," Elena said. She ran toward him and threw her arms around him, then pulled back when she saw the red stain on his arm. "You're bleeding."

"I'm fine. It's just a scratch." He wrapped his arms tightly around her and held her.

"Plenty of time for that later," Grange said. "There's a bomb about to go off. Let's get the hell out of here."

Jed grabbed her hand and they ran. Grange scooped Carla up in his arms and they made a wild dash to the boat, pushing off just as the explosion occurred, throwing up flames and smoke they could see long after they'd left the island. The Coast Guard and the military swarmed the island, searching for survivors.

"That's a hell of a lot of C-4," Jed said as the Zodiac zipped away toward the mainland, the Coast Guard as their escorts.

Elena leaned back against Jed's chest, listening to Grange and her mother talk.

She couldn't believe they'd survived. With a little luck and because of Jed and Grange, they were alive.

She and her mother could have been in that house when it went up.

She grasped Jed's hand tightly, never so grateful to feel the warm sun and sea spray on her face.


"All these years I spent trying to keep you two safe by staying out of your lives, when all this time the fucking enemy was in my own backyard."

Grange paced back and forth in Elena's living room, hands clasped behind his back, rigid military bearing so evident in the way he held himself.

Elena couldn't help being totally in love with her uncle. He'd helped save her life and her mother's life.

"I think you did what you thought was best. But I have to tell you, if you think I'm going to allow you to disappear from my life ever again, you're wrong."

He took a moment to stop pacing and graced her with that smile that was so much like her mother's it made her heart squeeze.

Her mother sat next to her on the sofa, her vision restored. In the past week she had been to the hospital, had been given I.V. fluids, antibiotics for an infection and all the rest she'd needed. She'd been sprung a few days ago and was more than ready to get on with her life.

"I agree with Elena. It's time I had my brother in my life again, and not just a few phone calls and visits here and there."

Grange crouched down in front of Elena's mother and took her hands in his. "I almost lost you." He looked at Elena. "Both of you. That would have been unforgivable. It's time I make some changes in my life. I'm retiring."

Jed, who was sitting in the chair across from Elena, arched a brow. "General?"

"You heard me. I've been at this long enough, and it's time to interject some young blood into the Wild Riders. With Mac and Lily getting ready to have a baby, I know Mac is ready to get out of the line of fire, so I think he's ready to take over the helm of the Wild Riders with Lily at his side. The two of them can run the organization as well as I ever did. I'm ready for fishing and more time on the boat. And maybe it's time I settle down and find a woman to spend my life with."

Carla laughed. "It's about time, old man. But do you think you can find a woman willing to put up with you?"

He arched a brow. "Are you saying I'm unreasonable, domineering, rigid and hard to live with?"

Jed coughed.

"Didn't ask you, smart-ass."

"Didn't comment, General."

Carla swept her hand across his cheek. "I think any woman would be lucky to have you. And I'd love it if you retired down here. You can help me finish that degree in psychology I've been spending the past few years working on, help me find a house, and help me settle down and become a good mother to my daughter."

Elena warmed. "You're already a good mother."

Her mother turned to her. "Not yet, but I intend to work on it every day for the rest of my life."

"You had all these plans I didn't know anything about. I'm sorry, Mom. I never took the time to ask you about your life. That changes now."

Her mother cupped her cheeks and kissed her on the forehead. "You have nothing to be sorry about. I'm the one who made such a mess of things. I was in and out of your life like a flitting butterfly, never settling on one thing, always off on another adventure." Her mother straightened. "My adventure days are over. I'm ready to be a responsible adult now."

Elena couldn't help the tears that fell. She laughed and hugged her mother, so grateful to have another chance with her, thanks to Jed and Grange.

After Grange and her mother took off to spend the evening together and talk about their own futures, Jed and Elena were left alone.

"So what's next for you?" she asked, not really wanting to ask the question, but knowing she had to be an adult about it.

He leaned back on the sofa and pulled her against him, throwing his arm around her. "Not sure. I'm supposed to report back to Wild Rider headquarters in Dallas."

"Supposed to?"

"Yeah. Grange's imminent retirement changes things."

She twisted around to face him. "In what way?"

"I signed on to work with Grange. He's been an amazing teacher, someone I've loved working under."

"You don't like the other people you work with?"

"I do. They're all a great group of people. Amazingly talented. Tough, tenacious, and I'd work with any of them on any assignment."

"Then I don't understand the problem."

"Grange recruited me, took me under his wing, trained me. He sought me out and asked me to come work for him. I look on him as a father figure. Stupid, I know. I should be able to work for anyone, especially at my age. And I can. That's not the issue."

"It's not stupid. I think with your talent and capabilities, you can afford to be selective. It's not like you're a rookie fresh out of school and you can't pick and choose where you work. I imagine a lot of people would be happy to hire you."

"Maybe. Maybe not."

"So what do you want to do?"

"Don't know yet. I'll have to give it some thought."

She climbed onto his lap and placed her palms on his face. "Jed. What do *you* want to do?"

He squeezed her hips. "Right now?"

She grinned. "Well, yeah, there's that. But honestly. What do you want to do?"

"Stay here, with you. Work with Grange. Have a family. I miss having a family. I'm jealous of what you have."

She arched a brow. "What I have?"

"Your mom. Your uncle. Marco. People who love you. I haven't had that in a long time. Never realized what I was missing until I saw it all around me. Until I met you."

Emotion swelled within her. "So you want a family?"

He skimmed his hands up her ribs, teasing her breasts. "I want you, Elena. I want to stay here with you."

"Oh."

"I told Grange I was falling in love with you."

"You did?"

"I did. He didn't take it well."

"He didn't?"

"Not at first. I think he might be used to the idea by now. Either way, I told him that's the way it was going to be, and you and I needed to have a real relationship that didn't revolve around an assignment."

She palmed his chest. "That would be nice."

"If that's what you want."

"It's definitely what I want. I don't want you to go back to Dallas. I just didn't want to ask you to give up your job for me."

"So what are you saying?"

"That I'm in love with you, Jed. You made my heart stop from the very first day you came into my shop. You've been turning my world upside down ever since. I don't want that feeling to ever end. But I'm also a little scared."

"Me, too. I've never done this before."

"Neither have I. I guess we'll just muddle through it together."

He flipped her over onto the sofa and came down on top of her, his lips on hers before she could even gasp a breath.

It had been so long since they'd been together. They hadn't had a moment alone in over a week. She'd spent all her time with her mother in the hospital, and he'd been with Grange, or they'd all been together. She'd loved all the family time, needed to be with her mother and had so enjoyed getting to know her uncle, but now she craved only Jed.

His kiss sent her senses reeling. She threaded her fingers into his hair, the other hand sweeping down over his arm, loving the solid feel of him. Knowing he was going to remain in her life balanced her world.

Part of her was unable to believe this man loved her. She hadn't been looking for love, but oh, had she found an amazing man. He'd risked his life to rescue her. It was the stuff of fairy tales.

His hand crept under her shirt to release the front clasp of her bra and tease her nipples. He lifted her shirt, put his mouth on her nipples to suck her between his lips, flicking his tongue over the buds until she arched against him, feeding her breasts into his greedy mouth. She heated up to a fevered pitch fast, rocking against his erection, needing him so much after everything they'd been through.

He raised her shirt over her head, took off her bra, then slid her shorts and panties off her legs, leaving her nakcd and throb-bing. When he put his mouth on her sex, she whimpered, holding onto his hair as he sucked her pussy, rolling his tongue over her clit.

"Jed. Yes, make me come."

She hadn't come since she'd been with him. For the past week she'd lain in bed alone, thinking about him, wanting to be with him again, and hoping he wanted the same thing but worried that she'd have to say good-bye to him, and wondering if she'd be able to. And now that he was with her, that he loved her, she was never going to let him go.

"Yes. This is mine," she said, half-crazed with the amazing things he did to her with his mouth. "I want this all the time."

He hummed against her pussy and she climaxed with a wild cry, bucking against his mouth as she rode out her orgasm, then pulled him up and kissed him, licking her come from his lips.

"I need you inside me, Jed. Please make love to me."

They made quick work of his clothes. She splayed her hands out over his chest, then lower, reaching for his cock.

"You're throbbing in my hands," she said, loving the way he looked at her.

"You make me hard."

"Then make love to me."

He grabbed a condom and slipped it on, then kneeled on the floor in front of the sofa, draping her legs over his shoulders.

"I love watching your pussy when I fuck you," he said, sliding inside her with a slow and easy thrust. "The way it grips me as if you never want to let me go."

She rose up so she could watch, too, could see his cock sliding all the way inside her, then withdrawing. She shuddered at the intimacy of their connection, then raised her gaze to his. "Make me come again. Make me come with you."

He reared back and slammed inside her, pumping furiously and grinding against her. She couldn't get enough of him, pulling him forward so she could wrap her legs around him and kiss him, his tongue licking against hers.

He pulled back to look at her, to sweep her hair away from her face.

"And this is mine," he said, bending down to sweep his lips against hers.

He ground against her, taking her right to the edge, slowing, and deepening his thrusts again with a maddening rhythm that brought her to the brink over and over. It was the sweetest tease.

"Oh, God, I'm going to come," she murmured against his lips.

He rolled his hips against hers, his pelvis sliding against her clit. She exploded in orgasm, bucking against him until he groaned out her name and came with her, shuddering against her as he glued his body to hers.

She stroked his hair, his back, kissed his face, his mouth. She'd never been so content.

"Stay with me tonight," she whispered.

"Always."

Tonight, she'd sleep.

# SIXTEEN

"What do you think about this piece?" Marco asked.

Elena studied it with a critical eye. It was a welded piece from a new artist that Marco had found at an art show the previous weekend.

"Kind of nautical, yet with a touch of fantasy. I like it, and the colors are unique. Very masculine. It should appeal to our male clientele."

Marco beamed. "Great. I'll let Paolo know you dig his work and have him bring more samples in."

Work had picked up with warmer weather moving in. Elena was happy to be back at work, though Marco had done a remarkable job handling the store while she was gone. He seemed to thrive on autonomy, so she intended to take more time off and let him manage the store more often, which fell in line with her plans to spend more time with the man she loved.

Not that he'd have as much time as she'd like, but that was

all right. She had other things to do, too. Her mother had found a house she loved, a cute cottage a few miles off the beach that she had bought and would be moving into within a month.

And with Grange down here now and his new retirement "business" getting off the ground—with Jed's help—she was going to be busier than ever, which meant she'd need Marco's assistance with the shop.

"Marco, can you handle things here for a few hours? I need to run a few errands."

Marco grinned. "You know it. Off to see your boyfriend?"

Now it was her turn to smile. "Maybe."

He waved her off and went to place his new client's piece in the window. "Have fun. Give Jed a kiss for me."

She laughed, grabbed her purse and climbed into the Chevy and headed down to the waterway after making a quick stop at the local deli. She parked in the lot, switched out of her heels and put on canvas shoes, then walked down the plank dock, where Grange and Jed were busily cleaning a boat.

"Must be nice having a job where you get to hang out in the sun all day getting tan."

Grange looked up and grinned, something he did a lot more these days. He still wore his hair in that severe military haircut, but he'd cut off his camos into knee-skimming shorts, wore canvas tennis shoes and a T-shirt that was a different color besides green. Today he wore a baseball cap on backward.

"Hey, we wear sunscreen. How's my favorite niece?"

"Your only niece." She climbed up onto the boat and kissed his cheek, then turned her attention to Jed, who looked mouthwateringly gorgeous in board shorts and a sleeveless tank.

Jed lifted his head from where he'd been busily sanding the deck. He was dripping sweat, and grinning like a kid.

"Afternoon, gorgeous. How's my beautiful woman?"

"Taking a break. I brought you two lunch and a cold drink. Figured you'd be too busy to stop and eat."

"We eat," Grange said.

"Chips don't count."

"Nutrition nazi," Jed said, but greedily took the sandwich she offered.

What he'd really liked was seeing the woman he loved showing up and making his day.

"Thanks," Grange said. "I think I'll take mine to go. There's a paint supplier at the store I want to talk to. Nice to see you, Elena."

"You, too." She smiled and waved her uncle off, then turned to Jed.

He ate his sandwich and admired her in her cute capri pants, polka dot top and tennis shoes, her hair pulled up high on her head in a ponytail.

He was a sweaty mess, and she was a fresh goddess. He was one lucky sonofabitch.

"The boat's coming along nicely," she said, glancing down at the well-sanded deck of the first boat Jed and Grange had bought as part of General's Fishing and Touring Charters, the business they'd started up together a month ago.

Once the general had asked Jed to go into business with him, it had taken Jed about two seconds to say yes.

Partly because it meant outdoors and adventure, something Jed had craved. Partly because it meant he could be with Elena, and mainly because now he had a family, and that family included Elena.

Maybe the general had known that, maybe not, but either way, Jed was damned grateful.

"What are you thinking about?" Elena asked as she wiped the corner of her mouth with a napkin.

"You. All this and how it worked out. How lucky I am."

"Really? I think I'm the lucky one. You stayed."

"I'd have stayed anyway, even if this job hadn't happened. I wouldn't have left you."

Her cheeks turned pink and her lips curved into a sweet smile that never failed to make his heart squeeze in a way that was still new to him. "I love you, Jed."

"I love you, too, Elena. It's a perfect day, I have my beautiful woman in my life, and we're on our boat. Life just can't get any better."

She leaned over, laid her hand on his heart and pressed her lips to his. "Oh, it will. This is just the beginning."